Praise for **EXPE**

. . .

"A fizzing, lip-chewing, collar-bone biting, palm-sweating roller-coaster of a rom-com that is both the sexiest book you'll read all year and the most heartening. A big, kind, horny love-in that will embolden readers to get some more experience of their own."

—Caroline O'Donoghue, *New York Times* best-selling author of *The Rachel Incident*

"A joyful, exhilarating romp of a romance! *Experienced* reminds us all that sometimes, the best of life—and love—is found where you least expect it. A beautiful celebration of love and identity."

—Ashley Herring Blake, bestselling author of *Iris Kelly Doesn't Date*

"Clever, sexy, and joyful, *Experienced* is filled with characters who quickly feel like old friends. A stunner of a debut novel—I loved it."

—Beth O'Leary, international bestselling author of *The Wake-Up Call*

"*Experienced* is fun, sexy, and smart. Kate Young's take on dating, relationships, and learning about your own queerness is wonderfully astute, her characters are warm and recognizable and importantly, deeply fanciable. I loved it."

—Laura Kay, author of *Wild Things*

PENGUIN BOOKS

EXPERIENCED

Kate Young is a writer and cook, whose award-winning Little Library Cookbooks feature food inspired by beloved works of literature. After a sunny Australian childhood (spent indoors reading books) she moved to London, which suited her much better. She now lives in a converted mill in a Gloucestershire town. *Experienced* is her first novel.

EXPERIENCED

a novel

Kate Young

PENGUIN BOOKS

PENGUIN BOOKS

An imprint of Penguin Random House LLC

penguinrandomhouse.com

LIBRARY OF CONGRESS CATALOGING-IN-PUBLICATION DATA

Names: Young, Kate (Food writer), author.

Title: Experienced : a novel / Kate Young.

Description: [New York] : Penguin Books, 2024.

Identifiers: LCCN 2024000850 (print) | LCCN 2024000851 (ebook) |
ISBN 9780143137986 (trade paperback) | ISBN 9780593512074 (ebook)

Subjects: LCGFT: Lesbian fiction. | Romance fiction. | Novels.

Classification: LCC PR6125.O8597 E97 2024 (print) |
LCC PR6125.O8597 (ebook) | DDC 823/.92—dc23/eng/20240109

LC record available at https://lccn.loc.gov/2024000850

LC ebook record available at https://lccn.loc.gov/2024000851

Printed in the United States of America

1st Printing

Designed by Nerylsa Dijol

For the girls eating noodles on the sofa beside me

I want the fireworks, I want
the chemistry
I want that girl right over there
to wanna date me
Ooh oh oh, that's what I want
There's nothing wrong with
what I want

"WHAT I WANT," MUNA

CHAPTER ONE

THE BREAK

...

Summer 2022

The conversation started, appropriately enough, in Mei's bed. It was a hot summer morning in mid-July, the light streaming in like a cliché through gauze curtains and warming Bette's skin. There was an undeniable luxury about being in bed together like this during the summer; they'd had long hours the evening before to take their time in the last of the daylight, to appreciate the golden glow on each other's skin.

As a general rule, Bette hated being sweaty, hated the summer. Her body felt big in the heat, like she took up too much space, as plump and warm as a rising ball of dough. But there was something—there was everything—about being there with Mei, about being flushed and warm in her linen sheets, that made her happy to overlook it.

There was a plan, at some point soon, for Bette to meet friends in the park, to enjoy the sun while they had it. But when she and Mei blinked awake around eight, the afternoon seemed so blissfully distant. They felt no rush at all. Mei disappeared to make tea, and Bette . . . Bette *missed* her. She'd been gone no more than ten minutes, just in the next room. Bette had heard her turn the radio on, had heard her fill the kettle with water. And still, she missed her. And so, quite without thinking how ridiculous it was, quite how soon she'd be back, Bette climbed out from beneath the sheet and followed her in.

She found Mei at the sink, looking out of the window, head tilted, fingers pressing into the top of her spine, where she was always tense after a week in the studio. One side of her robe had slipped off her shoulder, and she was humming along to something on the radio Bette could only identify as "misc. classical." Bette stepped close behind Mei, her lips finding Mei's neck, where her fingers had been. Still humming, Mei tilted her head, reaching back and working her fingers into Bette's hair, directing Bette to tug at an earlobe with her teeth, to trail her mouth around to the hinge of Mei's jaw. Bette pulled at the knot on Mei's robe, turned her and lifted her up onto the kitchen surface, right next to the pot of still-brewing tea. Mei raised an eyebrow as her eyes traveled down Bette's body; she was standing naked in Mei's kitchen, as though that were a thing Bette did with lots of people, as though this wasn't the latest in a long line of firsts. As though Mei wasn't entirely aware of all of the ways in which this was new.

Bette thought Mei hesitated then—it was the proximity of the steaming pot, probably, or the blinds being open in the kitchen, or Bette being so obviously, mortifyingly hungry for her that she couldn't wait ten minutes for tea—but a moment later Bette was sure she'd imagined it. Because Mei wrapped her legs around her, kissed her, soft and open, and pulled her close, enveloping them both in silk. They made it back to bed, eventually, abandoning the long-stewed tea. It seemed more important, much more important than tea, to bite down on Mei's plush lips, to focus attention on the sensitive skin above her hip bone, to push her back against the sheets.

In the hours that followed, Bette lost track of quite how many ways they fitted together. And it was just when Bette's heart rate was returning to normal, while she was deeply at peace with the world, that Mei mentioned it offhand. As though it were the natural continuation of a conversation they'd already been having.

"I love how much you love this," Mei breathed, voice still soft and intimate, as she reached beneath the sheets for Bette's hip. "Love how good it is for you. Makes me sad to think about the years you weren't having it. All those experiences you missed."

Her words carried a weight that was seismic, far too heavy for a Saturday morning, and Bette felt them fall onto the bed between them.

"You wish—you wish I had more experience?" Bette's voice was pitched strange and slow, unable to keep the horror from creeping into it. The glowing pride she'd felt at her sexual prowess mere minutes earlier, at the sight of Mei's hand twisted in the sheets beneath them, her whole body taut, vanished.

"No, no," Mei laughed, quick to reassure her. "More experiences. *Experiences*," she repeated, forcing the emphasis. "I mean, I just—I guess I wish we'd met after you'd had more time to figure out this part of yourself."

Bette nodded, feigning relaxed understanding and chill, but her mouth opened quite without her permission. "Okay, but that still sounds a bit like you want me to be better at this."

"Stop! You know that's bullshit. You're fishing now. All right,

4 · KATE YOUNG

make sure you're listening to this next bit. You're great at this. Fantastically, overwhelmingly great." Mei leaned over to kiss her reassuringly before carrying on. "I'm talking about all of it, not just the sex. I've been dating women forever. I know what I want. I want you to have had that opportunity too."

"I don't . . ." Bette started, but Mei put a warm hand over Bette's still-tender lips and jaw and leaned over to suck a kiss against her collarbone. It was infuriating that she'd figured out exactly which parts of Bette's body to put her mouth on when she wanted her to shut up. It was horrible (incredible) being so well known. Bette waited for her to continue.

"What we have is great. It's so great, and so easy. Which never happens to me this fast," Mei started. And despite the fact that Mei was blinking too often, oddly nervously, despite the fact that Bette's insides were still twisting anxiously, it was impossible not to feel gratified at the truth of it. To hear from Mei how unusual it was for her too. It had never happened to Bette at all. "But—look—I can't help thinking that, somewhere down the line, you're going to end up regretting not having given yourself the time to date, to sleep around when you came out. I don't want to take that opportunity away from you. I don't want you to resent me. Regret committing to the first woman you slept with. You know?"

Bette was quiet. No, she decided. She did not know. Three minutes ago her biggest problem had been whether or not they could fuck again before Mei left for her studio. How had a few minutes been enough to derail everything? Was Mei really talking about her regretting this? Regretting *them*? It was precisely the opposite of what Bette had been thinking. Should she tell her that she'd imagined them going to visit Mei's family together at Christmas? That Mei had mentioned her sister in Tokyo and Bette had looked at flights more than once? That she'd found herself wondering last week what them having a baby might look like? It felt, despite the nudges Mei had given her to be more open with her feelings, to share more of herself than she was used to, that it all might be too much too soon. It had only been a couple of months. And so she found another way to say it instead.

"I meant what I've said since the day we met. I'm a monogamist. I don't need to have time in some dating wilderness, shagging as many women as possible. I want you. I want this." On her back, eyes fixed on the ceiling, Bette searched for the right words to encapsulate it, to tell Mei how much it all meant to her. "Yes, you're the first woman I've slept with. But also I can't imagine it feeling this good—this right, I mean—with anyone else."

Bette turned her head and found Mei looking back, her face squashed into the pillow. Her blunt fringe was too short (she'd been furious on Tuesday when she'd had it cut), the dark hair sticking up where she'd been tugging at it earlier. Her eye makeup from the night before was smudged, the once perfectly drawn wings flaking and streaking across her cheek and beneath her bottom lashes. Bette could see the distinctive speckling of a hickey on her chest, just below her jutting collarbone, that Mei would feign being grumpy about once she spotted it. It was unbearably intimate, Mei was stupidly gorgeous, and Bette couldn't believe she'd still not told her that she'd fallen in love with her. Couldn't believe she'd held it back. She wanted to say it, wanted to tell her, but something about this conversation made it impossible. It wasn't the time.

Instead, Bette rolled fully on her side, reached across to curl an arm over Mei's waist and traced her fingers up her spine. She tucked a knee between Mei's, slotting their bodies together beneath the light summer sheet. Mei smiled, the good one that she thought showed too many of her teeth, and Bette kissed her open mouth. It was clumsy and awkward and it made Bette shiver. They both giggled helplessly. Mei pulled her even closer, her hand settling low on Bette's back.

"I get that. I do. I'm not trying to tell you how you're feeling. I've just been thinking about it, you know? About us, I suppose, about the future," Mei continued, her voice easy and light in a way that felt forced. "Our future."

"Right."

"It's just . . . I think if there was a time to do it, it would be now. To, you know, take a break for a bit."

"A break?" A faint ringing started in Bette's brain, a too-late warning of an imminent disaster; the bell that rang out on the *Titanic* long after the ship had any hope of turning.

"Not a breakup, obviously. Just a break. So you can have a bit of time to experience being out. Being gay. Have some fun before you settle down. Before *we* settle down."

Heart racing, Bette skittered over the scraps of the morning, trying to piece them together, adding them up and still coming up short. She pulled her leg out from between Mei's and shifted backward under the sheet. She realized she didn't even know where she'd left her clothes. This is why people shouldn't spend the night together naked. She was vulnerable. Exposed.

"You want us to stop seeing each other? So I can sleep with other women?"

It felt mad. Ridiculous. Surely she had misunderstood.

"Yes. Sleep with. Date, a bit, if you like. Have the time I had. To figure this out, you know? But yes."

The silence sat between them, stretching out until Bette realized that Mei was waiting for a reaction. She grasped at the first thought that came to mind, and regretted it almost as soon as she'd begun.

"Wouldn't—I don't know. Wouldn't an open relationship be a better way to do this?"

"I don't really want an open relationship," Mei said, her voice so calm and placating and definitive that Bette felt a rush of anger. She'd had the chance to prepare a response for everything Bette might come back with. Her tone seemed to suggest this was an unremarkable conversation, a chat entirely suited to taking place in the sheets they'd just had sex in. It was as if she'd already decided this wasn't going to be a big deal, as if that wasn't a decision Bette was allowed to make for herself. "And you just said it. You're a monogamist too. I think things would probably stay the way they are."

Things staying the way they were was *exactly* what Bette wanted. She felt sick. Worse, her clothes were, she was certain now, in the living room. All of them. She was going to have to walk out there, after this conversation, wearing nothing.

"So instead you think we should break up?"

"Not forever!" Mei said, as though she were throwing Bette a life vest while she sailed off away from her. "Just for a little while. And then after three months," Bette's eyebrows flew up and Mei stumbled for the first time, "or, you know, whenever—I just thought three months might be good, give us time to get back together a couple of weeks before Erin and Niamh's wedding? Anyway, after three months we can properly commit to this. But I want you to have time to figure out what you want first."

"*This* is what I want," Bette insisted. Mei had really thought this through, she realized; the plan was so detailed, so horribly considered. And so, *so* maddeningly stupid. And then she remembered Ryan, remembered breaking up with him while on the sofa together on a rainy Sunday afternoon. Remembered him fighting so hard for them that her empathy had morphed into pity. It wasn't attractive, desperation. It was mortifying to watch. She took a shaky breath and realized she was dangerously close to tears.

"I know you think that. And I'm not denying how wonderful this is," Mei was saying, all gentle sincerity. "But it might feel great with someone else too. You don't have anything else to compare us to. And I want you to know for sure."

It was impossible to argue with this. But it didn't seem fair. Wasn't there always a risk with a relationship? It was all hope and risk and jumping off a cliff together not knowing where you'd land.

"But—Mei, I—I love you," Bette said, hating the desperation in her voice, a tear slipping out with the words, determined not to be held back. It was agonizing to say it like this.

"Oh Bette," Mei said, her eyes sparkling and wet, as she reached across the bed to take her hand. Bette clung to it as though it could stop her from drowning. "I'm falling in love with you too. That's why I think we have to do this."

Maybe it all made a horrible sort of sense. How *could* Bette know? She felt suddenly weighed down, her inexperience hanging off her like an overstuffed weekend bag. Maybe it was right for Mei to want her to be rid of it. Maybe getting rid of it would make everything better. Easier. Less loaded.

She took a deep, steadying breath and pulled her hand away from Mei's, feeling the absence of it like a physical pain. "So. A break then. Okay. If that's—I mean, if that's what we're doing, then can I just . . . Do you mind turning round? I need to go and get my things."

And instead of Mei telling her to stop being silly, instead of Mei laughing and pulling her across the bed, she nodded and settled a hand over her eyes.

···

91 days to go

Bette was running. She hated running. But her route from Mei's to the park had taken her past the pub where they'd had their first date. And so Bette was late. She'd promised her flatmate Ash she wouldn't get distracted, that she'd be there to celebrate the end of term, that she hadn't become a person who met someone and instantly ditched her friends. Though, in the end, she'd rather be that person than this one: the one who was late because she was delayed having a long public cry about a non-breakup.

Because that was the thing. The whole morning with Mei had eventually boiled down to one salient point: this wasn't a breakup.

The problem was, of course, that it absolutely felt like one. It would be as though Mei were going somewhere technologically and physically remote for a while, as if she were setting up an installation at the South Pole. Except that she'd be in Bristol, and they often worked together, so there was every chance they were going to see each other in the interim.

It was going to be hell.

What would be ideal, Bette figured, would be to go home, crawl into bed, and emerge only after the mandated three months had passed.

Instead, the thread of messages from Ash made it clear that that was not the Saturday she was destined to have. She was, instead, late for the park. She was also supposed to be bringing crisps and a dip, which she didn't have, the procurement of which was going to make her even later. Bette had said yes to the plan days ago, when she imagined Mei joining them once she'd finished in the studio, imagined them lying on a picnic blanket together, imagined her head resting on Mei's stomach as they dozed. Imagined them posed like a bus ad for tinned G&Ts.

It wasn't going to be like that at all. Ash was already there, with Anton and Carmen. They were all going to assume she was late because she'd been in bed with Mei, and while that wasn't *technically* incorrect, she couldn't quite handle the disconnect between their idea and the reality of the situation. The thought of explaining it to them was appalling.

They wouldn't get it. She didn't get it.

And so, standing out of breath in front of the crisps in the corner shop, she decided that it was probably easiest not to mention it. If they asked about Mei, about the morning she'd had, she could keep it light. Breezy. Pretend that she'd got out of bed late and had to rush through getting ready and that the conversation in bed hadn't happened at all.

She caught a glimpse of herself in a fridge door as she was standing in line to pay, horrified at her lank hair, more dirty brown than red when it needed a wash. Beneath her sunglasses she could feel the crustiness of her eyes, certain last night's eyeliner was smudged beneath them. She was wearing a denim shirt dress that popped open relentlessly over her boobs, and was, predictably, doing so now. She was late *and* a mess, she thought, as she dumped the crisps on the counter, did the Sisyphean button-up and tied her hair back in a sweaty little bun.

It felt impossible that eighteen hours earlier she and Mei had been standing in a Van Gogh exhibition that was all light and colors and cushions.

It had been three months since their first date, and everything had been bliss: late-night text marathons and long walks around the quays and Mei cooking for her. There was a night when they'd laughed so hard that they'd been shushed in a restaurant, and another when they'd made out in an almost-empty cinema. When Mei's parents had come to visit they'd gone for lunch at a French place and Mei had put an easy hand on Bette's thigh under the table and Mr. Hinota had invited her to visit them in Cheltenham.

And then yesterday they'd gone out for a late lunch and walked through the exhibition hand in hand. They'd spent a whole hour in the corner of one of the rooms, letting the light fall on their intertwined arms, Mei resting her head back against Bette's shoulder. They'd talked about their favorite artists, about the prints they'd bought and built their personalities around during university. About Mei falling in love with Yayoi Kusama's mushrooms, with the cypresses Van Gogh had painted, and with Matisse. About Bette buying a print of Hockney's pool, of Paul Fischer's women by the beach, and of Klimt's woman in gold.

"*How* did you miss that you were gay?" Mei had said, as if Bette's cheap poster prints were revealing. And they'd both laughed. As though it wasn't a thing they needed to worry about, just a bit of Bette's past they could poke fun at.

Ash had dropped a pin, and Bette followed it through the park to a shaded corner. From a distance, she could make out Anton lying with his head on Carmen's stomach, and she briefly hated them. And then Ash waved and Carmen called out a hello and she felt an annoying rush of love for them instead.

"Afternoon," Ash said, the single word managing to contain genuine pleasure at her arrival and gentle passive aggression that was probably related to the time. She was on her feet before Bette could respond, wrapping her in a hug. Her black hair was shiny and sleek and twisted on her head, her sunglasses were enormous, and her shirt was so white it was hard to look at. She embodied a perfect summer afternoon. Bette was aware of looking rumpled and disgusting in last night's clothes.

"Sorry I'm late," Bette said, getting the first apology out of the way. "But I come bearing gifts." She reached into her bag and pulled out the bags of crisps, one after the other: Skips and Monster Munch and Pom Bears and Walkers and everything else she'd been able to find, tossing them into a pile on the middle of the blanket.

"Hero!" Anton said, cap low over his eyes as he reached for a bag of prawn cocktail and pulled them open with satisfaction. He found a particularly big one, angled it into his mouth, and then wiped his hand on the front of his gray T-shirt before reaching in for another.

"A beautifully curated selection," Carmen agreed, trapped in place by Anton's head but reaching a hand over to squeeze Bette's in greeting. "How've you been, babe? Feel like it's been ages."

It hadn't, really, maybe just more than a month since Anton and Carmen had last been round for dinner. But it felt like ages to Bette too—so much had happened that she didn't quite know where to start. She could feel what Carmen wanted her to address, could see the slightly suggestive quirk of her mouth. Instead, she decided on a place of relative safety.

"Yeah, work's been pretty full on."

Art's Aflame (a name so cringe-worthy that Bette used it as little as possible) was a charity that sent visual artists out into primary schools and community groups. She'd been working for them for a few years, long enough that the routine of it all was beginning to itch under her skin. But she'd managed to get some funding for a few new projects that would start in September, planning for which had made up a big part of her life in the past month. Carmen, a playwright, understood the grind of fundraising.

"I'm sure whatever project you've dreamed up is great," Carmen said, entirely severing Bette's train of thought. She squinted over from behind her gold-rimmed glasses, attempting to shield her eyes from the sun. "But this isn't really the content I was after. Your job is fine, but it's not new. Not new like your girl."

Bette would have relished it, a few hours earlier. It had still been such a thrilling little pleasure to find herself the center of conversation about sex, about romance. About love. Last time she'd caught up with Anton and Carmen it had all been so gloriously fresh.

There was plenty to fill Carmen in on. She could have told

her about meeting Mei's parents, or talk about how Mei and Ash's boyfriend, Tim, had made plans to go climbing, or tell her about the art school friend of Mei's they'd had dinner with. Her life had been so infused with Mei that it was impossible to scrub her from any corner of it.

Carmen was waiting, expectantly. She could tell them all. Tell them about the break. There'd be sympathy and warm hugs and they'd probably stay into the evening to make sure she was okay. Bette felt sick at the prospect of it.

If she said she was going to be dating new people, they'd get that. But a break from Mei, to have some one-night stands? She still didn't know how to couch it, whether she was saying *I missed out on an important experience and I'm excited to claim it* or *Is it a problem that it's so good with Mei that I can't even imagine being with anyone else?* She was mad at Mei, mad that Mei had entirely misunderstood what Bette needed. But she worried too that maybe Mei knew precisely what she needed, that Bette had, again, missed something fundamental within herself. It wasn't as though it would be the first time.

And so: "She's great. We went to see the Van Gogh exhibition last night. The lights one? I think you'd really love it."

"Ooh yeah, I was planning on booking a ticket for the next few weeks," Ash said, as she pulled an honest-to-god quiche out of a basket. Bette was so grateful. Get them all onto the exhibition and Ash's baked goods and she might get away with avoiding the Mei thing for the rest of the afternoon.

"Shall we book some tickets for August?" Carmen directed at Anton.

"God, yes! Freedom! We're finished," Anton said, stretching

his arms out along with each word, and only just managing not to clobber Carmen in the nose. She swatted at him and pushed at his shoulder until he was forced to sit up. "This year felt really long. Stupid long. Thought shit was supposed to go faster the older we get."

He reached over for the slice of quiche Ash was holding out in his direction, biting the point off and sending her a thumbs up while he chewed.

"It does. It's the perception of time thing," Ash said. "Each year we live is a smaller percentage of our life as a whole, so it feels shorter."

"That's—that's—Ash, that's really bleak," Carmen said, her mouth curling up in distaste.

"Truly chilling," Bette agreed.

"Shut up, it's a nice thing!"

"Nope, it's not," Anton told Ash, and she scoffed at all of them.

Bette bit into her own slice of quiche and sort of wanted to cry. It was great, and Ash was great, and Carmen and Anton were great too. It was all great, everything was great, except she was heartbroken, and tired, and at any second someone might ask her another question. She lay down on the picnic blanket beside Ash's hip and closed her eyes.

CHAPTER THREE

SUNDAY, 17 JULY

...

90 days to go

Bette found Ash in the kitchen the next morning, still in her tartan pajama bottoms, filling the kettle, a podcast blaring out of the tinny speakers on her phone. Ash had a faded fun run T-shirt on, and her hair hung round her face. It was a real end-of-term energy; even on Sundays Ash was normally up and dressed long before Bette got out of bed.

"Should I put coffee on?"

There was an exaggerated jump and shriek as Ash turned; she was prone to overreaction at all possible moments.

She threw an arm round Bette and kissed her cheek extravagantly before pushing her out of the way in search of the cafetière in the cupboard above the fridge.

"Morning! Nope, already on it. How'd you sleep?"

"Not bad," Bette lied. She'd spent most of it filling the notes app of her phone with drafted messages to Mei she knew she wouldn't send.

"Okay," Ash said, hand still in the cupboard, "you seem weird.

You were really weird yesterday. Are you just tired? Mei still blowing your mind?"

"Well actually we're . . ." Bette started, her voice strange and catching in her throat. It was time. "We're taking a break."

Ash almost dropped the cafetière as she finally laid a hand to it and looked over with incredulity splashed across her face.

"You're what?"

"Taking a break," Bette repeated, feeling the strangeness of it. "We're on a break."

"A break," Ash said.

Bette nodded.

"You and Mei broke up?"

"Yes . . . well, no. No we haven't broken up. She was—well—not clear but—we've not broken up. I don't think. We're getting back together in October."

"Hold on. I don't . . . Shit, Bette. *Shit.* Do you want to talk about it? Do you want to be alone? What do you need?"

Bette shrugged, a heavy feeling settling in her chest. Thank god it was still the weekend. The idea of going to work today, of feigning cheerfulness, of being charming and professional, was horrific. She was suddenly aware of Ash close to her, Ash who smelled of clean sheets and salt and summer, who was so warm and so soft. She buried her face in Ash's shoulder and allowed herself to be wrapped up in her. Bette let out a shaky breath.

"I'm okay," she said. "I'm okay."

Ash held her a bit tighter. "Would you feel better if we had coffee and freezer pastries?"

Bette nodded and trailed off to sit on the window ledge while Ash scooped coffee grounds into the cafetière, pulled a tray with two croissants on it from the oven, and put them on a plate. She pushed the plunger down on the coffee and carried it through to the front room with the posh little cups that Bette sort of hated—they were far too small—but which Ash thought "photographed well." Bette picked up the plate and followed. They fell into the sofa Ash had found online for a steal that they'd carried all the way home to Totterdown, flushed with how clever they were to avoid paying the £30 to hire a man with a van. It had taken them six hours to make it a single mile; they'd kept stopping and sitting down on it to watch clips on YouTube whenever it got too heavy. When they finally managed to maneuver it through the front door and into their flat, their phones out of battery and data, aching in places Bette was certain neither of them had muscles, they had agreed that staying in the flat for at least another year was the only way to make it worth it. It had been more than eight since then, in the five-room flat; a place that was unequivocally home. Though there was foam poking through the sofa in places now, Bette still felt sentimental every time they sat on it together.

Ash arranged the pastries on the table and poured the coffee. It looked, like everything Ash did, as if it belonged on Instagram. She had a tendency to make things beautiful, in a way Bette never bothered with, even on her best days.

"Okay, so—a break," Ash said, tucking her legs up beneath her. Marge deigned to jump up and sit between them, her striped tail tickling Bette's ankle. "Do you want to talk about it?"

The thing was, she really didn't want to talk about it. She still wasn't sure she understood it enough to be able to defend it.

"Not yet," she replied. "I just—I want to wallow today."

"Okay."

There was silence between them for a moment, and then Ash cocked her head to the side slightly, as if she already knew what was coming. Bette took a shuddering breath.

"It was so perfect. I was so happy," she said, the tears inevitable now, making their way down her cheeks.

And really, that was exactly it: she'd been so happy, and couldn't have imagined anything better. Mei had dropped by the office in February, after a year spent on a project in Italy. She was an artist who had once run workshops for them, in the years before Bette had started. She had walked in in a vest top and a pair of loose-fitting black trousers secured high on her waist with a thick belt, her fringe hanging down into her dark eyes. Bette had fancied her instantly. Her colleague Erin, a head shorter than Bette, her body built of compact muscle, eyes a pale green, had brought Mei over to introduce her. Bette was self-aware enough to recognize that, if it hadn't been for Erin's fiancée, Niamh, she might have spent her early lesbian months struggling to navigate an all-consuming work crush. So it had been quite an image, really, watching them walk over together. And when Mei had shaken Bette's hand and met her eye, Erin had smirked in a way that told Bette that her cheeks were pink. That she had entirely given herself away.

"I'm going to stay in Cheltenham with my parents for a couple of weeks," Mei had said. "I've been away for a while so they're desperate to look after me. But I'll be back in March, in case you need any sessions covered for the last bit of the year?"

She took the pen straight out of Bette's hand and found a Post-it on her desk.

"Just let me know, yeah?" she said as she handed both back.

Bette watched her leave, and then looked down at the Post-it scrunched up in her sweaty palm. *For a session, or a drink, if you like* it read, with a number printed carefully and clearly below. Bette sucked in a breath. She had been out only a couple of months, had been thinking about a way to ask Erin about the apps, or whether there might be any women Erin could introduce her to. It couldn't possibly be this easy.

She had texted Mei that night, and then with increasing regularity over the next fortnight. She was clever, thoughtful, and made Bette laugh. It had felt like a *drink* drink when she left the Post-it, but somewhere in the two weeks since, Bette had lost all confidence. They were texting daily about art, about food, about books they'd read, about their favorite places in Bristol. It felt good, charged. Full of sparks. But she couldn't be certain.

Finally there was a night when she drank just enough wine with Ash to consider getting on a train to Cheltenham to ask Mei herself. At Ash's emphatic rejection of the plan, she texted Erin instead.

> **Bette:** no worries if you're not sure but I wondered whether Mei ever dates women?
>
> **Bette:** installation artist Mei, I mean
>
> **Bette:** the one who was in the office a couple of weeks ago
>
> **Bette:** obviously don't out her or anything if she wouldn't be cool with that
>
> **Bette:** and sorry for assuming you might know

> **Bette:** it's not like I think all queer women know each other
>
> **Bette:** or that that's a label you use
>
> **Bette:** I mean, I don't even know why I'm assuming
>
> **Bette:** or what I'm assuming
>
> **Bette:** you know what, ignore me
>
> **Bette:** I've had wine
>
> **Bette:** sorry

It had taken Erin fifteen minutes to reply, and Bette felt every second of each one waiting for the response.

> **Erin:** she's gay and she fancies you
>
> **Erin:** loser
>
> **Erin:** see you tomorrow
>
> **Erin:** go to sleep

There had been a lingering little hangover, and Erin had teased her mercilessly the whole next day, but it had been worth it. And when Mei came back to Bristol, they went for a drink after work in the pub around the corner from Bette's office, sipping gin and tonics and talking in exactly the same way they had been via text. Bette couldn't stop looking at her mouth, at the way her tongue caught on one of her teeth when she smiled. How could Bette have ever thought this felt platonic? Once the sky outside was dark, and the ice in their final drinks had melted, Bette realized they'd gone without dinner.

"It's only a proper date if there's food!" she reasoned as she pulled Mei out of the pub, tipsier than she'd thought once up and on wobbly legs.

"I'm not sure that's a thing," Mei laughed. "But I wouldn't want you to be confused and have to ask Erin again. So we'll probably have to get something to eat."

There was something in there about Erin that Bette felt she should probably be embarrassed about. But she couldn't bring herself to focus on it. She spun round, a hand landing in the curve of Mei's waist, pulling her close, at once pleased and utterly flabbergasted by having nailed the move. "If we want to make it a clear and unambiguous date, there's probably another way we could do that."

"Is there?" Mei asked, her mouth close to Bette's, stretched wide in a smile. "What way would that be?"

Bette's heart was racing. This close, Mei smelled of coconut shampoo and something smoky, like burning wood chips, probably from her studio, and Bette had never wanted anyone more in her entire life. She leaned closer, her nose bumping against Mei's as she angled their mouths together. The kiss was chaste, a press of soft lip to soft lip, and Bette felt it in her knees. Mei smiled against her lips and pulled back slightly, only to press her lips to Bette's again.

"See?" Mei said, pulling back again. "Unambiguously a date."

"You know what? I'm not sure," Bette replied, her voice shaky. "That could have been a friendly kiss. You know? Nice little platonic moment between colleagues."

Before she could clock what was happening, she felt pressure on her collarbone, right above her heart, and realized that Mei was pushing her backward. Her feet scrambled to catch up, but

Mei's other hand had already found a place in the center of her back, guiding her carefully and expertly. It was so hot. Bette felt a brick wall against her back and was embarrassed to hear herself groan. Mei smiled, and leaned in.

It was nothing like the first kiss. Mei's mouth opened against hers almost immediately, sucking Bette's bottom lip into her mouth and gently biting down on it. It shouldn't feel this different, Bette thought. Men had mouths too. *Surely* Mei being a woman couldn't change things this much. But even more than the softness of Mei's lips, the sweetness of her tongue, it was the knowledge that it was Mei kissing her—a woman kissing her—that set Bette alight. She felt sharp relief, mixed in among all the rest of it. This was exactly how she hoped it might feel. The hand on her jaw angled her and she felt Mei's tongue tracing her lip. The hand on her back moved around to the base of her ribs and she was so distracted by everything that was going on with her mouth that she forgot to worry about straightening up or sucking her stomach in. Her head and her whole body were entirely consumed by Mei. There was no space for anything else. She kissed her and she kissed her and she kissed her.

"So?" Mei said, minutes later, as she stepped back. Her lips were swollen and wet, and Bette was pleased with her own foresight in not wearing lipstick. She already wanted to touch her again.

"Unambiguously a date," Bette replied, her voice steadier than she'd imagined it would be. "Very inappropriate kiss for colleagues. HR would have a field day. Or Amanda would, I guess," she continued, the company's office manager wandering uninvited into her head. "That's probably her role, given that we don't have an HR department. Should I be worried that we don't have an HR department?"

"Just to continue our commitment to being unambiguous, I'm refusing to acknowledge the HR chat going on right now." Mei bent down and picked up a tote bag she must have dropped between her feet when she pushed Bette against the wall. "So. Chips? Or home to mine?"

Bette shrugged. "Both?" she responded.

The next weeks, those early weeks, had been some of the most overwhelming of Bette's life. She woke fizzing with excitement to see Mei, to text her, to kiss her, to sleep with her. It was as if all of Mei's edges fitted hers. Every cliché she could think of—a puzzle piece, a perfect bit of furniture in an awkward room—felt inadequate, not soft enough to convey the blurriness of their edges, the way in which they fitted not just against each other but into each other. Bette had always dismissed the concept of soulmate, the suggestion of a perfect partner. But it was impossible to imagine anyone better suited to her than Mei. It had been so easy to fall for her, to willingly give herself up to the feelings that overwhelmed her. Four months had been enough to find herself somehow inextricable from Mei, as if she'd given too much of herself to be able to get it all back.

"Yeah," Ash said, dragging Bette from her reminiscence, her tone weird, almost dismissive. As if there was a question mark at the end of it. It was not what Bette had been anticipating. Ash stroked Marge absent-mindedly and, predictably, the cat jumped down and stalked off. Ash brushed fur from her dressing gown, a frown forming between her brows. "I mean, it was clearly so great in the early days, but . . ."

The implication brought Bette up short.

"What do you mean was?"

"It's just seemed more—I don't know, it's felt like you—no. Forget it. Forget I said anything. Sorry."

Bette wanted to demand that Ash tell her what she meant. But she could guess already. She knew that she'd been around less, that she'd canceled plans. But she'd thought Ash had understood. It was the first time she'd ever felt like this. It was normal, surely, to get lost in it a bit.

"Should we watch something?" Ash asked, reaching over for Bette's hand.

Bette nodded. It was easier than talking about it, exactly the right thing. "*Grey's Anatomy?*" she suggested. "Can we find an early Addison one?"

"Course," Ash said, reaching over for her laptop. "Eat a pastry. It'll help."

It did.

CHAPTER FOUR

MONDAY, 18 JULY

...

89 days to go

'I've put Tim on standby tonight," Ash said, when Bette flopped down on the sofa beside her.

"No, stop! Tell him to come," Bette said, and reached down to scratch Marge beneath her chin. The tabby acquiesced to the attention for a moment longer than she normally would, a small sacrifice. It was as if she could intuit the complicated feelings of the past day. It had been a long one. And then a message had been sitting on her phone when she had pulled it out late in the afternoon, and her heart had leaped.

> **Mei:** I think you're amazing. I just want to make sure you get the chance to know it too. I'm here if you want to talk. But I think you should take advantage of this time. xxx

She did know it. Sort of. And if the break was a non-negotiable, then what was the harm in figuring things out? In flirting and trying out something new. Mei was right. Bette was so new to this. And women were beautiful. And so much fun.

Since coming out she had imagined how much she might finally enjoy dating, now that there was a chance she'd fancy the person across the table. Maybe taking this time before settling down was the right thing to do.

By the time she'd pushed open the front door to her flat, her vague musings had begun to take shape. She would just have to go on some dates. Date a couple of girls. No big deal. A hot girls summer. Literally. And then, when autumn began in earnest, she could tell Mei it had been fun and that she was all in. The break would be over. They could move on with their life together.

"I didn't want to push him on us if you needed—I don't know. Whatever you needed," Ash said, and Bette thought of the dark mood she'd been in the day before, how gentle Ash had been with her. How little she'd pushed for anything.

"I'm fine. Really. Completely fine. My job for tonight is to set up some of the apps, and I feel like he should definitely be here for that?" she replied.

"Oh, I can't think of anything he'd like more," said Ash, meaning it sincerely. "He'd be so sad if we did that without him. But—do you want to talk about it? I mean, I'm very pro you getting back out there, and good riddance to her and I curse her with every power I have and everything but—are you all right?"

"I am. I think I am. And I need to get out there as soon as possible. It's kind of the whole point."

"The point?" Ash looked confused, sitting up straighter against the sofa cushions, and Bette realized she'd skirted the specifics the day before. She filled Ash in, with particular emphasis on the crucial bit: by mid-October they'd be back together.

When Bette had finished, there was a silence, a long one.

"Right."

"I've been thinking she's probably right, too. You know, it would be so much pressure on both of us, if I ended up with the first woman I slept with. I'm thirty. I've slept with more men than I have women, kissed more men. It's not like I'm keeping score or anything but—well. It probably matters."

Bette took a breath. The air in her lungs felt so good that she realized it must have been the first in a while. She turned to look at Ash. Her face was reaching for neutral, her forehead furrowed, her mouth twisted closed. Bette could see her work to contain it and then, like a tray of drinks that begins to wobble, then pitch, then fall, saw her lose control of all of it in quick succession.

"Bette, you seemed—I don't know—you seemed really sad yesterday," Ash said, picking at the pilling on her ancient tracksuit bottoms, avoiding Bette's gaze. "Really down. It's great if you're feeling differently now but I just—"

"It's fine, really. I'm going to go on a couple of dates, and then we'll get back together. And it'll all just be this fun story we'll tell at dinner parties one day. That time my wife sent me off into the dating wilderness. We'll laugh about it."

Ash's expression remained unconvinced. She pushed herself off the couch, heading toward the kitchen, and Bette followed, even though the conversation didn't feel finished. Sure enough, she was barely through the kitchen doorway before Ash started again.

"What's she going to be doing while you're off on this adventure then?"

It was an annoyingly good question, she thought, as she watched Ash pull ingredients from the fridge. Bette hadn't really considered that aspect of it. But Ash didn't need to know that.

"It's not really any of my business. We're on a break. She can do whatever she likes," she replied, coloring her voice with more flippancy than she felt.

"And after, what, a few months? You just get back together? As if it never happened?"

It was so easy for Ash, Bette thought, with a prickle of resentful annoyance. Ash, who had met Tim at twenty-six. Ash, whose British Indian parents had welcomed their only daughter's very white boyfriend with open arms. ("Bit of a racist assumption to have made, actually," Ash had said, when Bette had brought up that she'd been worried. And Ash wasn't entirely wrong, but there was relief all over her face, and her hand was tight in Tim's.) Ash, who had dated a couple of other perfectly decent guys before then. Ash, who had a ten-year plan with her boyfriend; who knew she'd be trying for a baby by thirty-three, once she'd made deputy head and could afford a year of maternity. It was all pretty easy, Bette thought, when you didn't stumble into a massive sexuality crisis in the dying days of your twenty-ninth year.

She had been quiet for a moment when she realized that Ash's question had been left unanswered between them.

"Yes?" she said, hating the way that the question mark attached itself to the word, hooking around the -es and tugging it upward into uncertainty. "Yes," she repeated. And then, to solidify things, "Exactly."

Ash nodded, hesitantly at first and then with a more confi-

dent certainty. "Okay. Noodles for dinner then? We'll call setting you up with a profile dessert?"

Ash cooked while Bette levered the tops off a couple of bottles of beer and tipped a bag of crisps into a bowl. When Tim
arrived, work polo shirt tucked into faded jeans, he joined them
in the kitchen. His hug let Bette know that putting Tim on
standby also involved giving him a heads-up.

"I'm fine," she said firmly, before he could ask, and felt him
nod against her.

"We're setting Bette up on the apps after dinner," Ash said, as
she abandoned the noodles briefly to land a kiss on Tim's cheek.

"These Bristol lesbians won't know what hit them," he said,
his voice both joking and tender. Bette wanted to be reassured
by it, wanted it to soothe her. But she was raw with embarrassment. It all felt too patronizing, the thought that she needed to
be buoyed up. She wanted Tim to take the piss, hated the thought
that she might be an object of pity.

She had struggled with Tim, in the beginning, with the time
he spent with Ash that usurped her time, with the way he walked
nonchalantly into their lives. He was easy in a way that neither
she nor Ash had ever been. It was, she supposed, perhaps part
of being a straight, white guy: assuming that your place was everywhere you wanted to be. The thing about Tim was that she
found it impossible to resent him for it; he was so sincere with
his affection. He felt like a brother, someone she could share
things with and who looked out for her, who she knew loved her
even when she annoyed him. Nothing at all like her actual brother,
now she thought about it.

Later, once Bette had run her finger around her bowl, collecting the last of the peanut butter and soy and chili sauce that Ash always made, and Tim had mined the best of his "clueless people buying hiking shoes and camping equipment" anecdotes from the shop—a rich seam as ever—Bette placed her phone in the center of the table.

"So," she said.

"So," Ash replied, her face serious.

"So," Tim joined in, his smile bright and thrilled as if anticipating a treat.

Bette downloaded a couple of options—Hinge, Tinder, Her—while Ash filled the kettle.

"Remember when I had *Guardian* Soulmates?" Bette said, clicking through the initial setup, allowing access to her phone and her data and briefly worrying, as she always did, that she should be more worried about it.

She couldn't remember how she'd advertised herself back then. She didn't know how she'd introduced herself to strangers before the headline was *I didn't know I was gay, but I do now; isn't it nice to fancy people?*

"Oh Soulmates! RIP. What a time," Ash said, distributing teas between the three of them and joining them at the tiny kitchen table. "Oh my god. That guy! Heart attack!"

"Heart attack," Bette remembered.

"Heart attack?" Tim asked.

"As in '*serious as a . . .*' I can't remember his actual name. How would we describe him?" Ash asked, looking at Bette thoughtfully. "I have nothing. He was entirely without personality and Bette dated him for six endless months."

It *had* been six months, Bette thought. Longer than she had been with Mei. It was unfathomable.

"Look, Tim. The thing about not fancying men—no offense, you know I think you're great—is that every single one I dated was completely fine. Nothing offensive. Fine men. But also entirely unappealing to me. It's all very obvious why now, but at the time . . ."

"So, you have to answer a few of these questions," Ash said, steering them back on track. Tim leaned over and scrolled through the list.

"Hang on. Your coming-out story? Your love language? Top, bottom, or switch? Just casual little openers then? Low-key getting-to-know you stuff?" he asked with a laugh.

"Welcome to lesbian Hinge. This is going to be a real eye-opener."

"Teach me *dot dot dot*," Ash pointed out another of the prompts. "I mean—"

"Yeah, I'm honestly not sure I can pull that off?" Bette replied. "Like, hi, teach me what sort of sex you like in case I like it too? Teach me how best to get you off so I can take my new skills back to someone else?"

"Yeah, it's maybe going to be better to wait for the date on that one," Ash said, pulling her back into the room.

Bette scrolled up and down, searching for prompts that felt casual, rather than instantly exposing. Tim and Ash were silent as she typed; the anticipation was tangible in the room.

"Okay, how about this then? My esthetic: wannabe Dana Scully circa season four. A life goal of mine: see Tegan and Sara play live. The way to win me over is: with bog-standard crisps and really beautiful collarbones."

"Perfect," Ash confirmed. "Nothing too serious, gay band name-checked, crisps name-checked. I like it. Now. Photos?"

"Hold on. Are we just skipping over collarbones?" Tim said, his hand landing on the phone in the center of the table, as though concerned they might simply breeze past it. "Seriously? Like . . . of everything, it's collarbones? Collarbones?!"

"Oh god yeah," Bette said wistfully. Mei had incredible collarbones. "They're so elegant. So hot. Absolutely no idea what it is because it's not like they're risqué or anything it's just . . ."

"Guys, please. If we're going to do photos before bed . . ." Ash started before trailing off with a tone of resignation. It was already far too late; Bette and Tim were lost to the undeniable attractive power of the clavicle.

CHAPTER FIVE
THURSDAY, 21 JULY

86 days to go

Bette matched with Ruth during her lunch break on Thursday. Ruth was hot; her profile was sparse in terms of information, but her pictures were great—candids rather than selfies, warm brown eyes, a glitzy dress in one photo Bette immediately wanted to buy for herself. Most importantly, Ruth messaged straight after they matched.

> **Ruth:** That pic of you on the beach is gorgeous.

The picture was one of Bette in a stupidly large sunhat and a loose buttoned shirt; Ash had scrolled back through her camera roll for it. She'd pointed out Bette's tanned legs, the breezy shirt, and how happy she looked. Bette had been unconvinced, certain her smile was too big and cheesy and that there was a visible spot on her chin and that she had an obvious squint behind the glasses. It was the opposite of sexy, and she was convinced that it undid all the work of the rest of the photos. But Ash was right; it looked like her, and it had been a brilliant week.

> **Bette:** Lisbon last summer
>
> **Ruth:** I've never been—always wanted to.
>
> **Bette:** You should!
> **Bette:** it was so good!
> **Bette:** custard tarts, incredible grilled chicken, amazing seafood, good beaches
> **Bette:** it was sunny all week, but not too impossibly hot, you know?
> **Bette:** the city is so great too, really beautiful, such a good city for walking
> **Bette:** I'd go again in a heartbeat

She looked at the string of messages, immediately horrified. Ruth hadn't asked for a TripAdvisor review. This was a hookup app. What was she doing?

> **Ruth:** Sounds brilliant.

She'd blown it, obviously. It was impossible to tell whether Ruth was being sarcastic or not, but a two-word response to what was basically a Lisbon long weekend listicle was definitely sending some sort of message. There was nothing left to lose.

> **Bette:** so I know this is kind of out of nowhere, but trying to get to know someone over text like this is weird
> **Bette:** do you want to meet in person?
>
> **Ruth:** That's not out of nowhere. It's an app designed for that specific purpose.
>
> **Bette:** true

> **Ruth:** Plus I like your gumption. Six
> enthusiastic messages about Lisbon and
> you're going for the date.

Bette wanted to crawl under her desk. The teasing was gentle but brutal: despite plans to be cool and casual in her messages, she'd instantly revealed a distinct absence of chill.

> **Ruth:** So yes, that sounds good.
>
> **Bette:** how about brunch? Sunday?
> Do you know In Brunch We Trust?
>
> **Ruth:** Hate the name, love their
> beetroot hash! Brunch it is. 11 a.m.?
>
> **Bette:** yes! Looking forward to it!

She regretted the second exclamation point instantly.

They didn't really text in the days that followed. It was important, Bette thought, not to get in too deep. It was a date, a hookup if she fancied Ruth as much in person as she did on-screen. Nothing more.

As the weekend approached, Bette could feel herself growing more anxious. What if she wasn't good without Mei? On a date. Or in bed. What if Ruth wanted something she hadn't done before or—god, what if Ruth wanted something she hadn't even heard of? But this, she supposed, was the point of the whole gambit.

It was her mantra as she arrived on Sunday morning: *just sex, just sex, just sex.* She was early; Ash had pushed her out of the door after her nervous anticipation had manifested in a fumbling awkwardness. They had lost two wineglasses to it before Ash had pulled the tea towel out of Bette's hand. It had been Ash's fault anyway, she'd spent the morning repeating the word "brunch" with ever-increasing incredulity. As if Bette didn't know how to plan a date.

She realized the coffee was a bad idea as she took the first sip. It was her third of the morning, on an empty stomach, and she could feel it pluck and play on every nerve in her body as though it were fingers on a harp. It had felt rude to take up a table empty-handed on such a busy morning, but now she was about to vibrate out of her skin. Perfect. Exactly what she needed.

Bette reached into her bag, her hands properly shaking now, and pulled out her phone.

"Bette?" a voice asked, tone low and soothing. If a voice could be the opposite of caffeine, Bette thought, this was it. This voice should do ASMR videos. This voice should . . .

"Hi, yes, sorry," she replied, the words running into each other. She could taste the anxiety and it tasted like coffee.

"Wannabe Dana Scully really helped. Well played. Your hair is stunning."

As her hand went self-consciously into it, as though it might be different to the hair she'd left home with, Bette looked properly at Ruth for the first time. At her center-parted dark brown bob, cut just below her chin. At her warm expression, at the laughter playing around the corners of her mouth. At her striped blue and white playsuit, the shorts turned up to show dimpled thighs kissed pink by the sun. At the sunglasses tucked into her bra, which dragged her top down just far enough to flirt with decency. She was somehow even hotter than her profile.

Bette put her phone away.

"It's dyed. Obviously," Bette said, and Ruth laughed. It was a lovely laugh. She sat down across from Bette and handed her a menu.

"Stole these from the counter as I was passing," she said. "I love this place but they're always rammed. And I'm starving."

"Me too," Bette said, relieved. "I think I've overdosed on coffee. I need to get something else into me before I have a heart attack."

"Oh yeah, if this was that Blind Date column, I'd be recording my first impression of you as 'jittery.'"

"Jittery, good hair," Bette corrected, relieved to be poking fun at herself. This she could do.

"Jittery, good hair," Ruth confirmed.

"Well I think my notes on you would read 'cute, playsuit,'" Bette replied, and was pleased to notice a slight flush on Ruth's cheeks.

"Is that cute comma playsuit? Or cute playsuit? I feel like that's an important distinction."

"Both, if you like," confirmed Bette. "But I definitely meant to include the comma." Ruth smiled at her and Bette took a breath, her heart rate calming a little. She really could do this.

"So, when did you move to Bristol?" Ruth asked, her eyes scanning her menu.

"How'd you know I'm not a local?" Bette replied, spotting the shakshuka and then deciding almost immediately against it, picturing peppers and tomatoes streaked down the front of her white shirt.

Ruth shrugged. "Lucky guess. More interlopers than locals here. I say that as an interloper."

It was a truth Bette had never really considered.

"God, you're so right. Almost everyone I know here grew up somewhere else. Anyway. Exmouth. On the coast in Devon."

"Oh beautiful! I love the sea."

"Me too, so much. And Exmouth's fine. I think I'd be more impressed by it if I hadn't grown up there."

"Oh sure, every time I go home to North London I try to imagine coming as a tourist. It's impossible; every corner down Kilburn High Road is a memory of some screaming teenage row with my mum."

"Did you fight a lot with your mum when you were growing up?" Bette regretted the question almost immediately, alarmed at how serious it sounded. This was a date, not a therapy session. She hoped desperately that Ruth wouldn't turn it back on her, wondered how to force the worms back into the can.

"No, she's great," Ruth said, running a hand through her hair and shrugging easily. "I was just doing a bit, usually. Imagining that we should probably fight more than we did. Felt mortifying to basically quite like my mum's company."

Bette laughed, and then the waiter arrived, and rescued her from having to segue away from mother-daughter dynamics. They ordered, and Bette even remembered to say decaf. After that, the conversation flowed easily. Ruth was halfway through a PhD in queer translated literature. She was sharp and quick-witted and self-deprecating. At one point she had a bit of maple syrup clinging to her top lip and Bette wanted to lick it off. It was a good date. Maybe even a great date.

And so she was feeling confident when she leaned over, met Ruth's eye, and said, "Do you want to get out of here?"

A laugh burst out of Ruth, so loud that people from the tables around them looked up from their eggs. Bette looked around uncomfortably, trying to work out where she had gone so quickly wrong. Ruth's forehead creased as her eyebrows crept northwards. "Oh wow, you're serious? That was a real line?"

A silence fell between them and Bette wished for a swift and comprehensive death. She was going to have to explain.

"I don't—sorry, I haven't really done this before and I—"

"Haven't done what before?" Ruth asked, sounding tentative rather than accusatory. Perhaps it hadn't been unforgivable. Maybe Bette could get away with it.

"A hookup, you know? Like, met someone on an app for a hookup?"

She realized that she had indeed stepped across a line into unforgivable. Ruth's arms crossed over her chest, and she looked down at her plate. "Oh," she said, that low and soothing voice suddenly heavy with clarity and understanding. She laughed, but not in the way she'd been doing since she walked into the café. Then she shook her head and looked up again, and Bette was certain she had imagined it. Ruth looked fine, amused even.

"Never?" she asked.

Bette shook her head. "Never. I met some people online when I was still dating men, but I was never particularly interested in the sex bit. Funnily enough. So I didn't really do casual."

"Right, that makes sense. And now?"

"Well now I thought—I don't know. I thought I'd . . ." She trailed off. Ruth waited a moment, and then sat forward.

"Look, I don't want to make assumptions here, but you don't strike me as a hookup person."

Great. Brilliant. This was mortifying. Was it just that she'd never done this before? Or was there something distinctly not-a-hookup about her? She had thought she'd been getting away with the *here for a hot hookup* persona.

"I'm not saying it's a bad thing!" Ruth said. "It's just that you've got wife and kids written all over you."

Bette felt herself flush, and tried to subtly wipe away the sweat that was tingling her top lip. She wished that she'd gone for tinted moisturizer, rather than the foundation that was almost certainly flaking off in the heat. She was a mess.

"What makes you think so?" she replied, aiming for nonchalant and landing closer to hysterical. Ruth smiled, and her crooked incisors showed. They were oddly cute. Could teeth be cute?

"You've looked up at every single pram that's been wheeled in since we sat down, you seem genuinely interested in my research, we've been here for nearly two hours and you haven't made a single suggestive comment—except for the getting out of here bit, I suppose. Plus, you invited me out for brunch."

There was no way to deny any of it, so Bette decided to tackle the most egregious statement first. "I love brunch! What's wrong with brunch?"

"Brunch is a getting-to-know-you date," Ruth said, gesturing around the café. And, all of a sudden, Bette saw it. The large windows and excess of light, the twee fonts on the blackboard, the mix of families and prevalence of dungarees. There was absolutely nothing about the café that felt in any way sexy. "A see-if-we-click-and-can-then-go-for-a-dinner date. Or a morning-after date, I guess. Brunch is not the sort of thing you suggest if your plan is a hookup."

That was why Ash had kept incredulously muttering brunch all morning. How was *Ash* better at this than she was?

"Okay, so what should I have suggested?" she said, pressing her shaking hands between her knees, distinctly aware that her tone was edging back toward hysterical.

"Drinks. Dinner, maybe, if you're feeling particularly confident or we'd been messaging back and forth about food. But if you actually want to hook up, then drinks. Or literally just invite someone round. To your house. And . . . hook up."

Bette was silent for a while, considering. Drinks, obviously. She should have said drinks. Of course. How was it possible to be so bad at this?

"Hey, it looks like you might be starting to panic a bit. It's okay! I didn't mean anything by any of this. I'm not trying to tell you how you should feel about it. No judgment at all, I'm just making conversation."

"It's just. I mean, you're right," Bette replied, too overwhelmed to try and deny it, exhausted at the thought of trying to be witty or flippant or make more conversation. "I'm a relationship person. That's why I'm shit at this! But I'm in love with this woman and she said I needed to have some more experience, some more *experiences* with other women before we commit to each other, and I—that's what I'm doing. I guess."

It was a lot to process, Bette supposed, and she waited for Ruth to work through it. It took a while; Ruth twice opened her mouth as if to say something, before moving her fingers across her lips and shaking her head with an air of incredulity.

"Wow. That's. I mean. Wow. Okay, so I thought you might be

new to this, but this is a whole other thing. Some woman you're in love with has sent you off on, what? A sex odyssey?"

"I'm really sorry, I don't want you to think I'm using you or anything." God, it all sounded awful, from the outside. And the inside too, honestly. "But I should have been clear that I want to date women who are looking for something very short-term. Like, one night, ideally. Women who want a fun hookup. I don't want to date anyone who might want more than I can offer. I just need to go on some dates and have a bunch of sex with new people. And then I can go back to Mei and she'll know that it's not just that she was the first woman I slept with, but that she is *the* one, and god I really didn't plan on saying all of that."

She was out of breath, she realized, her head pounding. It felt like the coffee high all over again.

"That is a lot to unpack," Ruth said slowly, wonderingly. She flagged down a waiter and ordered an Americano. Bette, who was still buzzing with the coffee or the adrenaline or a combination of the two, passed him their empty water jug instead.

"Sorry," Bette said, once he'd left in the direction of the kitchen. "I mean, about the . . ."

"Don't apologize. This is kind of amazing. I've been on a lot of dates in my life, and this is much more interesting than: *So what do you do in your spare time?*"

"Well, I'm glad you're getting something out of it at the very least." Bette hadn't been aiming for sarcastic and petulant, but had landed there regardless.

"Look, I don't know if you're going to want it, but can I offer you some advice?"

Relief began to outweigh the embarrassment.

"Please, please do. I clearly have no idea what I'm doing."

"We've established no more brunches, moving forward, right?" Ruth said, with the sort of authority that made Bette want to find a pen and a napkin for note-taking. "You need a good get-in-get-out strategy. So to speak. You don't want to get too attached, right?"

"Okay. I mean yeah, you're right." *Just sex, just sex, just sex* marched through her head again. She blushed as the waiter returned with coffee and water, as though he could hear what she was thinking.

"I don't want to stereotype and you might be absolutely fine. But if you're used to having sex in relationships, you might find it harder to not get attached. So you need to keep it casual. Drinks. Get to know them, obviously, but keep it light. Kiss them somewhere you feel safe—it's why I've always done this sort of thing in a gay bar, so you don't get interrupted by some leery old perv in a pub who thinks you snogging a girl has literally anything at all to do with him." Ruth took a breath, and Bette was suddenly impossibly grateful for her. For taking everything in her stride and for seeming to care. It would have been so easy for her to just stand up and walk out. "But you go where works for you. If that's good, if the kissing is good, then brilliant, work out whose place you're going back to, or how far you want to go without taking her home. If the kissing isn't great, if the chemistry isn't there, have a think about whether or not you might have a good time anyway. I'm not saying all first kisses have to be perfect, but it's not a terrible indication of whether or not you'll have fun in bed."

Bette couldn't help glancing down at where Ruth's sunglasses were still hooked in her bra. At the freckles scattered over her chest, at the sharp line of her collarbone. It was difficult not to, when she was talking about first kisses and being in bed. Ruth met her eyes as she glanced back up, and she knew instantly that she'd been less subtle than was ideal. Bette shifted her tone to businesslike.

"Right, that all makes sense."

"I don't want to patronize you here, so stop me if I'm wrong, but given that you're talking about this other woman being your first, you probably don't have much experience with one-night stands? But maybe you did before you started dating women?"

"No," Bette admitted. "Like, none."

"Cool. If it were me, then, I'd be really upfront. Your profile needs work, for a start, because you're definitely not clear enough about what you're looking for. You're newly out, and you want to date some people and work out what you like, right? You're not looking for anything more than a night. Just tell people that. If they're not looking for the same, they'll swipe left. But give them the chance to make that decision."

Bette realized that Ruth was talking about herself. She hadn't let Ruth make that decision. Her stomach churned guiltily.

"You're right. I'm really sorry. I should have thought."

Ruth waved her hand, as if batting the apology back. And really, Bette reasoned, now that things were clearer between them, she didn't seem to be terribly disappointed.

"It's fine. But yeah, this sort of setup wouldn't work for me, for instance. I've made a vow not to date emotionally unavailable people anymore."

There was a story there, one that hooked in somewhere in

Bette's brain, that she'd probably wonder about later. If she hadn't spent the past ten minutes deep in mortification, she probably would have asked.

"Thanks so much for the advice," she said, meaning it sincerely. "Honestly, I'd have been floundering without you."

"You're welcome. Consider it a gay mitzvah. I'm very pro you having as much fun and great sex as you like, but it's worth letting people know what they're in for. You'll have plenty of takers, believe me."

Bette felt her cheeks glow, and it took everything within her not to ask whether Ruth was absolutely sure about the hard-line "no" she'd already laid down.

"Also, I think you should give me your number too," Ruth said, smiling at the waiter again, in pursuit of the bill. "Because I am going to want to hear how this goes."

CHAPTER SIX

THURSDAY, 28 JULY

●●●

79 days to go

I t took Bette until Thursday to open the app again. It didn't mean she hadn't been thinking about it. She had, uncomfortably often. But each time her mind returned to the date, to her expectations, it was accompanied by a rush of guilt, of deep embarrassment. It was not a comfortable feeling, not one she welcomed, to be so awful at this. To have gone on a date that resulted in a hot woman having to explain dating to her. But by Thursday, thoughts of Mei and the task ahead of her outweighed everything else.

Ash had laughed when Bette had returned home following the date. Not kindly or sympathetically, but raucously and with relish. Bette wanted to be furious but it was, she conceded, objectively funny to proposition someone so baldly and be so sweetly and comprehensively rejected. And so she allowed Ash the laugh. But it was clear that she was going to have to update her profile herself, or risk being thoroughly mocked while Ash watched her attempt it.

Ash was at Tim's on Thursday, so Bette took advantage of having the run of the house. The evening was mild, cooler than it had been in a month. Mild enough to permit a scalding-hot bath and a very cold beer, to sip while her chin sat below the waterline.

Their bathroom was without question the worst room in the house, spots of mold blooming in the corners where the landlord had neglected it for too long. Ash and Bette, who had put loving effort into their living room and kitchen, who had sought permission to paint over the gross shade of magnolia she assumed all landlords must be issued with tins of, had long subscribed to the logic that there was nothing much they could do with their bathroom apart from keeping it clean. They'd had no hand in choosing it, and were resigned to the boxy, utilitarian nature of its design, which made the room feel even smaller and more crowded than it already was.

Mei's bathroom, on the other hand, was a dream. She had shelves and baskets fitted to the walls, plants everywhere, and piles of towels so soft and fresh that Bette wanted to bury her face in them. The walls were painted a deep navy-blue and the white tiles shone brightly alongside it. There were long hours spent talking in the bath there, late at night after the sun had set, knees knocking together in the center of the tub.

One Saturday morning she had arrived home from Mei's, walked into her own bathroom, and decided it needed work. Now, there was an IKEA shelf above the window, lined with pots that sent trailing vines and leaves down in search of light. She relegated all towels stained by her Real Red hair dye (the shade was anything but) to a "dye day" pile that sat in her wardrobe, and found a set of new ones to keep pristine. She'd bought a bath rack that balanced precariously over the sudsy water and a couple of fancy-looking candles that smelled of citrus fruits. The bathroom was no longer a room she hated.

She sank further into the water, and took a steadying breath before clicking back onto the app. It was clear, she supposed, scrolling down her profile, to see where she'd gone wrong. The part that said "What are you looking for?" was blank, and she'd skipped right past the "About me" section too, in favor of answering prompts and uploading a handful of photos. It was a profile entirely devoid of any tangible information. She was surprised that Ruth, so self-aware and clear about what she wanted, had swiped on her in the first place.

She clicked on "Something casual" and added it to her profile. But the "About me" was the real challenge. Every draft was like stripping off layers of her skin. "I'm newly out" made her feel prickly and embarrassed. "Not looking for anything serious" felt like an overused line. There was no way of including the word "sex" that didn't make her cringe. In the end she decided to go slightly retro, something that would be easy to pass off as a joke if it was laughed at in the wrong way.

disaster lesbian wltm hot queer women in bristol for casual fun, fucking, etc.

It would have to be fine. She dropped her phone onto the floor beside the bath and slid into the silence below the water.

SHE MATCHED WITH Jess on Saturday morning, before she'd got out of bed. The conversation opened with a hey and a winky face that Bette tried and failed not to judge. This wasn't a search for a wife, she reminded herself. This was casual.

Bette: hey!

Bette: gorgeous shot of you at the wedding

Bette: if that's a wedding?

Bette: kind of assume every fancy event is a wedding

Bette: which seems silly, actually

Jess: love your style

Bette: thanks! that's lovely of you.

Jess: you Bristol?

Bette: I am! 10 years now.

Bette: you?

Jess wasn't verbose, but that didn't necessarily matter. She was pretty. Hot, actually. Blonde hair sweeping down across her face, pouting at the camera. There was a guy in half her photos, a horrible yellow smiley sticker pasted over his face. Probably an ex.

Jess: my boyfriend and I love to play
Jess: wanna meet up?

Not an ex then.

Bette: not really my thing, sorry

Bette: no shade! Guys just aren't my jam!

Jess unmatched less than a minute later.

ON SATURDAY AFTERNOON, leaning on the trolley halfway down the biscuit aisle in Sainsbury's, waiting for Ash to return with the ground coffee they'd missed, she matched with Sophie. Her phone pinged with a notification, and Bette swiped instantly on the raven-haired pixie cut and the great orange lip.

> **Sophie:** Bette is such a cool name!
> I've never heard it before? Is it
> short for something?

> **Bette:** it is!

> **Bette:** Elisabetta

> **Bette:** I was Beth when I was little

> **Bette:** then I read Little Women and decided
> I didn't want to be the one who died

> **Bette:** so I started saying Bette instead

> **Bette:** spoilers, sorry

> **Sophie:** Haha

> **Sophie:** That's amazing

> **Bette:** didn't figure out until after I
> came out that I picked the name of
> an iconic L Word character

> **Bette:** should have known

> **Sophie:** Oh I've never seen it!

> **Bette:** it's great and fully insane

> **Bette:** are you based in Bristol?

> **Sophie:** I am! For a year now. I live in Clifton, which makes uni easy

> **Bette:** what are you studying?

> **Sophie:** Music! It's amazing. My sixth form didn't really have a great program, so I honestly still can't believe I actually got in

Huh. Sixth form.

She clicked out of their conversation and back onto the profile.

Sophie, 19.

Fuck fuck fuck fuck fuck.

"Ooh, she looks young," came a voice from close beside her ear.

"I know, I know! It was an accident, I didn't mean to swipe!" Bette said, her voice high and defensive. As Ash took over the trolley, laughing back at her, Bette found the age section in the settings tab. And unmatched from Sophie.

ON WEDNESDAY, on her walk home after work, she swiped on Netta. Netta had black braids twisted on her head, huge eyes and a smooth expanse of collarbone and shoulder on display that Bette wanted to sink her teeth into. She had clicked only on "Something casual" too, she was thirty-one, and Bette felt like she might be getting on top of the swiping thing.

It was late Wednesday night, when she was brushing her teeth, that the notification came through; Netta had swiped back.

"She's so beautiful!" Ash said, looking over Bette's shoulder, before spitting in the sink.

"I know," Bette said around a mouthful of toothpaste. Ash threw her an awkward wink (the other eye trying and failing to stay wide), and then left her to it. Bette's phone vibrated again.

> **Netta:** Hey! Thanks for swiping and sorry I'm late to swipe back! Great to sort-of meet you.

> **Bette:** it's nice to not-quite meet you too!
> **Bette:** what's your week been like so far?

She groaned. She hated that question, especially from a stranger. There was nothing to say, surely, but "fine." Why on earth had she led with that?

> **Netta:** Yeah, fine.

It was what she deserved. She clicked back onto Netta's profile. There were mentions of travel, and a love of romantic comedies. Confident she could recover from the most boring question possible, she clicked back on their chat.

> **Bette:** best Nora Ephron romcom?

The response was nearly instant.

> **Netta:** There's a right answer here

There was, Bette agreed.

> **Netta:** You've Got Mail, no question

That was not it.

Bette: whhhhhhaaaaaaatttttt

Bette: but . . . but . . . WHMS?

Netta: oh you're one of THOSE people

Bette: one of those people who recognize true brilliance?

Netta: It's an excellent film! Not denying! You've Got Mail is better

Bette: but Sally!

Netta: but Kathleen!

Bette: the rolodex!

Netta: the caviar!

Bette: he's never going to leave her!!!!

Netta: OK, I'll give you that one
Netta: A perfect line

Bette: all right, let's go
Bette: give me your thesis

Netta: it all essentially boils down to Tom Hanks > Billy Crystal
Netta: plus you get the greatest breakup in cinema with Greg Kinnear
Netta: plus books. And an ending that makes both characters truly happy

Netta: she gets to be an editor, or a writer, or whatever

Netta: gets rid of the albatross

Netta: let's face it if she actually wanted to save the shop there are so many other things she could have tried

Netta: she didn't try

Netta: he gets her and to run his nice little bookshop empire, at least until Amazon fucks them all over

Netta: and that's not even addressing the fact that I can practically guarantee that your favorite bit of WHMS (because she is without question the best part) is Carrie Fisher

Netta: She's amazing, she's perfect, but you can't ask her to carry the film. She's not the lead.

Netta: sure he basically catfishes her and sure he should tell her earlier and sure it's all a bit fucking icky

Netta: but TOM HANKS

Netta: in AUTUMN

Bette realized she was staring at her phone in delight, toothpaste now dripping down her chin and onto her pajamas. She washed her face and took her phone to bed.

Bette: that is . . . alarmingly convincing

Netta: Thank you. My goal on this app, from the beginning, has been to convert people to You've Got Mail

Netta: you're a Bristol local, right?

Bette: I am!
Bette: love it here

Netta: Oh yeah? What took you originally?

Bette: uni, years ago, and then I just never wanted to leave
Bette: you?

Netta: Just a meeting

Bette: lol and you never left?

Netta: No no I did
Netta: Home in London now
Netta: I'm in Walthamstow
Netta: you know it??

Confused, Bette clicked back to Netta's profile. Sure enough, she was 176 miles away.

Bette: shit, sorry, thought I had my settings at 10 miles

Netta: Sorry! I was in Bristol yesterday so it will have picked me up and pushed me in your direction
Netta: Was a real fly-in fly-out work visit
Netta: But, like, on a train.

Bette: of course

The disappointment settled in her. It had all been going so well. And now it was just one more to add to the week of disappointments and false starts.

> **Netta:** Are you ever up in London?
>
> **Bette:** practically never
> **Bette:** you in Bristol much?
>
> **Netta:** Not that often. But I might be in the next month or so? Trying to sign a deal there so I'll have to be back. Let's have a drink then?
>
> **Bette:** yes absolutely
> **Bette:** sounds great
>
> **Netta:** You're really fit, btw. Even if your Ephron opinions need work. Really glad we swiped.
> **Netta:** Anyway, looking forward to it

It could have been worse, Bette conceded. There was a spark; it felt like a date might be fun. But the disappointment ate at her nonetheless.

FOR HER BIRTHDAY, every year since she had moved to Bristol, Bette's mum had given her two swimming vouchers for the Lido in Clifton. She'd rolled her eyes the first time; certain it was a little nudge from her mother to immerse herself not just in chlorinated water but in an entirely different crowd. Her first visit started out precisely as she'd feared. It was a pool that felt far too fancy for her, a haven for people who had money for treatment packages and posh lunches. Who dressed in labels she didn't recognize and whose swimming costumes weren't pilling around the seams and sagging around their boobs. People, in other words, who weren't students. Who didn't work for arts charities. She wanted to hate it, wanted to feel above the whole thing, wanted to sneer at a pool that had a membership waiting list.

Unfortunately, it quickly became one of her favorite places in the world.

On Sunday, the first plunge into the water went straight to her head. It was a heated pool, but the air outside was so warm that it felt like a cool relief in contrast. She could feel the sweat wash away from her body and tried not to think too much about everyone else's sweat; sweat she was now swimming through.

Submerged in the water, her mind was normally blissfully empty. She had come to the pool to clear her head, but she thought immediately of the ten days of swiping, of every failed and aborted possibility. Of the fact that every time she wanted to text Mei she opened the app instead, and that it didn't satisfy the same desire. Her arms cut through the water, propelling her forward, and with each stroke she felt the frustration tense in her shoulders. She hated the apps. It felt so unnatural, so forced. So boring. She had been so lucky with Mei. To meet someone she clicked so instantly with, someone she fancied who fancied her. Who wasn't in another city, or already attached, or nine-fucking-teen. It all seemed so unlikely. How did people do this?

After twenty minutes of pushing herself up and down the pool the tension in her shoulders had eased, her arms beginning to ache satisfyingly from the repetitive movement instead. Her brain felt better too, buzzing less with general frustration and irritation and more with trying to solve the conundrum at hand. Ash was no help, in terms of hook-up experience, or finding-hot-people-on-a-dating-app experience. In fact, she knew surprisingly few people who had spent much time single in the past few years. She was an outlier.

Except Ruth. It occurred to her that Ruth, who seemed pretty au fait with dating apps, who had definitely referenced other dates, had given Bette her number. If not quite for this purpose, then not *not* for this purpose.

She'd lost count of her laps early on, but her shoulders told her she was finished. She pulled herself up out of the pool, wrapped the hired towel around herself and, despite the heat, made a beeline for the sauna. It was horribly, gloriously hot, and it was impossible to think about anything but the sweat dripping off her nose, by the fact that every breath in was damp and unsatisfying. Eventually, convinced she might faint, her head blissfully clear, she stumbled out, sucking in lungs full of fresh summer air. As her heart rate returned to normal, she showered off the sweat that had collected in every crevice of her body and then laid out her towel on one of the corners of decking in the shade. There was half an hour left of her slot, and although she felt like she probably should dive back into the pool, all she really wanted was to lie down out of the sun.

As she settled in, fiddling fruitlessly with the straps of her swimming costume in hope of it suddenly offering a suggestion of support, her mind returned to Ruth. Was it poor form to text? They had been on a failed date; it was probably tasteless to text her in hope of more dating advice. But then, on the other hand, Ruth had said she wanted to hear how things were going. Surely this was only offering what she'd asked for?

Bette agonized over it for another minute before reaching into her swimming bag for her phone. She could text hello. A simple hello, and then they could see where things went from there.

But when she unlocked her phone, in between a photo from Carmen of her and Anton at the Van Gogh and a reminder from Ash that they needed oat milk, there was a message already waiting for her.

> **Ruth:** So how goes the hunt?

Huh. Maybe she could have worried less.

> **Bette:** hunt makes me sound properly predatory

> **Ruth:** Sorry, didn't mean it like that.

> **Bette:** oh no, I wasn't complaining at all

> **Ruth:** Lol. Okay.
> **Ruth:** So how goes the hunt?

> **Bette:** is it terrible if I have a bit of a whinge about it?

> **Bette:** because . . . honestly?? a bit crap?

> **Ruth:** Is it all women who want someone to have sex with them (and their boyfriend) or they're twenty-two and make you feel ancient or they're women

who live 300 miles away who were in Bristol a week ago?

It was uncanny.

Bette: . . .

Ruth: I met you on the app, remember? I know the game.

Bette: it's not been all awful?

Bette: there was one woman who seemed great, but turns out she was only in Bristol for the day

Bette: but otherwise yeah it's women who want threesomes

Bette: or women who make me feel like I should be thinking about a pension

Bette: so, on the whole?

Bette: pretty slim pickings

Ruth: You don't have a pension?

Ruth: Not the point, sorry, I know. But also maybe worth looking into?

Ruth: Have you thought about meeting people in other ways?

Bette: like in person??

Bette: what is this?? 2005??

Bette: or whatever, I wasn't gay in 2005

Bette: that might not have been the vibe

Ruth: Oh it was all MySpace and hot people at college for me in 2005.

Bette: god I wish I'd been out at school

Ruth: I mean, it wasn't entirely smooth sailing. Section 28 was a pretty big thumbs down. But there was a lot of fun to be had.

It wasn't as if Bette didn't remember. But it had all been so theoretical to her back then.

Bette: sorry, really didn't mean to be flippant

Ruth: No! Not at all! Just . . . there's no one perfect way, I guess?

It felt so obvious, when Ruth put it like that. She had spent the past year feeling jealous of everyone who had come out sooner than she had. But there was something to be said for having been twenty-nine, for living with Ash, who had been nothing but thrilled, for not having to take a label into school with her and have it poked and pointed at.

It felt good, she realized, to talk to Ruth about things. Useful. These were things that, for all Ash's perfect, brilliant friendship, they couldn't share.

Bette: do you fancy grabbing a drink?

Bette: platonically, obviously, I'm not trying it on (again)

Bette: but I have about a thousand more questions and I have a feeling you've got the answers

Ruth: Ha! That is entirely possible. You can reap the benefit of my wilderness years. Friday? After work?

That was exactly it, Bette thought. She needed a guide. Someone who had been where she wanted to go. Someone who had ventured into the wilderness and had made it out the other side. Bette ran her hand over her swimming costume, trying to determine whether it was dry enough to wear home. It was still damp at the elastic seams and so she kept her head down, wondering how far she could push her slot, wanting to bask a little longer in the unexpected joy of having help and advice on the horizon.

CHAPTER SEVEN

FRIDAY, 12 AUGUST

...

64 days to go

It was Friday night, after work, and there were two pints sitting between them. The pub was crowded, but Ruth had managed to find a corner of a table in the beer garden and they guarded it ferociously as groups around them crept closer and closer. Bette should have anticipated it, of course; it was Friday, it was summer, and it was England.

When a man sloshed his pint down Bette's back for the second time in as many minutes, she morphed into the worst and most uncomfortable version of herself, apologizing again for being in the way. Ruth had rolled her eyes at the first apology but cut Bette off halfway through the second, staring at the man from behind her enormous sunglasses until he shrugged out a "Sorry, yeah?" and tried to shuffle a little further away.

It resulted in just enough space between them for Bette to be able to contort her arms behind herself and wring out her shirt. Of the two of them, thank god it had been her back to take the spillage. Ruth looked like some sort of platonic ideal of summer in a crisp white shirt dress, her yellow bra just visible beneath the fabric. Bette's trainers were streaked with mud from a walk to work through the park earlier in the week, and her navy buttoned blouse was an old one she had tucked into her shorts. It was a shirt she hadn't ever felt self-conscious about until she sat down opposite Ruth and thought suddenly about the very small hole under the arm, and the way the collar never lay quite flat, and the fact that she hadn't ironed anything since school. And though it would survive the lager (it had survived worse), she was now also destined to spend the rest of the evening smelling like a brewery.

Trying to ignore the stickiness, and at least appreciate the cool breeze against her wet back, she gave Ruth a rundown of the past fortnight, of her updated profile, of the aborted conversations.

"Nineteen? God, that's young," Ruth said, grimacing. "I was a proper rotter at nineteen. I would absolutely have swiped on a hot thirty-something."

"Fuck off. I'm thirty. Full stop. Not thirty-something," Bette replied, biting down on a smile.

"What were you like at nineteen?" Ruth asked. Her tone was casual, and Bette knew she wouldn't blink if she responded flippantly. But it was clear there was an invitation behind it. Permission to take the conversation from light, frothy bitching about dates to something more sincere.

"I was—" She hesitated, taking a gulp so large it threatened to come back out of her nose. "Fuck, I don't know. It's easy to paint over the reality with the benefit of hindsight, isn't it? Honestly, when I think about those first couple of years in Bristol my overwhelming memory is that I was just working really hard. Not even at uni, really. Just . . . working hard. You know?"

"I mean, I think so?" Ruth said, and then took a sip from her glass. "But tell me."

"I just want to go back and shake that version of myself. Not to try and wake her up about the gay thing specifically. Just tell her to give herself a break. I was trying so hard to fit into some version of . . . god, I don't even know. Whatever it was I was expected to be. Even though I didn't really work out what that was. Just trying. To be cool? Maybe? To be liked, to be fun, to be the girl you'd want to date? Regardless of how I actually felt."

"Yeah, I'd worked out the fancying women bit by then, but you're so right. It was such hard work. You couldn't pay me enough to be nineteen again."

Going back with the knowledge she had now was impossible to imagine. "No, me neither. Some of it might be more fun the second time round. But I've been a pretty big fan of thirty so far."

"Yeah? Did you come out this year?"

"Like a year and a half ago. But really only to Ash, my flatmate? It took me another year to tell my family, and then a bit longer than that to actually do something about it. To do what I wanted to do about it, I guess. I mean, coming out *is* doing something about it," she said, suddenly anxious of offending. "You know what I mean. Anyway. I met Mei. What about you?"

"I pretty confidently told my mum that I was going to marry a girl when I was eight or something. My aunt Rachel is gay. And I wanted to be like her and her partner Sid." She smiled, and Bette pictured a dark-haired kid with a blunt fringe prancing around with a lace tablecloth pinned to her head, certain she was going to marry a woman. She felt for herself at the same age. "I don't think Mum took it too seriously, just said that sounded good. I remember realizing as a teenager that I liked boys too. I was so furious about it. I dated my first boyfriend for three months before I could bear to tell my parents about him."

Bette laughed, thrilled, as she always was, by the existence of a parent who was entirely unfazed. She hesitated. It had felt different saying all this to Mei, when she was overwhelmed and naked in her bed—it all came out without her intending it. But here in the beer garden it felt trickier. Much more exposing. "I don't think I really knew what fancying people felt like until the last couple of years. I thought I was broken, a bit, I guess. Or that there was some giant conspiracy, and everyone felt the way I did about sex. Really underwhelmed."

"Heteronormativity is a hell of a drug," Ruth said, warmly and emphatically, touching her pint to Bette's in solidarity. "It's easy to get hooked on it really early on. And it's a hard one to wean yourself off, especially if you grew up without representation."

"And Catholic."

"And Catholic. Yeah, that'll do it," Ruth said, grimacing. "But you made it through. And now you've discovered the joys of women."

Bette could feel herself blush, and hoped she'd be able to pass it off as the beer, or the sun.

"Yeah, I guess I have. Or, I mean, woman. I suppose."

"Oh I meant more generally, just the whole—women thing. In general. I didn't mean—though yes. If you want to be specific. I guess."

"Ummm . . ." Bette mumbled, mortified, before realizing that Ruth had hidden her mouth behind her pint and was laughing at her. "Great, this is really great for me. Thanks."

She glared at Ruth for a moment before the corners of her mouth turned up too. She couldn't help it. She was having fun.

"Anyway. The apps. Basically, I thought this was going to be fun, now that I'm swiping on people I actually fancy. But instead it's just . . . admin. It's boring. Every time I open it there are about forty other things I would rather be doing. It feels like having a second job."

"Me too," Ruth agreed, sounding relieved to have the truth of it confirmed. "Every single person I know has a success story that happened to them or a friend, or a friend of a friend. So I feel like I can't give up. Like it would be the same as giving up entirely. On love, on romance, on the whole thing. I delete them all the time to make myself feel like I don't need it, but I always end up caving and downloading again."

"Have you met anyone interesting on it?" Bette asked, and then laughed and added. "Apart from me, of course."

"Apart from you, of course," Ruth repeated, less sarcastically than Bette thought she deserved. "No, not yet. I'm on it now to meet *someone*. Big, capital-S Someone. So it's new for me too. In a way. I've sort of always met anyone I've been serious about through friends or at work. I was only ever really on apps for something fun. But a lot of my friends have coupled up now, and the pool is just—smaller. Smaller than it was a couple of years ago. And I'm not lonely, not really, but it would be a really nice thing to have. I miss having someone."

There was a pause as Bette drained the rest of her pint. She wanted to say something reassuring, but everything she came up with sounded patronizing.

"So no, not yet," Ruth said, tipping her own glass back.

"You will," Bette said, leaning into the platitude. "You're really great."

Ruth smiled, but it was weary.

"So we've commiserated over our app failures," Ruth said, and Bette felt a rush of relief to be moving on. "You had a thousand questions, if I'm remembering correctly?"

Bette had. When she'd been sitting by the pool she'd had a thousand questions. And suddenly they all left her, except one.

"I—I just don't know how to do this without using people?"

Ruth nodded, fiddling with her empty glass. There was no instant reassurance, and Bette wanted to escape to the bar, suddenly keen for a task. But working her way through the rugby scrum was inconceivable.

"Sure, I get that," Ruth said, after another moment. "You're a nice person. So that's not surprising. But also, you kind of are? Using people, I mean." Bette opened her mouth to answer back, and realized she couldn't. She was using people. Ruth must have seen her face drop, because she reached across the table and clasped Bette's arm. "It's okay, don't beat yourself up about it. So long as you're open about what you want, it's not a problem. But, like, the intention here is to sleep with a bunch of women as a means to an end, right? Eventually you want to be back with whoever she is?"

"Mei. And yeah, that's the goal. Shit. That sounds really terrible."

"Stop apologizing. Sex is fun, and it doesn't always have to be more than that. It's okay to use each other. It's hot to use each other. To get what you want."

Bette flushed. It *was* hot, she knew that. And she wanted to talk about it in considerably more detail. But she was aware of everyone around them, of the too-close presence of the creeps. Sitting at the corner of a table in a packed beer garden didn't feel like the right place for an explicit conversation.

"Bette, absolutely no one is listening to us," Ruth said, apparently able to read Bette's mind now too. "I want to tell you about my new strap-on," she said, slightly louder. A couple of the guys in their vicinity turned, the beer slosher's grin lascivious.

"Okay, maybe they are," Ruth conceded. "Want to get out of here?"

Bette nodded and they abandoned their table and glasses; a couple were somehow sitting in their places before either of them had properly finished standing up. She managed to hold in the laugh until they tumbled out of the crowd and onto the street.

"Oh shut up," Ruth said, her grin wide. "What's a more appropriate location for this conversation then?"

It was getting late, Bette realized. She'd already taken up so much of Ruth's time. Somewhere in the direction of home probably made sense. "We could walk back up through the cemetery? I think it's late enough now that it'll be quiet, and they don't close it until sunset. We could take the long way back up?"

"Perfect," Ruth agreed, readjusting her bright-yellow crossbody bag in a way that meant it slapped against her with each step.

Bette fell into step beside her, ignoring a niggling blister on her pinkie toe in order to keep up with the brisk pace Ruth set. She was a walker, Bette realized. One of those women who managed to stroll miles without effort, who always had the right shoes on, whose thighs weren't sweaty and chafed from rubbing together. If you told Ruth to walk to Bath, she probably could, just keep walking from where they were and arrive ready for brunch the next morning. Bette would have to go home to change, spend a few months training for the endeavor, and even then would inevitably perish by the side of the road.

The tumble of thoughts circling in her head came out in one cohesive point. "How are you wearing a dress and walking this fast when it's this sweaty?"

"Shorts, obviously." Ruth stared at her, incredulous, pushing her sunglasses up from her nose to rest on top of her head. She pulled the hem of her dress up and showed Bette a line of white lace that circled the plump thigh beneath it. "You can't tell me you don't have cute little shorts to wear under your summer dresses? Why on earth would you put up with chafing?"

They *were* cute shorts, and Bette was furious. This is what came from spending all her time with a best friend and flatmate who only wore jeans. "Are you telling me that all the girls in Bristol whose thighs touch are just wandering around with shorts under their skirts and dresses all summer? And no one bothered to tell me?"

"Afraid so."

"Text me a link?"

"Of course," Ruth said, taking off again at a slightly more relaxed pace. "And the strap-on too, yeah?"

"Oh no, I'm fine," Bette said, then paused before adding, "I've got one already."

Ruth laughed, and Bette liked that she did.

"Actually, that was a bit of a lie. I don't have one, Mei does. Did. Does. They're not really for me, to be honest," she continued, pushing through the feeling that talking about sex like this should be awkward. Maybe it could just . . . not be. Ruth didn't seem bothered. "I tried with Mei because she liked it, but I wasn't really a fan of fucking her like that as much as I was of the other stuff we did. I was into it because she was into it. If you know what I mean?"

"Sure," Ruth agreed.

"So I'm not sure it's really that high on my list."

"You have a list?"

"Not, like, an actual list. There's not a checklist on my phone or anything. It's just a . . . like a metaphorical list. Really, it's just a single bullet point that says: have some sex," Bette said, and Ruth nodded sagely.

"Did she use it on you?" Ruth asked.

Bette thought back, wondering when she'd missed the moment with Mei when she might have asked. Wondered whether they'd made the decision together, or whether it had been made for her. "I guess—I mean—she didn't ever suggest switching. So I didn't really think about it."

"Well, maybe that's what she meant, by making sure you had this time? If you have any things in your head that you think 'Maybe I would like that,' then you could give it a go? With one of your . . . conquests?"

It was precisely the point, Bette thought. She nodded at Ruth as they rounded the corner past the stone gates. The cemetery was big and sprawling, the graves and monuments set far enough apart that in summer they were surrounded by a rich sea of green; grass and shrubs and flowers bursting through. It was always beautiful, but Bette loved it most as the sun just started to set. As they made their way toward the winding path that would take them up the hill, the temperature dropped significantly; the trees that lined the path broke the light until it fell on them in dappled patches.

"Look, you probably don't need me to say this. But . . ." Ruth hesitated. "The first time is not necessarily the best time. Not that it won't be good. Not that chemistry isn't a thing. But, you know. I mean—women are all—people are all different. Obviously."

"Obviously," Bette agreed with a nod she hoped looked reassuring, because Ruth had paused and was looking in her direction, and it seemed like she wanted her to.

"Like, I don't—I don't know if you're after specific 'sex with women' tips?" Ruth lifted her bag and settled it over the other shoulder, her eyes back on the path.

Bette didn't know how to answer. She absolutely did want specific tips, but it seemed very much like the wrong answer.

"Well . . . I mean . . ."

"Because I'm happy to be a sounding board," Ruth interrupted, "but actually my only advice is that there's no guidebook for correct lesbian sex. Or correct any sort of sex. Just, assuming anything based on gender isn't the one. You don't need to go in with a plan. You can just . . . ask. Listen. Figure out what the other person likes. Okay, sorry, this is starting to sound like sex ed, which really isn't what I was aiming for . . ."

"No, it's good. I mean, that makes sense," Bette said, suddenly feeling nervous.

"I'm not saying it's going to be bad! It might be great. But if I wanted to guarantee a bunch of really great sex, I'd probably find someone I clicked with. Someone I felt comfortable with, so I knew I could ask for anything I wanted. And have fun with them, trying things out."

She was blushing, a gorgeous pink, and Bette was charmed that it was a turn from strap-ons to intimacy that brought a flush to Ruth's chest.

"Well, sure," Bette agreed. It sounded enormously appealing when Ruth said it like that. But it also sounded a lot like a relationship. "It did keep getting better and better with Mei. Every time. But I couldn't do that to someone. I think I'd inevitably get attached. It's too messy. This is the best way to handle it."

"No, of course," Ruth nodded. "Of course."

Ruth's voice was more distant, and Bette couldn't work out what had changed. But a moment later Ruth continued, and it was as though she'd imagined it.

"You could add what you want to the profile then? Like, sex-wise. Specifically."

"What, 'working out whether I want to be fucked, so bring your strap-on'? I don't know if I could text that to one person with a straight face, let alone write it down on the internet for anyone to read."

Ruth laughed again, a little snort through her nose and then a grimace.

"You're right. It's not really the tone, is it? It's all taking baths together and what books are you reading and Sunday afternoons in the park, and here's a picture of my dog and let's take him with us on our first date. My flatmate has a dog breed checklist from her dating escapades."

"Oh that's *so* good. Hang on. I've just realized I know nothing about who you live with. I must have mentioned Ash and the flat fifteen times by now."

"Well, in fairness, your life is a hundred times more interesting. You're on a sex odyssey!"

Bette laughed. "Well, we need to rectify this imbalance. I get it, I'm amazing and fascinating, and we could talk about me for hours. But from this point, all the way up to the top, it's all you. Tell me about where you live."

"This is because we're hitting the worst bit of the hill now, isn't it? You don't want to be all out of breath. Leave the conversation to me instead."

"Exactly," Bette said, and then stared pointedly at Ruth.

"Okay," she said, a little out of breath already. "I live in a big, crumbling old terraced place. Not a single wall is at a ninety-degree angle, and most of them are sort of damp. I adore it. We do what we can with it. My flatmates have been there at least a year now, I think? We had a couple of duds a few years back, which wasn't great, but they're all really solid at the moment. The landlord reckons it's a four-bed, but we've turned the little box room into a kind of horrible storage space. We can close the door and pretend there's nothing there."

"Oh god, we need that room," Bette groaned.

"Yeah, in London some sad intern would be paying £650 a

month for it, but here it made sense to turn it into a shared storage space to hide things we don't want to see. Especially once Jody's boyfriend moved into their room and everyone's rent dropped a bit."

"So there's Jody and her boyfriend," Bette said, starting a count on her fingers.

"Their boyfriend," Ruth gently corrected. "But yes. Jody and Leon. They met when Leon was dating Jody's brother." She nodded at Bette's widened eyes, "I know, I know. I am privately *slightly* judgmental about it. But also, it's hilarious. I want to be a fly on the wall when they go back to Jody's folks for Sunday lunch."

"Wow," Bette exhaled with a shake of her head. "I'm trying to imagine my brother's wife leaving him for me. I mean, it would be horrible for both of us because she's an uptight bitch, but it's also *very* funny."

"Anyway, Jody is doing a law conversion course. Leon is a musician. He plays the double bass, which is, of course, the very nicest instrument for your flatmate to play."

"The girl next to me in halls in first year played the trumpet," Bette suddenly remembered. "I'm not musical so I guess I can't really judge, but she was so *so* bad. I haven't been able to hear one since without feeling a little sick. Like, my whole body rejects the instrument now. As a concept."

"I see your trumpet and raise you bagpipes," Ruth said.

"No!" Bette gasped in horror.

"Well, no," Ruth said, a smile breaking out. "But *imagine*."

"A nightmare," Bette agreed. "Okay, so that's Jody and Leon. Who's in the other room?"

"Heather. She's brilliant. The one with the checklist. I would suggest her for your sex project, if I didn't think she might ruin you a bit."

Bette turned to her, opening her mouth to protest that perhaps she wanted to be a bit ruined. Or a lot ruined, honestly. But Ruth shook her head, as if she knew what Bette was thinking.

"Nope. Absolutely not. But if you promise not to sleep with her, then you should meet her. She'll have loads of good advice, and probably people she'd introduce you to. It should have occurred to me before, actually. Anyway, Heather's gay and dates a lot. She's not that into relationships, but she really knows the scene."

"Wow," Bette replied, feeling oddly jealous of a woman she had never met. "What a crew!"

"Yeah, it's a bit of a queer house," Ruth said. "Always has been. Not deliberately, really, it's just part of having been out forever, I reckon."

Wonder bloomed in Bette, imagining the life she might have had, the chosen family she might have built. If she'd known. If she hadn't been so late to the whole thing.

"So, I'm this way," Ruth said, pointing off to the right when they reached the top.

"I'm just over there," Bette said, pointing vaguely in the direction of the flat, aware of the little prickle of disappointment in her, that they'd reached the fork in the road so abruptly. She hesitated, and then decided to throw out an offer and leave the ball in Ruth's court. She didn't want to be taking advantage. "Let me know if you fancy another pint at some point? Maybe somewhere less . . . Friday?"

"Absolutely," Ruth said, and then stepped forward, her arms wide. "I'll message you," she said as they hugged, the words close to Bette's ear, tickling down her neck. They pulled apart and in a rush of uncertainty, in wanting to do something with her hands, Bette found herself waving lamely. It was new, in terms of a level of awkwardness, she thought, as she moved her arm back and forth. She wasn't thrilled by it.

"See you later," Ruth called over her shoulder, her voice bright with laughter. Bette watched her leave, the yellow bag still bouncing against her with each step. And then she walked home in the last of the daylight, the cool evening air delicious against her skin. The shirt still stuck slightly, the stale smell of lager emanating from it. But she had made a proper new friend. She felt fantastic. Mostly fantastic. Almost completely fantastic.

There was something gnawing away at her, though, something she was missing.

When she pulled her phone out of her pocket to plug her headphones in, keen for something to soundtrack the last few streets home, she noticed a text that she hadn't felt buzz.

> **Mei:** Hope you're having a lovely
> Friday. Thinking of you. Xx

The bottom dropped out of her stomach, and she wanted to sit down on the footpath. It was Mei. The thing that was missing was Mei. Her thumbs hovered over her phone screen, poised, as though she had any idea how to respond. After a minute or so of standing still, she put Phoebe Bridgers on, dropped her phone back in her pocket, and walked home, utterly deflated.

CHAPTER EIGHT

SUNDAY, 14 AUGUST

•••

62 days to go

Once a month, on a mutually convenient Sunday afternoon, Ash and Bette cleaned the flat. It was a routine born of necessity; only once they had begun to add the day to a shared Google calendar did they manage to lift the house out of the state of malingering mess and dust it had existed in in the early years.

It helped too that their respective skills tessellated neatly together. Bette hated cleaning bathrooms, and Ash was grossed out by the thought of what could be found rotting in a back corner of the fridge. Bette had a mopping technique that left their floors gleaming, Ash somehow managed to polish their mirrors so they were streak-free. It wasn't the only reason she dreaded the thought of the inevitable future, when they wouldn't live together, but it wasn't an entirely insignificant part of it. She resented the knowledge that she would, one day, have to clean a bathroom again.

The Sunday after her drink with Ruth was a cleaning-the-shit-out-of-the-house Sunday. Bette had spent the Saturday in a funk, heartsore and missing Mei and drafting texts in her notes app and frustrated by the entire situation. Her period had arrived that evening, which helped explain quite how deep the funk had been. But the heartsore feeling, that desire for Mei, remained. By Sunday afternoon she still hadn't replied to Mei's text and had begun to spiral about having left it too long.

"It's not like it demanded a response," Ash said with a shrug, pouring hot water over a mystic blend—two bags of Earl Grey, one of their regular PG Tips—in the pot. The end of the tea would mean a start to the cleaning; Bette didn't mind the jobs, but an afternoon with her headphones in left her far too much time to think. She needed to solve the Mei conundrum before they started.

"Not explicitly, I guess? But it's been, like, four weeks since I've seen her." It had been twenty-nine days, and a couple of hours. But she could already see Ash's reaction to that sort of pronouncement, and so went for the approximation. "I miss her, Ash. I don't know why I haven't replied, except that I had no idea how to tell her I catastrophically fucked up the only date I've had so far, and that it's been a month and I'm failing and—"

"Okay, okay," Ash said, waving her hand in front of Bette in a bid for her attention. "I think that's probably more than enough of that. Far too much, honestly, but I wanted to hear where it was going so that I can effectively refute it."

"There's literally nothing in that you can argue with."

"Oh my god, *shut up*, you giant baby. I thought you got your period last night? Shouldn't this level of self-loathing be over by now?"

"Actually, in the past couple of months it's like my PMS has stretched out to cover those first days of my period too. Little bonus for my brain."

"Sure. Okay then, PMS girl, I'm going to spell this out. One—you aren't failing. There is no 'catastrophe.' You have *just* started thinking about dating, and already women are swiping on you and wanting to meet you. Whether you think they're the right women for this very very specific very very niche project is by the by. But this boring little 'poor me, no one fancies me' narrative is bullshit. Pure bullshit. Do better." Ash's love was tough when it needed to be. Bette craved it and feared it in equal measure. "Two—you don't owe Mei an update. This was her call, all of this, and if you aren't enjoying it then you don't have to do it. Forcing yourself to sleep with a bunch of other people because Mei thinks you should isn't healthy. Not for you, and not for the women you're picking up."

Bette bristled at the suggestion that she wasn't entirely aware of what she was doing, not entirely in control of the whole thing. "It's not that I don't want to. I think it could be fun. Should be fun. *Will* be fun, obviously. And that first date with Ruth, I really did want to. That wasn't me talking myself into something I didn't want."

"Well, I don't see the problem then. Don't reply to Mei. Let her wonder a bit. Let her come to you. And find another woman who is aware of your whole . . ." She paused and then gestured generally in Bette's direction—"Your whole *thing* and then shag her. Or text Mei and tell her you're done with the plan and that you want to get back together. Or that you're done with the plan but you need some time. All of these options are valid. Moaning self-pity all weekend is not."

She was, unfortunately, entirely correct.

"Sorry, Ash."

"You don't need to apologize to me. Stop whinging and let's get started."

Bette could feel Ash reaching the end of her tether, but she couldn't help it. "And you definitely don't think I should text Mei back?"

"I don't," Ash said, through gritted teeth. She was quite literally rolling her sleeves up, folding her hair up into a scarf and hanging her headphones around her neck. She was ready for the conversation to be over, ready for the bathroom to be clean. "But what I do think is that for every thirty minutes of cleaning we should do five minutes of swiping together. A little pomodoro method, but for cleaning and flirting."

"Pomodoro?"

"Pomodoro. Twenty-five minutes work, five minutes off. I try and do it with my class, and it turns out you're being a child today too, so let's try it. Okay? Sound good?"

Ash collected the cleaning caddy from beneath the sink and plonked it down in front of Bette, looking at her expectantly.

"Perfect," Bette agreed. "It sounds perfect."

LATER THAT WEEK, Ash's pomodoro swiping bore fruit. Bette arrived early for her date on Friday, scoping out the bar for a table they could prop themselves up at. The options weren't thrilling: the bar stools looked criminally uncomfortable and the single booth had already been commandeered. It was clearly a bar intended for standing. For dancing. For snogging in dark corners.

Still, she had a good feeling about the evening ahead. Charlie had been sparse in her use of emojis, was in her thirties, and, crucially, hadn't mentioned a boyfriend. It was a vanishingly low bar, but a promising start.

The bar itself was . . . fine. A bit too sticky, a bit too tacky, a bartender in a vest who looked as though he'd rather be literally anywhere else. But it was drag night and it wasn't one of Bette's usual haunts. It was a place that knew nothing of her, that expected nothing from her. She could be a one-night girl here.

Though, she thought as she looked around, 7:30 p.m. was probably far too early to have suggested they meet. Better than brunch. But only just. Bette felt out of place in the cavernous, almost entirely empty room, overdressed in a dark-green skirt that was slit up her thigh. It was a good few hours before the queens were due onstage, and the bar was alarmingly quiet. Pairs were dotted around, but Bette's attention fell on the group of young backpackers, all of them immersed in their phones, bags piled up beside their booth. They were done with Bristol, that much was clear, the bridge and the Banksys behind them, likely killing time before they piled onto a night coach bound for London and then Paris or Amsterdam or Brussels. Bette had caught that coach. She hated that coach.

She pulled her phone out and clicked on her thread with Ruth.

> **Bette:** longest coach journey you'd
> take if I gave you five grand

She could see Ruth typing almost immediately.

> **Ruth:** I need context. Am I alone
> on the coach? Do I get to choose

the scenery? How big is my seat?
Do I have food with me? Can I
take books? I think you're
expecting me to say eighteen hours
or something, but I think I could
do weeks, quite happily. I love a
road trip.

Bette: I've just been reminded of
the overnight coach I took to Paris

Bette: that's the context

Bette: this is not a road trip

Bette: this is a coach journey

Bette: not some luxury tour bus

Bette: all strangers

Bette: absolutely packed

Bette: one toilet

Ruth: Damn, I forgot that bit.

Bette: your seat is a coach seat

Bette: obviously

Bette: you can take books, but
the guy beside you hogs the
armrest and huffs every time you
turn a page

Bette: you can eat, but everyone
else can too

Bette: the woman in front of you
has tuna mayonnaise that she
pulls out after eight hot hours

Bette: for breakfast

> **Ruth:** This is a horrible game.
>
> **Ruth:** But also, I hate to lose.
>
> **Ruth:** Two weeks.
>
> **Bette:** fuck off
>
> **Bette:** no one would survive two weeks of that
>
> **Ruth:** Just for that, three.

Realizing that she didn't want to be on her phone when Charlie arrived, Bette pushed it into her bag and instead committed to familiarizing herself with the drinks menu. Midori was a key ingredient in three of the house cocktails, all of which were euphemistic in name. It was just after she'd talked herself out of a stabilizing crème de cacao and Kahlua shot that she saw her.

Charlie turned heads. She was tall, assured, and walked with a swagger that made Bette sit up a little straighter, a charge of anticipation running up her spine. There was leather and a swept-up fringe and dark curls and eyes lined with kohl. There was no bag hanging from her shoulder or her arm, and Bette was unaccountably turned on by it, by Charlie walking out of her house with only what she could fit in her pockets. She was a manifestation of Bette's very first lesbian fantasies.

When she met Bette's eye, her face cracked open in a crooked smile. "Bette, right?" she said, already pulling out a stool.

Bette nodded. "Charlie?" she confirmed, though she was already certain of it. "Can I get you a drink?"

"Sure, that'd be great," Charlie said, resting her chin on her hand and squinting over at the bar. "I'd say whisky, normally, but it's impossible not to notice the—well"—she gestured around—"so maybe something weird and sweet and frozen, while it's still happy hour?"

It was such a delicious reading of the room, a complete surrender to the environment, that Bette grinned back. "Perfect."

And so they sipped on frozen cocktails, and Bette watched Charlie's tongue turn bluer and bluer as they talked. During her first date with Mei the conversation had meandered all over the place, venturing into areas she'd never dared tread in her years of dating men: how she imagined parenthood, her relationship with her brother, the inadequacy she had felt in past relationships, the relief of figuring out why that was, her fears about Ash leaving her behind. When she left Mei's the next morning, it felt as though they'd fast-forwarded through months of a relationship.

There was none of that with Charlie. It was a relief, really, to flit around films they'd loved as teenagers that should have been gay—Charlie had correct opinions on *10 Things I Hate About You*—to hear about Charlie's trip around Germany, and tell her about the one she'd taken to Portugal. It was light, so light and easy that they were on their fourth round before it occurred to Bette that she didn't even know what Charlie did for a living. Didn't know anything about her, really, save that she was at the table across from Bette. And hot. It was perfect. She was doing it. This was exactly what Mei had been suggesting.

The conversation fell apart somewhat once Petty LaBelle took to the stage, which was hardly surprising. She was captivating, her eye shadow a thick layer of gold-and-green glitter that made Bette rub at her lids in itchy empathy, her heels and waist both impossible in their architecture. Fun was poked at the backpackers (who tried to sneak out unobtrusively midway through the act), a couple of guys from the crowd were pulled up onstage for reasons Bette could only assume were their fore-arms or thighs, a rousing lip-sync to Avril Lavigne's "Girlfriend" made everyone lose their minds. Between sets, while Petty changed backstage into ever more incredible outfits, the music was a predictable collection of crowd-pleasing '80s tracks and gay anthems. When the unmistakable opening notes from "Faith" started, Charlie stood, and Bette realized their drinks had been sitting empty for a couple of minutes. It was her turn to buy. Or Charlie's. Someone's. But instead of heading toward the bar, Charlie reached out a hand to Bette, pulling her up and toward the crowd that had formed around the stage.

She felt light, her head floating pleasantly above her. Why *didn't* this place know her? Why wasn't she here every night, los-ing her mind over Petty and her bubble act? Why had she never had a frozen Sex on the Beach before? It was easily the best thing she'd ever tasted. Charlie was pressed against her back as they danced, strong and hot and breathing a path down her neck, her hands guiding Bette's hips. Her arms were bare; the jacket must have come off when they'd abandoned their table. Bette's bag was still there too, she thought (she hoped). But Charlie was probably on top of things. Ideally, Bette thought, she'd like Charlie to be on top of *her*, and then hid a laugh at her own innuendo.

Fuck, she must be drunk. Yes, that's exactly what this feeling was. Frozen cocktail drunk was a whole other thing.

Really, though, it was impossible to care when Charlie was so close behind her, when she felt so desirable, like the alcohol and the music had finally lit whatever had been smoldering between them all night. She tipped her head back against Charlie's shoulder, inviting the breath traveling down her neck to become tangible: lips, tongue, the scrape of teeth. Charlie didn't need any further direction, and Bette shivered as she closed her mouth over the place where Bette's neck met her shoulder. Electricity spread from that point throughout her body and Bette relished the feeling of it, of being close to someone again, before turning in Charlie's arms to face her. She tipped her chin up, met Charlie's eyes, and caught Charlie's lips between her own.

It was good. Really good, if not quite the earthquaking, knee-shaking good that kissing always had been with Mei. Charlie tasted wrong, like sugar and like cigarettes. Ideally her teeth would be slightly meaner. But she wasn't looking for a new girlfriend. She was looking for precisely this: a kiss with a hot woman in a crowded bar. The press of her thigh, grinding and insistent between Bette's legs as soon as she had turned. The slide of her tongue against Bette's. The soft curls on the crown of her head between Bette's fingers. And Bette understood exactly what Ruth had been talking about. It wasn't a perfect first kiss. Too hard, not in the way she wanted, and far too much tongue. But she could tell they'd have fun in bed together. It seemed obvious, how good it would feel to pull Charlie even closer against her.

The bar had gone from busy to properly crowded now. Crowded in a way that allowed them to be blissfully anonymous. No one was watching them. No one cared. On one side of them, a cute round-faced guy in a vest top was entangled with a queen who towered over him, her lipstick smudged around both their mouths. On the other a guy with a closely trimmed beard was dancing between two blondes in sweaty T-shirts. Bette's tipsy brain supplied an appealing image: her burying her face in Charlie's neck, pressed up against the wall of the hallway that led out to the street. But they couldn't do that. Surely. Surely?

"Hey. Should we—?" Charlie asked, throwing her head over her shoulder in a way that Bette hoped meant they were on the same page. Bette followed her. And when Charlie pushed Bette up against the wall there was delicious confirmation they had been thinking exactly the same thing.

"Is this—?" Charlie breathed into Bette's ear, her hand finding its way inside the split of her skirt to run up Bette's thigh.

"Yeah," Bette replied, pressing her lips to Charlie's neck. "Um . . . yeah. God, yeah."

There wasn't anyone else in the dark hallway, everyone too distracted by the reappearance of Petty LaBelle. Regardless, Charlie had managed to land them right beside a hideous fake potted fern that probably masked them from view.

A little. From a certain angle, at least.

Maybe.

Bette reasoned that she probably had another twenty seconds to apply a rational brain to the inevitable next steps. Before she was having sex, in a bar, in a not entirely private fashion. There was still time to decide whether or not this was what she wanted. Whether this was how she wanted it. She and Mei had never had sex like this. But, of course, that was the point. This was the time for trying the kind of sex she'd never had with anyone else. Bette wondered how many other women Charlie had had up against this wall: a long-limbed femme in tiny denim shorts, a blonde girl with a heart-shaped face and an undercut. And, suddenly, Mei. Mei up against this wall, the plastic palm fronds tickling her shoulder, her thigh trembling. Bette shook her head, attempting to dislodge the thought.

"No?" Charlie said, her grip relaxing.

"Sorry," Bette replied, and shook her head again before she reached down and pressed Charlie's hand more firmly into her thigh. "No. I mean, yes. Yes, keep going. Please."

As Charlie's thumb traveled slowly around to the inside of Bette's thigh, and began the journey upward, Bette returned to the thought that there were probably tons of women that she'd had like this. And she realized too that she didn't care. It was fantastic. As far as she was concerned, Charlie should have everything and everyone she wanted. Bette was in such safe, practiced hands.

Charlie ran her thumb along Bette's knickers, where she was already wet, and Bette groaned, biting down on her own lip and dropping her forehead to Charlie's collarbone. She felt a rumble of laughter in Charlie's chest as her thumb played with the elastic, before pushing it aside and applying pressure exactly where Bette wanted it.

"Like this?" Charlie whispered, voice hot against Bette's ear. "How do you like it?"

"Softer—" Bette gasped, and then the pressure was perfect, a delicious tease. Exactly what she needed. "Like that—oh fuck," she said into Charlie's shoulder, her hips rocking forward entirely without her forethought or direction. All lingering thoughts of someone interrupting them left her; it was impossible to care.

A hand found her ribs, and Charlie's thumb grazed, soft and deliberate, up and down the side of Bette's breast. It was gentle, not firm enough to be hot, she thought, trying to maneuver herself more definitively into Charlie's touch. But Charlie kept her hand where it had landed, brushing imperceptibly back and forth. And gradually the heat of it built, making her feel desperate and short of breath. Bette found Charlie's mouth again, biting at her lip, gasping into her mouth.

The hand between her legs was similarly methodical. Patient. Entirely at odds with their surroundings, with being in public. She was getting Bette there by degrees, so delicately that her orgasm crept up on her, building and building and then hitting her with a force that made her screw up her eyes and shudder, pressing her face into Charlie's neck.

Charlie stayed close as Bette recovered herself, withdrawing her hand gently, shielding Bette from an audience that (mercifully) hadn't appeared while Bette readjusted her skirt. Bette kissed her again, spinning them so that Charlie was the one stretched out against the wall. She felt Charlie shake her head against Bette's lips.

"Don't think I'll get there like that tonight," she said, easily, slipping her hand into the one Bette had already hooked into Charlie's waistband. "But thanks. That was hot. I'll be getting off on the memory of it all week. Dance?"

Bette's mouth gaped open as she trailed off behind Charlie, their hands still linked. She'd done it. She'd had sex. With someone new. And now ABBA were playing, and they were going to dance a bit, and then maybe that would be it. They wouldn't see each other again.

She had done it. Underneath the smug pleasure, the glow of knowing she was walking back onto the dance floor with her thighs still trembling, she quashed the desire to call Mei, to tell her exactly what had happened. To tell her just how great it had felt. To tell her it had felt great, and brilliant, and wrong. To tell her she'd done it, and that all of it could stop now.

CHAPTER NINE

THURSDAY, 25 AUGUST

51 days to go

> **Ruth:** Hey, do you fancy coming to Jody's birthday party on Saturday? It's a big open house thing, and we've all invited people. Thought if you weren't busy it might be fun?

It had been a relentless couple of days at work and she'd let the swiping fall by the wayside, returning home each evening to Ash and the sofa and a bowl of pasta. Once Thursday hit, nearly a week since the date with Charlie, she wondered whether she should start looking for someone new. But the idea felt exhausting, even in entirely theoretical terms. Instead she had closed the app, slipped her phone into the pocket of her hoodie, put the kettle on and pulled a packet of biscuits from the kitchen cupboard. One weekend off hadn't sounded like the worst thing in the world.

But the universe (or Ruth, she supposed) clearly had other plans. The text arrived once she was on the sofa, tea and chocolate biscuits in hand. She could refuse the invitation, obviously, invent an excuse, tell Ruth she just wasn't up for it. She wouldn't question it.

But the alternative was that she could just . . . go.

Ash was spending the long-weekend weekend with Tim's parents. She had considered inviting Anton and Carmen round, before remembering that they were away too. The problem with most of your friends being teachers, or teacher-adjacent, was that the summer was either boom or bust. And this weekend was bust. She had visited her nonna the week before, clear-headed but aware of smelling of stale booze and sugar. There wasn't a long list of other people she saw on the weekends.

The reality was that one night at a time of doing her own thing, of having a long bath or watching the shows Ash couldn't bear or ordering from the deeply average kebab place that only she loved, was always enough. By the second night she was prone to spiraling, convinced she was destined to spend the rest of her life on her own, that all her friends had moved on and that no one had ever fancied her or found her interesting and probably never would, that she had perhaps ceased to exist entirely.

> **Bette:** I'm in!
> **Bette:** can I bring anything?
>
> **Ruth:** It'll be so great to see you! I've a list of people to introduce you to.

The party was becoming a more compelling prospect by the minute.

> **Bette:** yeah?

Ruth: Yes. And Heather has some
suggestions too.

Bette: if you'd led with that I
wouldn't have hesitated

Ruth: You hesitated? You replied
within a literal minute.

Bette: my brain works fast
Bette: there's a lot going on that you don't see
Bette: via text

Ruth: Clearly.
Ruth: Anyway, come from 8 p.m. and
bring a bottle or a plate of something.

A party. A party with new people to meet, in a house that
sounded like some sort of queer utopia. She was going to need
something incredible to wear.

RUTH HADN'T BEEN exaggerating about the party. When Bette,
keen not to be one of the first there, arrived after ten, she didn't
have to double-check her phone for the house number. She didn't
have to send a little text. In a street lined with Victorian terraces,
Ruth's house was surely the one from which Carly Rae Jepsen was
issuing, the one with a visible disco ball in the front room, where
the smokers perched on the brick wall outside were dressed in
combinations of leather, tulle and dungarees. It felt like she
shouldn't be assuming things about people based on how they were
dressed, but they seemed . . . queer. It lit something within her.

She hadn't been to a proper house party since coming out, and while she didn't want it to be some big thing, it kind of was. She nodded hello to the smokers on the wall and pushed open the door.

There had been a famous house party in Ash and Bette's second year of university, a mad, raucous, debauched party that everyone had talked about for the next eighteen months.

Jody's party was nothing like that party. They could never have imagined a party this good back then.

People had found corners in which to snog in twos and threes and a four that looked logistically tricky. An elaborate game of Twister was being played with dots taped out on the floor. A couple of beautiful guys had stripped off their shirts—had they had shirts? Did they need shirts?—and were doing body shots from each other's clavicles in the center of the front room. It was impossible to know where to join in, where to find her place among these strangers. There was a flash of wishing Ash was there beside her. It felt exposing to have arrived alone.

"Bette!" called a voice from behind her, and she spun round to find herself face-to-face with Ruth. She was flushed and warm as she pulled Bette into a tight hug, trapping the bag of crisps and condensation-wet white wine that Bette was clutching between them. Her sequined dress was cut low on her chest and high on her thigh, and Bette found herself wishing she could have the confidence to pull it off. Ruth's feet were bare, her toenails painted gold.

"This party is amazing."

"Yeah, Jody went all out. They decided at the last minute that the vibe was Bristol Bacchanal, so we all just bought some grapes and did some shots and made out with each other to kick things off."

Bette nodded, feeling slightly hysterical. She imagined a sort of spin the bottle, an infinite partnering with every woman here. The thought filled her with hope and fear. Mostly fear.

"I'll help you find a glass," Ruth said, a knowing smile on her face. "And then you can see what sort of—well, festivities, I guess, you want to take part in?"

Oh. Right away then. It was going to be like that. Bette had put time into her outfit—her highest-waisted jeans, a new corset top, her nicest lace knickers, a long silk kimono she'd found in a charity shop. Leaving the house earlier, she'd felt sexy; she had posed and pouted in front of the mirror in Ash's room and sent a photo to Ash that had prompted a line of heart emojis, and a few of the ghost head "I die" ones Ash employed with alarming frequency. But she was suddenly nervous, anxious and inexperienced and not ready for this and . . .

"Bette, calm down. I'm joking. This isn't an orgy. This is Jody's thirtieth. There's a group in the garden talking about a pop-up they went to. There is zero requirement to sleep with anyone."

"Oh thank god," Bette said, letting out the breath that had started to choke her. "Not that there's anything wrong with—you know—"

"I know, I know. Your commitment to not kink-shaming is noted. I just hadn't prepared you for a sex party. Absolutely fair enough. But I saw you watching Lukas and his boyfriend and I couldn't resist."

"Oh god, the guys with the tequila?" Bette guessed, horrified at the thought of what her face must have been doing. "They're so beautiful. I mean, aesthetically, you know. From an entirely theoretical point of view."

"Don't worry, you're not their type either," Ruth assured her. "Though you do look particularly gorgeous tonight. I refuse to believe that you might not be a little bit their type. Shocked every time I remember monosexuality is a thing, to be honest."

Bette flushed at the compliment. She had followed Ruth through to the kitchen and accepted the glass of wine she'd poured with a grateful "Thanks. You look lovely too."

Ruth twirled on the spot, showing off, as if Bette hadn't already admired every inch of the dress. "I know, right? Bought it a couple of years ago, it's my official party dress. My looking hot and dancing dress."

"Well, it's really working," Bette agreed.

She thought Ruth looked flushed too, for a moment, and then remembered the warmth of her face when they had hugged. Ruth had been dancing.

"Heather!" Ruth directed over Bette's shoulder. Bette turned as a tall Black woman with closely cropped hair and dark-blue lipstick came into the kitchen.

"Heather," she confirmed, air-kissing Bette once she was within reach. "You must be Bette."

"It's so nice to meet you. Your house is amazing."

It really was. The kitchen was quieter than the other rooms she'd walked past, and slightly better lit. It was operating as a thoroughfare to the garden rather than a space people had claimed as a venue, and she could finally take in the decor rather than guests. *It* was a wide galley, bottles and plates cluttering most surfaces. But it was clearly well loved; walls the rich yellow of the fancy butter Ash bought sometimes, open shelves lined with jars and crockery, pots of herbs crowded along the windowsills that were somehow lush and thriving. There were framed pictures on the walls, covers of *The New Yorker* that had food on them. It all felt purposeful, deliberate. Not like a shared house at all.

"It's pretty special, isn't it?" Heather said, smiling warmly at Ruth. "She's the visionary, the rest of us just added bits and pieces once we came in."

Ruth smiled, clearly pleased, and busied herself with finding a bowl and emptying the bag of crisps Bette had brought into it.

"So. I've got a shit poker face. Can't pretend I haven't heard about your project," Heather said, the air quotes hanging around the word "project" amused rather than judgmental.

"Yeah, it's—" Bette began. "It's been a real journey so far."

"Any success yet?"

Bette chanced a glance at Ruth, who was munching on a crisp and looking out into the garden. She hadn't told her about how the date with Charlie had ended up going. It was difficult to point to a reason, to label and identify it, but when they'd texted that week she hadn't mentioned the bar. And Ruth hadn't asked.

"Umm—yeah. I guess I have? I went out with a woman last weekend. She was really hot—it was really hot—sorry, she *is* really hot," she corrected, and Heather laughed. "I assume she's still hot now. It's only been a week."

"Name?"

"Oh. Charlie. Charlie . . . something. She's quite tall, your height probably? Curly hair on top, leather jacket."

"Oh I know Charlie." Heather sounded impressed. "She's been around forever. Very hot. Big top energy. *Exceptionally* good with her hands."

The way she said it made Bette positive that Heather had been fucked by Charlie too. A thrill zipped through her at being able to have this conversation, like she'd been accepted into a club she hadn't known was hers to join.

"Umm. Yep. Yep, that sounds like her," Bette confirmed, her blush now surely sweeping all the way down her chest. "Very good with her hands."

"That's brilliant!" Ruth said brightly. "A success!"

"I mean, if she's pulling Charlie, I'd say so," Heather said. "That's a pretty outstanding first time."

"Oh, it wasn't my first time," Bette rushed out, aware that her voice had become slightly high-pitched. "Because of Mei. I slept with Mei. She's my girlfriend. Sort of. I mean—it's complicated."

"Sorry babe, that wasn't clear. I just meant your first odyssey hookup. That's Charlie's vibe. I mean, I'm sure it was a great fuck, but I bet you've not spoken since, right?"

Bette shook her head. They hadn't. She had thought about messaging on Saturday, when she woke up, thought of sending a little note to say *thanks for the orgasm*. Or something. That she hoped it had been okay for Charlie too. But she'd already unmatched on the app.

"I might leave you two to it, now you've met," said Ruth, two glasses of what looked like whisky now in her hands. "I'm going to deliver a drink to our birthday royalty." She kissed Heather's cheek as she passed and left them alone in the kitchen.

With Ruth gone, Bette squirmed under Heather's gaze, aware of how intimidatingly stunning she was, of the way her eyes lingered over Bette's body. It didn't feel seedy or lascivious, more that she was considering her, trying to work something out. Bette couldn't help standing up straighter.

"So what's next then?"

She didn't have to wonder what Heather meant.

"Well, I probably have to get back on the app, right? That's the thing I kind of hate about this. It's so much phone admin. But I feel good about last weekend. About Charlie. So I think— more?"

"Oh, the apps are the worst," Heather said cheerfully. "But, yeah, that makes sense! Or I could introduce you to people here tonight you might hit it off with? I mean, you're fit, and you seem great. I can't imagine it's going to be difficult." She shrugged. "If I hadn't promised Ruth I wouldn't, I'd be hitting on you."

Bette couldn't believe the ease with which the compliments dropped from Heather's lips. As though they were irrefutable fact.

"Well, if I hadn't promised Ruth too, I'd absolutely be flirting back," Bette replied. It was fun to flirt, to feel hot. To feel wanted.

"Okay, well, let's head out before we go upstairs and shag against both our better judgments."

Bette laughed, trying to hide how strangled it sounded, and followed her back out into the hall.

NATALIA WAS HEAVEN: hair long and dark, eyes an impossibly pale gray, silk skirt falling over rounded hips. She was a city planner, working on making Bristol's public spaces more accessible. Her hands circled and gestured enthusiastically as she spoke, doing far more than half the work of communication. At Bette's request she was speaking deliberately slowly in her native Italian, the wine and the warmth and the overlapping languages making Bette feel a little fuzzy around the edges. After one too many instances of asking her to repeat herself, Bette gave up.

"Okay, sorry, sorry, English now. I'm too drunk. My nonna would be ashamed but I can't keep up."

Natalia laughed, her head falling onto Bette's shoulder. It was one in the morning now, but the party had yet to start thinning out. Bette and Natalia were crowded together in a wide armchair. It was not quite big enough to accommodate two women with hips that could be referred to as "childbearing," but they were making the most of it. Unsure whether it was the wine or the chair or the night generally, Bette could feel every place where Natalia's body was pressed against her own, as though she were sitting too close to a radiator.

They were going to fuck, she realized.

The night had been building toward it since Heather had been called off while showing Bette around. Bette had looked for Ruth, but she knew too that she didn't want to be *that* friend, the one who needed babysitting. Ideally she'd fall easily into conversation with someone, be impossibly charming. Someone who would text Ruth on Monday and say *Bette's great, isn't she?*

so that she couldn't help but agree. Instead she had found herself standing in the middle of a room, far too eager for a group to join, like the last person picked for netball. It was excruciating. And then she had caught Natalia's eye. They'd been squashed into the armchair ever since.

"I'm going to blame the wine too. I can't remember whether we've done this yet, so let's pretend we haven't. How do you know Heather?" Natalia asked, not lifting her head from where it had found a place against Bette.

It was as though the sound of her name had conjured her. Heather was suddenly standing in the doorway to the front room, an approving cock to her eyebrow and twist to her lips. She winked, with a guileless lack of subtlety, and walked out again.

"Oh, I don't, really. We met in the kitchen. Tonight. Like, a couple of hours ago."

"Oh right! So you know Jody then?"

"I've still not managed to meet them yet, actually," Bette said, looking around as if the whirlwind of blonde quiff and velvet that was Jody might materialize before them. Every time Bette had glimpsed sight of them they had been surrounded by a dedicated crew of well-wishers. "I really should make sure I say hi before I leave tonight though. No, I know Ruth. Not that well. We only met a month ago. But she's great."

"Ah, of course. Ruth is lovely."

And then Bette heard it, the question underneath the questions. "We're not dating," she said quickly. "I mean, we went on a date once, but we're friends. I'm not dating anyone right now."

"Yeah?" Natalia asked, lifting her head from Bette's shoulder, her mouth suddenly no more than an inch from Bette's. "That's great news."

"Yeah," Bette confirmed, though she wondered at the truth of it. The specific semantics and how they might play if picked at. It was true. She wasn't dating anyone. Technically.

Maybe it was better not to think too much about it. Natalia bumped her nose against Bette's cheek. They breathed in together, and then Natalia's lips were against hers, tacky and overly sweet with a gloss Bette might have worn when she was sixteen. It was strange and synthetic. But beneath the gloss her lips were soft, and Natalia's hand pressed onto Bette's thigh. She reached for Natalia's shoulder and traced her fingers along the skin, to the center of her back and down her spine. It felt good to be kissing her, easy and warm and, as Natalia moved her hand up Bette's thigh, veering closer and closer to hot.

She was aware, though, that it was a kiss that was a question rather than a statement. It was infused with softness rather than sex. And Bette felt uncomfortably aware that she'd not told Natalia the whole truth. Thought about how pleased Natalia looked when Bette had said she wasn't seeing anyone. Heather knew the plan. She wouldn't have smiled approvingly if she didn't think Natalia would be up for it? Surely? But Natalia was kissing her carefully, reverently, one hand now pressed into Bette's jaw. This felt like the end of a date, not the start of a hookup. She was kissing her like she'd walked Bette to her front door.

Then Natalia's fingers started to stroke gently over the thin skin behind Bette's ear, and she melted. Natalia wanted what Bette wanted. A shiver ran up her back and the hand that was still on Natalia's back pulled her closer still.

"I live pretty close by," Bette whispered, kissing her again before continuing, "if you want to come back with me?"

Natalia hesitated for a moment before nodding against her lips, and so Bette stood, reaching a hand out to Natalia to help her up too. She was shorter than Bette, by at least a couple of inches, though the masses of dark hair piled on her head made her seem taller.

"Do you need to say goodbye to anyone?" Natalia asked, and Bette looked at her, at eyes that were glittering with anticipation.

"Absolutely not," Bette said. "Irish goodbye, I think. No one will miss us."

Natalia led her out into the hall and, just before they walked through the front door, Bette looked back. Ruth was sitting on the stairs, talking with a guy Bette hadn't met, a guy with a clean-shaven jaw and lips that veered close to too full alongside his angular features. He was sort-of absurdly pretty, almost doll-like, and he was looking at Ruth with an expression that made Bette feel like she was intruding on something. But Ruth looked over and met Bette's eye, her brows raising infinitesimally before her hand came up in an almost-wave.

CHAPTER TEN

SUNDAY, 28 AUGUST

•••

48 days to go

Bette woke the next morning with more company than she had energy to handle.

Natalia was beneath the sheet beside her, in her shirt and knickers from the night before. Next to her, Bette was in full pajamas, top and trousers, which she only ever did when she was staying away from home. It was an uncomfortable juxtaposition. They had opened more wine when they'd arrived home, then talked on the sofa. For hours. They had kissed too. So much kissing. But something about the walk had cooled the heat of the party. The decision to take the wine to the front room had been the final nail in the coffin. It wasn't platonic, but it also wasn't in any way casual. A couple of times, Bette tried to move the kissing in a distinctly more sexual direction—at the very least toward her bedroom—but it hadn't felt right. There had been a moment, when Natalia was straddling her on the sofa, when Bette was holding tightly at her thigh, a hand buried in her hair, when things finally felt like they might be going that way. But Natalia had leaned back, looked down at her with an intensity that was mortifying, traced her thumb along Bette's lip and told her she was beautiful. Natalia wanted to get to know her. She asked about Bette's family, and accepted her deflections. They shared coming-out stories. Natalia talked about growing up with lots of siblings, about her plans to have children, about wanting at least three. She was pretty sure there had been a moment when Natalia said *I really like you,* as if that was a reasonable thing to say, as if it was okay to lay your heart bare and open on the first night. And then Bette thought of Mei, of the things she'd said to her the first night. She felt sick with guilt that Natalia thought it was that kind of night. There was no doubt that she'd fucked up.

There had probably been a moment when it might have been possible to draw a line under it all, to lay out what it was she wanted. But instead Natalia had asked to borrow a toothbrush, and Bette didn't say no. She was staying the night. It made sense, Bette supposed, given that it was close to dawn.

There was nothing much to say as they brushed their teeth and crawled beneath the sheets. Natalia kissed her once they were horizontal, her tongue fresh and minty, no trace of the gloss left. And then she rolled over and was breathing heavily almost immediately. Anxiety clawed at Bette. She should have said something, that much was blindingly clear. She should have told her that this was one night. That this was about sex. Sex they, crucially, hadn't even had. She should have mentioned that they probably wouldn't see each other again, at least not deliberately. That the whole point here was not to sleep over. Not to get attached. Seeing Natalia with a toothbrush in her mouth, making eye contact with her in the mirror above the sink, felt so like a relationship that Bette had looked away.

She managed to sleep around seven, a result of tiredness rather than any easing of her guilt. And when she awoke a couple of hours later Natalia was still there, lazy and affectionate in her sleep-addled state, curling herself around Bette's back, her hand resting on Bette's hip, tracing patterns over her skin where her pajamas had ridden down.

No.

No no no no. She couldn't allow it to happen. Sex after sharing a bed, kissing after sharing a bed, would be a terrible way to lead in to the conversation she knew they had to have. It would be taking advantage of the situation in a way she couldn't stomach.

"Tea?" she burst out loudly, sitting up on the edge of the bed and reaching for a robe to pull over her pajama set—a sort of aggressive opposite of nudity. She was uncomfortably warm, instantly sweating beneath her pajamas. "Coffee? Juice? I'm not sure we have juice, actually, because my flatmate's away. And it's really only her who drinks it."

"Tea is good," Natalia said, her voice a little bemused, still only half awake. "But you don't need to—there's no rush."

"No, I love tea. I'm desperate for one. Let's get up now," Bette said, before Natalia could suggest returning to bed with the mugs. She stood, cursing white wine and her churning stomach. There was time to boil the kettle, plunge her hand into the near-empty box to retrieve two dusty tea pyramids and pour the water into two mugs before Natalia arrived, her party clothes incongruous in the morning light.

"Great, you're dressed! What's your plan for today?" Bette asked, bright and chatty and angling for "not at all hungover."

"Oh I didn't really have one," Natalia replied, reaching for the mug Bette passed her, adding the milk herself. "But if you're keen to get rid of me before your next girl arrives, I'll be out of your hair as soon as I finish this."

She laughed easily, as if the idea of leaving was ridiculous, and Bette forced out a laugh in response. Natalia was still squeezing her tea bag against the side of the mug but at the sound of Bette's laugh looked up in surprise.

"Unless—oh—okay. Maybe you—I don't know, maybe you regret—? I'll just—"

"Shit, no, it's not that. No regrets at all. You were great. It was fun. I just—I'm not looking for anything serious, and I guess I really should have said that last night. I'm worried I should have told you that. Before. Before I brought you back here."

She was rambling, tripping over words and sentences as though she were back on the obstacle course she'd been useless at in primary school.

"Oh," Natalia said, nodding a bit too enthusiastically as she gulped down her scalding tea. She covered a little choking cough with her hand. There was probably tea in her lung now, which was something else Bette could feel bad about. "No, of course. I mean—there's no—no expectations. Of course."

"I'm really sorry," Bette said quietly, and she meant it. Natalia's face had fallen, and she was making only awkward, stilted eye contact. This conversation was better, surely, than dodging her texts in the days to come. Better than dragging things out.

But Bette still felt horrible about it. They could have avoided this altogether if she had been clear from the outset.

"Okay—so I'm just—" Natalia said, putting her mug down on the kitchen counter. "I'll just go. If that's—?"

"It was really nice to meet you," Bette said lamely, and wondered whether she should walk her to the door. Or whether that felt too much like a date thing. Staying in the kitchen cemented this as a hookup; walking her to the door—either side of it— left her open to the *Notting Hill* accidental-unexpected-kiss thing. Or Chandler's *"This was great! I'll give you a call! Let's do it again sometime!"* thing he did to Rachel's mascara goop boss. And there was really no way back from that. She couldn't kiss Natalia again, after making things so uncomfortable. She couldn't be that person.

The door slammed. While she had been working out whether or not to walk Natalia to the door, Natalia had made the journey herself. It hadn't seemed like a long moment of thought. She must be more hungover than she thought; her brain working at half capacity. Bette leaned against the kitchen counter, feeling sick with regret and furious with Ash for being out, and Ruth for inviting her in the first place, and Heather for blithely leaving her in the vicinity of hot women who ended up snogging her, and Mei for the whole stupid thing.

And with herself, most of all.

BETTE HAD BARELY moved over the course of the day. She'd decided against returning to bed, not wanting to climb back into the sheets she and Natalia had spent the night between. Realistically, she was going to have to strip them before bedtime because they still smelled of Natalia's perfume, but she was putting off the guilt spiral the scent would induce. She was already considering sleeping on the sofa just to avoid the task. Rather than dealing with any part of the situation, she had dozed in front of *Married at First Sight Australia*, held Marge against her until she finally stalked off in disgust, drank eight half-cups of tepid tea, and had eaten endless rounds of Marmite on buttered toast. If there hadn't been bread in the house, there was a real chance she might have starved.

All the things she had been saving for Sunday—her laundry, a long-overdue call to her parents, the reorganization of her closet—had fallen by the wayside in favor of being horizontal and feeling sorry for herself. The hangover had faded by 3 p.m. but the shame hadn't, and both feelings roiled her belly in exactly the same way.

She had, all things considered, rarely been happier to hear Ash's key turn in the lock. The relief hit her as though it were physical, and she could feel tears pricking at her eyes. It wasn't what she wanted, was impossibly frustrating, but by the time Ash was standing in the door to the sitting room, the tears were trickling down her cheeks. All she had been waiting for, apparently, was Ash leaning against the door frame, a look of affection clear beneath the judgment.

"Have you moved at all today?" Ash asked. There seemed no point in lying; it wasn't a question so much as it was a well-formed assumption based on clear evidence.

"No. I think I might have a bedsore on my hip."

"You don't have a bedsore."

"I might."

"Okay, well then I think you should get off your hip, put some outdoor clothes on, and come for a walk. It smells like a brewery in here. I refuse to spend my Sunday evening on a sofa that smells like this. There's a reason I don't go to pubs with carpet. It's a hard limit. We need to air the house out."

"Can't you just open a window and then I could stay here?"

"No," Ash threw over her shoulder as she carried her weekend bag down the hall. She returned a moment later, while Bette was still resolutely in the same position. "If you lie there any longer you're going to fuse to the sofa. And I'm attached to you being able to get up to go to work and pay your half of the rent. I'm attached to the sofa too."

"That's . . . fair," Bette admitted reluctantly. "Give me five minutes."

It was ten minutes, at least, before she left her bedroom in leggings and a long T-shirt. Fifteen before she put her shoes on. Ash waited impatiently, leaning against the hallway wall, rolling her eyes at Bette's grumbles, tsk-ing in an uncanny impression of Bette's mother while she laced up her shoes.

Annoyingly and inevitably, the fresh air felt good on her face and in her lungs. She gulped in big breaths of it, as if she hadn't properly taken in oxygen since before the party. It cleared away the last vestiges of her hangover. The guilt, she worried, was probably there to stay.

"So come on." Ash nudged her shoulder against Bette's. "This isn't just a hangover, is it? We're not that old yet, right? We can still have a good Saturday night without wanting to die the next day? Right?"

"It's not just a hangover," Bette replied. She stopped at the edge of the footpath, waiting for a clear run across the street, even as Ash scooted around a car.

Ash stopped midway through crossing the street and looked back at her expectantly. "Well?"

Bette shrugged, and pushed herself to jog for a moment to catch up. It was torture. Her body hated her.

"I brought someone home last night. She seemed great at the party—like the right person to bring home. For this—whatever. But I probably should have been a bit clearer about things. Before we got to the kissing bit."

"Ah."

"Yeah, I told her this morning that I wasn't looking for a relationship, and she didn't seem thrilled about it."

"So you Ruth-ed her. After the fact. Which is probably worse."

Bette didn't appreciate her date with Ruth becoming a verb. "Ugh, fuck. Yeah. Yeah, I suppose I did. *Fuck.* I feel awful."

"Was there not a moment it would have made sense to have the conversation?"

"Of course there was, Ash," Bette said, her voice climbing a register both in pitch and volume. "Obviously. There were so many moments I should have mentioned it. I get it. I'm the worst."

"Not the worst," Ash said, her voice kinder. She always seemed to struggle with playing bad cop when Bette did such an effective job of it herself. "But it's not ideal behavior."

"She's a friend of Ruth's too, I think." Bette paused, realizing she had no idea what Natalia's connection to the party was. "Or Heather's, I suppose. Or Jody's. I have no idea. I probably should know but I wasn't really listening. The headline is that I should have told her and I might run into her again and I fucked it up. I was a bit drunk, and she was just *so* beautiful . . ."

"Yeah, but you think everyone is beautiful." Ash was smirking.

"Look, I just . . . really like women," Bette said lamely.

"I just think they're neat!" Ash parroted, a perfect imitation of Marge Simpson holding up a potato.

"Oh shut up."

They were quiet as they walked down into Perrett Park. The heat of the summer, and the rain they had had in the past week, meant that the grass was lush and green underfoot. The sun had almost disappeared from the sky, the faintest pink glow still visible along the horizon, the evening suddenly cool. The park was empty but for a handful of guys on their backs, cans in their hands, and a few joggers doing laps around its perimeter.

"You know I'm always going to cheerlead you getting exactly what you want. I want you to be happy. I spent two weekends watching you try on jeans to find those black ones you love. I queued with you overnight, Bette. For Coldplay tickets," Ash said, her voice unusually gentle. "And so if this is what you want you know I'll shut up. I'm on board. I'll do whatever you need. But you waking up filled with regret and feeling terrible—Bette, I don't think that's . . . I don't know . . ."

She wanted Ash to keep laughing, to poke fun. To imitate Marge Simpson. To commit to the full bit and whinge about the Coldplay queue, ten years after the cursed night in question. She didn't want the concern and mothering and attempt at understanding. It felt sticky and saccharine; honey poured over the horrible mess of Bette's life. Instead of soothing and reassuring her it made Bette prickle and bristle, as if her body wanted something bitter to course through her, something to cut through the sweet.

"I want Mei," Bette said firmly, cringing slightly at the words even as they left her mouth. "And this is the way to have Mei."

"I just—I'm not sure—"

"Look, I fucked up last night, but I'm still figuring out how to manage hookups. It's not like I've had a lot of practice. I'll do it better next time. I don't need to have some big existential crisis about it. I'm fine."

"Okay," Ash said. "But I—"

"It's fine, Ash." Bette spoke over her with a note of finality in her voice that she hoped could draw a line underneath everything. "I'm fine. What do you want for dinner? My shout."

She pulled out her phone and started scrolling through the Deliveroo options. And, mercifully, Ash let her.

BY THE TIME they finished their lap of the park and returned home, Bette's feelings had softened. An irresponsible amount of curry was arriving imminently, which made everything a little better and a little easier, as an extravagant takeaway was always wont to do. Once back through the front door, Ash disappeared to put her pajamas on and Bette set up *Grey's Anatomy* on her laptop. As she scrolled down season two, preparing her argument for watching "It's the End of the World" again, her phone buzzed in her pocket.

> **Ruth:** So!!
> **Ruth:** Successful night for you then?!?!

The overuse of punctuation was entirely un-Ruth. Ruth was deliberate and clear with her punctuation and capital letters, in a way that made Bette feel every bit of the three-year age difference between them. Ruth used full stops as if they were appropriate in texts, as if they meant the same thing they did in a book.

> **Bette:** ha
> **Bette:** exactly as you'd promised
> **Bette:** it was fun!
> **Bette:** heather's great

It occurred to her that she hadn't seen much of Ruth at all after she had left the kitchen. She wondered how the night might have progressed if she'd found Ruth instead, in that moment of searching. Probably a lot less complicatedly.

> **Bette:** thanks so much for inviting me
>
> **Ruth:** Of course!! Glad it went well.
> **Ruth:** (It went well, right?! Did I see you leave with Nat????)

The punctuation marks. Unbelievable. It was as though Ruth had been kidnapped, as though someone who didn't know her was texting in her place.

> **Bette:** you did
> **Bette:** she's lovely
>
> **Ruth:** She's fantastic! We were at university together!

Shit. She should have known Natalia would be Ruth's friend. Avoidance seemed like her only option.

> **Bette:** of course! I think she mentioned
>
> **Bette:** how was your night?

> **Ruth:** It was good—lots of people I haven't seen in ages, so that was nice. And I think Jody had fun, which really was the whole point.
>
> **Ruth:** And so did you by the sound of things?!

She was relentless. Bette wasn't going to be able to avoid it. She needed to be vague. Noncommittal.

> **Bette:** yeah, it was good!
>
> **Bette:** thank you again
>
> **Bette:** couldn't have imagined better wing women than you and heather

There was a beat, long enough that Bette started to put her phone down.

> **Ruth:** Hey, I have a spare ticket to a dinner next weekend if you want to come with me?

She should be planning another date, really. A stranger this time, another Charlie. But—

> **Bette:** msg me the details
>
> **Bette:** I'll be there

CHAPTER ELEVEN

FRIDAY, 02 SEPTEMBER

...

43 days to go

I t had been precisely the sort of day in the office that Bette should have been readying herself for since the break. Pure chance meant that she was on her way to the photocopier when she overheard Erin buzzing Mei up. It was just enough time to prepare herself. To her surprise and horror, the only option seemed to be to run into the bathroom stall, crossed legs beneath her on the seat, hidden from view in case someone came looking. She remained there for an hour; long enough for her leg to go to sleep, long enough to engender some distinctly odd expressions from her colleagues when she finally stumbled out. Long enough that the phone she had left behind on her desk had a couple of texts from Mei that she didn't know how to reply to. Long enough that (as Bette discovered over lunch) a very confused Erin had had to tell Mei that Bette had simply vanished, her print job still awaiting her in the tray.

But it was the weekend now, and she didn't want to think about having not explained herself to Erin, about not having texted Mei back, about the endless hour in the toilet. Bette had plans.

Ruth was already at the bar when she arrived, her ankles crossed, wearing a black dress that scooped down her back in a way that showed off her lipstick-pink bra, her hand resting next to a martini glass filled with so many olives that it looked like an optical illusion. She was laughing with the bartender as he prepared drinks, her head thrown back, her neck long. Bette had never seen anyone look more effortlessly glamorous. She belonged in a black-and-white film.

Bette shook herself slightly, realizing suddenly that she'd been watching from the doorway for a beat too long. She walked over and pushed herself up onto the stool next to Ruth's.

"Well, this place is amazing."

"Bette! You look gorgeous," Ruth said, leaning over to kiss her on the cheek, her now-familiar perfume fresh and bright. "Isn't it incredible?"

It was. The decor was cozy and plush: polished wood, dark-green velvet, cushioned banquettes. The lighting was low and warm in a way that made everyone glow.

"How did you know about it?" Bette asked.

"Haven't been before, but I know the chef. He's only doing a couple of nights, trying out a new menu. His wife is a colleague, actually, so I bought a couple of tickets when he announced it months ago. Honestly, I'd forgotten about it until she texted last weekend."

Bette looked around, her eyes falling on a menu on the bar. "What are we eating? Stupidly didn't even ask." Everything on the tasting menu was a list of four ingredients separated by commas, at least one in each list that she'd never heard of. Ash had had to explain a similar menu to her when they'd gone for a fancy dinner once; nothing had arrived looking like she expected. "Tasting menu means we get it all, right? I'm so glad I don't have to make any decisions. This all sounds amazing."

"Me too," Ruth said. "I had dinner with them once and made him tell me everything about cooking in San Antonio. I was so jealous."

A download of their respective weeks took them through the margaritas that came with the menu, and to a table by the window. A plate of stuffed and fried jalapeños appeared, Ruth took more than her fair share, and Bette couldn't even begrudge her them when she saw the bliss on her face. More plates hit their table and they shared them out. In the brief conversational lull that followed, as they both ate, Bette remembered the question she'd planned, to avoid them getting stuck too soon on her dating life.

"Look, I know we've established the apps are the worst, but have you met anyone fun lately?"

As Ruth finished chewing she fiddled with the menu to the side of her plate, rolling the corner between her fingers. She looked down at her hand, watching as she manipulated the paper, and then up into Bette's eyes. Bette waited, wondering if she should regret the question.

"I mean, no one world-rocking," Ruth said, shrugging, clearly already keen to change the subject. "But some—I mean, yeah. Some fun people. There was one woman I met a couple of weeks ago, but I don't think it's going to go anywhere."

"No?"

"No, I don't think we're right together," Ruth said with a shrug. "She's a real Aries, you know?"

"I—" Bette paused, and resolved not to lie. "I really don't. What's an Aries supposed to mean?"

"Nothing," Ruth said after a moment, a smile tugging at the corner of her mouth. "It means absolutely nothing. Just that star signs are a thing with most women I've dated. So I've ended up obsessed against my better judgment." Bette's skepticism must have been showing on her face, because Ruth's tone shifted toward defensive. "I don't want to; they just make sense! I guess I've dated a lot of really convincing lesbians. Anyway, this woman was a real Aries in the sense that she was ambitious and lit up the room, but also she sort of needed to be at the center of it."

"I'm a Capricorn, so does that mean anything?" Bette asked, vowing never to mention any of this to Ash, a dedicated zodiac cynic.

"Sure, if you want it to. Anything can mean something if you want it to. Like, I'm a Cancer, so I'm loyal and sentimental but I can also get a bit . . . intense. Obviously I know, rationally, that that probably doesn't have a huge amount to do with the fact that I was born at the end of June. But I also kind of like to think of myself as a textbook Cancer. It's a nice feeling. A club of intense weirdos I get to belong to."

"I see that," Bette replied and, much to her surprise and slight dismay, she sort of did. "So tell me about Capricorns then."

"Well, you're persistent. Disciplined. Ambitious too—"

"Ha, okay," Bette said dismissively, waving the words aside with both hands. "You should talk to my mother."

"What?"

Fuck. She'd not really meant it to come out like that. She just wanted to cut through the zodiac sincerity. Poke a little fun, deliver an easy line. It had seemed fun and flippant and self-deprecating in her head. But it didn't sound as if Ruth was going to let her get away with laughing it off.

"Yeah, I mean, it's not a big deal. Just—persistent, disciplined and ambitious is not the way my family would describe me. At all."

"No?"

Bette recognized the tactic from the single therapy session she'd attended at the beginning of university: one-word prompts that encouraged someone to talk. She resented the effectiveness of it.

"No. No, I—oh I don't know," she started. "I think I'm a pretty big disappointment to them. There's a life they thought I'd have that I—I mean, they're convinced I've wasted my twenties in Bristol. That I'll eventually figure things out and go back home. Work out that I'm supposed to have a more conventional life. It's not like I'm even radical! I work a nine-to-five. I've not joined a cult. I just don't think they got over me not marrying at twenty-three and going into teaching or something more—I don't know. Secure. And the gay thing hasn't helped. They're fine with it, obviously. Apparently. But I don't know . . ."

She took a breath, and realized as she did the false brightness in her tone. She felt exhausted, like she'd run for a bus. She hated running for a bus. Ruth was looking at her, considering but not pitying, and Bette felt a rush of relief.

"I mean, that's pretty common, no?" Ruth replied. "Our parents' generation was a whole different thing. It's hard for them to look at us and what we're doing and try to map it onto their lives. For them not to worry, not to apply their own timelines." Ruth paused, rolling her menu between her fingertips again, taking a breath before she continued. "My parents were the last of their friends to have children. They tried for me for a long time before it happened. Before I happened. So they were in their mid-thirties when I was born. But now I'm thirty-three. I only have one friend with kids. I'm still studying. I'm renting. There is absolutely no place in my life for a kid right now. I know they love me, and they just want me to be happy. They're trying. But they don't get it."

Nothing she was saying was particularly revolutionary. But Bette felt a warmth behind her ribs, at Ruth understanding. At knowing she wasn't alone.

"I'm not trying to apologize for them!" Ruth said, and Bette realized she hadn't replied, hadn't shared any of the warmth aloud. "Especially about the gay thing. It's shit that they're weird about it, and I'm sorry. I'm on your side. If there are sides here. I think you're great, and ambitious and focused and also—well—clearly *very* sensitive about how people perceive you. Touchy, even. A classic Capricorn, one might say. But all of that aside, it's important that you know it's not just you, that the parents not getting it thing isn't *about* you. Its bigger than that. *You're* great."

A silence landed between them, one Bette didn't know how to fill. She didn't know how to tell Ruth how much her words

meant. She couldn't fathom why Ruth should have any diffi-
culty at all finding someone. Finding a big capital-S someone.
She was fantastic. How could anyone *not* want Ruth?

"Thank you," she said, throat thick, feeling entirely and impossibly inadequate. "I—thank you."

"Plus, look at how determined you've been about the project!
You could have just been on your own for a bit, or something.
But you're really committing to it. Leaning in!"

"How have we ended up back on me again?" Bette wondered.
"Okay, you said the dating hadn't all been awful, and then we
only got through one weird Aries. Anyone else?"

"I mean, yeah. There kind of is, actually, but it wasn't an app
thing," Ruth replied, and Bette watched her throat and the top
of her chest prickle into pink. "It's new. He's new, and we're taking things really slow. His name's Gabe. He's a journalist, mostly
zones of conflict, and he took a series of photographs on his last
assignment. The university organized an exhibition of them a
few weeks back, and I met him there."

Gabe. Gabe the journalist, who didn't just take photos but
took a "series of photographs." Gabe, who in two sentences was
already alarmingly impressive. Some part of Bette's brain offered up a memory from the haze of cheap party wine that had
been obscuring it: the guy from the stairs, the night of the party.
She thought of how great they both looked, of Gabe's face as he
looked at Ruth.

"Did I—was he with you last weekend? When I was leaving?"

Ruth nodded, the blush reaching her cheeks now too. It
might be new, but Ruth clearly liked him. Bette found herself

hungry for details, wanting to know what it was that made Ruth flush like that.

"So you've had a few dates?"

"A couple, yeah. We're not rushing into anything, that's basically the whole point. For me, anyway. I like him. I just—yeah. Slow was the plan. Is the plan."

"Slow is good," Bette said, not knowing whether she agreed even as she said it. Slow felt kind of ridiculous.

"We went to a roller disco," Ruth said, her smile slightly embarrassed.

"A roller disco? Like, lights and roller skates and disco music?" Bette repeated. "Are we in a teen film from the eighties?"

"I know. Turns out I'm also appallingly bad on skates."

"Yeah?"

"Oh yeah," Ruth said, with a nod so sincere that Bette couldn't help laughing at her. "No idea why I thought I'd be sort of all right. Put them on, fell straight down on my bum. Like, straight down. Still at the counter. I had to hold onto the side for the next hour, like a child."

"No."

"Yes indeed. He tried to help, but I was pretty much a lost cause. Plus, turns out Gabe can literally dance. Like, moonwalk in roller skates. He brought his own with him."

Bette wasn't sure why the first image that came to mind was of the guy from the stairs, looking unfairly good in denim shorts and an open shirt and hot-pink roller skates, and of her sticking a foot out and tripping him as he skated past. It probably didn't speak well of her.

"I almost saw Mei today," she said instead, and then regretted it almost immediately. Keen for something tangible to do, she pressed her finger into the sauce left on her dinner plate and transferred it to her mouth. "I mean—I didn't actually see her. She was in the office. And I—I hid in the toilets."

"Right."

"Yeah, I kind of knew it would happen at some point, but I wasn't . . ." she began, no choice but to commit to it now, but Ruth cut her off.

"Bette, I don't want to talk about you having to hide in a toilet. I don't want to talk about Mei at all. Oddly enough."

It was as though shutters had crashed down between them, as if Ruth was closing up shop. The warm flush on Ruth's cheeks was gone, and her eyes seemed distant. There was an edge to her voice, so instantly altered, that felt sharp against Bette's skin. There was danger here, suddenly. She'd stumbled down a bad road.

"What?"

"I don't want to talk about her."

It made sense, of course. Ruth didn't know Mei. Disinterest made sense. But Ruth seemed . . . weirdly mad. And that made no sense at all.

"I just wanted to—" Bette said, trying to backtrack, desperate to reverse away from the harshness in Ruth's voice. But she couldn't even finish the sentence. Why *had* she brought Mei up?

"Look, if she were your girlfriend then sure, I guess. We could talk about her. But all I really know about her is that she's given you an ultimatum and forced you to do something that, no offense, you're not very good at doing. And that's enough for me to know I'd really rather not talk about her."

It seemed incredible that mere minutes before she'd felt Ruth so entirely on her side. Embarrassment rushed in, her face and neck flushing, but it was quickly overtaken by anger. Ruth had no idea what her relationship with Mei was like.

"I'm not sure what you're saying."

"Look, I know it's been weird for you. I know you've struggled with it. But—I mean—with Nat . . ."

So that *was* it. She'd talked to Natalia. And underneath the nice invitation to dinner and the conversation about fucking star signs she was simmering away. Bette had hurt her friend's feelings, and now Ruth was mad. She could feel tears prick at the corner of her eyes. They were in a restaurant. She absolutely could not cry.

"Did you invite me out here tonight to tell me I'm doing a bad job at hooking up with people? Because, frankly, I don't need you to do that for me. I felt awful all day on Sunday."

Ruth looked uncomfortable, her shoulders creeping closer to her ears, her eye contact avoidant.

"Well, I'm kind of glad you did? I mean, I hate the idea of you feeling awful. But there's a better way to go about things than the way you are. Than the way you did."

"You're talking like I don't regret it," Bette said, aware of how crowded the restaurant was, aware of her voice tipping toward hysterical. "Like I'm asking for your opinion."

"I thought you messaged me to get advice on how to pick up other women. Surely we're only here because you wanted my opinion."

The accusation coursed through Bette, her stomach churning and skin itching. There was no denying that her first texts had been a request for help. But it had been weeks since she'd first texted Ruth for help. Weeks since that had been all they were. She'd thought there was more between them now than that.

"And I thought we'd become friends, actually, but I guess I'm shit at all relationships? Not just romantic ones." Bette stood, reaching into her purse. And then she sat down again, her jaw clenched, her teeth gritted. "For fuck's sake. I don't have any cash. I'm not going to leave you with the bill because I'm not that person but I want you to know I would be walking out right now if I could."

They sat in silence, the seconds ticking over, inexorably slowly, until there had been a full minute of them.

"In fairness, no one carries enough cash to make that kind of statement anymore," Ruth said.

"No," Bette agreed. "No, they don't."

"Also, I've already paid. I bought the tickets."

"Oh."

They sat in silence again, the air between them tense and uncomfortable, until Bette decided that she could be the bigger person. If she absolutely had to be.

"Should we have coffee with our dessert?"

Ruth's head flew up, her brows knitted together, her eyes wide. She nodded, the action odd and childlike when coupled with her expression. She looked so grateful that Bette could feel the relief of it behind her ribs.

"Yeah," she said. "Let's order some. Bette I didn't mean to—"

"It's fine," Bette replied, certain that a sincere apology would either grate against her or make her cry. Potentially both. "We can just—let's just forget it."

"No, I shouldn't have—I mean, it's really not any of my business. I don't know where that came from."

"Really, let's just—please can we just not?"

"Okay," Ruth said, nodding reassuringly at her. "I'm done."

Bette made eye contact with one of the waiters. Dessert would fix things. It had to.

CHAPTER TWELVE

SATURDAY, 03 SEPTEMBER

●●●

42 days to go

They had reached a semblance of an understanding before they left the restaurant. Enough, at least, for Ruth to have apologized again, pink-faced, as they were leaving, and promise to text over the weekend. Enough for Bette to have apologized too, in lieu of being able to apologize to Natalia. But the hurt of the conversation lingered like an unfamiliar bruise, one that she couldn't help poking at. And so, hoping for a sympathetic ear, wanting reassurance that Ruth had lost her mind, she brought it up with Ash the next evening.

"I told Ruth about the Mei thing," Bette said, dinner bowl on her lap, heels balanced precariously on the edge of the coffee table, *Grey's Anatomy* on again.

Ash picked up a few flakes of salmon with her chopsticks, dipping the fish into the sauce pooled in the base of her bowl before lifting it to her mouth.

"Sorry, are we calling you skiving off work for an hour to sit on top of a toilet 'the Mei thing'?" Ash said, mildly, apparently engrossed in Izzie and ghost Denny mooning at each other on the laptop screen.

"Yes."

"Sure," Ash nodded. "Bet Ruth was thrilled to hear all about it."

"Actually, she was really weird about it. She basically told me I'm terrible at dating, and then refused to talk about Mei. Like, I know the Natalia thing wasn't my finest moment. I'm obviously going to avoid stuff with any of Ruth's friends from now on. But it was like she was taking it personally." Bette was self-aware enough to recognize that the reason their conversation still ate at her was because she wasn't entirely blameless; she could have handled the Natalia situation differently. But she resented Ruth for calling her out on it.

"Can't imagine why that might be. Total mystery."

"Guess they must be closer than I realize. If anyone did that to you, I'd take it *very* personally."

"Yeah, no, that's not what I meant."

Ash was looking smug, and Bette suddenly realized the implication.

"Ash, for god's sake. You've not even met her. So you have no idea what you're talking about," she said, aware of how defensive her tone was, furious that the conversation hadn't gone in the direction she had hoped. Ash had missed the point entirely. "Also, she's seeing someone. Gabe. He's a journalist. So whatever your eyebrows are suggesting, it's not that."

"Oh! Interesting," Ash said, shrugging as she lifted a bundle of noodles toward her mouth. "And how are you feeling about that?"

"It's nothing to do with me," Bette replied, exasperated, wondering how on earth they'd ended up here. She thought back to Ruth's flushed cheeks, to the embarrassed smile. It was good, obviously, to see Ruth happy.

"Right."

"She seems to like him. So that's—that's good," Bette said, and Ash smiled around her noodles, the chopsticks still between her lips. Bette refocused on the screen, wishing fervently that she'd never opened her mouth at all.

PART OF THE initial appeal of Bette's job had been the overnight work trips. It was an odd joy to have a room at a Premier Inn, with a window that overlooked a car park. A small per diem that she could spend on an M&S meal deal from the station, dinner in a pub she'd never been to before, a pint that someone would reimburse her for. A couple of hours on a train, away from the distraction of the office, to try and fail to catch up on emails. It was a little reset, an almost-holiday when she couldn't afford one. At the very least, an occasional night in a bed she hadn't made.

Over time, the little jaunts had lost their shine; the happier she felt at home, the less she felt the need to be away. But after a couple of years of barely leaving Bristol, of barely leaving her street, the idea of being somewhere else was undeniably appealing. And so when Erin emailed to ask for cover, while she was up in Edinburgh for wedding-planning, Bette claimed the trip within minutes.

It was too crowded on the train to pull her laptop out of her backpack. Most of the journey passed by instead in a blaze of green fields and gray skies, two episodes of a podcast Ruth had put her onto in her ears.

But as the train approached Weymouth, her hand hovered over her phone. Maybe it was worth a swipe. She was working, sure, but they didn't own her evenings. Looking for something casual here, where she was unlikely to run into the woman again? It made a lot of sense.

She clicked in and refreshed her location. There was a new ten-mile radius, and new women. Women who had taken selfies with their dogs, women by the sea, women pouting in front of their bathroom mirrors, women clutching cocktails, women in boxing gloves, women at festivals covered in glitter, women in big round glasses. She paused. The woman in big round glasses. A receptionist, a dog-lover. A switch. Evie. As the train pulled into the station, she swiped yes.

The station to the care home wasn't a difficult journey, and she had time to make it on foot. It was an awful day, the sky a swollen and threatening sort of gray. The sea reflected it back, cross and uninviting. It was a relief, really, not to feel the pull to the sea that she did on a sunny day. Work was so much easier, she thought, as she turned into a large car park and walked up the path to push open a heavy glass door, when summer was shit.

A woman with a shaggy haircut was behind the desk at the end of the corridor, a phone pressed to one ear. A pair of large round glasses kept slipping down her nose, and she wore an open shirt knotted over an olive-green tank top. It was the woman she'd swiped on the train. It seemed impossibly unlikely. But it was either her or an impressive doppelgänger.

Maybe-Evie tucked her hair behind her ear and looked up, meeting Bette's eye. A mouthed "One minute" and an apologetically raised finger stopped Bette in her tracks a few meters from the desk, and she hovered awkwardly.

"Can you send both for us to check?" knotted shirt was saying. She nodded, almost dropping the phone in the process, and rolled her eyes self-deprecatingly at Bette. "Yes. Yeah, that's great. Okay. Talk next week. Thanks."

Once the phone was back in the receiver, she looked across the desk and tucked her hair behind her ears again. "You must be Bette? Nice to meet you. Do you need to leave anything back here before we head through?"

Bette shook her head, turning and popping a hip to show off her backpack, instantly regretting the primary-school energy of the move. "It's fine. I've only got this. You're—" she said, and then paused, realizing that she was about to reveal herself and her swiping and potentially weird-out a complete stranger. A new colleague. "I mean, sorry, what's your . . . ?"

"Evie," the woman replied, confirming Bette's accidental detective work. She walked out from behind the desk to shake her hand, firm and confident, and then led Bette down the hall. "I'm the receptionist. I know Barbara's supposed to be here for you this afternoon but honestly it'll mostly be me. She's pretty up against it. We'll try and catch her later."

"That's fine! It's really the session and the group I wanted to see—I can phone Barbara next week to talk if she can't get away."

Bette spent the next few hours sandwiched between two women: one so tall and pinched and the other so short and soft that they belonged together in a picture book. They were deliciously sarcastic and cutting about each other's work, and sweetly brutal about Bette's attempts at making something of her own. She spent most of the afternoon in peals of laughter, thinking of her nonna.

"Told you it was all going well," Evie said from the doorway, as Bette crammed feedback forms into her backpack following the session. She had dropped in and out of the session all afternoon, but Bette had found herself deliberately looking around in the final hour; she'd begun to worry she might have missed her going home. "Barbara actually has forty minutes before she has to leave, if you want to hear how things have been from her end?"

"Oh that'd be great," Bette said, picking up her backpack and following Evie out. She fell into step beside her; now that they were close, Evie had the distinctive clinical smell of a soap that probably disinfected everything it touched. But she could also see the light freckles that scattered along her collarbone, and the thought flickered back across Bette's mind: receptionist, dog-lover, switch. Could she just . . . ask her out? Ask her what she was doing later? She was just gearing up for it when Evie rendered the line forming in her head obsolete.

"Hey, you're staying over, right? Do you want someone to show you around town tonight?"

It was an easy walking distance between the care home and the Premier Inn, and there were maybe two pubs on the way. It was hardly Paris. She could survive without a tour guide, and Evie had to know that. This wasn't an obligation offer, Bette realized.

"Sure," she replied, a smile taking over her face. "Sure, that'd be really nice."

———

TWO PINTS AND two and a half games of pool in, Bette made the decision to sleep with Evie. She was aware of the slightly questionable professionalism, but it wasn't as though they were in the same office every day. And Evie was hot, in a Dr. Ellie Sattler kind of way. Hot, and unequivocally flirting back. It all felt like an unbelievable win on a night when she had a hotel room and a reasonable start time the next morning.

And the thing was, Evie was good at pool. Astoundingly good, making all sorts of impossible shots that utilized the sort of physics Bette almost understood in theory but could never make work in practice. Evie leaned over her pool cue, her shirt slipping off one shoulder and revealing the bare skin beneath. It was compelling, watching her make her way around the table, resting a hip against it while Bette fumbled her cue and hit a ball near-ish to the pocket. And then, just as easily as she'd made every other shot, she sunk the black from behind two of Bette's reds, and smugly drained the rest of her glass.

"Another?" Evie asked, her body suddenly slightly too close to Bette's to be polite. Bette wasn't sure if she meant the pint or the game, but she glanced down from her eyes to her lips and watched Evie's smile stretch wide.

"Or that's fun too," Evie said, and cupped a hand around the side of Bette's jaw.

The kiss was confident, no prevaricating, no question in it. Bette could smell Evie beneath the sterilizing hand wash, like salt and summer, as if she'd swum in the sea before work that morning and it had dried on her skin. Bette fumbled with her pool cue in a bid to get her hands involved, and felt Evie laugh against her lips as it bounced on the floor at their feet. They both looked down, and then up at each other again, and Evie licked her lips. Ruth's warning, to be wary of making out with girls in pubs, reverberated in her ears, but it was difficult to care. And so she leaned in again.

Evie groaned slightly as she bit gently into Bette's lip, and Bette realized she had something she needed to say before they got too carried away.

"I'm not looking for anything serious," she said far too loudly, cringing inwardly. "If that's okay. I mean, I'm basically never here. But you're gorgeous, and disarmingly good at pool, and this has been really fun, so if you're up for it then—"

"Hey," Evie said, tapping Bette on the shoulder with her pool cue, still grasped in the hand that wasn't tangled in the hair at the nape of Bette's neck. "I'm not looking for another girlfriend either. I have a partner. We're ethically nonmonogamous. I'm looking for authentic connections, meaningful encounters with people I find interesting. No expectations from my end beyond tonight."

Bette nodded, realizing that in any other context someone who said "authentic connections" or "meaningful encounters" with a completely straight face was not really the woman for her. But it was one night. It hardly mattered.

"Shall we—" Bette gestured toward the door. "I mean, I have a hotel room. Which might be better than the pub. If that's—I mean . . ."

Evie laughed, sharper than was entirely kind, and Bette felt her face flush. But then she leaned forward and kissed her, hard and certain, and Bette decided not to worry about it. If she

EXPERIENCED · 139

could manage to just shut up, she could probably pull this off.
Evie stepped back, a grin still firmly in place, and raised an eyebrow at Bette. It was a clear challenge to take the lead again.
And Bette loved a challenge. She picked up her backpack from
beneath the pool table and walked out of the pub, determined
to play it cool, not to look behind her to check that Evie was following. Near the door the Orpheus impulse nearly won out, but
she walked determinedly through it and breathed a sigh of relief
as she heard the door swing again behind her.

"You're at the Premier Inn, right?" came Evie's voice from behind her.

It was a performance, but she was determined to be sexy, to
claw things back after fumbling in the pub. She looked back at
Evie.

"Yep."

Ten minutes later Bette was swiping her key card across the
lock and pushing open the door. The performance was becoming harder and harder to maintain; she was nervous. Somewhere
between the pool table and the brightly lit Premier Inn hallway,
the sexiness had been chipped away from the evening. The hotel felt too clean, too stark, like an office. Bette wanted to throw
a scarf over a lamp.

"So, do you want a drink?" she offered.

Evie laughed. "I don't think that cupboard is a minibar."

She was right, obviously.

"I could just go out and get . . ." She trailed off.

"I mean, you could try. But it'll be a good twenty-minute walk
to a corner shop. Everywhere else will be closed by now." Evie

shrugged, a sort-of explanation and apology for the town, for the lack of late-night options. "It's fine though. I don't need a drink."

Bette nodded, knowing she must seem jittery and strange. They were still standing in the middle of the room, and her backpack was still on her back. She glanced around. There was a tiny desk, but otherwise there were no options for sitting that didn't result in them being immediately in bed together.

"Hey, are you okay?" Evie asked, stepping forward and squeezing Bette above her elbow. "There's no pressure at all. Honestly, if you just want me to go home, I can. No issue. Or we could watch something for a bit?"

Bette felt so grateful that she didn't quite know how to convey it. "Yeah. Yeah, sorry. Just—yeah, let's watch something?"

She kicked her shoes off, dropped her backpack to the floor and climbed onto the bed, on top of the duvet. Evie followed suit, bringing the remote with her. She scrolled through and found an old episode of *Grand Designs*, then put the remote on the bedside table.

"Okay, this is perfect," Bette said, leaning back against the headboard and crossing one ankle over the other.

"Yeah? Kevin McCloud do it for you?"

"Ew, no. But any mention of underfloor heating really does."

Evie looked over at her and grinned. "So, how did you imagine this going then?"

"Honestly, I didn't think much beyond wanting to kiss you in the pub," Bette said. She pulled her eyes away from the modernist cliffside build and suddenly pregnant owner, and over to Evie. "I mean, I did. I asked you to come back here. But I don't . . . What do you like?"

It was a bit of a cop-out. But she realized the truth of it as she said it. She hadn't imagined anything specific, wanted Evie to have the ideas. There were things that had worked for her in the past. But did they work because they were what Mei liked? When faced with the question, she couldn't articulate what it was that she fantasized about, what she wanted. Not beyond: women. What if she asked for something and then couldn't get off? What if she did something with Evie that she'd done with Mei and it didn't work for her? Then Evie would know—that she was new, that she was inexperienced, that she was still figuring it all out. She wanted, desperately and with sudden clarity, to skip this whole phase. To just be done.

To her relief, Evie took the lead, moving with a confidence that felt reassuring. And so Bette made herself relax, tried to enjoy it as Evie maneuvered her body, as she stripped her of her Breton top. Tried to enjoy it as Evie kissed vaguely at her chest, missing the places she most wanted to be touched. As Evie settled on top of her, positioned her legs and started to rock, Bette didn't say that it wasn't really doing anything for her. She just tried to follow the rhythm. And then Evie sat back and pushed a hand inside Bette's jeans, beneath her knickers. It was too dry. Too hard. But she looked so sure, so determined. It was probably supposed to be good. And so, after a reasonable length of time had passed, Bette pretended that it was.

THERE WAS AN M&S near the station, a little further along the front. And there was time for her to walk down to it before her train onward to Bournemouth, tasting salt from the sea on her still-kiss-swollen lips. Lizzo was in her ears when she stepped in front of the open fridge shelves, reassured by the familiar array of packet sandwiches, by the bright lights. She liked a sandwich shop, liked looking at the various fillings and constructing what it was she wanted for lunch. But she liked even more that she could already taste the prawn mayonnaise and the brown bread, and the salt and vinegar crisps she'd fill it with.

Once the sandwich and crisps were secure in her bag, she left the footpath and stepped down onto the sand that led to the sea. She walked back to the station along the shoreline, squinting behind her sunglasses and sweating through the back of her T-shirt. How was it possible for such a cold, gray day to turn into this one? It was harder, this morning, to avoid the fact that all she really wanted was to be in the sea. She took off her shoes, relished the feeling of the sand between her toes, and waded in.

Her skirt was too long, really, for her to be walking shin-deep in the waves. The hem was drenched by the time she pulled it up and tucked it into the lace-trimmed shorts Ruth had got her hooked on. But it would dry. There was a whole train journey for her to dry out. It was hard to regret anything when she could feel the sand between her toes and sun on her face and salt stinging where she'd just shaved her legs in the shower.

It was, of course, difficult to push her feet back into her shoes (her shirt from the day before was sacrificed to the sandy dusting-down), and she made it to the station with barely a minute to spare. There was a seat on the train, at a table, that was blissfully unreserved. Her quarter of it was soon a mini-office, her charger running across the table, her laptop open, work tabs and emails open.

By her feet, her phone buzzed relentlessly in the outside pocket of her backpack. There was a chance it could be Erin, and so although she had planned to ignore it, to get some work done, she contorted herself in her chair until her phone was in her hand.

It's a match! Her notifications read. It was Evie, of course. In everything that had followed, she had almost forgotten about the swiping.

> **Evie:** Such weird and perfect luck that I saw you here before the workshop finished yesterday
>
> **Evie:** Anyway, had a great time last night, thought we had a really special connection
>
> **Evie:** It'd be great to see you again
>
> **Evie:** xxxx

There was a text too. And a voice note. A fourteen-minute voice note. She felt her skin prickle uncomfortably.

> **+447535******:** Hope you don't mind me texting too, got your number from work! Messaged you on the app. Would be great to hear from you when you're next back!

Nope. Absolutely not.

All she could think of was how silent everything had been once they had switched off *Grand Designs*. It was unnerving. With Mei, with Charlie, with Natalia there had been so much conversation. It had struck her, after a decade of sleeping with men, that women were really good at talking to each other. Or at talking, anyhow. Maybe not at communicating directly, at saying what they meant—there was too much equivocation and uncertainty and protecting of feelings for that. But she had never been so consciously silent in bed with a woman. None of the laughter and filth and endless slipping from talking to fucking and back again that there'd been with Mei. None of Charlie's heat whispered in her ear. Not even, for all that it made Bette cringe with regret to remember it, any of Natalia's praise and pleasure and sweetness. None of the conversation, the spark, from the pub earlier in the evening. None of it.

And now. Fourteen minutes of, she assumed, the very opposite of silence.

Careful not to click on the message, she swiped at it to move it out of her notifications, and opened her texts so that Evie couldn't see her on WhatsApp. Her finger hovered. Her initial impulse was to text Ruth, but it had only been a couple of days since their dinner. They'd messaged over the weekend, but things still felt a little delicate. So she texted Ash an SOS and then stared at her phone waiting for a reply. Her eyes fell on the clock top-left: 11:14 a.m. Ash would be in class. For hours. Bette sent a brief explanatory text so Ash didn't panic later, swallowed her reticence about texting Ruth about a girl she'd slept with, and opened a new text thread.

> **Bette:** you around?
>
> **Ruth:** A text! Vintage. To what do I owe the honor?
>
> **Bette:** oh thank god

Bette: thank you for having a job you
can text during

Bette: that wasn't supposed to be a dig

Bette: you know what I mean

Ruth: I do. I have exactly that job. For the
next six minutes, and then I have a tutorial.

Bette: thank you, incredible, statues
are being erected in your honor etc

Bette: anyway, I'm avoiding going
online on whatsapp

Bette: hence the texting

Bette: because I met this woman at
work yesterday

Bette: we went out for a drink
afterward and . . . you know . . .

Ruth: Sure. A euphemistic . . .

Bette: yeah

Bette: it was fine

Bette: anyway I was really clear this time!

Bette: about not wanting anything beyond
last night

Ruth: That's great!

Ruth: I think that read slightly
sarcastic but I really mean it.

Bette: but I get on the train this morning

Bette: and she's sent a string of messages

Ruth: Sure

Bette: and
Bette: a FOURTEEN-MINUTE VOICE NOTE
Bette: that's a podcast
Bette: a whole podcast

Ruth: Hahahahaha
Ruth: Look, it's a good thing women are hot. Because they're also just entirely insane.

Bette: obviously I'm going to listen to it at some point, I'm not a monster
Bette: but I just needed to say to you:
Bette: FOURTEEN-MINUTE VOICE NOTE

Ruth: I want a full podcast review from you by the time I get out of this tutorial.

What with the crowded train and the emails that needing answering and the taxi and then the session, there had been no chance to find the fourteen minutes that the message required until she was walking back to the station in the last light of the day. By then it had been bumped down the list in her notifications by exclamation points from Ash accompanied by an all-capital-letters *FOURTEEN MINUTES?! GET OUT GET OUT GET OUT*, by a text from her mother with train suggestions for her next trip back, by a link to an article about the Arts Council from Carmen, and by a—a—

A fourteen-minute voice note from Ruth. She plugged her headphones into her phone, and pressed play.

"Just thought I'd give you a little end-of-the-day palate cleanser as I walk between classes. In case you're still avoiding another special little podcast you've been sent today, and you needed a lead-in. An *amuse bouche*, if you will. But for your ears. Ooh, an *amuse oreille*? Shit, that's so lame. I regret saying that. I don't have time to start again. Anyway. It's a lovely late-summer evening in Bristol, and the city misses you . . ."

Bette rolled her eyes, feeling oddly smug that Ruth had given the quarter-hour she had between classes to Bette. Not to enjoying some silence, or listening to something herself. Not to Heather or Jody. Not to Gabe. But to Bette. She couldn't stop the smile breaking out on her face.

CHAPTER THIRTEEN

SATURDAY, 10 SEPTEMBER

●●●

35 days to go

Y ou should come to football with me," Ash said. They were in the kitchen, a pot of coffee brewing on the counter while they worked their way through bowls of cereal. Bette was up unusually early, but it had been bright, and Ash had been loud, taking out her frustration at having to go to work on a Saturday by letting every door in their flat slam as she walked through it. "I think you might enjoy it."

Ash had joined a ladies' team the winter before, rediscovering her old love for it, like falling for a childhood sweetheart all over again. Things had been quiet over the summer, but autumn was coming now and the season was starting up again.

"I thought we'd agreed that my athletic skills are exclusively aquatic?"

"Not to join the team. I want us to keep winning," Ash said, clearly horrified at the thought. "No, because there are so many gays on the team. Might be fun?"

"Oh!" Bette replied. It hadn't even occurred to her. It should have, but the last season had been pre-Mei, and back then she'd been so intimidated by the idea of spending time with them all. Ash would come home with stories of her teammates, of their fun girlfriends, of a whole big group of women with their shit together. It had felt unfathomable to consider that Bette, mere months into figuring out how she felt about women, might get there too. Might find that confidence.

"Wouldn't it be weird for you? If I slept with one of your teammates?"

There was a long pause.

"Funnily enough, I wasn't actually thinking about you sleeping with any of them," Ash said, the sentence leaving her with the energy of a protracted sigh. "Just thought it might be nice for you to meet some new people."

Bette cringed. Tunnel vision. It was probably good to meet new people regardless, outside the project of it all. Because people were good, and interesting, and fun. Not because they were prospective shags. Fuck.

"Fuck, I'm sorry, Ash," said Bette, sincerely and seriously.

"Not a big deal," Ash said. "Just—this does seem to be taking over your life a bit. Like, it doesn't have to be a thing that that's where your mind immediately went. But—maybe—I don't know, there's something . . ."

Bette nodded into her bran flakes and banana.

"Do you want to finish that thought?" she asked, uncomfortable and embarrassed and determined to take Ash down with her.

"Not really," Ash replied, standing up with her bowl. She brought the coffee pot back to the table and focused on pouring out two mugs. "Just—no, you know what? I really don't."

Bette took a coffee and they both drank in silence. Ash was quick to finish; she drank as though desperate to escape.

"Well, it sounds like it could be fun."

"Sure," Ash said, noncommittally. "It is. It's the start-of-season party Thursday. If you want to come."

Bette nodded and pulled her phone out, ostensibly to check the date. But the air between them felt stilted and strange. Bette wouldn't go to the party. She knew she wouldn't. She went to Jody's party because there was the promise of being introduced to someone fun. But parties full of new people didn't tend to be her favorite places to be.

"Bleurgh," Ash said, "look, can we just imagine that neither of us said anything? Just—a reset? Or something? I have to leave now and I don't have time for us to get into it. But I'm sorry I made things weird."

"I made it weird first!" Bette said, loving Ash so much she could barely stand it. "I'm sorry, I really am, it's just—it's just been a lot lately."

"Okay, well, let's just ignore any weirdness and pretend I was already gone when you got up this morning and just—shit," she said, looking at her watch. "I really do need to go. This meeting starts in half an hour. They'll murder me if I'm late. Okay. I'll be home with ingredients by midday. They promised we could all be gone by eleven."

Bette nodded and waved at her as she hurried off, a mouth full of the last of her cereal. After a beat, Bette pushed her chair back so that it scraped along the floor and ran out after her. Close to the door, she pulled Ash into a hug and squeezed her hard.

"Love you," Ash said into her shoulder.

"You too," Bette replied. "See you for lunch. Can I do anything?"

"Make the table nice? Put that wine we bought in the fridge? But it's all fine otherwise. They're not coming until two. I'm looking forward to getting out of school as soon as I can and coming home to cook."

THEY SHOULD HAVE known, in hindsight. Any time Ash assumed that things at school would run on time had ended in tears. And this, a Saturday morning of meetings to start the term that the teaching staff had fought against and lost, was bound to overrun. Sure enough, at half-ten Bette's phone vibrated relentlessly on the kitchen table. By the time her tea had brewed and she picked it up, Ash's messages filled the entire screen.

> **Ash:** Bette there is literally no way I'm going to be done in time
>
> **Ash:** I hate this day
>
> **Ash:** Carmen is going to meet us here when we're done and she and Anton will come straight back with me
>
> **Ash:** Tim too
>
> **Ash:** But that probably won't be until two
>
> **Ash:** I know I said I don't need your help but now I need your help
>
> **Ash:** If I send you the recipe could you shop for me and get things started?

Ash: It's not a difficult recipe

Ash: But I hate asking

Ash: This was supposed to be on me

Ash: I know it's not your ideal Saturday

Bette picked up her phone and laughed at the escalating panic on display.

Bette: sorry

Bette: was making tea

Bette: just joining the meltdown now

Bette: course I can cook, I'm not completely useless

Bette: just send the recipe

Ash: You're a lifesaver and I love you and I'm naming my firstborn after you

Bette: obviously

CIRCLING THE SUPERMARKET in frustration, Bette pulled her phone out of her pocket. Ash was busy, and Bette didn't really want to bother her anyway. What she wanted to do was have a bit of a bitch.

Bette: been to three shops now and no one has clams

The reply was almost immediate.

Ruth: Why on earth are you shopping for clams?

Bette: it's Ash's plan but she's still at school

Bette: we're having people to lunch

Bette: there are going to be five of us

Bette: I don't really cook for five very often

Bette: it's supposed to be easy

Bette: but I have been looking for clams for an hour now and I am more and more certain they don't exist in Bristol

Bette: or in the sea

Bette: like, at all

Bette: they're a hoax

Ruth: Send it to me

Bette: ??

Ruth: The recipe

Bette felt a prickly little rush of embarrassment. It was one thing to play up the frustration, to make Ruth laugh and sympathize and tell her it was going to be fine. But sending the recipe felt a lot like being useless. Like asking for help. But it wasn't as though Ruth was leaving her with an alternative. She pressed forward on Ash's recipe and then pushed the phone into the back pocket of her jeans, ignoring the buzz of reply as she looped around the biscuit aisle in mild despair. Once she had three chocolate-covered varieties in her basket, she felt strong enough to look.

> **Ruth:** Yeah, you need clams for that.

> **Bette:** great this has been really helpful

> **Ruth:** You could make something else?
> You're still in the supermarket, right?
> What looks good? Surely Ash will be
> fine with anything you want to make?

Of course Ash would be fine with that. That wasn't the problem. The problem was that she had said she was on top of it, that she had things in hand.

> **Bette:** of course she would
> **Bette:** it's not a big thing
> **Bette:** I just like having a recipe
> **Bette:** don't worry, I'll figure
> something out! I'll do some googling!

The exclamation points saved it, Bette thought. The exclamation points were Monica Geller's "breezy." Only . . . effective.

> **Ruth:** Send me a picture of the fish counter.

Or perhaps not so effective.

> **Bette:** ??

> **Ruth:** Fish counter. Come on.

Bette walked back over, pointed her phone at the fish, and made uncomfortable and apologetic eye contact with the guy behind the counter as she snapped a couple of blurry pictures. She sent the best one. *Ruth is typing* . . . appeared and then hovered over their conversation for what felt like an age.

> **Ruth:** Right. Buy three sacks of those mussels, a 300ml pot of single cream, a bag of tarragon from the herb section in the fruit and veg, three little shallots (or a brown onion if you can't find any), and a jar of grainy French mustard. I'll bring wine and bread.

Bette wanted to be annoyed by the suggestion she wouldn't know where tarragon could be found. But she didn't, so it was an irritatingly helpful text. And in addition to the tarragon information, it included an implication that she wouldn't be alone.

> **Bette:** . . . what

> **Ruth:** I'm coming round to help

> **Bette:** you're coming round to help?

Ruth is typing . . . appeared again, and flashed in and out. Over and over. A woman tutted loudly behind her, and Bette apologized and pushed herself and her trolley up against the cheese section.

> **Ruth:** I live round the corner. You're spiraling. I've got most of a

bottle of white we can cook with and
I can get to Harts before I come.
Mussels and crusty bread. It's a breeze.
And if Ash likes clams, you're probably
safe with mussels too.

Bette: okay

Ruth: Buy the mussels. Hurry up.
See you in 30.

Bette: okay

Bette generally responded well to direction. But the rush of relief at being told exactly what she needed to do was surprisingly overwhelming. It was hot. Why was it hot? Ruth was a friend, coming round to help her. It was important not to make things weird. She and Ruth were friends, and Bette didn't only think about sex. Plus, Ruth was seeing Gabe.

It was a little weird when Ruth arrived, she decided. Weird in the sense that Ruth walked in with a bottle of wine under one arm and two baguettes poking out of a tote bag, and looked so capable that Bette instantly wanted to cry or hug her or something; an impulse she couldn't really identify. Weird in the sense that it felt immediately as though she'd always been in Bette and Ash's kitchen, as though there existed a place in it that was carved out for her.

Weird in the sense that it wasn't weird. At all.

They stood shoulder to shoulder at the sink and Ruth showed her how to pull the gross stringy bits from the mussels. *The beards need a good tug. Be confident, come on.* They scrubbed the shells and Bette chipped her orange nail polish and hoped they wouldn't end up eating it. Ruth asked for the biggest pot they had and it wasn't big enough, so they decided to use two. And then Ash walked in with Tim and Anton and Carmen and the kitchen was suddenly filled with so many of her favorite people, all of whom she was cooking for. Technically. She was, at the very least, helping. It felt good.

Carmen, always infinitely softer than her tall, brittle frame suggested, wrapped herself around Bette's back and scattered kisses on the top of her head. She smelled as she always did, like bright, citrusy perfume; the expensive kind that lingered all day in the way that Bette's never managed to. Bette turned to see Anton (his scruffy Saturday beard growth flecked with a gray he pretended not to be pleased with) open the fridge, find a jar of olives, and pull them out with his fingers. Ash rolled her eyes and handed him a fork. They looked exhausted, Ash and Anton both, and Bette wanted to pour them wine and sit them down. But it was good having everyone in the kitchen together.

"You're amazing," Ash said, peering over Bette's shoulder and into the seafood-filled sink. "I love mussels. This is perfect. Honestly, I don't think I've ever loved anyone quite as much as I love you in this moment."

"Me neither," Tim called out from across the kitchen. His hand was buried in a share bag of crisps and he looked weighed down, as if he'd taken some of whatever had happened from Ash's shoulders and was now struggling beneath it.

"Well, it's actually . . ." Bette started, and then Ruth interrupted.

"Sorry, I've sort of crashed things! I'm Ruth," she said, and Bette realized the problem with feeling like someone belonged in your kitchen and in your home: you forgot to introduce them. "This was all Bette, but it was sort of a two-person job, so I dropped in for a bit. It's so nice to meet you all!"

"You'll stay, right? For lunch? Bette?" Ash said, her eyebrows raised.

"Yes?" Bette said, looking over at Ruth, who shrugged and nodded, looking pleased.

"I've got plans tonight, and I'll need to be picked up at six. But I could give this address, if that works? I'd love to stay."

"Of course!" Ash said. "So pleased to have you."

And then once Ash had poured everyone a glass of wine and Tim had found a second bag of crisps, she shooed everyone into the front room and they left Bette and Ruth to get on with things. Ash squeezed Bette's elbow as she walked past, and Bette felt immeasurably pleased that she had sent the message in the supermarket. That she had said yes to Ruth's offer of help. That she had found a way to be here in their kitchen keeping things together while Ash drank wine and took a breath and was looked after.

"Okay, so give me the headlines," Ruth said, once they were alone, sipping from her glass.

"Headlines?"

"Tell me about Anton and—Carmen, was it? I think I can get away with the Ash and Tim knowledge I have, but give me something about the others."

It was the thing she liked most about Ruth, she realized. How thoughtful she was, the effort she put into every single interaction.

"So, Anton works at the school with Ash. He's the Year Five

teacher. They both started at the school at about the same time, so he's been a friend of ours for years. He started dating Carmen maybe a year ago? I think? She's a playwright. I think she's got something happening at the Old Vic at the moment, but don't quote me on that."

"Year Five, dating a year, playwriting," she nodded. "I can work with that."

"Anton also has a secret aspiration to leave teaching so he can be one of those Formula One tire-changing guys. And Carmen has lived in nine different countries because her mum's a diplomat, so she's got amazing stories."

"Now *they're* the headlines I really wanted. Perfect." She clinked her glass against Bette's. "Okay, should we finish up?"

Ruth helped her fry the sliced shallots in butter and they divided the mussels and wine between the two pots.

It all smelled fantastic. And when Ruth nudged Bette to pull the lid off a couple of minutes later it all *looked* fantastic too, the mussels plump and vivid, their black shells glistening. They poured over the cream and sprinkled in the chopped tarragon and then Ruth added more spoonfuls of the mustard than Bette would have dared to. She looked so good cooking, so competent and comfortable, her hair tied up out of the way on top of her head, and Bette thought about Gabe, wondered if he had seen Ruth like this. They stirred the whole lot with the big soup ladle and carried both pots straight to the table.

It all kept feeling weirdly comfortable once they sat down, as if they'd done it a thousand times. As if Ruth fitted in easily with them, not complaining that she had somehow ended up straddling an awkwardly placed swinging table leg, refusing to switch with Bette. Ruth caught Tim's eye and topped up his glass, and asked Carmen about her latest play, and Anton about his Year Fives. She complimented Ash's earrings and they ended up violently defending vintage jewelry that irritated their skin because they were both idiots.

It made her think, entirely without meaning to, of Mei being at the dining table, that first time they'd had dinner with Ash and Tim. They'd been dating only a couple of weeks, and Ash basically demanded she come round for dinner to be approved of. It had been lovely; Tim and Mei had hit it off, and Mei had brought a cake that she had made herself that completely won Ash over. Late in the evening, after dessert, Ash had shot Bette a look as they cleared the table that said *follow me*. When they made it into the kitchen she mouthed *marry her marry her*, and Bette had blushed so pink that Mei had noticed when she sat back down at the table. God. Fuck. She missed her.

"So how did you two meet?" Tim asked. The grin that threatened at the corner of his mouth told Bette that Ash had obviously already filled him in. They'd all been to the pub, a few weeks earlier, and Bette had broken the "break" news to Carmen and Anton. She'd shied away from details, and they'd not pushed. But now, with Tim very definitely pushing, Carmen looked interested and leaned forward eagerly, her glasses slipping down her nose. With a gentle nudge she shushed Anton, who sounded like he was hovering around the same school-focused rant that he and Ash went on every time they all sat down together. Ruth turned to Bette and sat back, and she recognized the passing of the story baton, the expectation falling on her to explain it. She'd not previously considered how to put it.

"As one of the architects of my profile, Tim, you should know that Ruth was one of its first—how would we put it?" She turned toward Ruth, who shrugged. "Appreciators, I guess? Anyway, we went out, and then an hour or so in she came for my entire life, and we decided we were probably going to be friends instead."

Everyone laughed, and Ruth bumped her shoulder reassuringly against Bette's.

"To be fair," Ruth said, "you were going about finding some no-strings-attached sex in—well, not the way I'd do it. So I helped you rethink it. And now look at you! The girls are lining up!"

"They're not lining up," Bette said, feeling the blush bloom on her throat, even closer to the surface than normal after the wine in the kitchen. "Don't listen to her. I've had a couple of dates."

"So Project Shag for Mei is going swimmingly?" Anton asked, and Ash sent a furious expression in his direction. He looked indignant. "What? That's what you've been calling it! It's been a hit, Bette? Right?"

Bette's stomach flipped over, her skin prickling uncomfortably. She wanted to feel fun and flippant about it, to laugh with them all, to be casual and easy. But that pang of Mei-lessness, of imagining her at the table, was vivid, and all of a sudden none of it seemed especially funny.

"Fine, yeah," she said.

"Oh come on," Ash said, warm and keen as she topped up glasses. "It's a bit better than fine! You're in demand! Tell them about Charlie, Bette."

"I just—sorry—" Bette said. She realized, suddenly, what the problem was. Talking about it like this made it feel like a game. It was one thing to have had a laugh making the profile with

Ash and Tim, to finally listen to Evie's agonizingly long voice note and send Ruth a mock-serious review of it. Sitting around the table, with all her happily partnered-up friends, it felt distinctly more exposing. Like she was an oddity, her life a thing to be considered and discussed. She thought of sex against the wall and Charlie's hand, of Natalia on top of her on the sofa, of faking it with Evie, of Ruth's face at the restaurant. Of all the swiping and the shit conversations with women who barely warranted a mention.

She didn't want her romantic life pulled apart and analyzed like some sporting . . . thing. All she really wanted was to have Mei back beside her. That was the point of the whole gambit, and it was also decidedly not the bit that anyone wanted to hear. "Sorry. It's not—I feel kind of weird talking about it."

"Shit," Carmen said. "We're horrible little gossip gremlins. I know we shouldn't push. We're just boring and living vicariously."

"Boring?!" Anton said, mock outraged. "Piss off! I am *fascinating*. Or I can make things less boring for you. See how you fancy the single life again?"

"Oh, I absolutely dare you," Carmen laughed, reaching forward to dip the end of her bread into the pot.

"Yeah, mate, I'm not sure you want to see how that would end," Tim said.

Ash, her expression apologetic, steered the conversation back to school. Bette exhaled in relief. Under the table, Ruth reached over and squeezed her arm, and Bette felt her heart jump into her throat.

It was easier after that. There were other things to say, things that had nothing to do with Bette's romantic life. It had been a

big week; a good one in terms of providing endless topics for discussion. Parliament was a mess. There was a TV show Carmen
was watching that Ruth had opinions about. Anton and Carmen
had been to Ireland, and were brimming with anecdotes and
recommendations for pubs to visit and long walks to do. Ruth
pulled out her phone to make notes and Bette couldn't help thinking about Gabe, about the fact that it was probably him that
Ruth would go to Ireland with, and felt suddenly resentful that
she and Mei had never gone anywhere together. Tim and Anton
were planning a weeklong hike in Yorkshire during the next
school break and, as they often ended up doing when they were
together, talked for an inconceivably long time about tents and
boots. Bette wondered, only half listening as everyone else
asked interested questions about the route, how she'd ended up
with so many friends who walked. Not to get somewhere, not to
look at a nice bit of green and then sit down and have a pint, but
walking for the sake of it, as though it were fun in its own right.

In the early evening, when the mussel shells were cleared
away and the last bottle of wine was open, Bette considered
whether she could convince Ruth to stay and watch a film. It
would be great to offer her a reason to stay around.

And then the doorbell rang, and Bette remembered. Ruth
had plans.

"Oh, that'll be Gabe! He's early," Ruth said, and Bette felt a
combination of indignation and nervous anticipation. Gabe was
here, with no time for her to prepare, and she was going to have
to play charming host.

"Do you want to get him, Bette?" Ash suggested. "Bring him
through for a glass of wine?"

"Oh, no," Ruth said, her tote bag already on her shoulder. "He's just collecting me and we're off! I wouldn't have invited him round without asking."

"Come on, we'd love to meet him," Ash said, looking at Bette expectantly. "Wouldn't we, Bette?"

"Of course we would," Bette replied, finding her voice somewhere in the back of her throat. "Of course. I'll just—I'll go get him."

Gabe was waiting on the doorstep, his white T-shirt tucked into his jeans, his dark hair curling around his ears, his face somehow slightly less beautiful and much more compellingly human than she'd remembered. He wasn't a doll at all. He was an attractive, spicy-cologne-scented, annoyingly friendly-looking man. He put a hand out for Bette to shake.

"You must be Bette? You're just as she described you. It's a pleasure to meet you," he said, his accent unplacable, his words warm and deliberate.

"And you," Bette replied, though Ruth hadn't described him at all. "I mean, she's talked a lot about you, and it's a real pleasure to meet you. Do you want to come in for some wine? Ruth's inside. I know you have plans so you don't feel like you have to—"

"Thank you. I'd love to meet some of Ruth's friends, of course," Gabe said, stepping up and through the door. She pointed ahead of him down the hallway and heard the cry of welcome as he found the front room. She paused in the hallway for a second, staring hopelessly at her own reflection in the mirror. He seemed like a demonstrably good guy. There was no reason for her stomach to be twisting uncomfortably. None at all.

Back in the front room, Gabe had taken her seat beside Ruth, and Ash was midway through introducing him to everyone. He caught Bette's eye as she walked back in and stood up from the chair. It was somehow worse than if he'd just stayed put, hadn't realized that she was now without anywhere to sit.

"Sorry, Bette, I realize I've—" he started, but Bette cut him off.

"It's fine! You stay there, I'll sit on the sofa for a bit," she said, gesturing at him to sit down again. And he did, so she perched on the edge of the sofa, feeling entirely out of things, as though she were watching the conversation at the table on a television. The sofa was too soft to sit up properly on and Bette felt herself curve over, felt her knees too high and her arse too low and her mussel-and-bread-and-wine-filled stomach too squashed up. It was so horribly and oddly lonely that it made her chest ache. Or maybe that was the wine. Gabe and Ruth would head off soon, and she'd be back in among everyone.

"Ruth mentioned you're a journalist?" Ash was saying, as she passed Tim's unused water glass to Gabe, and tipped a couple of fingers of wine into it.

"I am," Gabe nodded, with a gesture of thanks. "Though it's becoming increasingly difficult to make a living from it. Sometimes feel like 'journalist' isn't quite as true as 'journalist-photographer-events-and-wedding-waiter.'"

"All the good people are hyphenates," Carmen said. "Playwright-usher-language-tutor-occasional-gardener here. My CV's a total mess."

"What's your plan tonight then?" Anton asked them, and Gabe looked at Ruth with a smile.

"We're going to the drive-in," he said. "They're showing *Jaws*."

Who *was* this guy? Roller disco and the drive-in and a white T-shirt and jeans and dark curls like he might break out into a rendition of "Greased Lightning" at any moment.

"And if we're going to pick food up on the way . . ." Ruth started, her tote bag back on her shoulder.

"Already sorted," Gabe replied, and Bette felt an odd flash of triumph, at having no doubt in her mind that Ruth would have preferred to be involved in the snack curation. She had a lot of opinions about food. Opinions that Gabe should probably listen to.

"Well, have a great time," Bette said, standing up, and everyone at the table looked over, as though they'd forgotten she was there. "I'll show you out?"

It took a moment for Gabe to shake everyone's hand again, for Ruth to give Ash a hug and a thank-you, for Bette to shepherd them back into the hall.

Bette stood back to let them pass, and Ruth kissed her on the cheek as she did. It wasn't the sort of air-kissing Bette was used to: two cheeks touching briefly and a demonstrative "mwah" in her ear. It also wasn't the loud smack of lips on the meat of her cheek that Ash would land on her most days, at some point or other. This was pure warmth, the press of Ruth's soft lips close to her mouth, a gust of breath hitting Bette's jaw as Ruth pulled away.

"Thanks for today," she said to Bette, and she turned back as she reached the tiny iron gate. "I had so much fun. Your friends are lovely."

"I couldn't have done it without you," Bette said, realizing how sincerely she meant it. Ruth grinned and pressed a hand to her chest over her heart.

Bette waved, feeling oddly bereft, and then watched them

leave together down the street, shoulders brushing up against one another.

"They're such a great couple," Carmen was saying when Bette returned to the front room.

"It's casual," Bette replied automatically, feeling oddly weighed down, dropping heavily back into her chair. "They're not technically a couple."

There was a pause.

"Sure," Ash said, her tone curious. It was a curiosity that should have stopped Bette continuing, but her mouth didn't get the message in time.

"I mean, yeah. He seems great. It's just that Ruth's been really clear about wanting to take it slow with him. So she probably wouldn't want you all thinking they're a couple. You know? They're just dating, casually."

She cringed, regretting having started, biting the inside of her cheek to try and stop the steady stream of words coming from her mouth. The semantics were irrelevant. She didn't need to be making some big deal out of this.

"Sure," Ash repeated, with a significance Bette couldn't bear to think about. Maybe that was the feeling from the hall; all of a sudden Ruth was one more friend who had a default person to spend Saturday night with. Everyone she knew had a someone again, a big capital-S Someone. Ruth might not want to be serious yet, but that's the direction it was heading. At some point soon, Gabe would want to be serious with Ruth. Anyone would. And so of course Bette couldn't help feeling a bit miserable, a bit left behind. She only wished that she'd managed to conceal it better. She couldn't stand the pity written on everyone's face.

"Anyway," Ash said, clearly keen to take the conversation in a different direction, to save Bette from herself. "More wine? Game of cards? Or do you two have plans?"

Anton shook his head, Ash left in the direction of the kitchen in pursuit of another bottle, and Bette took a long drink from her glass.

CHAPTER FOURTEEN

SATURDAY, 17 SEPTEMBER

...

28 days to go

The train to Devon took ninety minutes of her afternoon and more than a decade off her age. Not in the good way that a hyaluronic acid face mask and a nine-hour sleep did, but in a way that made her *feel* like a teenager again: petulant and moody, angry with the world, wanting to put headphones in her ears, pull a hood down over her eyes and ignore everyone. A visit home was all too rare, though; she wasn't going to be able to pull off anything but resigned politeness. Despite how close Bristol was to Exmouth, she hadn't been "home" all year. She had seen her parents when visiting her nonna, but even that had been less often since Mei. The guilt sat heavily in her. Other people managed to make time for their families. But it had been too easy to make excuses, to blame a work event or weekend plans with Ash, or with Mei.

Inevitably, eventually, there was a weekend that was unavoidable. Her brother's birthday fell in the middle of September, and her mother had been adamant about a family lunch. They'd even booked the tickets for her, a bright-orange open return arriving in the post with an ominous note that read *For the 17th. See you then.*

Bette's mother collected her at Exeter station; navy dress starched and pressed, glasses settled atop her head, skin smooth and unlined, arms toned and tanned. Bette could have picked up a connection, but the timings were awkward, and her mother insisted it was easier to come and collect her. What she really wanted, of course, was time when Bette was a captive audience, where she couldn't wander off to make tea, when there was only half a meter of space and half an hour of time in the car between them. Sure enough, ten minutes in busy traffic allowed her mother to touch on her favorite topics: Bette's hair: *such a shame to see that color over your lovely brown*; her career: *it should be illegal for them to pay you so little*; and her home life: *soon Ash is going to move in with that lovely boyfriend of hers, and where will you be then?* At least she didn't ask about Mei. Before the break her mother's silence on the subject would have rankled her, but it was a relief not to have to pretend. Bette hummed in vague confirmation that she had received the information, and then turned her attention out of the window toward the approaching sea.

It was a shame, really, that she came home so infrequently. Not in terms of being picked and prodded at, of the relentless judgment. But in terms of the coast. She missed the pressure of hot stones underfoot, the feel of salt drying powdery on her shoulders, the taste of ice cream when caught by a warm breeze before it reached her mouth. It was whispering to her, calling her over; she just had to get through a hello with her father and then she could spend the afternoon on a towel.

But her mother was talking about lunch: *your brother wants lamb for tomorrow, Elisabetta*, her voice forceful on Bette's name, as if she knew Bette was only half listening. "And you can help me with the cake this afternoon, yes?"

"I was thinking I might go down—"

"You're not home since Christmas and then you go out this afternoon?" her mother cut her off. "No. No, you're helping today. If you want time out there you can wake up before everyone else tomorrow."

They just couldn't comprehend her love of it. They were the only people she had grown up around who hated the English beach. Who, a generation after their families had moved from Puglia to Bedford, had relocated in search of a coastline. And who had chosen to remain despite their deep resentment of what they considered to be an inferior bit of sea.

"We're so glad to have you home," her mother said, reaching over to put her hand on Bette's knee. Bette felt a rush of guilt. It wasn't her mother's fault they didn't have anything in common, she thought.

"Sure, Mum," she replied. "We'll make cake. It'll be lovely."

Her mother's smile was painful to watch, so grateful and pleased. It was impossible for Bette to make up for her perpetual absence in the course of a single weekend. But she could bake a cake.

Three hours later, they had drunk a pot of coffee down to the dregs and the cake sat cooling on the rack. It was her mother's favorite, an Anna del Conte orange and almond one. The kitchen smelled like Christmas, of the citrus fruit they'd boiled, of memories of making the cake for New Year's Eve when she was young. At home, cooking wasn't something she did with any confidence or enthusiasm, but being back in the kitchen with her mother (fetching ingredients out of cupboards, washing up and doing precisely as she was told) felt like muscle memory.

After popping his head in for a cup of coffee and a warm pat on the shoulder, her father had retreated to the shed, a thousand Saturday tasks that needing tending to. Tasks that couldn't wait for a weekend she wasn't visiting. It was all fine, really, better than she'd prepared herself for. Until her brother's key turned in the lock.

"Fede!" her mother called, voice easy, "we're in the kitchen!"

Her brother's tall frame filled the door to the kitchen. A pair of glasses were newly present on the bridge of his crooked nose; he'd been wearing contacts since their teenage years. But otherwise he was as he always had been, his hair in tight curls, his skin golden brown from the sun. He enveloped their mother in a hug.

"Hi Federico. Happy birthday," Bette said.

"Beth," he said, the only one who hadn't abandoned the childhood nickname that felt as though it belonged to someone else. "It's good to see you. We weren't sure you'd make it!"

Bette tried to imagine having not come, after the tickets that had arrived in the post, of the weeks of familiar guilt, of the calls from their mother.

"I wouldn't have missed it," she said.

"I'll go and get your father," their mother said, swatting at her son's arm in affection. She stepped out into the garden, leaving Bette alone with her brother. The distance between them, him still at the door, her leaning against the sink, was a gulf.

"No Sara?" Bette asked, grateful for the absence of her sister-in-law.

"She's at church this afternoon. Choir rehearsals. She'll be here tomorrow. Notice you've not brought anyone, though," he countered, and Bette's skin prickled uncomfortably. Of course that was why he had dropped by. "I just wanted to—I wanted to be here. In case . . ."

"In case I brought my girlfriend?"

"Yes," he admitted, clearly aware of their limited time, launching straight in. "Yes, in case you brought your girlfriend. Look, we love you. Whatever you do. Of course we do. But Dad hasn't been well. They're trying to get his blood pressure down. So I thought I'd just come by. I worried that you might—I don't know."

She'd known, vaguely, about their father's blood pressure. But the idea that she might have an impact on it was new.

"You worried I might hold hands with my girlfriend and give him a heart attack?"

Bette thought about telling him about the break, about the casual sex, about being fucked against a wall in a club, and in a Premier Inn by someone she knew she'd never see again. She tried to picture his response, imagined his golden face draining of color.

"You're being dramatic," Federico replied, his voice tinged with frustration. "We're happy to see you. You should visit more often. They miss you. I just don't know why you're so determined to . . . I mean, Beth, why even tell them? Why did you have to make some big thing about it?"

She knew what came next. They had had the conversation before, of course: explicitly with her brother, implicitly with her parents. Each time she'd been back since coming out. She'd tried to ignore it, tried to see it from their side. Tried to focus on the bit where they made it clear they were trying to love her, in spite of whom she was attracted to. Tried not to let it all bother her so much. People had it far worse than she did. And it wasn't as though she was going to stop visiting. Certainly not when they might make it harder for her to see her nonna. It was worth just coming back a little bit less and keeping the peace.

"It's not like you've ever even brought anyone back," Federico was still saying. "It's all so theoretical. Just . . . you don't need to make a big deal of it. They don't need to hear it. They love you so much, they really do."

There was something about the word "theoretical" that burned, that she could feel digging in at her side and underneath her ribs. Her parents still weren't back yet. And so there was a moment left to say it, to dare him to deny it. Fuck trying to ignore it. Fuck keeping the peace.

"Well, sure, but not me. Not the actual me. Just some fictional version of me who takes Communion. One who got married ten years ago and who doesn't require prayers and apologies and explanations. Who isn't destined for Hell."

Their parents arrived back in the kitchen before he could answer. It was just as well, Bette thought, as she boiled the kettle for a pot of tea for all of them, as her brother drained his cup, made his excuses, and went back out of the front door. There was no doubt his response would have made everything worse.

LATE THAT NIGHT, Bette lay on her side in bed, the glow of her phone illuminating her childhood bedroom. The bed was still the same single, but the meager floorspace in the room had been given over to her mother's sewing desk, a folding exercise bike that stood resolutely open, and a pile of what she thought might be Pilates paraphernalia. Bette had been back in her old room enough times to know that there was a thinly veiled message here. They had turned her brother's room into a proper guest double. They had painted over the navy-blue he'd subjected the walls to at thirteen with a neutral cream and replaced the carpet with a plush gray one. Her brother was married, after all. They couldn't pretend that he had a sexless, single-bed existence. He had grown up. Bette hadn't.

It had been an hour since she'd climbed beneath the sheets, and forty-something minutes since she'd given up on sleep as a sure thing. Instead, she was making herself deliberately miserable, picking at a scab that was especially painful after the confrontation with her brother. She hadn't looked at Mei's social media in weeks, had deliberately avoided it. But alone in bed, miles from a friend to help distract her, she had exhausted Mei's Instagram feed instead. The only new content was a couple of work-in-progress shots, but it hadn't demanded much scrolling to find herself in the months they'd spent together. A shot she'd taken of Mei beside a finished piece. Their shadows side by side on the wharf. Before that were the photos she'd obsessed over when Mei was just a girl in her phone—her art, a couple of selfies, the tattoo on her shoulder that Bette had traced her fingers over. When she'd exhausted the feed, she scrolled back through her message thread with Mei. Her heart jumped at every *x*, every *thinking of you*, at a string of messages encouraging her to touch herself, not long before everything had fallen apart. She scrolled, eventually, all the way to the top, through their flirting, through the messages they had sent when she had left Mei's after their first night together, through their snippets of Italian. She was turned on, and angry, and unhappy. Masochism. That's what this was.

She clicked out of their conversation and opened a dating app instead. There was a niggling worry refreshing it here, in the place she'd grown up. That announcing herself as looking for girls to shag might somehow get back to her parents, to her brother.

It was only once she'd swiped on the ninth woman that Bette realized she might not be going about things in the best way. The local lesbians weren't sitting at home on the apps on a Saturday night. They were out. By the time they saw her profile, could swipe back, she'd be back in Bristol. Maybe one more. She swiped again. Two more.

She stopped.

It was Stephanie. Steph. From school.

The face in the photo was one she hadn't seen in over a decade. It hadn't changed much; Steph's round face and pink cheeks and straight bob still made her look absurdly young. It was undeniably her. The words under her face read *Steph, 30*.

Bette hovered, considering, her thumb poised for action, before swiping yes. She didn't want to sleep with her. It would be too weird, too close to home, too personal, despite the fact that they didn't know each other anymore.

But she wanted to talk to her.

She stared at the screen, resigned to the fact that Steph was probably asleep. Or out. Or . . .

It's a match!

Or looking at her phone at 11 p.m.

> **Steph:** no way!!!
>
> **Steph:** are you back for a bit?
>
> **Bette:** just the weekend
>
> **Bette:** how has the past . . . decade been?
>
> **Steph:** lol
>
> **Steph:** yeah all right
>
> **Steph:** what are you doing now?
>
> **Bette:** everyone here went to bed an hour ago
>
> **Bette:** was thinking about going out
>
> **Bette:** but no idea where people go now
>
> **Steph:** the front
>
> **Steph:** nothing's changed
>
> **Steph:** wanna meet up?

The front wasn't too far; fifteen minutes' walk, probably a bit longer in the dark. It wasn't a bar. It wouldn't result in a snog.

But it was distinctly less pathetic than lying awake in her child-hood bedroom, scrolling through Mei's Instagram.

> **Bette:** I'll bring a bottle of
> whatever I can find
>
> **Steph:** great
> **Steph:** 30 mins?

She pushed herself out of bed, pulled on clean knickers and climbed back into the jeans that hung over the back of her old desk chair. Her bra was lace-edged, with a longline band that grazed her ribs and approached the dip of her waist. With higher jeans, or a slightly sluttier attitude, it was practically a top. Wishing she had a slightly sluttier attitude, she tied her buttoned shirt over it, leaving it open from her throat to her boobs. It was, at the very least, a nod toward the slut she wanted to be. The sort of cool Bristol lesbian she wanted Steph to know she had become.

Bette turned the handle of her bedroom door and grimaced at the creak. The whole house was alarmingly noisy to move through. Was there a house in England that didn't creak or groan at the smallest attempt to exist within it? Perhaps she could—was it ridiculous? To consider climbing out of the window? She crept over and looked out, onto the flat roof of the kitchen, and pictured jumping off it and into the back garden. It was absolute madness. Ridiculous behavior. She was a thirty-year-old woman. She could go out of the front door. Plus, she'd promised booze. And there was no booze in the garden.

And so, socks on and as light-footed as she could manage,

she did, swiping a nearly full bottle of Amaretto from the side-board on her way past.

It was an easy downhill stroll to the front. A walk familiar from countless after-school afternoons and late nights and lazy holiday days. She made her way past the chippie, past the off-license (checking to see that the same dusty boxed bottle of Moët was still in the window—it was), past the bus stop where she'd wasted so many hours waiting to head into Exeter. Waiting to be somewhere else.

As Bette made her way toward the sea, "the front" began to feel more and more vague. She was imagining a specific bench, but Steph didn't know that. And then, just as Bette pulled out her phone to message her, there was Steph. On the bench. She was wearing tracksuit bottoms and a cropped sweater, the sleeves pushed up to her elbows, half her hair in a knot on top of her head. Bette felt overdressed. She wanted to do up a button, but it was too late for that.

"Hey," Steph greeted her and opened her arms for a hug. It was a little awkward, a little forced, and Bette felt a rush of regret. It *was* weird, to come out in the middle of the night and meet someone she'd not really known at school. And she'd been the one to swipe. Maybe Steph thought that this was a date thing? A date thing, on the front, like they were sixteen again.

"Hey," she replied.

"Must have been, what? Five years?"

Bette remembered the last Christmas pub hangout she'd attended, remembered deciding that she didn't need to do it again. She'd been twenty-one.

"I think that was more like ten."

"Fuck," Steph breathed, low and long. "We're so old."

Bette laughed and felt herself relax. If this was a date, Steph wouldn't be in tracksuit bottoms. Surely. This was much lower-key. And it was sort of nice, actually, seeing someone from the past. Someone from the past who was also looking for women on a dating app. She sat down on the bench and twisted the top off the Amaretto.

"You made plans with anyone while you're back?" Steph asked, as she folded her legs up beneath her and reached over for the bottle.

Bette hesitated, wondering how to respond. Bristol wasn't that far away. It didn't speak well of her that she wasn't in touch with anyone anymore. She could lie, could mention someone. But they might be friends with Steph now. She was setting herself up to fail.

"To be honest, I don't really—I mean, I've been pretty crap at keeping in touch with people. I've kind of lost track of who'd be around."

Steph handed the bottle over and Bette took a long drink, the sweetness instantly reminiscent of school parties, of the weirdness and the loneliness of being sixteen. There was a reason she didn't drink it anymore.

"Fair enough."

It was the start, it turned out, of Steph filling her in on the lives of people she hadn't thought about in years. Someone's kid, someone's wedding, someone's new job, someone's divorce. Bette nodded in feigned interest so much that she started to feel the onset of a headache. All she really wanted to hear was Steph's story: When did she come out? Was she seeing anyone? Had it all been all right?

But you couldn't just ask about someone's coming-out story. Maybe it was one that Steph didn't want to tell.

"So how long are you back for?" It was the first sentence in a while that demanded a response.

"Only a night. It's my brother's birthday."

"Oh shit, I didn't message him."

"It's on Monday, actually," Bette replied, wondering when he and Steph had become close enough for her to have his number. At school her brother had very much had his own crowd. And she'd never heard him mention Steph in the years since. "You haven't missed it."

"Oh great. I'll see him tomorrow. Actually, on that, Fede said something last time I saw him at church."

Church. Of course it was church.

"Oh yeah?"

"Yeah, think he was angling for me to give you a call and tell you it's still all right to come and take Communion," she said, and shrugged. "Like, maybe you thought it wasn't? Anyway, forgive us our sins and all that. It's fine. Or, like, he wanted me to tell you it works for me. So this is me telling you. I guess."

"Oh yeah?" Bette asked, feeling oddly hopeful. She didn't want to atone, didn't want to go back to church. But there was something soothing about hearing that someone else from the community was queer, and that it wasn't some big thing.

"Sure. I mean, I'm going tomorrow morning. And you saw me on a dating app. And I was out at the Vaults last night. It doesn't have to be that complicated."

The Vaults was a gay bar in Exeter. Bette had heard about it growing up. She'd never been. Of course she'd never been. She should probably go. It might feel good to go.

"Oh yeah? I've never been."

"It's fine. Full of dykes though," Steph said, as she took another swig. The suggestion that this was in some way less than ideal brought Bette up short, and her confusion must have shown on her face. "Oh you know what I mean. You're not, like— you're not one of *those* lesbians. Like, you wear lipstick. I can tell."

There was a definitiveness about the statement, as though this was an irrefutable fact. The end of the discussion. As if lipstick was somehow solid evidence. Bette stared. *Was* she one of those lesbians? She didn't know. No. Probably not. Almost certainly not, actually. But she liked those lesbians. She fancied those lesbians. She wanted to be in a bar being chatted up by those lesbians.

"It's easy, you know, when you're not one of them. You don't have to make some big thing about it."

Something heavy dropped into her stomach. It was, in many ways, what her brother had been saying. To be gay was fine, just a quiet family matter, so long as you weren't too obvious about it. To be a lesbian wasn't technically a problem so long as you were femme. Or so long as you could reasonably pass as straight.

It was the closest they were going to come to Steph's coming-out story, and Bette realized she didn't want to stay on the beach. She wanted to go home. She stood up so fast that for a moment she felt drunk.

"I have to—I mean, no one knows where I've gone, so I should . . ."

"Sure. Mind if I?" She took a long drink before Bette could answer, and then handed back the bottle.

"If you could—if you could not . . ." Bette started.

"Not mention to your brother that I saw that you're looking for casual sex on a dating app?"

"Yeah."

"Sure," Steph shrugged, easily. "I'll see you around?"

"Yeah. It was good to see you," Bette lied, and then lied again. "Maybe I'll catch you at church sometime."

It felt so much longer, somehow, going back. The odd thrill of recognition was gone, and the streets seemed endless. Endless, and so so empty.

Her heart raced; it always did a little, when she was walking home alone. It was one thing in Bristol, where there were street-lights and cars and other late-night walkers heading to work, or from work, or home after a night out. Here, she was alone. Everything was dark.

She pulled out her phone, her silly little safety net. Women with friends in their phones didn't get murdered. She started typing.

> **Bette:** are you awake?

Nothing changed under Ruth's name, no *typing* . . . no *online*. She had last looked at her phone at half-ten, like a normal human person who hadn't snuck out of her childhood bedroom to sit on a bench by the sea and drink Amaretto.

And then, suddenly:

> **Ruth:** Having cocktails with Gabe and Heather!!! Come meet us???
>
> **Bette:** I wish!
> **Bette:** visiting my parents
> **Bette:** back tomorrow night

Ruth: Well, we wish you were here!

Ruth: Next time??

Ruth: Let's make a plan!!!

They were drunken exclamation points this time. Bette wished fiercely that she were there too. She stared at the phone, at Ruth's message, until her eyes were damp and the light issuing from it began to blur.

LUNCH WAS FINE. It wasn't warm or easy, like it was when she visited Ash's family. There was an awkward distance between her and everyone else at the table. But it was fine. The lamb was good, and no one had yet mentioned the fact that Bette, who had survived her first year of college on baked beans and crumpets, had offered to stay home and supervise the cooking instead of coming to church. Most of the conversation revolved around Sara's work; her sister-in-law had recently finished training as an optometrist, and it turned out eyes were just begging for something to go wrong. All in all, smiling and nodding every now and then seemed to be all anyone expected of Bette, which suited her just fine.

And then there was a moment when Sara lifted her glass. Bette knew, just before it happened, exactly what was going to come next.

"We wanted," Sara said, taking hold of Federico's hand, "to take the opportunity, of all being together, to let you know some very exciting news." Say it, Bette thought, as Sara looked around the table. Say it. "We're pregnant."

Bette felt her mother's shout of joy before she heard it, her whole body exploding open in excitement. Everyone was out of their chairs, holding onto each other and existing under the pretense that they were a good, happy family. Which, if she took scissors to the picture and cut herself out of it, they probably were.

Fuck fuck fuck fuck. She should be happy. This was unequivocally news to be celebrated. She should suck up her worst instincts and hug her brother. But she sat in her chair, a dead weight. They'd done it again, another step in the textbook perfect life they were building together. Another reason for them to look at her in pity and concern.

She smiled, eventually, hugging the appropriate people and ignoring the "sympathetic" pats her mother kept landing on her arm. Her father suggested a toast, but Sara wasn't drinking and so it was quickly decided that no one else would either. Bette boiled the kettle for a pot of coffee (Sara had brought decaf for all of them), and stuck half-melted candles from the drawer into the cake. Her mother arrived to light them and carry the glowing cake through, Bette trailing behind with the coffee. They sang, Federico cut the cake into small slices, and they sat eating them in silence.

"We're going to see Nonna on the way to the station, right?" Bette asked, directing her words toward her mother. Her nonna was in care in Exeter, close to the station, and when Bette visited it was on Sundays. It felt right, seeing her nonna when she would once have gone to church.

"I went yesterday morning," her mother said, focused intently on her cake. Bette could feel the tension radiating from her. "Before collecting you. Mornings are better for her now. And we couldn't go this morning."

"But I—I want to see her. That's why—I mean, can't we just go again? You could just drop me off? I could always walk back to the station."

She'd been depending on a lift, had assumed it was a given. They'd talked about going when she'd first spoken to her mother about the weekend.

"I don't think it's a good idea to go again. We don't want to confuse her. She's often asleep in the afternoon."

Bette nodded, her teeth grinding and a pain sparking behind her forehead. She knew what "confuse her" meant. As if she would walk in and plant the word lesbian in each sentence. As if they needed to shield her nonna from the reality of her, as if Bette couldn't be trusted.

"We'll go next time you come home. They said you've been down quite often lately," her mother continued, moving the last of her cake around her plate.

Oh. It was a punishment then. Punishment because she visited Nonna and didn't visit them. Bette chewed at the inside of her lip until she tasted blood.

She would be back in Bristol soon. Back on the sofa, back with Ash. Back home.

CHAPTER FIFTEEN

WEDNESDAY, 21 SEPTEMBER

···

24 days to go

There were a few more women in her phone that week. There was a quiet weekend on the horizon, and less than a month of the whole dating gambit left. It felt good to know she was close to the end. But she couldn't finish on sex and voice notes with Evie or beach Amaretto with Steph. It was far too tragic.

Bette had options. Fine options. There was Esther, who captained a netball team (and who unfortunately reminded Bette vividly of the PE teacher who had once forced her to finish the cross-country after she threw up halfway round). Lily seemed great; bright and clever, if a little too interested in yoga, right up until she went full conspiracy-theory mad with a string of links about 5G. Sonya had seemed like a real possibility until she started working her dog into every message, and then casually mentioned she was going out of town and needed someone to "hang out" with Pickle.

Bette didn't want any of them. She wanted to know it was

going to be good, wanted a safe pair of hands. Wanted, ideally, another Charlie. She didn't want fine.

And then, late on Wednesday night, Netta messaged. Ephron-loving, sparky-texting, 176-miles-away Netta.

Already in bed, Bette pulled her phone as close to her face as the charger would allow.

> **Netta:** Hey, I'm back in Bristol tomorrow
>
> **Netta:** Late notice, I know
>
> **Netta:** But let me know if you'd still be up for hanging out?

Her photos were the same: braids twisted on her head, Disney-huge eyes, a smooth expanse of shoulder and collarbone. They hadn't messaged since that first night, but Bette's response was instant, instinctual.

> **Bette:** yes
>
> **Bette:** need a tour guide?
>
> **Bette:** happy to show you around?
>
> **Netta:** Yeah, take me to your favorite pub
>
> **Netta:** Or I'm staying near the Cabot Circus shopping bit?
>
> **Netta:** You could come and have a drink?

It was unambiguous. Netta was looking for something casual. She'd been so clear about it. She was exactly what Bette had been hoping for.

"WE DIDN'T TALK last night about what you'd like. What we'd want. So I brought a bunch of stuff with me, just in case," Netta said, throwing a large overnight bag onto the low seat at the end of the bed. She was in half a suit, her jacket slung over the back of the chair behind her, her shirt more unbuttoned than Bette assumed it had been at work that day. She was even more striking than her profile pictures, and just as clever and as funny as her messages. Bette had worried before the date that she might feel like she had with Evie; like she was performing a role. But it had felt right and easy from the first moment she'd seen Netta. They'd met for a couple of drinks in the hotel bar, which was even fancier than Bette had prepared herself for. They'd talked about late-'90s romantic comedies, and about Netta's work as a construction lawyer; about plans for a new development near the wharf she had been drawing up contracts for. And then they had taken the lift straight up to the third floor.

"What do *you* like?" Bette said, sitting up on her knees on the bed, her wrap skirt falling open to expose her thighs. She followed Netta's gaze down to the lace-topped hold-up that was now entirely visible and decided not to readjust it. She felt sexy, high on the fact that she could tell that Netta thought she was fit. That she had, in fact, told her exactly that downstairs. She had a sense too that any honesty might be rewarded; Netta seemed unflappable, easy. She could say it here. "Maybe we could start with you. I—I'm still working out what I want."

"Oh?" Netta replied, cocking an eyebrow.

"Yeah. Not, like—I mean, I like women. This isn't an experiment. Not in that way, anyway. I'm just—I guess I'm still figuring out what I really like. You know. Specifically."

"I do know," Netta said, a smile spreading across her face. "Okay, so this is going to be fun. We can just . . . play."

Bette let Netta undress her slowly, surrendering herself to it and trying not to take over. They kissed for a long time before Netta moved her hands from Bette's face and hair, blazing a path slowly along her body. It had taken so long that by the time she did, Bette was already desperately turned on, wanting Netta to touch her everywhere, wanting to touch her in return.

She reached over to unbutton Netta's shirt, taking in every inch of revealed skin as she did. She was gorgeous, each part of her round and curved—the perfect crescent of her cheek when she smiled, the swell of her breast above her bra, her hip once she lay on her side.

"I want to take a bath," Netta said, her fingers tracing gently down Bette's spine, her mouth on her throat.

"Okay," Bette said, pulling back, suddenly tense and aware of being naked. "I can just . . ."

She caught Netta's eye and saw the perfectly raised brow above it.

"Oh," Bette said, on a relaxed breath out. "You mean together."

"Mm-hmm."

Bette clambered out of bed and followed her, trying to ignore the impulse to hold her boobs in place as she walked across the hotel room. Netta certainly wasn't holding anything down. Or covering anything up.

It was darker in the bathroom, the only illumination the light from the bedside lamps in the other room. Netta filled the bath with water so hot that it sent clouds of steam into the cool of the air conditioning. Bette wished for a moment that she'd lingered on the bed a little longer; it was awkward to be naked in the bathroom, with the admin of filling a bath. But then Netta moved to sit on the edge of the tub, as the bubbles rose behind her, and reached for Bette.

As Netta kissed her, Bette felt a hand on the inside of her knee, felt it rise impossibly slowly up her thigh. She dipped her fingertips into Netta's collarbone, ran them back and forth across the skin. And then, just as Netta reached the top of Bette's thigh, right where the skin was softest, she pulled her hand away and turned off the tap.

"Oh come *on*," Bette groaned. "You're a tease."

"Mm-hmm," Netta agreed, her smile wide as she stepped into the water. "You coming in?"

Bette sat across from Netta, the bubbles up to their chins. There was maneuvering to be done: the bath was big enough for two, but only just, and placement of feet and knees had to be negotiated. But once they'd relaxed into it, it was a pleasure to sit in the dim light and admire Netta's kiss-swollen mouth, the braids twisted on her head, her insanely long eyelashes. It was a thrill to try and perv on her through the bubbles, to know that Netta was doing the same, her eyes tracking up and down Bette's body. It felt incredibly intimate, not at all what she'd expected. It was difficult to reconcile this moment with the knowledge that, theoretically, she'd never see Netta again. But the water was hot, and the bath was deep, and it felt good to be sleek and clean and still turned on.

"After we get out," Netta said, her foot pressing into Bette's thigh, "I want to eat you out."

"Okay," Bette said, certain that she'd have said yes to anything Netta suggested. It helped that this particular plan was exactly what she'd hoped for. Netta was still looking at her, hungry, and Bette shivered, struggling to remember being so nakedly wanted. It was intoxicating. "Okay but like . . . now? Can we get out now?"

The water was still hot, and at home she wouldn't have wasted it. But it was a hotel. There'd be more hot water later, if they wanted to get back in. And so Bette pushed herself up, felt Netta's eyes on her as she climbed out of the bath and wrapped herself in a towel from the pile. There were robes hanging from hooks on the door and, once Bette had rubbed haphazardly at her body, she pulled one on.

Bette leaned against the edge of the sink and watched Netta climb out of the bath, watched her rub her dimpled thighs, the swell of her belly underneath her breasts. It was only when Netta put a foot up on the side of the bath and started drying between her toes that Bette lost hold of the last threads of her patience.

"Um, I think you said something about . . ."

"I did, didn't I," Netta said, her body utterly lacking in urgency. She pulled the other robe over her shoulders and left it hanging open before stepping closer to Bette. "Come on then," she said, her mouth so close to Bette's that she was sure they were going to kiss. Instead, she trailed after Netta, let herself be handled and positioned, let Netta push her to sit on the edge of the bed. Let her undo Bette's robe, spreading it wide. Let her push Bette back against the sheets and kneel on the carpet in front of her.

And then there was a distinct lack of teasing, only Netta's tongue, relentlessly present. Netta sucked and stroked, slow and soft and perfect, and Bette couldn't do a thing but lie back on the bed, one hand over her face, one grazing teasingly over her own puckered nipples. She was aware of her thigh trembling, of her toes clenched against the carpet, of the groan she couldn't control deep in her chest.

Netta's fingers were technically inside Bette, she realized, but only imperceptibly so, teasing the sensitive skin at the entrance to her cunt. She'd never been fingered so tenderly. Never by someone who touched her not as though they were seeking something deep inside her but had found it already. Was marveling at it, just at the edge. The feeling of Netta's fingertips and the wet warmth of her tongue were an overwhelming combination. Bette's whole body tightened and she gasped, coming before she even realized she was close.

"Oh my god," she panted, Netta's mouth still relentless. "Oh my *god* you're really good at that. You know that, right? That can't be news. Like, people must tell you that all the time."

Netta pulled back, her cheek resting against Bette's thigh. She was shaking with laughter.

"They do," she confirmed. "Yeah. But it's always nice to hear."

Bette hauled her up the bed, pulled her down to blanket her and kissed the taste of herself from Netta's mouth.

"What do you want," Bette asked, a hand resting where Netta's arse met her thigh, the other pushing the toweling robe from her body.

"Can you fuck me?"

Bette nodded. "Yeah, I mean, I kind of assumed that was a given. But with my fingers or . . ."

"No, I've brought a strap. Can you fuck me with it?"

In hindsight, she probably should have thought more about the bag, the one still at the foot of the bed. But it had been so easy to get swept up in the nakedness and the bath and the frankly outstanding orgasm. And in that state, body still quivering a little, it was hard to get worked up and nervous. Netta was good at this. Great at this. She'd tell Bette what worked for her.

The harness fitted better than Mei's had; it didn't dig in distractingly around the top of Bette's thighs. Bette thought of Mei telling her she should wear it around the house, to do the washing up, just to get used to it.

Netta was sitting at the edge of the bed, her knees spread wide. Bette looked down at her from where she stood between her legs.

"I wondered if . . ." Bette started and then paused. Netta didn't try to fill in the gap. She waited, patiently, her hand on Bette's chest, above her breast. "I wondered if—would you ride me?"

Netta smiled wide and nodded, the hand on Bette's chest grounding and warm. "Love to. Lie back."

When Bette did, her back against the cool sheet, she was struck by the sight of Netta high up on her knees, a bottle of lube in her hand. She swung a leg over Bette and sat down on her thighs.

Bette pulled Netta's mouth to hers. For long minutes she kissed her, eventually encouraging Netta back up to her knees before slowly pressing two fingers inside her. Groaning into Bette's mouth, Netta rocked her hips forward.

"Come here," Bette directed, taking care of the lube, of positioning Netta where she needed her. They kissed as Netta sank down onto the dildo, as Bette relished the whine that built up at the back of Netta's throat. Bette lay back, hands squeezing Netta's thighs, watching Netta rock back and forth, and pushed up beneath her. She was gorgeous: breasts heavy, face screwed up in pleasure, the incredible expanse of neck as she let her head drop back.

"Don't stop," she said, as if Bette had any intention of it. Instead, Bette trailed her hands higher, her thumb delicate against the soft skin between Netta's legs. She rubbed gently back and forth, and Netta's head dropped forward with a gasp. "Don't stop."

She didn't; kept thrusting, and touching, keeping up with the pace Netta had set, determined not to fuck it up. The pressure felt good against her too, sparking around her body, but it was somehow less important that the sweat beading on Netta's chest, than the way her breath kept catching. Bette thrust up more firmly, and then Netta was crying out and falling forward.

"That was perfect," she said a minute or two later, working her fingers into Bette's hair and tugging, still straddling her. "Perfect."

Bette glowed, warm beneath Netta, warm with all of it.

At midnight they ordered room-service chips and ice cream and ate them in the laughably huge bed, swigging bottles of beer from the minibar. Smiling, her eyes alight, Netta dipped a finger into the melted remains of her ice cream and brought it to

Bette's mouth. Bette sucked, her teeth scraping at the skin. And then there was ice cream on Bette's collarbone, on her left nipple, down the joints of her spine, in the dimples that sat at the lowest point of her back, in the ticklish crevice behind one of her knees. Netta's mouth followed the sweetness down her body, lingering whenever Bette squirmed or cried out.

Bette forgot to worry about whether or not it was working for Netta. It was, it so clearly was, and she could lose herself to the sensation of it. Of her mouth, of her expert fingers, of the sparks within her own body that traveled the length of it.

"What do you want?" Netta said, biting into the meat of Bette's thigh, soothing the sting with her tongue.

It felt easy to answer, this time. She wanted Netta to pin her down, wanted not to be able to take over and get on top, wanted the firm pressure of Netta's fingers deep inside her. She wanted to feel the pain of teeth on tender skin. She wanted to be pushed and teased. Wanted Netta in control.

Afterward, she turned to Netta, who was grinning at the ceiling, her chest still heaving. "You're amazing."

"Oh, I know," Netta said, not a hint of sarcasm in her voice.

Bette put her hands over her face and laughed, deep and long, pure joy filling her lungs. It had been good. Really, really good. She could have great sex with someone who wasn't Mei. "Can I—" she started, looking over at Netta again.

"Do you want to?" Netta said deliberately, asking her to consider. And Bette felt a rush of affection for her so strong that it threatened to drown every other feeling in her body.

Bette nodded and rolled over, ran her lips along Netta's collarbone, and then kissed her way up to her ear. "I really *really* do."

The next morning, Bette couldn't stop smiling. She watched Netta reassemble the suit over her body and felt a pang that she'd never see the skin beneath her shirt again. But that was, she reasoned with herself, the whole point. She'd nailed it, this time. This was exactly what the break should have been about. No strings attached, entirely fuss-free fucking. Mutual attraction, mutual satisfaction, clarity between them. A hotel room so nice that she still couldn't believe her luck. This was it, probably the last woman before she and Mei were back together. It had been perfect. Netta had been the perfect woman for it.

"I'm on a train back to London tonight," Netta said, zipping up her bag and placing it by the door before stepping into her heels. "But checkout isn't until ten, so if you want to take a shower or something before you leave, you can."

She walked back over to the bed and kissed Bette softly, cupping her jaw. Bette surged up toward her, her hand finding a home again at the base of Netta's ribs. Netta grinned but shook her head against Bette's.

"No time for that," she said. "But this was fun. I'm really glad I messaged."

"Me too," Bette said. "Thank you—for everything."

"We probably don't need to go that far," Netta said, and Bette laughed.

"Okay, that's fair. Thanks for last night then. Thanks for the sex. It was really good."

"I'll take that," she said, halfway toward the door. "Look after yourself, Bette."

CHAPTER SIXTEEN

MONDAY, 26 SEPTEMBER

•••

19 days to go

Ruth was just returning to the table when Bette's phone started to ring in the pocket of her jeans. They had been to a late cinema screening, and the gin and tonic heading toward her was her second, so it was now very late. Late enough that Bette's heart began to race, imagining all the potential disasters on the other end of the line. No one called late at night.

As Ruth sat down beside her at their tiny table, already launching into another rant about the ridiculousness of the plot they'd been subjected to onscreen, Bette pulled out the phone and looked at the lit screen.

It was Mei.

It had been more than a month now since Mei had last texted, since the messages Bette had ignored after the day in the office. The closer they got to the end of the break, the clearer the jumbled collection of emotions felt, the important ones having made their way to the surface. She missed Mei, missed being her partner, missed what they had. She felt a rush of anxious anticipation when she thought about the coming weeks, about seeing Mei properly again. She was ready, theoretically. Ready for them to go back to how things had been. But Mei's name on her phone made her heart jump and her hand shake. She hadn't prepared herself. She wasn't ready for it tonight. But here it was.

"Bette," Ruth said, abandoning her rant, her eyes on the screen too. "Are you—I mean . . ."

"I—I'm going to get—" Bette said, and watched Ruth bite on her lips, as if trying to stop herself from saying something. Bette tried not to think about it.

"Mei?" she answered.

"Oh, you're awake," Mei said, her voice thick. "I wasn't sure— I thought maybe I'd just—I convinced myself you wouldn't—"

"I'm here," Bette reassured her, even as she wondered what she meant by it. "What do you need?"

Ruth was looking at her, and it was impossible not to meet her eyes. But she could hear Mei take a couple of deep breaths on the other end of the line. The sound was heartbreaking, horrible to listen to. The distance between them, over the phone, felt infinite.

"Could you come meet me?" she asked, her voice barely above a whisper. "I don't—I need you, Bette."

She could tell instantly that Ruth had heard it, had at least caught the gist of it. Bette watched as Ruth twisted her hands in her lap, her eyes now fixed across the bar. She thought of how shuttered up Ruth had become when Bette had brought Mei up over dinner, all those weeks ago. It was not ideal, obviously, to be having this conversation in front of her. But, ideal or not, it was happening.

"Where are you?" Bette asked.

"Hospital. In the waiting room. The ER. It's—it's my dad. They were visiting and—"

Bette's heart nearly leaped out of her chest. She thought back to Mei's parents at lunch, ordering a second bottle of wine and insisting on dessert. Her father was compact and serious, a deceptively powerful man, firm edges where her mother was soft. The idea of him in a hospital, in the ER, was unfathomable.

"I'll be twenty minutes. Fifteen. Text me which hospital? I just need to get a cab. Just—are you going to be all right until then? Have you got someone with you?" Ruth was fiddling with her straw, folding the top of it over, wrecking the paper. She would understand, Bette thought. Of course she would.

"I'll be all right. I'm not alone, Mum's here. I just really need you."

"I'll make it in twelve," Bette promised, trying to ignore the way her heart had jumped when Mei said "need." "Mei's at the hospital. It's her dad. I'm really sorry but I—I have to . . ."

"Of course. Go," Ruth said. "Talk later this week?"

Bette hugged her, one eye already on Uber over her shoulder.

IT WAS MAYBE fifteen minutes later that Bette arrived outside the hospital. In fact, she knew precisely how many minutes it had been (seventeen), because she had been aware of every single one of them, each second piercing her spine as she sat in the back seat of the cab. Her phone buzzed relentlessly with messages as she clambered out onto the footpath.

> **Mei:** I'm really sorry
>
> **Mei:** I'm so glad you were awake
>
> **Mei:** I can't believe you're coming
>
> **Mei:** Text if you can't find us

A sign in front of her pointed toward the ER and she headed down the hallway, trying not to peer into any rooms as she passed. She looked instead at her phone, at a second string of messages from Mei.

> **Mei:** My mum doesn't know about this
>
> **Mei:** about what happened with us, sorry
>
> **Mei:** She thinks it's all like it was, so could you not tell her?
>
> **Mei:** I just don't want to have to explain tonight
>
> **Mei:** I'm sorry to ask

Bette couldn't imagine striking up a conversation about their break in front of her mother, in a hospital waiting room. But it was helpful to know where she stood. She was Mei's girlfriend again, at least for the night. She tried not to feel pleased about it. She failed not to feel pleased about it.

It was long after visiting hours had ended, and Bette worried for a moment that, visibly injury-free, she might not be allowed through. But in the ER, it was clear, time ceased to exist. A young woman was bouncing a grizzling toddler on her knees, two booze-jolly guys were holding a blood-soaked towel to the forehead of a third, a couple with indeterminate injuries or illnesses sat with fingers knotted together, a child with a hacking cough was being read to by their father.

And then there was Mei. Her face was puffy and swollen, and there were tears fresh on her cheeks. Bette stepped forward and embraced her before she could dwell on how long it had been. Mei smelled familiar and comforting and Bette wanted to kiss her. It couldn't have been a less appropriate time for it. She pressed her lips to the top of her shoulder instead, rocking Mei back and forth.

"I'm so sorry," Bette said, realizing suddenly that she didn't know the context, that she had no idea what she was trying to reassure Mei about.

"We still don't—I—" Mei replied, her voice quavering. She swallowed twice in quick succession, clearly trying to calm down. "He fell. He was on the ladder in the dark, trying to fix the light. The one above the back door?"

Bette nodded. She could picture the light exactly; it was above a concrete step. The thought of falling onto it was horrifying; she felt sick, her stomach burning.

"We said it could wait but he just . . ." she trailed off.

"He doesn't like to wait," her mother said from her chair. Bette stepped back, letting go of Mei, and put a hand out for Mrs. Hinota to grasp. She stood, her gray hair hanging limply, her skin so pale it looked almost translucent. Her grip on Bette's hand was impressive nonetheless.

"It's good to see you, Mrs. Hinota. I wish it wasn't—well—" Bette said, gesturing helplessly around them. "How long has he been—?"

"They took him back an hour ago for scans, and to set his shoulder too. We should have been able to go through with him but . . ." Mei trailed off. "They're supposed to come and find us at some point. Take us through."

Bette nodded. "Can I do anything? Do you want tea? Or something?"

She had no idea whether what she was offering was possible, but surely there was a vending machine somewhere. There always was in films.

Mei shook her head. "Not sure I could handle anything. But thank you. No—just—can you sit?"

She backed up toward her mother's seat, tugging Bette along with her. And then they sat, Mei between Bette and her mother, the three of them falling into silence.

"Mei said you've been busy with your work," Mrs. Hinota said eventually, as her hands clasped and unclasped in her lap.

Bette hummed in confirmation, happy to go along with it, to nod blithely in agreement to anything Mei might have told her parents.

She wanted to feel useful, wanted to have walked in and made things better. But it felt obvious now that there was no way to make this situation better. That sitting beside Mei, pushing a shoulder against hers, was perhaps the best she could do. Mei had pulled her phone out, and Bette couldn't help glancing down at the screen. She was scrolling down a list of search results: head injuries after head injuries after head injuries. Bette hesitated and then reached over, taking her phone out of her hand.

Without it, Mei fussed and fiddled. She kicked her legs as though she were a child on a swing set, her trainers grazing the floor beneath her seat with each back-and-forth. Her mother rested a hand on her knee to calm her, and Bette watched her take a few big, deliberate breaths, her chin trembling as she did.

Bette opened her mouth to ask a question. But the content flew out of her mind immediately when she heard "Hinota?" from between a set of doors across the room.

Mei was on her feet before Bette could even process what was happening. Once standing on shaking legs, she reached out behind her, and Bette laced her fingers through Mei's. Mrs. Hinota was standing too and took a step forward toward the approaching doctor, as if it might make the news reach her more quickly. The doctor's scrubs were rumpled but clean, and Bette had watched enough *Casualty* during university to be oddly reassured by the expression on her face.

"Mrs. Hinota?" she said, directing her speech toward Mei's mother. "You can see your husband now."

Bette felt Mei's exhalation through her hand, felt the entirety of her tense and anxious body let out a breath.

"He's suffered a serious concussion, has three broken ribs, and we've had to set his shoulder. The scan took longer than anticipated; we're sorry you've been waiting without an update. We're going to keep him at least overnight for observation. We'll reassess tomorrow, but it's likely you'll be able to take him home then. If you would like to be with him tonight, we can organize for one of you to stay?"

"Thank you," Mrs. Hinota replied, glancing at Mei. "I will stay."

"Thank you," Mei said, her voice tender and strained. "Thank you for—thank you."

The doctor nodded, her movements tight and efficient; she

had no expendable energy to spare. "I can take you to him now, if you like?"

Mei squeezed her fingers more tightly, and Bette realized their hands were still linked. She looked up at Mei; she couldn't remember making the decision to stay in her seat while everyone else stood, but it had felt like the correct decision. She wasn't family. She shouldn't be part of this.

"I'll wait here," she said, hoping to save Mei the awkwardness of asking her to remain behind. "Take your time, seriously. I'm not going anywhere."

Mei nodded distractedly and hurried off after her mother, leaving Bette alone in the waiting room. It felt wrong to be there, a witness to the horrible nights of the people around her, no reason to still be sitting among them. But just as she made the decision to text Mei that she would see her outside, she looked down into her lap to find Mei's phone staring back up at her accusingly. There was no option but to stay.

She'd been sitting for a couple of minutes, scrolling listlessly through Instagram, when Mei's phone buzzed in her lap. She resisted the temptation to look.

Bette returned instead to Instagram and watched a video of a woman applying zombie makeup. Twice. It was a weirdly attractive zombie.

Mei's phone buzzed again.

It was past midnight, and Bette wanted to know who was messaging her. The phone lay face down in her lap, and her fingers itched to pick it up. She thought of Ash asking what Mei was allowed to do in all these months; whether she was allowed to hook up too.

And then the phone buzzed again.

It struck Bette that it might be Mei, actually, on Mrs. Hinota's phone. Mei, who couldn't get in touch with Bette directly because Bette was holding her phone. Mei, texting herself, assuming that Bette would see it. She wouldn't know Bette's number by heart—who knew anyone's number by heart? It was almost certainly Mei. She should check it.

She flipped it over and swiped a finger across the lock screen. The phone begged for a fingerprint or a pin, and Bette had neither. The WhatsApp icon sat there, right in the middle, but there was no way of seeing the message. It was unusually late for a message, but Mei had a sister in Tokyo. It was her, surely. Mei would be back eventually, and Bette should probably just ignore the phone until then.

It was half an hour, many more makeup reels, and a good amount of time Googling "unlock phone in emergency" before Mei returned. Bette had prepared herself for longer, but had been starting to feel antsy; she'd left for the cinema with a phone low on battery, and it was now hovering dangerously close to zero.

"He's okay?" she asked, feeling stupid even as the words left her mouth. He clearly wasn't. He was spending the night in the hospital.

"He will be," Mei said, her voice calmer and steadier than when she had left. She moved toward the exit and out into the ambulance bay. "He looks—but yeah. Yeah, he will be."

The steadiness of her voice changed things. This was no longer the Mei who had reached for her when she walked into the waiting room, who had threaded her fingers through Bette's. The brief reunion had an end point, and it was imminent. Maybe Bette had already missed it. She walked a step behind Mei, resigned to it.

The night was cool, the lights of the hospital bright against the inky sky. Mei was silent as they walked out of the hospital grounds, but once they were out on the street Mei turned toward her, looking up and meeting Bette's eyes.

"I have a favor to ask. My car is in the car park but I don't want to drive alone. I have to collect some things from my parents' house so they can stay for a couple of days. Could you drive it? Drive me?"

"To Cheltenham? Now?" Bette said, the questions rushing out of her before she could stop them.

"I know, it's a lot. I just—I need you."

She couldn't ignore the leap in her chest this time, the word settling warm within her. Bette nodded.

The drive out of Bristol was quiet. Mei was turned toward the window, her forehead resting on the glass. There was a moment when Bette thought she might have fallen asleep, but she mostly shuffled in the seat, readjusting her sweater, straightening her trousers, exerting control over tiny, inconsequential things.

It was almost impossible, not saying anything. Bette wanted to respect whatever Mei needed, and silence seemed to be it. But she chewed at her cheek, swallowing back all she wanted to say. It wasn't the time for it.

But as they drove further and further up the M5, the silence in the car began to border on ridiculous. On comical, as they approached the turn off for Cheltenham. She had to say something. Anything at all. And then Mei turned to Bette and cleared her throat.

"You look really well. Are you well?"

"I look really well? I look . . . really . . . well," Bette repeated slowly, as if she needed to consider each word on its own merits.

"God, I don't know. This is hard! I called you in the middle of the night. We're in a weird place. I had forgotten how long this drive actually is."

Bette couldn't help it. She laughed. Long and hard. The tree-lined streets were nearly empty, it was approaching 1:30 in the morning, she and Mei were on a break, and she was realizing that apart from "Cheltenham" she had no idea where she was going. They'd never been to Mei's family's house when they were together.

"Thank fuck you said it. The whole journey has been this horrible weird silence vacuum and obviously I didn't want to say anything because you can't say 'I miss you and it's so good to see you and to hold your hand' to the woman whose father is in the ER because tonight isn't about me. But Mei, look, I really miss you. And I know I didn't reply to your messages that day you came to the office but, honestly, I didn't know what to say. And I need you to know that I miss you, and I'm so glad this break is almost done, and that I still—even though tonight . . ."

"Bette, I have to . . ."

"No, sorry. Let's not. Tonight's not about me, or about us. Let's just—let's get your dad's pajamas or whatever we're here to do. And we can talk tomorrow."

She chanced a glance to her left, where Mei was clearly wrestling with not saying anything.

"I mean it, seriously," she reiterated. "I'm not going anywhere, and we can talk another time. Tonight is about your mum and dad."

"Okay," Mei said, her voice thick. "Thanks. It means a lot."

"Of course," Bette replied, sitting comfortably in fourth gear and reaching over to take Mei's hand.

It eased something between them. Mei directed her through the outer parts of Cheltenham, and eventually into a driveway Bette couldn't help raising her eyebrows at.

"Wow," she said, looking up at the trailing flowers and vines hanging from the Regency property.

"I know," Mei replied, clearly primed for this response from new visitors. "I should have—I know."

"This is—this . . ." Bette started. She wanted to say that the house she'd grown up in would fit maybe four times in Mei's. That it was closer in size to her church. But when she looked over at Mei, she was still buckled in and her eyes were glassy. She reached over and held her hand. "Okay. What do you need?"

"Nothing. Just . . . come with me?"

"Of course."

Inside, the house was somehow even more overwhelming. Bette felt strange in it, too small in the cavernous hall. She was used to moving through a front door quickly; both at home and in the house she'd grown up in, hovering in the doorway held everyone else up. Here Mei stepped around her, kicked off her shoes and headed for the polished staircase. Bette toed off her trainers and, desperate to be useful, called out after Mei.

"Tea?"

Mei turned, looking tired and so grateful, and Bette loved her. "Yes. Yes please. Tea would be brilliant."

It was one thing to offer tea, Bette thought, and quite another to be able to follow through. She utilized the only logic she could: head toward the back. There was a closed door she didn't touch, and one through which she could see an uncomfortable-looking sofa and an honest-to-god piano. And then, mercifully, there was a door that had a tiled floor behind it, and a kettle obvious on the counter. Everything would surely fall into place from there. It was reassuring that even in an unfamiliar kitchen there was some innate logic to the location of the mugs, of tea bags, of milk (the milk, to be fair, had been a pretty sure bet).

She saw it as she was returning the milk to the fridge. There, between a Ruby Wedding invitation and a couple of John Lewis vouchers held in place by a magnetic mouse, was a photo of her and Mei. They were in the French restaurant in Bristol, the only time she'd met both Mei's parents. The face that looked back at her from the photo was so happy—breezy and summery in the green and white shirt she remembered tucking into a denim skirt. And Mei. Mei looked so good. Eyes bright, skin soft against that linen dress. The one Bette had pushed up later that night, when she'd pushed Mei out on the table at home and eaten her out. Here, the red lipstick she'd ruin later was still perfect on Mei's mouth, even after the meal. Mei's arm was in front of hers as they sat close in the booth. She could remember Mei's hand between her knees under the table, could remember worrying that it was too intimate for Mr. Hinota's phone. But he'd brought it home, and had it printed, and had pinned it to the fridge. The rest of the house didn't have a "things pinned to the fridge" energy. It was too curated, too fancy, looked too much as if it belonged in a magazine. But here, in such a tangible family space, Bette had found herself. It made her heart clench in her chest. It was everywhere she wanted to be: on the fridge, beside Mei, grinning goofily at her dad's phone.

There was a creak from somewhere above her and she shook herself, squeezing out the tea bags and carrying the mugs through into the hall. Mei was on her way down the stairs, a soft leather holdall in her hand.

They didn't speak as she handed Mei a mug, as they both blew on and gulped down the far too hot tea in the hall. There seemed to be a silent agreement that they were too tired to consider sitting down to drink the tea, that there was a real chance they'd fall asleep where the mugs landed. Instead, as soon as they were close to drained, Bette took them back into the kitchen, rinsed them both out and left them draining on the rack.

"Should we head back?" Bette asked, her voice as gentle as she could make it. She took the bag from Mei's hand, made her way toward the door and tried not to draw attention to the fact that she could hear Mei's stifled sniffles.

It was the choked sob that was finally too much for her to ignore, too much to politely pretend she couldn't hear. She turned round, dropped the overnight bag and pulled Mei toward her. The sobs became more pronounced then, less careful, less controlled, and it was only once Mei's face was pressed against Bette's collarbone that she let herself properly cry. Bette held her, stroking her back, lips buried in the hair at the top of her head.

Eventually Mei's sobs calmed, and she reached up to wipe her face.

"Sorry, I'm gross."

"Don't apologize. You want a tissue?"

Mei shook her head, pulling her sweater up over her face and wiping her tears away with it. Once her face was clean she settled back against Bette, curling her arms up under her chin, allowing herself to be held, burrowing her way into Bette's body.

"I was holding the ladder," she said, barely above a whisper. "He slipped. I couldn't stop him. I couldn't help."

Bette's mouth hung open, uselessly.

"The sound, Bette. His head, when he landed," her voice wavered again, and she choked in a breath. "I can still hear it."

"But he's okay," Bette said, pulling her closer. "He's going to be okay."

She felt Mei nod into her chest, her arms trapped between them. They breathed together, and Bette worked to keep hers deep and even, hoping Mei would follow suit. Eventually, she felt Mei's tense form loosen against her. And then, just as she was easing her hold so that they could head back to the car, Mei tipped her head back and placed a soft kiss at the underside of Bette's jaw. Bette's heart stuttered.

"Mei?"

"I just," she said into Bette's shoulder. "I just want it to feel like things used to."

It was exactly how Bette had been feeling for months. How was she supposed to refuse now, when Mei was offering her exactly what she'd wanted? The line drawn between them was one Mei had sketched out and then reinforced in bed that morning in thick ink. She had resented and hated the line. But crossing it seemed like risky behavior, especially on a night when Mei was all vulnerability, a thousand raw nerves poking through her skin. Bette didn't want it this way, she realized. Mei had been adamant, and nothing had truly changed. Bette wanted to celebrate the moment they got back together, not feel conflicted about it.

"I don't think—" Bette said, feeling responsible for doing the right thing, the thing that neither of them would regret tomorrow. "I don't want you to—I don't know, I mean, I feel like we shouldn't—"

"No, I'm sorry, you're right," Mei said, her voice resigned, and Bette didn't know whether to feel disappointed or relieved. She settled on an overwhelming combination of both. "Let's go home."

"Home," Bette agreed. It wouldn't be long now. After all, she was on the fridge, she thought, feeling warm embers flare in her belly. Sitting there, on the fridge, confidently, waiting for the break to be over.

13 days to go

It felt, for the next week, as though Bette was living in limbo. She went to bed early and slept late. She didn't feel great about it, but passing as much time as possible asleep made complete sense. She filled up the waking hours too, determined not to be stuck at home in her own head. She went to see Carmen's new work in progress, and stuck around for a drink with the cast. She went for a long walk with Ruth, up the hill and across the suspension bridge, high on endorphins. She spent Saturday afternoon playing a board game with Ash and Tim.

But really, she was waiting. Willing time to go faster. Wanting to fast-forward through these final two weeks.

As the credits rolled on *Grey's Anatomy* on Sunday night, Ash apparently reached some sort of limit.

"So are you okay?" she asked, without preamble, as she separated a bourbon biscuit and dunked the non-iced half into her tea. "You've seemed off this week. Sort of . . . manic, maybe?"

Bette bit into her own biscuit and sipped her tea.

"I miss Mei," she admitted. "I have been, the whole time.

Missing, I don't know—missing the domesticity and it being easy, and having her at the table with us. I don't really want to be having sex with lots of different people. I really loved having someone."

"Sure, that makes sense," Ash said, turning more fully toward Bette, resting an arm along the back of the sofa.

"That night at the hospital? Last Monday? Mei needed me, asked me to help. It was late and she was tired but she tried to kiss me and I stopped things. And now I'm just waiting. I mean, there's a photo of us on her parents' fridge. I know we're going to be okay; I know it's just a matter of time. But really? I just wish I could sleep through the next two weeks."

"Have you talked since?"

"No," Bette said. "I drove her back, and then I walked home. I sort of thought she might have been in touch. Just to talk about it. Where we're at. But she hasn't. And I don't want to push."

"I mean, you could text her, right? You don't have to wait for her to call?"

Bette shrugged. There was no reason she couldn't be the one to make the call.

"I could."

"But you won't, will you?"

"No," Bette confirmed. "I won't. I'll wait it out. I want to know she's done with this too, I want her to want me back. But in the meantime, I'm not doing any more dates. I had sex with other people. Some of it was even good. Really good, actually. But it's not surprising, I guess, that I ended up knowing it's her I want. Nothing's really changed."

Ash took another biscuit, pulling the halves apart.

"Why have you started buying these again? I miss those chocolate and ginger ones. Bourbons are fine, but they're mid-tier. At best."

"I've been eating too many biscuits this week to be buying the chocolate and ginger ones. I'm not made of money," Bette said, reaching into the packet for another. Ash snorted.

"Is there part of you that's going to miss the dating? When it's all officially done?"

"Not really, honestly. I mean, not that it hasn't been fun. Charlie was great."

"Hot, biker jacket, sex in the club?"

"Yeah. It was a great story, too. I'm glad it happened. And Netta was amazing. And I'm so glad I met Ruth. That's probably been the best bit. She's brilliant."

"She really is," Ash agreed.

"It feels weird to think about it like this, but honestly, the whole thing has been sort of worth it, to know that I'm sure about Mei. And to have found a friend like Ruth."

IT WAS A nothing sort of Tuesday, but it was finally October, and it was sunny. Next Saturday, the one after this one, would be the end of the three months. It was so close now that Bette could taste it. Her mood matched the weather: bright and hopeful. And so when Erin caught her eye and suggested an M&S lunch in the park, Bette jumped at it. Her packed lunch glared disapprovingly at her from the under-counter fridge and she ignored it.

"This was supposed to be a non-working lunch," Bette complained, once they were on the grass with crisps and sandwiches.

They'd spoken of nothing but work since leaving the office. "We might as well have stayed at our desks at this rate. Tell me about the wedding."

The next ten minutes were almost enough to convince Bette that marriage wasn't for her. That perhaps it shouldn't be for anyone. There were problems with some supply-chain thing that affected the menu, drama with cousins and aunts and people who hadn't been invited far enough in advance, the fact that Niamh's suit had been returned three times and still wasn't quite right. Bette could hardly believe couples survived it.

"I'm so glad you're still coming," Erin said, tessellating crisps carefully over the egg in the second half of her sandwich. "I know I've known Mei longer, but I'd be so gutted if you decided you couldn't be there just because of her."

"Oh, we're fine. I mean, we're good," Bette said. Mei must have finally told her about the break. But it was okay. It was almost done. And she was Mei's person, the one she called in the middle of the night.

"Well, I think that's really big of you. Not in a patronizing way!" Erin added. "Just, you know—I don't reckon I'd be okay being at a wedding with my ex and her new girlfriend."

CHAPTER EIGHTEEN

TUESDAY, 04 OCTOBER

...

Who even knows?

Bette wasn't quite sure, later, how she got home. She hadn't returned to the office, had given Erin some vague excuse there was no way she believed. En route to lunch, blithely unaware of what awaited her, she had walked out with only her wallet, keys and phone, and so her backpack sat under her desk, awaiting her no longer imminent return. She trundled home in a daze.

When she finally stepped into the kitchen, Ash took one look at her face and wrapped her up in a hug so fierce that she could feel herself fighting for breath.

"Sofa?" she asked. "Tea?" she added, seeming to understand without instruction that full sentences might be too much. Somewhere among the sadness and the mortification and the sick feeling, Bette felt overwhelmed to be so known. She nodded.

There was something soft around her shoulders and a mug in her hands faster than she could fathom. It was too warm, really, to have both at once. But Bette was happy to be blanketed, to be covered and cosseted. Ash encouraged her to take a few sips, and then guided her gently until Bette's head was pillowed by Ash's thighs, until Ash's hand was buried in Bette's hair, until Bette's arm was hooked around Ash's knees.

"Do you want to talk about it?" Ash asked, her nails scraping gently on Bette's scalp.

"I don't—I just—" Bette started, the words stuck in her throat.

Ash waited, and Bette lost track of time as she tried to form sounds into words and words into sentences and sentences into some sort of explanation for what had happened.

"It's Mei," she managed.

"I thought that must be it," Ash said. "Oh love, I'm so sorry. What happened?"

"She's bringing someone else to Erin's wedding. She has a girlfriend. Her name is Tamara. Erin and Niamh have had them to dinner. They've been together more than a month."

"Fuck *off*," Ash breathed, low and shocked.

"I know."

"But—but—"

"All of that too."

"I can't believe this. That poisonous snake *bitch*," Ash said through gritted teeth now. "Hold on, was she seeing her—"

"A week ago?" Bette knew exactly where this was going. "When she called and then I went to the hospital and pretended to her mum that we were still together and drove her to Cheltenham? Was she seeing her when she tried to kiss me in her parents' hall? When she didn't reply to my text checking in on her dad? When she didn't call all week, which I assumed was about her family being around but was actually probably . . . this?"

"Yeah."

"Yeah," confirmed Bette.

The hand that had been moving through Bette's hair tightened as Ash took a shaky breath.

"Ash," Bette said, squirming to get away from her nails. "Ouch."

"Shit, sorry."

They fell into a silence. Bette felt sick and out of control, like she was approaching the first plummet of a roller coaster, full of regret and dreading what was next. She was trapped; there was no way to avoid the fall. She focused on trying to breathe, which had ceased being purely instinctual when Erin had said Tamara's name. She could hear Adriene, the YouTube yoga woman, telling her to *take the deepest breath you've taken all day* and she tried it, over and over, until her head felt cleaned out. Empty.

"It's only three o'clock," Bette realized.

"Inset day," Ash said, by way of explanation, sounding miles away.

"Thank god," Bette said, with deep sincerity.

It was a sign of how bad Ash thought things were that she found the first series of the American *Married at First Sight* and cued it up. Ash hated reality dating programs, no matter how many different ones Bette tried to get her into. But she moved only to refill their mugs, not complaining about the unreality of the format, or the participants who only wanted to boost their Instagram following so they could shill beauty products. She didn't even look up the couples online, to prove that they hadn't lasted after filming. They simply stayed on the sofa, Bette's head on Ash's thigh, as afternoon became evening, and then night.

"I texted Ruth," Ash said, voice gentle, hours after either of them had last spoken. "She's bringing ice cream when she gets home."

"What the fuck?" Bette said, sitting up with a start, rubbing at her eyes. "Why would you text Ruth?"

"Honestly? Because you need to eat something, and I thought I could probably convince you to have ice cream, but I didn't want to leave you alone and Tim's working late tonight and then I remembered Ruth lives near the stoner Tesco and took a punt she might be around." There was a Tesco down the hill from them that sold a range of Ben and Jerry's that Bette had never seen rivaled by any other supermarket in the country. It was open late.

"Since when do you have Ruth's number?" Bette asked.

"Since she cooked the mussels, obviously," Ash replied. "I text her every now and then. Mostly for recipe advice. That's all right, isn't it?"

Bette wanted to say no. Wanted to say that Ruth was *her* friend. But it was impossible not to feel warmed by the idea of them conspiring together to look after her.

"It's not—of course it's okay. I just . . . I don't want Ruth seeing me like this," Bette said. Ash looked at her for a moment.

"Sorry," she replied, truly sounding it. "I didn't think you'd mind. You've been spending so much time together, so I assumed it wasn't going to be a big thing."

"I know we've been hanging out," Bette replied, head in her hands. "But it's—it's not—ugh I don't even know. Fine. Thank you. In advance, for the ice cream. Do I look okay?"

Ash considered for a moment.

"Do you want the truth or do you want something gentle and reassuring?"

"Gentle and reassuring. Obviously. I'm not nearly stable enough for truth."

"You're the most beautiful person I know, Bette," Ash said, her voice entirely genuine. "And I love you."

Bette was silent for a moment.

"Truth?"

"You look horrendous. You're a horrible crier. One of the worst I've ever seen. I'm running a flannel under cold water for you. Maybe your eyes will calm down."

She dumped Marge into Bette's lap and ran down the hall to the bathroom. Marge hovered, rather than committing to comfort or risking ridicule by making it clear she wanted to be petted. But Bette ran a firm palm down her throat anyway, over and over, until Marge was pushing back into Bette's hand, purring. As Ash arrived with a flannel and passed it to Bette, Marge jumped down, embarrassed to have been caught seeking affection. She stalked off.

"Better?" Bette asked, her face scrubbed, handing the flannel back to Ash.

Ash grimaced. "Not—I mean—no. No, definitely worse. Your mascara is now everywhere too. And you look sort of scrubbed raw. Shit. Sorry. But look, it's fine! Ruth's just coming to drop off ice cream and then she can go home. It's fine. You don't have to see her."

"We can't make her walk up the hill with ice cream and then kick her out once she's here!"

"I mean, I'm very much of the opinion that you're calling all the shots today," Ash said. "Whatever you need. If you want her to just go home, then we can send her home, we can eat the ice cream and we can go to bed."

"No. No, she should come in. It'll be fine." And it would be, surely. Ruth would come, she'd give her the ice cream and a spoon, she'd commiserate and then she'd leave. It didn't matter that Bette's eyes were puffy or her makeup was all over her face or that she'd slipped out of her jeans at some point in the late afternoon and that beneath the blanket was in pants and her top from work. It was only Ruth.

The show reached its inevitable finale, and the interviews happened. A couple of the couples committed to making it work, were more in love than anyone ever had been, apparently, and Bette vaguely considered stalking them on Instagram. Just to see how they had fared, to see how they felt about their "soul-mate" and "best friend" after the cameras had left. But it was a task for another time, not for this tender, bruised horror of a day.

Without the reassurance of the next episode, Bette felt at a loss, already anxious and determined to fill the room with noise. Her head was back on Ash's thigh, but the silence seemed to suggest that she should sit up, figure out what was next. And next was probably a conversation about Mei. And she didn't want that. She was about to suggest they put *Parks* on, one of the good Ben Wyatt–rich episodes in the third season, when Ash pulled the laptop toward them and balanced it on Bette's head, where it still rested in her lap. When she put it back down there was an hour-long Scott Moir and Tessa Virtue ice-dancing compilation starting and Bette felt herself tearing up.

"This is perfect," she said, her voice choked up. Ash's hand tightened in her hair.

"I know," she said gently. "Loser."

They stayed like that until the end of the video, Ash's hand comforting against her head. And when it was over, she felt like it was probably time to sit up. She pushed herself up off Ash's thigh and stretched out her back. It felt as though she was one of those spring-loaded snakes, her spine contorted and compressed. She was sitting, but she wasn't quite ready to move on from the ice-dancing.

Bette found a video of her favorite performance, from 2018, and put it on. She sat back on the sofa, cross-legged, and fiddled with the blanket over her lap. And then when the video was over she dragged the timing bar back to the beginning and started all over again. Ash tutted but indulged her, picking up their mugs and heading, inevitably, in the direction of the kitchen to refill them. Left alone, Bette let the video play again, tears dripping silently down her cheeks.

A knock at the door shook her out of her stupor, and she paused the video and wiped her face with the blanket. But gathering herself to stand up made her realize just how desperate she was for the loo. She dashed down the hall to the bathroom as Ash squeezed past to let Ruth in.

Once behind the closed door, she risked a glance at herself in the mirror. Ash hadn't been exaggerating. She looked awful. She splashed clean water on her face, which was supposed to help. Her mother always told her to splash cold water on her face when she was upset. Or tired. Or anxious. Or when her throat was sore before school. Or when she'd hit her elbow. It was her foolproof cure for everything.

Bette blinked through the drips falling from her eyelashes and buried her face in a clean towel from the shelf. Mei might have been a liar, a manipulative arsehole. But at least, thanks to her influence, they always had the shelf of fresh towels in the bathroom now. Bette slipped into her room and pulled a pair of pajama bottoms on.

Ash's and Ruth's voices were muffled from the front room, and Bette felt uncomfortable about how long she'd been gone. Determined not to be pitied, she walked in with a smile plastered on, stretched over her teeth.

"That's such a gorgeous fake smile," Ruth said, by way of greeting. "Hope it's not on my account. I was promised despair in exchange for the ice cream."

"Don't worry, I can get back to despair pretty quickly," Bette assured her, aware of how crackly and strange her voice sounded.

"Glad to hear it," Ruth said, but her tone was kind. She was curled up on the sofa, and Marge had taken up residence on her lap.

"I know," Ash said, following Bette's eyeline. "Cat whisperer."

There wasn't really space for three polite friends on the sofa, and the two armchairs they rarely used weren't where she wanted to be. Ash, of course, saw the whole situation in moments and pushed herself up.

"Really early morning for me," she said. "I'm going to take my leave of the emotional invalid and hand things over. You two will be okay?"

"Course!" Ruth said.

"Yeah, thanks Ash," Bette agreed. "Thanks for this afternoon."

She leaned over and pressed the space bar, and the final thirty seconds of the video played out. With a glance back at the sofa, and a quiet laugh, Ash waved them both good night.

"I love you," Bette called out, and she heard Ash shout it back. The video came to an end and she clicked back on the beginning, starting it all over again. Scott Moir raised his eyebrow and the *Moulin Rouge* music started playing, all curtains and pantomimes. And then they were off.

"How many times have you watched this video?"

It hadn't really occurred to Bette that Ruth might find it weird that she was sitting, wrapped in a blanket, watching a video from the PyeongChang Winter Olympics on a loop. She realized, briefly, that this was perhaps something to be defensive about. Or to lie about. But she had been stripped raw by the day, all defenses worn down.

"Today? Or ever? Either way, I don't really know. I've lost count. A lot. Look at them. They're perfect. They're so in love."

She could feel Ruth's eyes on her, and Bette wanted to direct her back to the screen, didn't want her to miss a single bit, wanted her to understand.

"Bette, surely they're . . . colleagues? Teammates? Friends, maybe? I guess?" Ruth pulled her phone out, evidently invested in having an answer to offer. A moment later, she held it out toward Bette. "Look, they're both in relationships with other people, see? This is ice-skating, it's not real life. They're acting!"

Ice-*dancing*, Bette's brain grumbled. And anyway, she wasn't interested in evidence, in harsh and horrible reality. She felt something settle in her throat. Mortified, she talked around it, sure she could control it if she could only get her thoughts out.

"Of course I know that. But look at her flip up and sit on his face!" she said, and heard Ruth choke back a surprised laugh. "Look at him catch her! Imagine being able to trust someone like that!"

There was a long silence, and Bette turned to find Ruth still looking at her, her head cocked to the side in contemplation, her face serious and considering. But when she finally spoke it was with barely held back laughter.

"I am genuinely concerned that you've gone a bit mad here. What's really going on?"

"*This* is really going on!" Bette shouted, far too loud so late on a weeknight. The lump in her throat was back and she was going to choke on it. "What if I never have this?"

Bette looked down at her hands, twisting in her lap, and heard Ruth take a deep breath.

"Look, I don't want to be a dick. But Bette. You are never going to have this." Bette opened her mouth in indignation, but Ruth reached out and covered Bette's clasped hands with her own. "This isn't aspirational relationship stuff. It's a performance. They're acting. Also, these people have been doing nothing but skate together since they were kids. They've won gold medals doing this. I think your gold medal chances are, well—look, I'm going to say it: they're slim. You are absolutely never going to have this. *No one else* has this. Literally only they have this."

It was impossible to argue with Ruth's logic, and Bette was furious. The fury swelled, bubbling and coursing through her, until it finally burst out in the only way it could—a half laugh, half sob that she couldn't quite get control of. Ruth reached over and put an arm round her, pulling Bette into her side.

"You're such a sap," she said, affection written so clearly in her voice that Bette was certain she must be imagining it. Sure enough, when she looked up at Ruth, her face held mostly exasperation. Eventually "Come What May" came to an end, and the American commentator sounded overwhelmed and talked about how lucky they all were to have seen this partnership, and Bette leaned over to start the video again.

Ruth reached over and closed the laptop, almost trapping Bette's hand inside.

"No! But . . ."

"I'm cutting you off. That's plenty for one night. No more getting sad over ice-skating. It's depressing and I refuse to watch you doing it to yourself. Pick something else to watch. I'm getting the ice cream."

"Ice-dancing," Bette muttered under her breath.

"Whatever," Ruth threw over her shoulder, as she left the room.

It was ridiculous, Bette thought, as she listened to Ruth's careful footsteps down the hall, to get choked up about the idea of someone making fun of her YouTube habit and scooping ice cream into bowls. But, to her credit, it had been a really emotional day.

CHAPTER NINETEEN

WEDNESDAY, 05 OCTOBER

...

What's the point in counting?

I t was difficult to dwell too much, in the days that followed. Work was busy, which was a relief. Ash stayed in on her usual Tim night. Tim even called, once, which was odd, and sort of stilted. Neither of them were really phone-call people. Carmen texted and made plans for Sunday: a drink just for the two of them, "my treat" (Ash had clearly filled her in). There was a message from Ruth on her phone every time she looked at it too—a hello, a check-in, a little prompt (best school-set film of all time, top-three pastries she'd ever eaten, most underrated song of the early '00s).

It was sort of all right, then, when everyone else was awake. The problem was the time after she went to bed.

On Wednesday, when she still wasn't asleep at two, she took four of the accidentally-not-non-drowsy antihistamines that had sat in the bathroom cupboard for years. An hour later she was still awake, with *The Office* filling half her screen, and the fourth page of Google search results for *antihistamine overdose death?* on the other.

When Ash flagged even earlier on Thursday, Bette climbed into bed and lay in the dark in her room. She willed herself to sleep, determined not to open her laptop.

It didn't take long to accept it wasn't happening. She unplugged her phone and brought it back to bed with her.

> **Bette:** I can't sleep
>
> **Bette:** tell me what I should do
>
> **Ruth:** What do you normally do when you can't sleep?
>
> **Bette:** normally?
>
> **Bette:** I roll over
>
> **Bette:** and I sleep
>
> **Bette:** I love to sleep
>
> **Ruth:** You're the worst. Okay. Have you tried audiobooks? Soothing voice, quiet story, nothing too gripping, no screen glare?
>
> **Bette:** never really tried

A link arrived a minute later, an audiobook gifted to her: *The Remains of the Day*.

> **Ruth:** Okay, give this one a go. McNulty reading it (fit), great story even if you've already read it, every single sentence beautiful, but not exciting enough to keep you awake.

Bette: oh I've heard great things!

Bette: never read it before

Bette: thank you

Ruth: It's nothing! Hope it helps,
And fingers crossed you sleep
soon!

The book, it turned out, was not nothing.

Fucking Stevens. Stevens wandering about the big old house and feeling a thousand things and doing precisely nothing about any of them. *Fucking* Stevens. By the time he was preparing a tea tray and Miss Kenton was talking about her engagement, playing some horrible game of marriage chicken with him, Bette could feel tears slipping down her cheeks and onto her pillow. By the time he was sitting by the bus stop she had been reduced to sobs so loud that Ash knocked on her door. She managed to say *It's not Mei, it's this stupid book*, and Ash set her mouth in a firm line, nodded with an attitude that felt both sympathetic and exasperated, and left.

It was morning, then, which wasn't ideal. But people with much more complex jobs than hers could survive without any sleep, she reasoned. Nurses, parents, long-haul drivers. And she'd been lying down the whole time.

Bette: absolutely fuck you

Ruth: Good morning! Are you . . .
all right?

Bette: I did not sleep

Bette: but at least Stevens is going

232

232

to die alone in the horrible sad
Nazi house

Ruth: Ah.

Bette: AH

Ruth: So you listened to the book.
It did not send you to sleep.

Bette: I listened to the book

Bette: I listened to seven hours
and five minutes of the book

Bette: I may never recover from
the book

Ruth: I'm . . . sorry?

Bette: correct

Bette: at least I know that things
could get worse

Bette: this breakup?

Bette: nothing

Bette: I've barely scraped the
surface of human devastation

Ruth: See!? You're welcome.
Things could always be worse.

THAT SATURDAY NIGHT, Ash pulled two bottles of beer from the fridge, popped their tops off and brought them over to where Bette was sitting on the kitchen counter.

"So, Ruth texted. She and Gabe and her flatmates are going bowling tonight. They thought we might want to come?"

"Why didn't she just ask me?" Bette said, her chest suddenly tight and anxious.

"Oh, she said that she didn't know if you'd be in the mood but that you're not great at saying no. Which is true, before you get all weird about it. So if you're not up to it, I can text no from both of us. I'm great at saying no."

"So they're going bowling? Like, bowling bowling?" Bette asked. "I thought we'd agreed I'm not coordinated enough for sport."

"I'm not entirely sure we'd call bowling a sport," Ash replied, thoughtfully, as she took a sip from her bottle. "But I think it probably doesn't matter if you're crap at it."

"Oh great," Bette said. "Another punishing humiliation on the cards for me."

Because that was the whole point, really, wasn't it? She was heartbroken, yes. She kept thinking about the lost future with Mei, about the fact that she would never kiss her again, would never sit across the sofa from her and hear about the plan for the latest sculpture. Would never again walk into a restaurant proud that of everyone in the world Mei could be at dinner with, she had chosen to be with Bette. But all of it was amplified by the mortification, by the humiliation. The shame of having shouted so loudly about being so in love, and to have been proved incorrect. Of having been found inadequate. Far too easy to let go of and move on from. Inconsequential.

"So that's a yes?" Ash said, her voice sounding very far away.

"We can get an Uber and get drunk on cheap beer and both agree to be bad at it?"

Everything in Bette was screaming no: she wanted a Saturday night in bed, wanted to catch up on the sleep she'd missed. But Ash looked so excited about it, like the idea had so much promise. And Ruth was right. She was terrible at saying no.

"Really, really bad at it, Ash. Promise?"

TWO HOURS LATER, what was entirely apparent was that Ash was either an exceptional liar or an incredibly lucky amateur bowler. The bowling alley had a vaguely ridiculous Saturday night energy: remixed '70s classics and disco lights, but also endless teenagers pouring bottles of what was probably vodka into their cinema-size cups of coke.

"It's like riding a bike, isn't it?" Ash said, her grin after her third consecutive strike stretching out past pleased and into smug. "I haven't done this since I was a kid, but it's pure muscle memory!"

"The master!" Jody said, falling in a mock bow. The quiff Bette remembered from their birthday was slightly softer, swoopier, and they were wearing jeans and a white tank top that looked unreasonably good with bowling shoes. "You're wiping the floor with us."

It was kind, Bette thought, to include everyone in this summation of where things stood. There were some very decent totals on the board, none of which were hers. She picked up an orange ball with a ten carved into it, lined it up and rolled it firmly and devastatingly straight into the gutter. The indignity was only amplified by having to repeat it before they could move onto Ruth's turn. She knocked down a single pin with her second throw, which felt somehow worse than none. Like she couldn't even commit to truly failing.

"I thought this might be a fun distraction," Ruth said as Bette sat back down across from her. "I didn't think you'd be so awful at it." There was a supportive energy somewhere in her tone, but mostly Ruth was laughing at her. Gabe was sitting alongside Ruth, an arm flung easily along the back of the plastic booth, his face all warm sympathy. Bette fought the impulse to tell him where precisely he could shove it.

He had been making such a clear effort, and Bette felt bad. She was tired, in a weird mood. Having to put on a face for Gabe, for someone she didn't know that well, who kept focusing attention in her direction, felt beyond her.

"At least you're not that guy," Gabe said as Ruth stood to take her turn. He gestured over her shoulder, toward a tall, broad guy who'd thrown the ball so hard that it had bounced across two of the lanes, taking out a cluster of pins that were definitely not his.

"At least he's hit some pins down," Bette said with a shrug, turning back toward him.

"Oh, come on," he said. "You've done all right!"

She looked at him, brow furrowed, trying to figure him out.

"Okay, you haven't. I've never seen anyone bowl a worse game. You know, if you can keep your total below twenty by the end, that's probably some sort of lanes record. They'll hang a picture of you."

Bette couldn't help it. She laughed.

"So, are you a natural, or a stealth expert?" she asked.

Gabe shrugged, his plump lips pursing and holding back a

smile. "Stealth expert, I'm afraid. I bowled a lot as a kid. Couldn't believe my luck when Ruth told me the plan. Hadn't prepared myself for competing with Ash's skills"—he saluted Ash, and she grinned back over her plastic beer cup—"but hopefully I've done all right. I wanted to be able to show off a bit."

His eyes moved to Ruth, lining up her second shot. She bent over, and Bette looked away.

"Yeah, that makes sense," Bette said. "She's pretty impressive."

"Intimidatingly so," he agreed, clapping Ruth's entirely respectable seven pins and high-fiving her as she returned to the booth.

"You talking about me?"

"Heather, actually," Bette lied. "Mortifying to assume we were talking about you."

Ruth rolled her eyes and Heather snorted, splitting the jug of increasingly warm lager between their plastic cups. Unlike the rest of them, all in assorted jeans and dungarees and T-shirts, Heather had clearly taken the bowling lane as an opportunity to dress up. Her pleated skirt flirted with being too short whenever she leaned down to roll the ball down the lane. Her socks were pulled up over her knees. It was an outfit Bette would have been jealous of when she was seven. It was an outfit she was pretty jealous of now. Heather looked long and sexy and irreverent as she flung the ball in the general direction of the pins, turning back to the group before it connected, missing the moment when eight pins took a fall. There was a cool insouciance about it that floored Bette.

But then, when Heather's second ball missed the pins entirely, she didn't watch that either. Bette couldn't imagine being so cool about . . . anything, actually.

Maybe, if she'd been a bit cooler about Mei, she wouldn't have lost her. Maybe she could have just refused the whole thing from the start; laughed at Mei in bed that morning and kissed her instead and told her no. Maybe she wouldn't be single all over again, wouldn't have people looking at her with pity while she bowled a terrible game. Maybe she wouldn't have given Mei an opportunity to leave her for someone else. To realize just how much she didn't need Bette.

"Bette," she heard, distantly. She blinked a few times, her vision blurred, and Ash's concerned face came into focus near hers. She was crouched in front of her, and Bette was aware that she had almost certainly been there for a while. That, from the way Ruth was looking at her from over Ash's shoulder, from the way that everyone else was avoiding eye contact, Ash had probably been trying to get her attention for a while. Bette reached up to touch her cheeks. They were wet. Fantastic. Truly, just what the evening called for.

"Sorry—I—" she started.

"It's okay," Ash said. "It's hard watching me be so good at this, I know."

It eased things, and they all laughed. Bette took a breath.

"Do you . . . want help?" Ruth asked, clearly already cringing at her offer. "Bowling-wise? If it would keep you from tears?"

"Sure," Bette said, as she stood and found the orange ball. "I probably can't get any worse."

Ruth followed her, pulling her jeans up to settle high on her waist. An emerald-green shirt billowed over them, a bra in the same shade revealing itself every time the shirt slipped from her shoulder. Bette couldn't stop looking at it.

"To be clear," Ruth said as they approached the lane. "I have no advice to offer. I mean, any advice beyond: try and roll it straight, or straight-ish, so that it doesn't go in the gutter. If it goes straight, it will maybe knock some pins down."

"Great," Bette said, the word damp with sarcasm as she walked toward the line and brought the ball up to her chest. "Don't know how I've been doing this without you."

There was a horrible moment just before she let go of the ball when she realized something had gone terribly wrong. Instead of leaving her hand, instead of rolling straight into the gutter, the weight of the ball pulled her arm forward and her knees hit the ground, her fingers trapped in its tiny, ridiculous little holes. She was on the ground, in the lane. There was a moment of shocked silence, and then Bette could feel her shoulders start to shake.

"Laughing or crying?" Ruth said from behind her, her voice on the edge of full hysterics. "Are we laughing or crying?"

"I don't fucking *know*," Bette said, as tears of . . . something ran down her cheeks.

"Yeah, okay, that makes sense," Ruth said, and then crouched down beside her and pulled her into a hug. Ash and Heather and Jody and Gabe joined them, collapsing on top in a sort of scrum, as if Bette had done something impressive rather than utterly mortifying.

"God, this is a size four," Jody said, laughing so much that their breaths had turned to hiccups. "It's for a child, Bette." They pulled the ball from Bette's hand and Bette could tell, once it was loose, that it was much smaller than the ball she'd been using for the rest of the evening. It was impossible not to see it now, how small it looked alongside the others.

"Lane Nine. Please do not sit in the lane, Lane Nine," an exhausted voice said over the tannoy.

"Yeah, I think we're done," Ruth said, pushing herself to her feet and reaching down for Bette's hand. "Kebabs?"

THEY WAVED GOODBYE to Gabe outside the bowling alley, Jody wolf-whistling as he pulled Ruth aside and kissed her. He hugged them all in turn, and Bette really wanted to like him. There was absolutely no reason for her not to.

As they walked toward the kebab shop, Bette looked round at everyone: Heather and Jody arm in arm up ahead, Ash's fingers threaded through her own, Ruth (whose heels she kept treading on) half a step in front of them. It was nice, just the five of them. She pulled Ash forward, and they fell into step with Ruth.

"Was it my fault he left?" Bette asked. "Gabe, I mean. I'm really sorry for crying. And I know I don't have much chat tonight. I should have made more of an effort."

"Oh! No, no. He's on deadline, nothing to do with you. He just wanted to spend some time with everyone, even if only for a couple of hours. And I'm trying to be better at inviting him into different bits of my life."

"Ooh, yeah, crucial step," Ash said, nodding sagely.

"Think I wanted to keep it all separate for a while? It was easy to have him at Jody's birthday, when there were so many people. But it feels like a bigger deal to have him in a smaller group. And look, there's just no doubt they were all going to love him. And that—you know? It might make things more—I don't know. Serious."

"Yeah, I get that," Ash agreed.

"He's a good guy though," Ruth said. "Really good. I like him. He fits right in."

"He seems great," Bette said, wanting to be generous. "Really great. I can see why you like him."

"Yeah, he's—he's exactly the right sort of person for me," Ruth said, her tone odd in a way Bette couldn't place.

The lighting in the kebab shop could only reasonably be described as glaring. After the disco lights of the bowling alley, it was stark. Everyone's sweaty, patchy faces made Bette anxious about her own. Bowling might not be a sport, but dancing around under disco lights and throwing heavy balls around was exercise of a sort. Surely. But the end-of-the-night makeup— the flaking, the smudging, the damp sweat—suited everyone else. They looked, honestly, like they'd had fun. So perhaps it was suiting her too. Maybe she looked gorgeous, like everyone else did.

They claimed the middle table in the kebab shop, pulled up an extra chair and ordered falafel stuffed into flatbread with vinegar-soaked cabbage and shredded carrot with extra chili and garlic sauce. And as Bette was looking around the table, marveling over the beauty of everyone with their smudged makeup, Ruth returned with two baskets of bread and two bowls of chips. Bette groaned in appreciation and realized, as she did, quite how tipsy she was.

"Fuck, yes," Jody said, splitting open a piece of bread and

filling it with chips that left salt on their fingers. "The dream. Do you have—" They looked up at Ruth and reached for a tub of what looked like garlic sauce.

"Okay, brief review?" Heather said, once they had all followed Jody's lead and Ruth had pulled a second pot of the garlic sauce from her pocket.

"You know I love this place. The bread's soft, plenty of vinegar, chili sauce is hot, falafel crisp," Ruth began.

Heather shook her head. "No, no, no. Your boyfriend's review."

Bette wasn't sure when she'd missed Gabe's upgrade from "guy I'm taking it slow with" to "boyfriend," but Ruth didn't deny the label.

"Hey! We don't need to do—" Ruth started.

"Oh, we absolutely do," Jody agreed. "I missed him at my party, and he's been a proper little ghost the past month."

"He's not a ghost! Just because he's not constantly around doesn't imply ghost. We're taking it slow. Plus, unlike you lot, his flatmates aren't entirely lacking in boundaries. So—"

"So you've been staying at his," Heather shrugged. "Fine, you can be all squirrely about him, but we've met him properly now, and we have some opinions."

"Ugh, fine," Ruth said.

Heather and Jody looked at each other. Bette looked at Ruth, watching the tension radiating from her as she waited with raised eyebrows. Ash looked at her kebab.

"We loooove him," Heather and Jody said together, looking at Ruth with wide grins.

"Oh god," Ruth said, and Ash laughed.

"We loooooove him," Heather emphasized. "He's great. Up for

a laugh, good sport, confident but has the stuff to back it up, clearly adores you. Tick, tick, tick."

Bette thought back to him wanting to impress Ruth, to how he'd spent the evening always seemingly aware of her even when in conversation with someone else. Thought of him with a hand on Ruth's thigh.

"He really does," Bette said, and Ruth looked over, her eyes wide and surprised. Hopeful.

"Yeah?" she said, as though hearing it from Bette somehow confirmed it.

"Oh, absolutely," Ash agreed. "Couldn't take his eyes off you."

"Plus that mouth," Jody said. "That's a mouth you could really—"

"Okay, okay, let's leave the review there," Ruth said, eyes closed and head shaking, as if hoping to wipe the last ten seconds from her mind.

"Ugh fine. But this isn't over," Jody said, and they all munched in silence for a moment, Ruth's cheeks and chest pink.

"So, Bette. I've been gagging to ask. How are you?" Heather had redirected her attention, and Bette saw Ruth breathe a sigh of relief.

She had been anticipating it, ready for the sympathy, for the kindness that she thought might tip her over the edge into tears again. But instead Heather was simply hungry for drama, was ready to bring opinions. It made Bette want to be honest, even in the company of people she'd only met once before. She didn't have to perform misery here, or feign nonchalance either, if it wasn't what she was feeling. And so:

"Honestly, and it's nothing to do with tonight. This has been great. But yeah, pretty miserable."

No one reached out to take her hand or pat her on the shoulder, just nodded at the truth of what she had said. Bette loved them.

"It just hits me at weird moments," she said.

"Ruth hasn't said anything, except that you maybe needed a bit of a cheer-up crew," Jody said, biting into their kebab and smearing sauce on their chin. "Which isn't a nudge for information. Just didn't want you to think we've all been gossiping about you at home."

"Oh," Bette said in surprise. "I just assumed. But then, I'm a terrible gossip. I would have been telling the story if the situation was reversed."

"It's true," Ash interjected, mouth full of cabbage.

"Oh, I think we all are. Normally," Ruth said. "But it just didn't—it wasn't my story to tell."

"My girlfriend," Bette started, and then corrected herself. "My ex-girlfriend has a new girlfriend." She looked to Jody, the only one she hadn't clarified the situation with. "We were on a break, but—"

"Oh no, sorry. We obviously know that bit, about the shagging around," Jody interrupted. "Like, Ruth's not a gossip, but we have definitely discussed the odyssey. Your odyssey. A bit— well, a lot."

Ruth's head dropped dramatically into her hands as Heather and Ash laughed.

"Okay, well, that's fair enough," Bette conceded. "So the update is that she has met someone else. And didn't tell me about it. And in three weeks I have to go to our friends' wedding and they're going to be there together. And I could just not go, I guess. But I made a big show of being fine about it to one of the brides. And also, I don't want her to win."

"Sounds like you need a girlfriend for this wedding," Heather said, head cocked to the side and voice thoughtful.

"Or she could just go on her own and be charming and brilliant and it will be fine," Ruth said, firmly.

"No, I'm with Heather," Ash said. "Fuck, Bette, you need to *win* here. And showing up with some gorgeous woman on your arm is the way to do it. It's bullshit and privileges couples and you shouldn't ever need someone. But . . . maybe here you do."

"Sure, well, I'll just get over Mei and quickly fall in love. You know, with one of the many lesbians in Bristol who are angling for a shot at an emotionally fucked-up complete mess of a woman."

"Exactly," Jody said. "That's a great plan."

CHAPTER TWENTY

SUNDAY, 09 OCTOBER

...

Limbo

Bette thought about it. About how much easier weddings were when you had someone to split the cost of the hotel room with. When you had someone to travel with and chase canapés with and mock the best man's Beat poetry speech with. Quite apart from the emotional aspects, the heartbreak, the devastation, the inability to do literally anything else, Mei dating someone else had put a real logistical spanner in the works. They were bound to run into each other on the same train and Bette's last-minute hotel room was now significantly shabbier than the one she and Mei had originally reserved.

And she couldn't quite believe that Mei hadn't been in touch. There had been no messages, no calls. They hadn't spoken since the night of the hospital. Erin must have confessed to her that she'd spilled the beans, because the last time Bette and Mei had spoken about the wedding they were traveling together, they were staying together, they were attending together. Mei hadn't seemed the sort of person to just vanish. But without so much as a conversation, everything had changed. It helped, in a way, in terms of making Bette furious. It was harder to be quite so desperately in love when Bette was so disgusted by what Mei had done. She couldn't pine, couldn't fathom wanting to spend any more time with someone who could do this.

Mei should have had to have the difficult conversation. Should have had to *do* the breaking up. Instead, Mei had allowed a break to slide into a breakup without any effort or communication on her part whatsoever.

One night in front of *Grey's,* so angry that her hands were trembling, Bette had passed her phone to Ash. She had spent days opening and closing their thread on WhatsApp, hovering over the call icon, drafting messages and opening lines in her head. Ash didn't hesitate in deleting Mei's number, in archiving their conversation, in blocking her on Instagram.

BETTE HAD HAD a string of fine days in a row. Days when she had slept seven hours, and then got out of bed in the morning in an okay mood. At work that day she had happened across Mei's name on the calendar and didn't have to take a little walk away from her desk. There'd been days when she thought about it, sure, but didn't feel overwhelmed by it. But now it was late, Ash was asleep, and Bette was hopelessly far from being so herself. Her phone was on mute across the room, because that's what the sleep health website had told her to do. Giving in, desperate for something to distract her, she got up and swiped across the screen.

> **Ruth:** Taking a shot you're awake.
>
> **Ruth:** Nothing specific it's just you mentioned you still weren't sleeping that well.

> **Ruth:** And I'm awake and bored and so just thought I'd text.
>
> **Ruth:** But you're probably asleep! So no worries!
>
> **Ruth:** You don't need to reply to this in the morning.

There was unfamiliar anxiety bleeding through Ruth's texts. It was clear that this was less checking in and more Ruth needing something from her.

> **Bette:** I'm awake
>
> **Bette:** so awake
>
> **Bette:** if I had to drive straight through to Scotland I could do it
>
> **Bette:** I'm that awake
>
> **Ruth:** I'm so awake that I've given up on sleep entirely. I'm in the front room. I've got a book. A dull book, and even that's not putting me to sleep.
>
> **Bette:** do you want to chat?
>
> **Bette:** I kind of hate talking on the phone
>
> **Bette:** but I think I'd rather that than the glare of the screen

Her phone rang in her hand.

"I'm so honored that you deigned to speak to me. That my voice is the lesser of two phone-related evils."

"Just barely, but you're welcome," Bette replied. She put the phone on speaker and placed it on the pillow beside her. "So what's keeping you up?"

"Oh nothing in particular. How are you?"

"Yeah, no, we're not doing me tonight. I'm fine. Let's do you. What's keeping you up?" she repeated, with slightly more force this time.

There was silence on the end of the line and Bette thought for a moment that Ruth might deflect again, might avoid the conversation entirely.

"It's the PhD," she replied, her tone already apologetic. "It's so boring."

"Yeah?" Bette said. It felt useful, good, warmed her to be able to be an ear for Ruth. Since they had met she'd been the one in crisis. But Ruth had texted her. Not Heather. Not Jody. Not Gabe. Ruth had come to her for help. She tried not to bask in the glow of being that person, of Ruth knowing she could be helpful as well as a bit of a mess.

"Yeah," she said, and then exhaled audibly. "I just don't have enough time for everything I have to do. The funding is so shit, and I have to take on so many tutorials just to keep my head above water, and the last thing on my list is always my research."

"God, that's so hard," Bette replied.

"It is. I had a meeting with my supervisor today. She basically said she thought I'd be much further along. I don't know how I possibly could be. Now that term has started again I have constant classes. But she's right," Ruth said, her voice speeding up, tangible panic creeping into the edges of it. "I should have made more use of the summer. I've got to get everything done in the next six months. I should be finalizing things and I'm not. It just feels impossible. I can't . . . I can't . . ."

"Hey, it's okay," Bette interrupted, working to keep her voice as soothing as possible. "I mean, not that I have any idea what you're going through, but I do know that you don't have to have all the answers now. You're not going to fix everything at eleven-thirty on a Monday."

"No, but maybe if I sit here and let myself freak out I'll just decide to quit instead and then I won't have to worry about it at all," Ruth said, her voice still pitched high, her breaths coming too fast. "I can just find something else to do, something that doesn't stop me sleeping and doesn't make me feel physically sick. I—"

"Breathe, Ruth," Bette said, cringing at how patronizing it sounded. She thought of what helped her when she got worked up: Adriene, the YouTube yoga lady, and her breathing. "Breathe really really slowly. In for four, out for five. Deep as you can."

Ruth did. Her breaths were shaky at first but soon evened out, steadier and steadier as Bette breathed with her. The relief Bette felt was tangible.

"Thanks," Ruth said, eventually. "Sorry."

"Stop," Bette said. "It's really fine. It's more than fine. You're okay."

"Yeah. Yeah, I am."

"Would it help to talk stuff through? Do you want to tell me about your research? Tell me all the translated novels from the twentieth century that are going to change my big gay life?"

"I can't believe you remember what my research is. We haven't talked about it since . . ."

"Since the first date. The date," Bette corrected.

"Yeah," Ruth said, her voice soft and intimate. "Thanks for remembering. But maybe—I'm not—can we talk about something else? I'm not trying to deflect, I think it just might help to talk about something else for a bit."

"Okay, should I outline my PhD for you?" Bette replied. "It's actually really clever; I've been working on it for ages."

"Absolutely. I can't think of anything I'd love more."

"Okay," Bette said, turning over onto her side, looking at the phone on her pillow. She imagined Ruth there instead and felt her stomach flip. "It's called You're My Person, colon, an examination of platonic love and female friendship on screen, and it's foregrounded against the rise of young women marrying later and living alone around the turn of the millennium. It utilizes, as its key text, the cultural significance of the relationship between Meredith Grey and Cristina Yang on *Grey's Anatomy*, with supporting documentation that includes that season four *Sex and the City* episode where Charlotte says the girls can all be each other's soulmates. I have a whole section, called crying laughing face crying laughing face celebration face, addressing the fact that Sandra Oh and Kim Cattrall both left their shows, and had to remain really important soulmate friends via sort-of in-character texts and one-sided phone conversations at important narrative moments."

There was a long pause, and then: "I would very much like to read this thesis," Ruth said.

"Well, settle in," Bette said. "I have thought about this . . . a lot."

Bette sent her feet to the bottom of her bed in search of a cool patch and launched into it.

CHAPTER TWENTY-ONE

WEDNESDAY, 19 OCTOBER

···

15 days post-revelation

The thing about making your murky way through a devastating breakup was that it did rather fuck up your ability to do or think about literally anything else. Like having food in the house.

And so, when Ash suggested meeting at the big Sainsbury's after work, Bette jumped at the idea. They had eaten egg fried rice three nights in a row. It was time.

It made sense that Ash was in charge when they shopped together; Bette had a tendency to commit to a basket she regretted, hauling around the supermarket without a plan. They were halfway down the dairy aisle before Bette realized that Ash's motivations in going together weren't entirely about having a lackey to do the fetching.

"You seem okay today," she observed.

Bette snorted. "As opposed to?"

"As opposed to the absolute steaming pile of misery you've been for weeks now."

"Well, yeah," Bette conceded. "I do feel a bit better."

"Anything changed? Or are you just gradually feeling like you're on the mend?"

"I don't know. I mean, I've been thinking about it a lot. I've still not quite pinpointed where it went wrong. And I know she messed up, obviously. But in the beginning, all Mei was trying to do was to give me this opportunity to make up for lost time. Have the wild gay adolescence I missed out on."

"Making up for the straight years?" Ash said, and though she kept hold of the trolley, Bette could hear the inverted commas around the word.

"Yeah. Like, it wasn't a bad thing for her to do. I really do get it. I just didn't know then how to articulate to her why it felt wrong. Hold on . . ." Bette dashed down an aisle and returned with an armful of ramen noodle packets, looking at Ash as if daring her to challenge it. "I don't even know if this is going to come out right. I still haven't quite worked this out myself. Okay. So, on the gay adolescence thing, I'm not a teenager. Right?"

"Sure," Ash agreed, sounding unconvinced.

"I don't feel like one, at all. I'm still the same person I was before I came out. I still want kids, and someone to be really domestic with. I want someone who's going to be my person, the one I call if something horrible happens at two a.m." It was coming out wrong, Bette worried. Her "in case of emergencies" contact for years now was standing right beside her. But it was complicated. Ash had Tim. "I know I have you and I know that couples aren't the be all and end all. I know that compulsory heteronormativity is a scourge on all of us. But I *want* it. That didn't change when I figured out who I'm attracted to."

"That makes sense," Ash said, a little hesitatingly.

"Yeah? I think maybe I can be mourning that time I lost, all those years I could have spent having fun and figuring out what I wanted, without wanting to make up for it." Bette waited for Ash to respond, to agree and marvel at this frankly genius realization, but she seemed determined not to make eye contact. Bette forged on. "Anyway, for the sake of that, for the sake of being free to sleep around for a bit, I lost Mei. I let her tell me what I needed, let her make that decision for me. And I sacrificed the life I wanted for one I might have wanted ten years ago, or one she thought I *should* have wanted. I'm mad I can't have both things. Or I'm mad I didn't get to have both. But if I'd known I had to choose, the choice was easy. I always wanted Mei. I just didn't want to let her down."

They'd reached the freezer section and went overboard on frozen dumplings, paratha, the ice cream that was on offer and bags of frozen vegetables that would be destined either for noodles or for Ash's regularly creaky football knee.

"Do you ever wonder whether you might be overthinking things a bit?" Ash asked, dropping a second bag of peas into the trolley.

"Constantly. I worry about that all the time. Obviously."

"I'm not saying it's simple, or that I understand every nuance here. I'm obviously never going to. Straight-person privilege, I guess. But I think that what's happened is that your girlfriend left you for someone else. You didn't sacrifice Mei. You got dumped. In a really shit way. You're allowed to be sad about that. But it doesn't have to be some big gay lost adolescence realization."

It was difficult to be so called out, and even more difficult to argue with the truth of it.

"I miss her. I mean, I miss us," Bette paused, wondering

whether it was still true. It was, or at least: "I miss when it was good."

"Yeah. You can be sad about that. That's allowed. But let's consider being sad about one thing at a time, maybe. We can mourn your lost slutty teen years next month."

"Well, to be fair, I've kind of done it now. Maybe it doesn't need to be mourned."

"Well, we can mourn it drawing to a close. Or we can mourn the version of you who might have been good at it. Although, let's face it. It never really was you."

"Hey!"

"Oh come on. You don't do casual. You fall in love straight away. I mean, look at us. Intense from day one."

Bette was silent as she leaned on the trolley, considering.

"I guess you're . . . not entirely wrong."

"Of course I'm not. Speaking of—well—all of this, have you worked out what you want to do about Erin's? Do you want to take someone to the wedding with you?"

It had been ten days since the bowling. Ten days during which Bette carefully hadn't mentioned it.

"Are you offering?"

"Of course I am. I'll come if you want me to come. I'll call in sick to school. I'll be there beside you, and tell Mei that I've left Tim," she said, sounding so sincere that Bette couldn't even laugh at her. "But maybe think about who you actually want to take. Like, in an ideal world. Who you'd have the most fun with."

And then, like the knowledge had been there the whole time, she knew exactly whom she wanted to take: Who would make her laugh, who wouldn't let her dwell and mope. She thought back to Ruth on the other end of the phone earlier in the week, Ruth vulnerable and honest while she was battling a panic attack. She thought of Ruth at the bowling alley, making sure Bette was laughing before she laughed too. She thought of Ruth with the mussels, and on the sofa watching ice-dancing, and walking through the cemetery, and sitting at the bar drinking a martini and making friends with the bartender, and in the playsuit she'd worn on the first date. Their only date.

The right answer, the only answer, was Ruth. Gorgeous, sparky, fun Ruth. Bringing Ash wouldn't work. Mei wouldn't be jealous of Ash. Bringing Ruth said: *I've met someone new, and she's extraordinary.*

It had to be Ruth.

"SO. I'VE DECIDED that casual dating isn't really for me," Bette said, apropos of nothing, spreading the split yolk out over the crushed peas on her toast. She missed it when cafés were obsessed with avocados and hot sauce. Mashed peas were a crap substitute. "I'm just . . . not good at it. I've been thinking a lot about it and it's not me. I mean, it was fun. Sometimes. It was fun with Charlie. And Netta. Did I tell you about Netta?"

Ruth shook her head, catching the eye of one of the waiters and miming out a far too elaborate water jug and drinking glass tableau. The waiter approached their table in confusion, and Ruth looked up apologetically.

"Sorry," she said. "If we could get some water? That'd be great."

He smiled the smile of someone halfway through a brunch shift, someone bored with hungover diners and splitting bills into awkward ratios and useless attempts at mime. There was silence between them for a moment after he walked away, a silence long enough to make Bette question Ruth's timing in asking for the water. To wonder whether she hadn't wanted to hear about Netta. But it would be even stranger to draw attention to it, not to continue the conversation she'd begun.

"Anyway, she was hot. The sex was great. Really—I don't know. I got into it. But I also spent the whole time reminding myself it was a one-off, that I needed to play it cool. I felt weird, knowing I wouldn't see her again. Knowing that wasn't the deal. It's not the sort of dating I'm used to."

"It felt like you were trying to be someone else?"

"Exactly. Sex sort of—well, it means a lot to me. I spent so long not really enjoying it, wondering what the fuss was about. It was always a performance. I could never lose myself in it, you know?"

"Sure," Ruth agreed.

"Anyway, I tried really hard with the dates to pretend that it was all meaningless, like I could be that person. A Charlie, or a Heather, maybe. But it's not meaningless, not to me. Not now that I've figured out the attraction bit."

Bette waited, expecting Ruth to agree again, expecting a nod, a visual encouragement to continue. It didn't come.

"I don't know if meaningless is fair," Ruth said instead. "You had this very specific plan where casual wasn't *allowed* to become anything else. But sex doesn't always have to be either life-changing or meaningless. It's not a binary. It can be something fun with someone you're attracted to. And I don't know. I'm not sure Heather would say that the sex she has is meaningless."

Bette flushed. "Meaningless was the wrong word. Sorry."

"I mean, it's possible that it really isn't your thing. But maybe it was the very specific . . ."

"The odyssey of it all?" Bette interjected.

"Well, yeah. Honestly, I couldn't imagine you going back to something you mostly seemed to be resenting, without someone waiting for you at the end of it."

Ruth was right. Casual or not, the next person she dated wouldn't be someone who fit inside the parameters she'd agreed with Mei, but someone who was right for her. Bette found herself nodding, and Ruth continued.

"I've had a fair bit of casual sex, mainly after my first boyfriend and I broke up. And I had a really good time." Bette raised her eyebrows, could feel the corners of her mouth turning up. Ruth smiled too, her cheeks pink. "He was the first person I ever fell in love with, and I was obsessed with him. With feeling like that. He was offered a graduate position in Singapore after we finished undergrad, and of course it made sense for him to take it. We tried long-distance for a year. And then, and trust me, I know how boring it sounds, we grew apart. I felt it running through my hands like water, spent so much time furiously trying to stop it draining away. But he froze on Skype one day and when his video kicked back in he was halfway through ending things. For a while after him I didn't want a future with anyone else. I couldn't see it. I wanted to put less pressure on meeting people for a bit."

Bette thought of the future she'd imagined with Mei, of the family she had started to visualize, and thought of how devastating it might be, how exhausting, to do that over and over again. To put that much pressure on everyone she slept with.

"Yeah. That makes sense."

"It *was* fun, too. I met some great people. Just, no one I fell for." Ruth sounded wistful, fiddling absent-mindedly with her hands as she spoke, and Bette realized that this was the most she'd ever delved into her romantic life. Short of knowing that Ruth was looking for something serious, that she had been taking things slowly with Gabe, Bette didn't know anything else about her history. It had felt like territory Ruth didn't want to explore. But there was an opening here. And Bette couldn't resist.

"Have you been in love since?"

"Oof. Okay. I—yeah—actually, you know what? That's not a question for here." Bette was about to apologize, about to walk it back. But Ruth made eye contact with their waiter again. "Let's go sit on the wharf instead."

Bette nodded. It wasn't a brush-off. It was a change of location.

It was, she thought as they sat down, a great one. The midday sun was still present enough to cut through the October chill. When they arrived at the wharf, Bette shrugged off her jacket and sat down cross-legged on top of it. Ruth followed suit, her legs dangling over the side, and opened the tins of whisky and ginger they'd bought en route. She took what sounded to Bette like a deep, steadying breath.

"So. Being in love. Yeah. I have. It was . . . it was pretty recently. It ended earlier this year."

"Yeah?"

"Yeah," Ruth said, her voice tight. "She was a colleague. We were together three years. Nearly four. We met doing our master's. But she was seeing someone else too. For quite a while."

She paused and Bette bit her tongue, longing to interject. "For the whole time."

It didn't sound like Ruth, the story, the telling of it. There was none of her usual warmth, no segues, no self-deprecation. Her tone was that of a coroner in a TV drama, laying out the facts for the visiting detective, cold and sterile as the slab.

"Ruth, I'm so sorry," the words utterly inadequate. Bette took a sip, to give her something to do with her mouth, and coughed as a rush of bubbles invaded her throat. "That's—I don't know how—I mean—fuck . . ."

"It was her ex. The other person she was seeing. I'm still not sure whether they ever stopped sleeping together. She was working in the States. The ex. So I was a placeholder, or something. I guess. Until she came back. They're together now, I think," Ruth was fiddling with her hands again, pinching at the skin between thumb and forefinger, hard enough that her skin turned white under the pressure. Bette wanted to reach over. Her own itched in her lap as she fought the impulse; she didn't want Ruth to feel embarrassed that she'd noticed.

"I mean, she's clearly a fucking idiot."

Ruth laughed, short, sharp and surprised. "She is," she confirmed. "But I was an idiot about her for a long time too. I should have trusted myself. I felt like something was wrong, especially in that final year. And I ignored it."

"The old sunk-cost fallacy?" Bette said, thinking back to a half-remembered lecture. "You'd invested too much to leave?"

"It wasn't even that considered. It was just . . . denial. I couldn't believe it of her. I couldn't believe how lucky I was when I met her. If I'd listed out everything I thought I wanted, she would have ticked every box. Clever. Compassionate. Cared about the same stuff I do. Made me laugh, even when I was in a horrible mood. She came to synagogue on Rosh Hashanah, with my parents. She was great with my cousins' kids. Everyone adored her. I adored her."

"But she was sleeping with her ex," Bette said, entirely unnecessarily, before she could question the impulse. There was something hot coursing through her, and she was suddenly desperate for Ruth to look at her instead, to list out *her* good qualities. She wanted to meet Ruth's family, wanted them to adore her. She wanted not to have to Google Rosh Hashanah, wanted to know already what the rituals were and why it was important. She hadn't gone back to church since her brother's wedding, since they had used one of the blessings during the service to pray for Bette. Specifically. But she could go to synagogue, if Ruth wanted. She liked that it was important to Ruth.

"She was sleeping with her ex," Ruth repeated quietly, her gaze squarely on Bette, her expression curious. It was as though she could see right through all Bette's layers. Straight to her heart.

Fuck.

Oh *fuck*.

She fancied Ruth. The thought didn't hit her like a train, or like a bolt of lightning. She just . . . saw it. Knew it. Realized consciously what the rest of her had known since the start. It wasn't news, not really. She had thought Ruth was gorgeous since the app. Certainly from the date. She'd lingered on the low cut of her playsuit, on the way the fabric sat on her thigh. She'd noticed her. She'd thought about kissing her. She'd wanted Ruth from the moment she'd approached the table.

And then they'd become friends. Of course she could be friends with someone she found attractive. Bette found a lot of people attractive. It wasn't particularly complicated. Ash was fit. Carmen was too. Erin was beautiful, in a pretty intimidating way, and it had never been an issue at work.

But there was a difference, she realized, between thinking someone was attractive and being attracted to them. A difference between appreciating someone's outfit and wanting to strip them out of it.

She didn't just like Ruth. She didn't just think she was clever and sparky and fun and beautiful and brilliant. She didn't just enjoy spending time with her. She *liked* Ruth. Ruth was gorgeous, and now Bette thought about it, the image did come to mind every now and then of running a hand through her hair, of how warm and soft she'd feel pressed up against Bette. She wanted to kiss her, to bite down on her collarbone, to suck on the tender skin beneath her ear. She wanted to see her make tea first thing in the morning, and take her to visit her nonna, and argue about where their children should go to school. All things considered, they weren't particularly platonic feelings to have for a friend.

And now she'd reacted in a weirdly jealous way, *and Ruth knew.* Maybe Ruth knew? She was looking at her as if she might know. But maybe she was looking at her oddly because Bette hadn't spoken in a while, because she'd said the weird thing about the still-unnamed ex-girlfriend. Because Bette was *still* staring at her. Without saying anything.

"Um—sorry," Bette said, not knowing how else to address it. "That was a really weird thing to say. I was just—I hate that she hurt you. I'm really sorry."

262 · KATE YOUNG

"It's okay," said Ruth, her voice soft and careful. "I'm okay now. Mostly. But it's why I need to be really careful with myself. Why I need to take things slow, and look for the right person this time. I jumped off a cliff with her, you know? Trusting that I'd land safely. It felt like I'd ended up so deep in something that it was hard to breathe, but I thought that at least she was there beside me. That we'd both jumped. But she hadn't. I was just down at the bottom of the cliff, drowning alone in the sea. I can't fall head over heels into something again. It's what I'm do-ing with Gabe at the moment: acclimatizing as I go. I'm consid-ering every step. He's nice. I like him. But I'm not losing my head over it. I'm nowhere near the cliff."

The twist in her stomach at the mention of Gabe's name felt familiar. It was so obvious now, what it was. What she'd felt as far back as the party, watching him on the step with Ruth. She felt stupid. And also so thrilled about the banal nothing that was the word "nice" that she wanted to jump up and scream in joy. "Wow. That's . . . vivid. You've really thought about this."

"Oh sure, like you've never spent an afternoon coming up with the perfect metaphor for a feeling."

"Yeah. I have. I really, really have."

The silence that settled between them felt heavy and loaded. This realization had changed . . . everything, really. And also nothing. Ruth was already seeing someone. She was looking for slow, for sensible. Not someone so recently out of a relationship, who'd fallen for her already, who'd been anything but sensible in the past few months.

The original plan for brunch had been to warm up to asking Ruth about the wedding. Could she still ask Ruth to go with her? Now that she'd realized how she felt? After she'd risked letting Ruth know it too? Maybe this was her chance to reassure her, to let Ruth know that what she was asking was clearly platonic. That she was confident that they were friends who could do something ridiculous without the threat of it changing anything.

She liked Ruth. But it hardly mattered. Even if they hadn't settled into a friendship she was determined to keep, even if it was what Ruth wanted, it was far too soon. Bette was still bruised by what had happened with Mei. She wasn't ready. Ruth deserved better than this version of her, a version who was still trying to figure things out. She could get a handle on the other feelings.

"So, I have a favor to ask," Bette said, digging her nails into her palms. "It's a big favor and you can absolutely say no. Honestly, I'm kind of expecting a no, so really it's not a problem."

"Bette, stop saying no for me and just ask."

Bette forced a laugh, peering over the edge, wondering whether orchestrating a fall into the water might be less embarrassing than what she was about to do. It was, she decided, on a par.

"Jody was right, I think. I need a date for this wedding. It's— I'm going to be all right. It's not that I want to get back together with her. But I can't go to the wedding alone. I just don't think I'm going to survive seeing Mei, and watching her dance with this new woman, while I'm standing in the corner alone. Very Robyn, and not in the good way. So I—"

"Bette, do you want me to go to the wedding with you?" Ruth interrupted.

"Yes."

"Okay," Ruth nodded.

"Okay?" It would have been so easy to smile. To say thank you. But they needed clarity. Ruth deserved clarity. Or . . . at least . . . a bit of clarity. "I mean, that's amazing, but I need to make sure we're completely on the same page. I want you to go to the wedding with me, but I also want you to go to the wedding *with* me. Like, I want it to appear, for all intents and purposes, like I've brought my hot new girlfriend. I want Mei to look at us together and think: *fuck*."

Ruth was silent for a long time, looking out at the buildings opposite, squinting against the glare. Bette gave her time to process. Ruth didn't make eye contact, didn't turn back toward Bette, and Bette focused on the strong line of her jaw, the curve of her throat, the wide neckline of her Breton top. It was incomprehensible to think back even half an hour, to a Ruth she wasn't entirely aware of fancying.

"You want me to act like your girlfriend? Tell everyone we're dating? Behave like we're a couple? The whole bit?"

Bette was suddenly convinced that Ruth was about to change her mind. That she'd just heard how ridiculous it all was. That it had been too much to ask for. She wished that Ruth didn't have her sunglasses on, that she wasn't facing the water, that it wasn't impossible to read her.

"Yes," Bette replied, hope tight in her chest.

"Okay."

"Okay?"

"Yeah. I mean, it's Edinburgh, right? I love Edinburgh," Ruth finally turned back to her, and offered Bette a small shrug. "And

I love a train. And . . . I don't know. I think we'll be able to pull it off. I mean—we could be convincing. With the whole . . . thing. We like each other, right? Shouldn't be that hard to extrapolate that. Exaggerate it, I mean."

Bette's heart was racing, her mind struggling to keep up.

"Do you think Gabe would mind?"

Ruth paused, and Bette let herself imagine that Ruth had only just remembered that she was seeing someone. Let herself imagine Ruth saying, *I don't care* or *this is more important. You're more important.*

"I mean, we're not in an exclusive relationship. And also, us being together in Edinburgh isn't real. He's going to think it's very very funny."

It wasn't real. Bette's heart dropped. She was suddenly aware of her body, of being scrunched up over her crossed legs, of the folds of her belly. She wanted to stretch out, wanted to look casual and easy, the way Ruth did, resting back on her hands, her legs dangling. It was the first time since their single aborted date that she had thought about how her body might look to Ruth, had wanted Ruth to think she was hot. She was so fucked. Bette looked at Ruth, so overwhelmed and so entirely enamored with her that she didn't quite know what to do.

It wasn't real, she reminded herself. It wasn't real.

"Okay then," she replied. "Okay."

CHAPTER TWENTY-TWO

FRIDAY, 28 OCTOBER

•••

24 days post-revelation

There were a scant five minutes before the train was due to depart, her phone kept buzzing in her pocket with texts she assumed were from Ruth, and Bette categorically did not have time to stop and check them. The road up to Temple Meads felt endless as she dodged her way through slow-moving tourists and uncertain drop-offs, her heart racing in her chest. She was going to make it. Almost certainly. Probably. So long as there wasn't a huge queue at the ticket barriers, or a group blocking her journey through the tunnel under the tracks, and so long as the little suitcase she was hauling behind her didn't break a wheel or burst open or break where the long metal bits connected from her hand to the case. Oh god, what if the long metal bits broke?

She ran through the tunnel, feeling as though she might vomit, wondering whether she would be able to keep running if she suddenly couldn't hold it back any more. She'd never run and vomited at the same time before. It might be interesting.

And then she was on the platform and up the step and

through the doors and on the train and it was moving forward
with her in it. She sat down in the bit between the carriages,
blocking everyone, gulping in stuffy, air-conditioned air. On her
phone, Ruth's gentle, polite, nudging messages hovered closer
and closer to panicked but never quite crossed over. Thankfully,
what the messages did include was a carriage and seat number;
Ruth had found them two together for the first leg of the journey. Bette took one more deep breath, tapped out a quick reply
confirming she was at least on the train, and made her way
down the narrow aisle, trying to avoid hitting her case against
the ankles that spilled into it as she did.

And finally, there was Ruth, her bag in the seat next to her,
clearly reserving it for Bette. She had a plastic M&S bag on the
tray table in front of her and was staring ahead, white headphones over her ears, her head nodding slightly with the movement of the train. It was the first time she'd seen her since
they'd hugged goodbye at the wharf, and Bette was tangibly
aware of having spent the week thinking about Ruth, about her
jaw and her collarbone, about her ability to laugh at Bette and at
herself, about her clear eyes and the silk of her thick hair, about
her asking for details of Carmen and Anton in Bette's kitchen,
about the line of her spine in the dress she'd worn to dinner.
And here she was.

And Ruth, of course, knew none of it. She jumped when
Bette picked up her case and flopped down next to her, and
then exhaled in apparent relief. She pushed off her headphones
and left them sitting round her neck, a tinny voice issuing faintly
from them.

"Oh thank *god*. Really thought you might have missed it."

"I'm the worst. I'm on time for everything. I've spent weeks of my life scrolling through my phone because I'm waiting for someone. But when it actually matters I'll sleep through an alarm or get stuck in an impossible traffic jam, or leave my bag on a bus."

"I woke up to the buzz of my phone once, thinking it was my alarm. It was actually the calendar reminder for my flight to Budapest, telling me it was time to board the plane."

"Ouch."

"Yep. Went from being a cheap, easy holiday to a really stressful, really expensive nightmare. The hot baths were nice though."

They settled back into their seats, and Bette caught sight of the ticket on Ruth's phone screen, open and ready for inspection. Bette had paid for it on her "only for emergencies" credit card, had forwarded it through, and had then felt sick about it all week. This close to the trip, it was almost eye-wateringly expensive for Ruth to journey up with her. It would have been far cheaper for her to fly. But it was part of the whole thing; it wasn't unrealistic to imagine Mei was on her train, probably with her new girlfriend. Traveling solo was not an option. And she wasn't about to ask Ruth to pay for her own ticket.

She planned to ignore the M&S bag for as long as possible, at least until they were past the Bristol stations. But, as soon as her heart rate returned to normal, inevitably, eventually: "Okay, so I didn't bring a packed lunch, and it appears you very much did."

"I thought this would get us to Birmingham at least. Then we can restock." Ruth looked sheepish for a moment. It was an intimate expression, one Bette hadn't seen before. There was an admission in it. "Whenever I go somewhere, I like feeling on holiday immediately. And I know it's eight a.m., so I should have bought pastries and coffee or something. But a train pastry says work trip to me. Crisps and a G&T at eight a.m. are a holiday."

It was a shame, really, to have already realized that she fancied Ruth. The better story began . . . *she pulled a bag of salt and vinegar crisps, a pot of ricotta-stuffed peppers and a can of gin from an M&S bag first thing in the morning and then I knew.* Except, of course, they'd never be telling the story. Because, clearly, she'd never be telling Ruth. She had to live with the fact of fancying her and be fine with it. It didn't help to watch Ruth pull open the bag of salt and vinegar crisps and offer her one. It didn't help to wonder whether Ruth knew they were her favorite or whether it was just a coincidence, and what that said about them, about how Ruth might feel and about how much it didn't matter because Ruth deserved someone so much better than her. Already *had* someone better. It just didn't make things easier, was all. It wasn't easy to fancy her friend, the one who was sucking salt from her fingers, her elbow nudging against Bette's on the Great Western Railway armrest.

"Salt and vinegar," said Bette, fishing, leaning into making her own life more difficult. "I love them. No better crisp."

"I thought so!" Ruth said, the sides of her eyes crinkling as she smiled. "They're what you brought to the party. Anyway, it seemed like a thing that the girl you're dating should get right. So. Well done me."

Oh great. She was perfect.

"Yep. Yeah. Well done you," she said. Her voice sounded odd to her ears, too high, too bright.

"On that, though," Ruth said as she pulled open a bag of prawn cocktail crisps and used one to scoop the cheese from a pepper. "It's Erin and Niamh, right? Tell me what I need to know. Tell me what your girlfriend would know."

Bette inched her elbow away, aware of being too close, of her heart jumping every time Ruth's skin brushed against hers. There was only so much she could handle. She nodded and launched into a potted history of Erin and Niamh, accepting as she did quite how comprehensively fucked she was.

SEVEN HOURS WAS a long time to be seated side by side. The train was long and trundling, and they chatted about nothing much. Eventually, Ruth pointed out that taking a book out wouldn't be rude. It might have made her worry, Bette thought, coming from someone else. But it was exactly what she wanted too.

Ruth had something called *My Year of Meats*, by another Ruth. Bette made a joke about it that sounded clever in her head and utterly stupid once she let it pass her lips. In her bag were two Jilly Coopers that she had pulled off her shelf before leaving. They had felt like a good idea at home, the exact sort of familiarity and comfort she was going to need in those first Mei-anticipating hours. It hadn't occurred to her to feel embarrassed when packing them, but once Ruth was beside her with something she'd never heard of, probably some challenging literary masterpiece, she second-guessed herself. But Ruth looked over and hissed out a *yes* of appreciation and then followed it with *Harriet's the best one*.

She hadn't always been this perfect, surely? This was Bette reading into things and being weird and obsessed. This was her falling for someone and instantly writing the whole perfect narrative in her head. But then she remembered Ash and her thousand smug glances. Ash had seen it, had long approved of this coming agony. Bette put *Harriet* on her lap, leaned her forehead against the jostling and jolting window and allowed the movement to send her off to sleep.

She woke somewhere before the Scottish border, along a stretch of sea that took her breath away. Ruth was writing in a large spiral notebook, the type Bette had had at school, filling the page with lines of untidy scrawl in green biro.

"'S a serial killer pen," Bette mumbled, brain still slightly behind her voice. As she spoke she realized how intimate it felt, for Ruth to hear the voice she had when she first woke up. Bette shook herself a little, willing her brain to catch up and join the conversation properly.

"It's actually an *I've never been without a black biro in my life and today I can only find this stupid conference pen in my handbag and I've been wanting to die for pages* pen," Ruth said, hand still moving across the page.

"Yeah, that's awful. It's not even a nice, easy-to-read green. Nightmare. What kind of disgusting company commissioned that?"

Ruth turned it over to read the name. "It's a thesaurus app, I think? Or something? Look, I don't know, but I didn't have another option and now it's making me question my whole career."

"It's not that bad."

"Serial killer, Bette. That was your first reaction. I have to read back over this at some point, and all I'm going to be thinking is: serial killer."

"Do you want my pen?" Bette asked, rummaging in her backpack. "It's black."

Ruth turned, not just her head but her whole body, knee bumping against Bette's. "I cannot believe you've been holding out on me."

"I was asleep."

"You've been awake for at least a minute now. You've watched me write full sentences."

Bette handed the pen over and they settled back into a comfortable silence, black slowly overtaking green on Ruth's paper. The words swam in front of Bette's eyes, so she turned away and looked out of the window again, pulling open the final bag of crisps.

By the time the train crossed over into Scotland, Bette was full of crisps, her mouth dry and salty, and full of nerves too. Somehow, in the midst of the feelings that had arrived in the last week, she'd not really considered what she planned to say to Mei. Bette had somehow managed to avoid her on the same trains, waiting on the same platforms, making all the same endless connections because it was cheaper. But they were basically in Edinburgh now. And even if they managed to avoid each other at the station, there were only a couple of hours until dinner.

She hadn't seen Mei since leaving her and her car behind at four in the morning. The drive home from Cheltenham had been even quieter than the one there. What had Mei been thinking, in that hour? Had she been agonizing over all she hadn't said? Had she tried to say it, in that moment before they'd reached her house? When Bette had stopped them from discussing it? Or was she relieved? Relieved to have got away with the lie, of begging a favor from Bette and knowing she'd get whatever she wanted?

She was going to be at dinner. And she was going to have to smile and be polite and be the bigger person. Because she sure as hell wasn't letting Mei win.

A hand on Bette's arm made her jump. Ruth was holding a bag of chocolate buttons in her direction.

"We've got ten minutes left, I think. Last little chance for a train snack?"

Bette took a pinch of buttons from the bag and put them in her mouth all at once, comforted by the way they melted, the chocolate blandly familiar on her tongue. She wanted a cup of tea. A cup of tea and a bath and six back-to-back episodes of *Grey's Anatomy* and a takeaway and all of it with Ruth still beside her.

But instead they began to gather up their things, readying their bags and watching people crowd the aisles, as if the seconds they might save by being the first off were worth the passive-aggressive crush of bodies.

Edinburgh Waverley was sprawling and huge, and she stepped onto the platform feeling suddenly overwhelmed. This wasn't a trip where she could disappear. She felt exposed, on display, like everyone would be able to see that Ruth wasn't actually hers, that Mei had broken her and rejected her, that she was unfanciable and unloved and . . .

A hand slipped gently into hers, warm and soft and safe. "Let's go check in before dinner, yeah?"

She nodded, squeezing Ruth's hand back before letting go. It was far too early to be taking advantage. She should save that for the wedding itself. There was so much advantage-taking ahead of them.

———

THERE WERE, much to Bette's relief, two beds. The woman on reception had been adamant about that, to the point where, if they 'had been a real couple, Bette would have been inspired to kick up a pretty significant stink. The hotel desk was oddly low—an office desk, rather than one the right sort of height for propping up on, a chin cupped elegantly in a hand. It made the reception area feel as if they'd been called to the headmistress's office, an unsettling sensation reinforced by the unmistakable air of prim assuredness coming from behind it.

"We'll pop you two in our twin room. It's the *Wind in the Willows* suite. Very popular. Girls' trip to Edinburgh is it?"

"Oh yes," Ruth replied, her voice drier than an unbuttered rice cake. "Just two gals being pals."

The woman stared, her lined forehead growing more creased by the second.

Upstairs, Bette's first impression of the room itself was of a crowded Oxfam surplus depot. She had never been to one before, wasn't even sure they existed. But if one did, it would be this: a graveyard of dusty, mismatched furniture, with not nearly enough space for anything to be functional. It was the esthetic opposite of a Premier Inn, uncomfortably personal and esoteric. The walls were covered in supremely weird paintings and prints of toads that contrasted horribly with the floral wallpaper. Bette turned to Ruth, who was shaking with laughter, her bag still hanging from her shoulder.

"The *Wind in the Willows* suite?" she said, gasping for breath. "I thought it might be a bit Tory. A bit Union Jacky. I was surprised! It's Edinburgh! But I was not prepared for . . . toads."

Bette flopped down on the bed closest to the door, leaving the nicer (nicer? the bar was impossibly low) bed under the window for Ruth.

"At the very least, I've now seen the ugliest room in all of Scotland. So if the rest of the weekend is a bust, we've had this."

"Well, *we'll always have the framed toads* can be our *we'll always have Paris*," Ruth said, her voice wistful. She sat down on her own bed and it sank in the middle, both sides of the mattress popping up to form a V around her.

"So, pub before dinner?" Bette asked, pushing herself up on her elbows.

"God, yes," Ruth replied. "The only way through this is whisky."

THEY WERE TWO rounds in before Bette could properly look Ruth in the eye. Once they had decided to leave the toad room in search of warmth and alcohol and sanity, Bette had retreated to the bathroom to change, leaving Ruth with space to maneuver. And then, before her brain could stop her, she walked back into the room without knocking, to find Ruth in a black bra and her jeans. Ruth didn't seem bothered and so Bette feigned easy nonchalance—it wasn't different from seeing someone in their swimming costume. It was just a bra. Not even a particularly revealing one. But it was longline, and low-cut, and Bette wanted to run her fingers under the band that hit Ruth at the top of her waist. Wanted to pull the strap off her shoulder and kiss the skin beneath it. It was not, in any way, a useful step in the journey toward assuring herself that Ruth was her platonic gal pal. It was one thing to know, objectively, that Ruth was hot.

It was quite another to be faced with continuing evidence of it, to have Ruth half dressed in front of her in the room they were sharing.

Thankfully, it didn't seem to have had an impact on Ruth at all. She was sitting in the pub, cheeks pink from the cold and the alcohol, recounting the story of the last wedding she had gone to. It was a huge one, near her parents in North London, and there was something in the story about a live chicken. It was a great anecdote, funny and unexpected; Ruth was a brilliant storyteller. Bette knew that she would be able to recall precisely none of it once the moment had passed, that she would be entirely incapable of reassembling any of the vague component parts into a cohesive whole. Her mind was too full already, too occupied with the exact line of Ruth's plunging black top and the shade of pink her lipstick left on her whisky glass.

"We should go," Bette realized, glancing at her watch. Her voice betrayed her, quavering slightly and destroying any suggestion that she was fine. "The dinner."

"Hey," Ruth said, laying a hand over Bette's on the sticky table between them. "You look great. You're charming and brilliant. You've got a cool girlfriend on your arm. You've won. You've unequivocally won."

Bette puffed out a breath. Of course Ruth would think it was about the dinner. It was. Sort of. And she couldn't know about the rest of it.

It was a hike to the restaurant. Everywhere in Edinburgh was a hike. By the time they were on the correct side of town, Bette was feeling significantly less put together, and Ruth was out of breath and flushed down her chest. As they reached the top of the steps behind the station, Ruth shrugged off her coat.

"I love this stupid thing," she said, tucking miles of fluffy leopard print fabric under her arm. "But it's the most synthetic coat in existence. The sweatiest I've ever owned."

"It looks warm, at least."

"Oh no, not at all. The wind goes right through it. It's worn away in big patches. But I'll be wearing it until it falls directly from my shoulders into landfill."

While they stood to catch their respective breaths, Bette pulled her phone out to check the address.

"Right, it's up here, I think," Bette pointed, and kept glancing down at the map until they were outside the restaurant, watching the distance between her and Mei narrow in real time. As she reached the door Bette took a deep, steadying breath.

"It's okay," Ruth said, and a hand squeezed her elbow.

"I know. I'm almost relieved now, I guess? Like, I just want it to have happened. I want to have seen her and survived and then get on with things. The anticipation has been the worst bit."

"You're brilliant. You can do this. I'll be right beside you."

They weren't too late arriving, but the sound as soon as they entered the restaurant made it clear that most of the rest of the group were already there.

"Bette!" Erin called, running over in a blur of teal and leather and hugging her tightly. "You're here! You're here! And you must be Ruth?"

"Thank you so much for making space for me," Ruth said, holding her hand out to be shaken.

"Oh, don't even mention it," Erin said, brushing her hand aside and pulling her in for a hug too. Erin been a complete hero when Bette had floated the idea of a plus-one who wasn't Mei, not poking for details, accepting the "new girlfriend" as though she had no idea what Bette's month had been like. "We assumed there would be dropouts, and we'd already paid for everyone's meal. It was easy. You're doing us a favor, honestly."

The conversation was background noise to Bette, who was looking again at a table that had only two unclaimed seats and a distinct lack of dreaded ex-girlfriends.

"Shit, did I not warn you?" Erin said, looking intently at Bette. "Mei's not here tonight. Family something. I meant to text you. Sorry, sorry. It's been a real day."

Bette felt Ruth reach down and squeeze her hand again, and forced a smile onto her face. It would be fine. One more evening of anticipation. And, really, it was impossible not to find herself distracted by the hand in hers, by the feeling of Ruth's thumb running back and forth over her fingers.

CHAPTER TWENTY-THREE

SATURDAY, 29 OCTOBER, JUST

•••

25 days post-revelation

Bette's glass had been topped up all evening; the hum of alcohol was running along every one of her veins. They'd eaten small plates of nice things, none of which she could now remember. She'd been between Niamh's sister Louise and a friend of Erin's from university—Maggie or Maddy or something. It was impossible to ask her to repeat it a third time. They had all told stories about Erin and Niamh; Bette had recounted the one about Niamh doing karaoke at the work Christmas party, about Erin shouting *I love you* (for what turned out to be the first time) from the crowd, about Niamh abandoning Blondie mid-verse in order to snog Erin silly. Bette had caught Ruth's eye more than once while telling it and felt her stomach clench.

And now they were in a bar draped with Pride flags, the music too loud for anyone to be talking. They were still loosely in a group but there was only one person who had all Bette's attention. Ruth was a whole-body singer, Bette had realized as they all shouted together on the dance floor. Every part of her joined in, her hands in the air, her head thrown back, her sweaty fringe plastered to her forehead. She was flushed again, the drinks bringing out a delicious pink that ran down her throat and chest, disappearing into the deep V of her top. Bette wanted to lick her, to run her teeth along her collarbone, to tug an earlobe into her mouth. She wanted to kiss her, up against the wall of the bar.

She definitely couldn't do that. She was an enormous perv. She should probably go to the bar. Order a pint of water. Or outside. She could go outside. Fresh air would be good.

But a distinctive guitar twang through the speakers caused everyone around them to scream in delight, so loud that Michelle Branch's first lines were almost drowned out. Ruth practically squealed.

"God, I *love* this song," she yelled, squeezing Bette's hands and pulling her closer as the drum kicked in and the crowd jumped and sang and played a hundred air guitars. The last time Bette had danced to "Everywhere" had probably been in college, ironic and too cool for it, laughing self-consciously and rolling her eyes the whole time. Now, surrounded by a sweaty mess of drunken queers, there was no scrap of equivocation, only the deep joy of realizing that she meant the words she was shouting. She got it. Ruth was everywhere. Was everything. The thrill of it filled her up.

The song was quieter, suddenly, and Ruth pulled her closer still, one hand around her waist. She'd been touching Bette so often since they'd arrived in the bar that Bette felt drunk on it, heady and delicate and almost able to convince herself that Ruth wanted her too. It felt inescapable, now, the tequila coursing through her, the lyrics intimate and low, Ruth's face right next to hers as she sang with drunken sincerity. Ruth let out a breath, close enough to Bette's ear that she could feel it down her spine. It was an absolutely terrible idea, Bette thought. Truly impossible to recover from. Exactly what Ruth had said she didn't want. Except, maybe Ruth did want. Maybe it wasn't such a terrible idea to just . . . check.

And really, the drink and the heat and the song and Ruth's breath and her warm hand on Bette's waist were louder than every other objection Bette's brain offered. The objections had long been half arsed anyway.

She turned her head, just slightly, lips brushing lightly across Ruth's cheek. There was plausible deniability, still. An excusable level of contact. She felt Ruth take a shaky breath in. Bette waited, and then Ruth turned her head too. Everyone around them was still jostling and shouting as Bette moved her hand to the base of Ruth's throat, as she watched her eyes flutter closed, as she pressed their lips together. Ruth tasted of tequila and of lime and of sweat. Her mouth was tender and open and warm and it was probably a huge mistake to keep kissing her. But her hand settled under Ruth's jaw, fingers brushing along the shell of her ear, palm angling Ruth exactly where she wanted her.

They definitely shouldn't be kissing like this, regardless, here on the dance floor. But then Ruth's hand traveled down her spine to the small of her back and it was impossible to care about anything that wasn't Ruth's hand, or Ruth's tongue making its way past her lips, or Ruth pulling her even closer, or the noise Ruth was making low in her throat.

"Ruth. I want you. So badly," Bette said, abandoning everything but hopeful honesty, and pulling back to speak into Ruth's ear.

She felt Ruth let out a breath that was almost a laugh and

then nod, grasping her back more firmly, pressing their bodies together. "Yes. Okay, yes. Let's get out of here," she said, reaching down to clasp Bette's hand in hers and turning to pull her out of the throng.

They tried hailing a cab for a couple of minutes outside the club, and then abandoned the plan in favor of walking. It felt faster, in the moment. It almost certainly wasn't. Their speed wasn't aided by the fact that they kept turning toward each other to kiss again and again. Ruth's hands were everywhere, hot on Bette's hip, tracing the inside of her wrist. But they kept moving forward, determined to reach a bed of some sort, stumbling over each other's feet, missing each other's mouths, ending up on streets Bette had never seen before.

She wanted Ruth, wanted to press her down into the sheets of the twin bed. She wanted to taste her, to feel her shake, to run her fingers along every part of her. She couldn't understand how they'd never done this before. Nothing had ever felt better than Ruth's mouth, than Ruth's breath tickling her ear, than Ruth's hand on her skin.

By the time they reached the hotel, Bette had to actively remind herself that they were still in public. The same woman was still behind the reception desk, her eyebrows knitted together disapprovingly. They stumbled up the stairs, Ruth flushed and laughing and holding tightly onto Bette's hand.

Once down the hall and outside their room, Bette crowded in along Ruth's back as she struggled clumsily with the key in the lock. Ruth's hand shook slightly until Bette's covered it, helped her pull the key back and jiggle it until it turned right.

The lock clicked and Bette smiled, her lips pressed against Ruth's neck.

"Come on, then," Ruth said, grasping the handle and pushing the door open. They were the first words either of them had spoken since they'd walked back into the hotel, and the thrill of anticipation that had been running through Bette amplified. The words were a cup of Ash's fancy weekend coffee: clarifying, grounding. Utterly delicious.

Bette swallowed and followed Ruth in, grateful to finally be able to watch her the way she wanted. To see her hair sway to reveal the vertebrae at the top of her spine, to feel the memory of her hands twisted in Ruth's belt loops, still tasting Ruth on her lips and tongue.

Ruth's huge coat had trailed from her hand since they had reached the top of the stairs, and she laid it down across the chair by the window before bending over to unlace her boots. The momentum they had had in the street, in the foyer, everything that had threatened to boil over in the club, had reduced to a simmer now that there was a door between them and the rest of the world. Now that they could take their time. Bette worried, for a brief moment, that the simmering tension might have cooled down completely, that Ruth might have decided against it. That there was a line coming about compromising their friendship. But Ruth looked up, her eyes finding Bette's. There was want written in a thousand languages across her face.

Quite suddenly, Bette realized that she might die if she didn't kiss Ruth again. Right now, actually.

Right.

Now.

Ruth was already moving too, and when they met in the middle of the room they did so with their mouths already open, their hands already rising to bury into hair, to touch cheeks and jaws, to pull and grasp and seek out new skin. Their teeth clacked, and Bette laughed into Ruth's mouth.

There was something about it, about the awkwardness and brief pain of it, about the stark reality of it, that jolted through Bette.

"Fuck. Gabe," she said, before she could stop herself.

Ruth, already flushed, was suddenly even pinker, looking down at the threadbare carpet.

"It doesn't . . . it's not a problem. Don't—let's just . . ."

She trailed off without finishing any of the sentences and looked at Bette, her eyes clear.

"Okay," Bette said, because it felt very definitively like Ruth didn't want to talk about it any more. And it wasn't like Bette really wanted to either.

And so she kissed her again.

It was nothing like the kiss in the club. There must have been an awareness of propriety, of going too far, of an unwelcome audience, that she hadn't quite registered. Because their kisses in the club felt suddenly restrained in comparison. Ruth kissed exactly as Bette had expected, when she'd allowed herself to think about it: invitingly, warmly, teasingly, a smile evident and turning her lips up, even as she devoted her whole attention to Bette's mouth. Too late, Bette realized that Ruth had gently been guiding her backward toward the bed, and stumbled back to sit down on it, utterly without grace. It didn't seem to bother Ruth at all. She moved closer to stand between Bette's legs, at least a foot taller now, her fingertips grazing Bette's jaw and collarbone.

"Bette," she said, considering, almost to herself.

"Yes?" Bette replied, her hands slipping from Ruth's waist down onto her hips and then round to trace the pockets of her jeans.

"What do you want?" Ruth asked, her fingertips trailing lower and lower, from collarbone to cleavage, across the tender skin of her breasts, tantalizingly close to Bette's nipples.

It was an impossible question, Bette thought. But not for the reason it had been when Evie had asked it. Not like it had been at the start with Netta. Not because she didn't know. The truth was that she wanted everything. There were endless plans in her head. She wanted to make sure that Ruth never forgot this. And she wanted Ruth to help her lose control, so she could let go of all the plans, to get out of her head. There was a glistening spark of hope in her that this might change things. But she couldn't shake the prickling, uncomfortable fear too that they'd wake up in the morning and one or other of them would blame it on tequila, on Edinburgh, on the weird wedding magic. And so, if that was going to be the outcome, then she wanted all of Ruth now, regardless of the consequences. She wanted to be reckless.

"I want to taste you," she said, and felt Ruth shiver.

"Yeah?" Her voice was strangled, delicate, barely audible.

"Oh god, yeah," Bette replied, pulling Ruth closer toward her, leaning her forehead against the swell of Ruth's belly beneath her breasts. She was so soft. But the hand that grasped Bette's hair, pulling her head backward, positioning her for a kiss, was firm. Strong. So sure and certain. It made her tense and throb in anticipation, and she groaned into Ruth's mouth.

Bette inched backward, pulling at Ruth's thighs as she did, encouraging Ruth to straddle her. They kissed again and again, mouths hot and lush, Ruth biting at her top lip and sucking on the bottom one. Their bodies moved closer together, Bette's hands still behind Ruth's knees, pulling her legs tight around her own hips. Ruth's weight was grounding and thrilling. She felt caught, entirely hemmed in by Ruth around her and above her. She felt overwhelmed by want. Her desire to take things slow, to draw everything out, warred with her want to be naked against each other as soon as possible.

Ruth's hands were everywhere; at the nape of Bette's neck, fisted into her hair, trailing down her back, flirting along the neckline of her top, her fingertips finally slipping into Bette's bra. Bette's hands moved from behind Ruth's knees, up her legs and then down to the seams that ran along the insides of her thighs, pressing her thumbs into the fabric, teasing and gentle. Ruth gasped and groaned, breaking the kiss to drop her forehead against Bette's shoulder.

"Please," she panted. "Please, please fuck me."

Bette could do that. She grasped Ruth with both hands, lifted her out of her lap and, before she could question the impulse, give in to the fear of messing it up, flipped her over onto her back. Ruth burst out laughing as her back hit the bed.

"What?" Bette said, breathless and feeling herself blush.

"Where did that *come* from?" Ruth asked.

"I don't know," Bette admitted, the corners of her mouth

turning up too. "I've—I've never done it before. I'm actually
staggered it worked. I half thought one of us might end up on
the floor. Or with an elbow to the face."

She lay down beside Ruth, a hand possessively across her
stomach, and hauled her closer by her waist.

"Well, the night is young," Ruth said, her voice like a silver-
screen goddess, an indeterminate mid-Atlantic accent making
the words seem both cheesy and silly and somehow oddly pro-
found. The night *was* young, Bette thought. They had all the
time in the world.

"There's still time to elbow you in the face. Later. But I want
to—first I want . . ." Bette replied, her smile turning into a laugh
too. She leaned down and then they were laughing and kissing
again, mouths wide and clumsy. The hand that had found its
way to the curve of Ruth's waist started moving down, tracing
along the waistband of her jeans. Ruth inhaled sharply, everything suddenly more weighted, more filled with intention. Bette
felt Ruth nod in response to the question that lay within the
gesture, and she popped open the button and pulled the zip
down. Ruth hummed in approval, and Bette moved to suck on
her neck as she pushed her hand down into Ruth's knickers,
seeking heat, seeking slick softness. Ruth grasped at Bette's
arm, her fingers pressing into her bicep as Bette found where
she was wet. She touched her for quiet minutes, so gently and
delicately that Ruth hummed and sighed in frustration against
Bette's cheek, her hips angled to try and draw Bette into her.
But it was wrong, the jeans too tight to touch her properly. And
so with a kiss to Ruth's shoulder, her neck, her nose, her mouth,
Bette made her way down the bed.

Ruth sat up as she did, pulling the black top over her head, revealing the bra Bette had seen earlier in the evening. She looked, Bette realized, apprehensive. Nervous. As if this, the taking their clothes off bit, might be a dealbreaker, the moment when Bette decided she wasn't actually that interested. It was incomprehensible.

"I've been wanting you like this," Bette said, surging back up the bed to kiss her mouth, bending down to press her lips to the top of each breast. "Thinking about this all day. For—for way longer than today."

She pulled Ruth's jeans down, along with her socks. There was an odd moment of awareness, of realizing she was still completely dressed as she stripped Ruth beneath her. But they could focus on her later. She settled herself between Ruth's legs, pushing them wider to give herself the room she needed. The thighs on either side of her were pale, the skin delicate and soft, and she sucked kisses onto them, higher and higher as Ruth's breaths became more ragged, her hips rocking up in pursuit of Bette's attention.

Bette looked up and found Ruth propped up on her elbows, looking back at her, her hair hanging down into her eyes. She tucked her fingertips beneath the seam of Ruth's knickers that sat at the very top of her thighs. Ruth gasped and nodded, muttering something that sounded like *please, please, please, please*. And so Bette ran her fingers beneath the fabric, the angle right this time. Ruth groaned.

"I want to go down on you," Bette said again, reveling in knowing and articulating exactly what she wanted, her cheek pressed against Ruth's thigh. "Is that okay?"

"How are you *still* asking?"

Bette laughed and then knelt up and dragged Ruth's knickers down her thighs, down her calves, off her feet, before settling back down between Ruth's legs. She ran a gentle thumb where she was swollen and slick and soft. Ruth groaned again, flinging an arm up and over her face. Bette pressed with more surety, holding her open, and dragged her tongue over her. She tasted of sweat and heady sweetness. Bette took her time, and when she had added to how wet she was, when she could feel her tongue gliding effortlessly over the delicate skin, she began to suck.

"Bette, fuck—oh—" Ruth breathed, a hand traveling down to grasp the back of her hair, as if there was danger of her stopping, of her ever wanting to be anywhere else.

She kicked the blankets off the bed entirely, until the sheets were all that was left beneath them. They were so starched and stiff, and Bette could feel them along her forearms. It should have been uncomfortable. It should have been too cold; November was days away. But all she could feel was the warmth of Ruth, was Ruth's body making space for her. She took her time, her lips soft, kissing and licking and sucking Ruth over and over, aware of her hips pressing up in search of more.

Ruth's hips were right; it still wasn't enough. Bette wanted to be closer. She pulled Ruth's leg tightly over her shoulder, encouraging her to dig her foot in. Ruth took the hint, pressing her heel into Bette's vertebrae as Bette moved a hand under her, digging her fingers into the soft flesh of her arse. Her tongue was working over Ruth, finding the places that made her keen and squirm, learning a rhythm that sent her voice higher, that made her lose control of her hips and breath. Ruth's hand was firmer in Bette's hair, her heel pressing down harder. She worked her way further down and pressed a firm tongue inside her. Ruth's hips jerked and she shouted out.

"Bette—can you—" There was nothing more, but Bette took a guess, closed her mouth back over her and sucked. She ran her tongue back and forth as she felt Ruth tense and then shake beneath her, crying out as the hand in Bette's hair tightened and pulled. Bette kept her tongue gentle but relentless, not letting up, until the hand in her hair tugged her backward, Ruth gasping and whispering, "Stop, stop, I can't—too much—"

The leg that had been over her shoulder fell to the side and Bette knelt on the bed, stroking gently at Ruth's thighs, trying to calm her trembling. Her breathing was labored, her skin covered in goose bumps, her eyes squeezed tight. Instead of soothing, Bette's touch seemed only to intensify things, and Ruth shook her head back and forth beneath her arm, flushed all the way down her chest to her belly.

"No, Bette. I can't. You can't," she said, sounding strained and desperate.

"Unless, I mean—I definitely could? If you want?" Bette said, sweeping her hand higher, her fingers moving back through the hair that grew at the junction between Ruth's thighs. She laughed, as Ruth's body shook, as her hip rocked, as she sought Bette's hand. "Tell me to stop, Ruth. I mean, you could tell me to stop. You *should* just tell me to stop. If you want."

A groan started in Ruth's chest as Bette touched her gently, bringing just her fingertips back to where she was tender and still slick. She rubbed in gentle circles as Ruth's leg began to shake again, before bending over and biting a kiss to her belly.

She closed her mouth over the lace of Ruth's bra and sucked on her nipple, feeling it pucker and harden beneath her tongue.

"Come here, come up here," she heard Ruth say above her, and Bette lay down on the bed next to her. Ruth wrapped an arm around her neck and kissed her fiercely, desperately, her tongue seeking out the roof of Bette's mouth. They kissed and they kissed. Bette's fingers continued their gentle circling until Ruth's mouth slackened and their kisses became little more than breathing and gasping into each other's mouths. She pushed two fingers into Ruth's mouth to suck on and bite as she came again, her eyes still squeezed tight, her face screwed up, every inch of her gorgeous. Afterward, her mouth open, eyes still closed, catching her breath, she turned her face toward Bette and buried it, hot and damp, into Bette's neck.

"Just give me—" she started, "and then—sorry—" Ruth said, still out of breath. "It's your turn. Oh my god. I can't believe you're still dressed." She looked down. "Bette, your *shoes* are still on. Get it off. Come on. All of it."

"You don't have to—" Bette started, but Ruth cut her off with a kiss.

"Off," Ruth reiterated.

Bette stood beside the bed and Ruth watched her, one eyebrow cocked, still in her bra without any knickers on. It was absurdly hot.

"Come on then," Ruth said, expectantly, pushing herself up onto her elbows with what looked like real effort.

"You don't have to watch. This isn't some striptease or—I don't know—oh fuck off," Bette said as Ruth laughed wide and bright. She kicked off her shoes without unlacing them and pulled her top over her head, tossing it to the side. "I'm taking my clothes off, but I don't want you to think this is me trying to be sexy. Like, if I wanted to give you a striptease, I would, and it would be incredibly hot, but it's not the time and so this is just me getting naked."

"And yet it's still incredibly hot," Ruth said, her eyes trailing down to where Bette was unbuttoning her skirt, pushing it over her hips. She unclasped her bra and stepped out of her knickers, and then lay down next to Ruth again before she could think too much about the nakedness.

Ruth's hands knew exactly where to travel to make her feel sexy: her collarbones, her nipples, the side of her rib cage, the dip of her waist, her inner thigh. Bette rocked her hips into Ruth's, and a thigh pushed up between her legs. They moved together, sweat between their bodies, searching for a rhythm, Ruth's breath ragged again already.

"You're so wet," she said, gripping Bette's earlobe between her teeth.

It was impossible to argue now that her knickers were off. She was already so sensitive, and shuddered as soon as Ruth's hand found her.

"Sorry, yeah, I mean—well. You're hot. Watching you was hot. It really did it for me."

"How could you possibly be apologizing to me? It's so hot, Bette." She kissed her, hard, biting. Bette tasted blood. "Can you—? Actually—come on." She guided Bette onto her knees, encouraged her to sit astride her shoulders. Bette's arse rested on Ruth's chest, the lace and metal of Ruth's bra imprinting themselves into Bette's flesh. "I'm still not sure my limbs are working enough to fuck you with my hand. Which is absolutely your fault. So just—yeah—yeah, that's it."

She ran her hands down Bette's back, gripping onto her arse and encouraging her to kneel a little higher.

"You okay?"

Bette nodded, forgetting that Ruth couldn't see her face any more, and then gasped as she felt Ruth's mouth. It was hot and wet, and her thighs quaked. It was going to be over so quickly. She was far too worked up already, and Ruth's mouth was perfect. Ruth's hands were gripping far too tightly, tightly enough to bruise, and that was perfect too.

It all went hazy impossibly quickly; she'd been determined to remember every moment, but she felt drunk on Ruth. Later, she would remember that she was technically still a bit drunk on tequila too. But at that moment it felt as if all that existed in her body was connected to Ruth, as if she'd taken over every part of her. Long before she wanted to come she was falling forward into the headboard, every extremity in her body tingling, every nerve set alight, her chest heaving.

She eased herself up and collapsed down next to Ruth, her feet against the headboard, both of them facing the ceiling, top to tail in the bed. Her body was emptied out, ringing and clear, a crystal glass traced with a damp finger. Ruth reached for her hand and threaded their fingers together.

They would talk about it in the morning.

CHAPTER TWENTY-FOUR

STILL SATURDAY, 29 OCTOBER

...

Still 25 days post-revelation

I n the morning, they didn't talk about it.

Bette slept poorly. She woke frequently, shuffling around in hopes of finding a more comfortable position. There was a distinct lack of space in the twin bed, but moving to the other bed wasn't an option while Ruth slept beside her. It seemed too much like abandoning her. Like it could be read as a statement. At half-four she slipped out of bed and pulled her pajamas on, hoping they would make her feel cozier, that she might finally drop off. But what was worrying her wasn't her back on an unfamiliar mattress or the pressure on her hip or the flat hotel pillows or even the presence of someone naked in the bed beside her. It was the churning in her stomach. They should have spoken before they fell asleep. Would Ruth pass the night off as nothing but a bit of tequila-influenced fun? Would she regret it entirely? Settling on her side, Bette looked at Ruth, her mascara smeared thanks to a cursory face-washing, her hair a mess, her mouth lax. She wouldn't. Surely she wouldn't. Ruth had made it clear she didn't want anything casual, that she wasn't interested in a one-night stand. But she'd also been pretty adamant about taking things slow. And last night didn't feel particularly slow.

Sleep found her near dawn. When she woke, the sheets beside her were empty, the awful mattress still indented where Ruth had slept. There was no light creeping out from beneath the bathroom door, but Ruth's suit for the wedding was still where she'd left it the day before, the hook of the hanger balanced precariously from a metal toad that protruded from the wall. Bette breathed a sigh of relief. At the very least (and it really was the very least, the worst of the scenarios that she'd spent the night panicking about), Ruth hadn't left.

She was probably just getting a coffee. In fact, as soon as it had occurred to her, Bette realized what a great plan caffeine was. There was a tiny kettle, on a plastic tray patterned with horrible toads with bows around their necks, and she walked it to the bathroom to fill it. The sink was shallow, with an impossibly small tap, and Bette spent fruitless minutes trying to angle it under the running water. It was useless; any water that ended up in the kettle flowed straight back out again. She stepped into the shower instead and held the kettle up to the shower head, getting away with only a minimal spray to her face, feeling indecently pleased at her own cleverness. But by the time she had boiled the kettle and poured the water over an ancient tea bag, she had very much lost the will to live. Certainly for being up and out of bed. The teacup was absurdly small, but she took it back with her beneath the duvet. She would drink it, and do a crossword on her phone, and then Ruth would be back. She was sure of it. And then they could talk.

The next thing she knew, she was damp and groggy and something was shaking her arm.

"Hey, Bette. Bette, wake up, we're late." She blinked her eyes open. Her shoulder was wet. Oh god, the tea. It was everywhere. Oh god, the wedding. They were late for the wedding. Oh god, Ruth. Ruth was there, shaking her shoulder. She was back.

"Fuck, fuck, *fuck*," she said, which seemed to encapsulate it.

"Yeah," Ruth agreed, looking frustratingly put together already.

"I need a shower," Bette managed.

"You really do," Ruth confirmed. "I had one earlier so the bathroom is all yours. I'm going to get ready here, but we really need to leave in the next twenty minutes? If we can? I went for a walk. I'm sorry, I thought you were up or—"

There was no time for Ruth's polite worrying. "It's not on you, not your fault. Should have set an alarm when I got back in bed," Bette shouted over her shoulder as she turned the taps to their hottest possible setting, stripped off and squeezed an obscene amount of toothpaste onto her toothbrush before clasping it between her teeth. The water pressure was uneven, and Bette contorted herself in an effort to keep her hair out of the spray. Twenty minutes. Enough time to finish up in the shower, to dry off, to spray a can of dry shampoo over her head, to swoop it up or pin it back, to throw her outfit on, to try and cover up the circles under her eyes, to cram her feet into her shoes, to—

There was absolutely not enough time.

She turned off the water and jumped out, sliding a little on the bathmat. Fantastic. Smacking her head on the tiles and giving herself concussion would really set them back. Heart pounding, slightly more gingerly, she stepped over to the mirror and ran a hand through the condensation. She looked exhausted, her skin dull and her eyes glassy. Ideally, she'd spend the next thirty minutes pretending she knew what to do with makeup to disguise it all. Instead, she probably had four minutes to cover everything up and then paint it all back on.

It was only once her eyeliner was in place, her powder settled on her cheeks, that it occurred to her that she'd hurried into the bathroom without her knickers, without her dress, without anything she was supposed to be wearing. Her pajamas were hanging from the hook and she could put them back on, but then she'd have to navigate stripping off and redressing in front of Ruth. It wasn't that she hadn't seen it all now, she supposed. But it was different in the morning light, shoulders still damp from a shower. She pulled back the bathroom door enough to speak through the crack.

"Ruth?" she called. Before she could step away from the door, Ruth pushed it open a little, and the hanger carrying her dress and bra were suddenly in her hand.

"Oh," she said. "Thanks. I'm—"

"Three minutes," Ruth said in a tone not to be negotiated with, and a thrill at the instruction ran through her. It was not at all the time for that. There was simply no time for—whatever that did for her.

Finally, almost dressed, she stepped out of the bathroom and made a beeline toward her overnight bag. She had packed high-waisted Spanx to wear under her dress, but she couldn't put them on in front of Ruth. There was no sexy way of pulling Spanx on in front of someone. She stepped into a black-lace pair

298 · KATE YOUNG

of knickers instead and pulled them up her thighs. It wasn't until she was straightening the skirt that she looked up and caught sight of Ruth.

Ruth looked—Ruth was—

Ruth.

Her suit was cut wide at her hips and shoulders, soft and flowing, but was cinched in at her waist with a thick bow. She wore a cream silk top under the navy, and a pair of towering gold heels that meant Bette was, for the first time, looking up at her. There was a hickey at the base of her throat, just visible beneath the makeup Ruth had painted over it.

Yesterday, before the—before everything—she would have told her, unequivocally, entirely without thinking, how beautiful she looked. But they still hadn't talked. She had no idea where they stood. And so, as it was, all Bette could do was nod and blush in approval and stutter out a "You look—yeah—" It was hopelessly inadequate. Absolutely not what she wanted to say.

"You too," said Ruth, her voice caught in her throat, barely making it out past her teeth. Bette looked down, so distracted by Ruth that her conscious brain needed to be reminded of what she'd put on. The dress was velvet, tight, a red so dark it was nearly black, held her boobs up in a way she'd struggled to believe and was split up her thigh. She had worried about it, for weeks. Worried what Mei would think when she saw her. Hoped it ruined her life a bit.

The look on Ruth's face told her it might. Just a bit.

"Should we—" Bette started, stepping toward her.

"Not—I mean, we don't—" Ruth said, glancing down at her wrist, as though there were a watch there. She was right, Bette knew. They were so late. And if they got into everything now, for one reason or other, they'd never make it downstairs.

"Later?" Bette asked, wanting to make it known that, in her mind at least, there was a conversation to be had.

"Come on, let's get downstairs," Ruth replied, which wasn't an answer at all. The nerves in Bette's belly leaped, and she chewed at the inside of her cheek.

"Yep. Yeah, let's," she said, falsely bright, tucking her bank card, phone and the room key into her clutch.

BALLOONS FILLED THE venue in a hundred shades of green and white. It made what was clearly an uninspiring multipurpose hall feel cozy and warm, fairy lights and festoons glowing through the translucent plastic of the balloons.

"Erin said their plan had been to fill the whole place with plants," Bette remembered. "But someone quoted six grand, and then the next person said eight. So they went with balloons."

"It's really beautiful," Ruth said, looking around the room as though determined not to meet Bette's eye. Their cab ride to the venue had been torture; Ruth had made polite conversation with the driver and Bette had sat anxiously chewing at her lip until she could taste blood. And now that they were in the venue they were surrounded by people. There was no possible way to delve into the *hey, we slept together last night and you don't seem okay* conversation they needed to have. And, of course, everyone at the wedding thought they were together. That had been the whole point. They'd been greeted by Louise, elegant in a black jumpsuit and perfectly defined eyeliner, whose winking welcome had reminded Bette that they had left the night before without saying goodbye to anyone. That they'd left mid-snog, their hands all over each other.

So she made small talk about balloons, trying to push through the strangeness between them. And then Ruth's hand slipped into hers, a thumb brushing across her knuckles, fingers tangled together. Ruth took a step closer and Bette let out a sigh of relief that she felt to her toes. It felt like she'd been holding her breath since she'd woken up. It was going to be okay. Ruth was holding her hand.

"I think Mei just saw us and thought *fuck*," Ruth muttered beside her. Bette looked up and met Mei's surprised eyes across the room. Bette had worried for weeks about how it would feel to see Mei again. Imagined that her heart might leap, entirely out of her control. Imagined that the anger that had been simmering within her might bubble over. But though she looked over at her and felt a pang—a vague sort of longing, a mess of attraction and lust, smothered by tangible disappointment and sadness that it had all gone wrong—it was like trying to look at the moon when the sun stood beside her, holding her hand.

She thought again of the whole point of the fake relationship, thought of how she'd pitched it to Ruth back on the wharf. Remembered how preoccupied she had been twenty-four hours prior. It had worked. Mei looked entirely wrong-footed, and Bette had technically won. It couldn't have mattered less. All she wanted was for Ruth to be holding her hand of her own accord.

"That's the point, right?" Ruth said, her voice tight, her smile horribly fake, still holding tightly onto Bette's hand. "Have someone—anyone—on your arm."

It was awful, her forced tone. Belle and Sebastian were playing, one of the songs from the first album Bette could never remember the name of. She wanted to cry. Wanted to walk out of the wedding and fix whatever had gone wrong between the moment they had fallen asleep and now.

"It's not—I mean. You know—you have to know. That's not the point. Anymore. I want . . ."

Ruth took a breath that looked like an effort and met Bette's gaze properly for the first time since the night before.

"Bette, I . . ." she started, but the tinkling of a glass reverberating through a speaker forced their attention toward the front of the room. Bette wanted to scream.

"If everyone could find somewhere where you can see," Louise was saying, pointing them all toward the windows at one end of the room, where things were clearly set up for the ceremony. "I've been reliably informed that the brides are outside. If you'd prefer to be seated, take some space on the benches!"

"Ruth?" Bette said, squeezing her hand as they made their way over.

"Not now," Ruth shook her head, and pulled her hand free. She met Bette's eye again. "We're okay. I just—not now, okay?"

Bette nodded, pathetically grateful for the reassurance, comforted by Ruth's *we're okay* as though it were her last 2 percent of phone battery, just barely keeping her going.

They found a spot somewhere near the back of the crowd, and the chattering around them quietened. The opening drum beats of a song Bette loved from *Dirty Dancing* started, and the doors at the back of the hall creaked open. Erin and Niamh were on the other side, hands clasped together, smiles stretching their faces so wide that Bette felt a sob bubble its way up her throat. It had been a lot, the morning, was all. She was hungry, and anxious, and tired, and probably in love with Ruth, and still, despite herself, mourning everything she'd had with Mei, and she couldn't reasonably be expected to survive the happiness on display, as well as the lyrics of "Be My Baby."

"Those *suits*," Ruth breathed, and Bette nodded, blinking furiously. Erin was in sharply tailored white, her hair scraped back at the sides and a mess of curls on top. Niamh's suit was softer, a pale green that matched some of the balloons overhead, the trousers wide and swishing as she walked. They looked so in love, gazing over at each other every couple of steps. Halfway up they got the giggles and Bette ached longingly, and by the time they reached the front of the room she had abandoned any pretense at being all right, staring up at the ceiling in an attempt to stem the tears, wishing she'd brought a proper handbag stuffed with tissues rather than cramming everything into a tiny clutch.

She got things under control by the time Erin and Niamh reached their vows, but the sincerity and list of promises threatened to take her under again. Finally they exchanged rings, and everyone cheered; once the guests reassembled around the bar at the other end of the room, Bette was able to catch her breath. She decided against checking on her face in the loos, took two glasses of something fizzy off a passing tray and handed one to Ruth.

"You okay?" Ruth asked.

"Oh just great. Really fantastic," Bette replied, taking a drink so deep that she could feel the bubbles burning her throat. Ruth nodded, gulping from her own glass. Before either of them could say anything else they were joined by Maddy/Maggie and her partner, Simon, and someone arrived with a bottle to top them all up. It was easy, then, to slip into conversation, to gossip about the other guests, to chase the cute waitress carrying the haggis-filled sausage rolls.

It was easy, once it wasn't just the two of them.

There was no seating chart, so when it came time for dinner they followed Simon and Maggie (thank god for Simon's clear enunciation). They were introduced to Mike and Harry, two more of Erin's university friends and, inevitably, just when Bette was looking at the two final seats on the table, Mei slid into one of them. Beside her, she heard Ruth cover up a resigned laugh with a cough.

"Mei," said Bette, unsure what the next words that left her mouth might be, finally deciding against adding anything.

"It's really nice to see you," Mei replied.

They were going for polite friendship, then. It was reassuring to recognize that she did not agree with Mei. There was no latent part of her that thought it *was* nice to see Mei.

"This is Ruth," Bette said, figuring it was worth getting the introductions over with.

"Mei, right? I think Bette mentioned you," Ruth said, her voice easier than it had been all day. It was such a line from a film, such obvious bait, that Bette almost laughed out loud. But Mei looked shaken and flustered; the jibe had landed exactly where Ruth had aimed.

"Oh, right. Yes." Mei looked around wildly and pointed to a woman at the bar. Bette realized she hadn't even registered the woman who had been standing beside Mei earlier. A month of panic and anxiety and hating this stranger, and she'd not given her a second thought. "And that's Tamara. I'll introduce her properly when she comes back. I just—yeah, that's Tamara. And you're Ruth."

"And I'm Maggie," Maggie said, and Bette snorted out a relieved sort of laugh.

"Yes, this is Maggie. And Simon, and Mike and Harry," Bette said. "Everyone, this is Mei."

Maggie raised an eyebrow, like she could tell there was subtext, but the men were already too deep in conversation about someone from university to do much more than nod in Mei's direction. The awkward silence that fell over their half of the table was broken by the arrival of Tamara, her short dress flipping around her toned thighs, a bottle of white in one hand and red in the other.

"Thought I'd get us started," she said, in a voice that would have sounded most at home on *Made in Chelsea*. "Hi, I'm Tamara."

Dinner was fine, mostly because Maggie, Harry and Mike filled any of the silences with stories about Erin from their first year at Hull. Tamara seemed entirely unaffected by the fact that she was sitting across the table from her girlfriend's ex, and Bette couldn't work out whether to be offended or relieved. Ruth was perfect. Charming and easy, an instant comrade to everyone on the table. It was all exactly as she had hoped, exactly as they'd planned. Ruth's knees bumped occasionally against hers, and there was a moment when she linked her fingers through Bette's on the table. It felt real, for those brief moments, and it was almost enough to balance out the panic Bette had been feeling since the early hours.

There were speeches—Louise did a rap that went down

shockingly well, and Erin's mum had Harry reaching for a serviette to wipe away his tears. And then there was a cake, and then a first dance to Taylor Swift's "Stay" that Bette wished Ash had seen, and then she was standing next to Ruth as everyone else flooded the dance floor.

"Do you—?" Bette asked, holding out a hand.

Ruth looked down, and for a moment Bette was sure she was going to refuse. She wondered whether her heart could take it.

"Sure," she replied, finally, and Bette's whole body was flooded with relief. "Yes. Yes, let's dance."

The lights were still too bright, the dance floor nothing like the one they'd been on the night before. But Ruth's body, pulled close to hers, the feeling of Ruth's heart beating against her chest, was almost too much for her. She wanted to kiss her again. They had to talk, away from all these people. She had to figure out what was in Ruth's head, find the root of the problem that had made Ruth pull her hand away from Bette's on the table.

They danced for so many songs that Bette stopped counting them, lost track of everything that was happening around them. If they had danced for one song, Bette might have thought it was for the performance of the thing, purely for Mei's sake. But they were still slow-dancing, Ruth's cheek pressed to hers. She had stopped worrying after the first song that Ruth could feel the roll of flesh above her arse, that she should have put the Spanx on back in the hotel. Ruth was touching her, running her fingers back and forth over the line her knickers made where they pushed into her back, over the bits of her she'd wanted smoothed out. She was grateful for the lace, for the fact that it meant she could feel Ruth properly, for the distinct lack of Spanx between them.

Eventually Bette pulled back.

"I'm going to get a water," she said. "Do you want something?"

"That'd be good," Ruth nodded. "I'm going to go to the loo. Meet you at the bar?"

She stood on the dance floor and watched Ruth leave, kept an eye on her until she was out of the door, heart horrible with hope. There was a queue for drinks and Bette joined it, replying to a message from Ash with barest details; it wasn't the time to get into the whole story. She had just opened a message from Carmen begging for wedding selfies when she felt the presence of someone far too close beside her. It was a someone who wasn't wearing Ruth's perfume, and Bette turned toward them.

It was Mei. Of course it was Mei.

"Are you having a nice night?"

There was no one they knew around, and Bette was too tired and too anxious to pretend.

"Are we really doing this?" she asked, her voice cold in her throat and between them. "We're just pretending we're friends who want to know how the other is?"

"No," Mei said, her eyes focused and clear. "No, you're right. I fucked up. Monumentally badly."

"You really did," Bette agreed.

"I can't believe—I wasn't thinking."

"You weren't thinking? You just—what? You accidentally got a new girlfriend? You accidentally invited someone else to Erin's wedding? You accidentally turned a break into a breakup and forgot to tell me about it?"

"Look, I wish I could give you a reason. I went mad, I think. I texted you and you didn't reply. And then I thought I'd see you at the office and instead you'd vanished somewhere and ignored all my texts. So I just assumed you didn't want to see me at all. By then, I already regretted it. I regretted sending you off to have a good time with women who weren't me. I wanted you to have a chance to leave me, if you were going to, before I got in too deep. But I was already in too deep. And then when you didn't message me back that day—I just thought I should step aside. Do the right thing. Let you have what you wanted."

Bette remembered it so clearly, remembered not knowing how to see Mei, remembered hiding on the toilet, heart pounding in her throat.

"Why didn't you just *say* that? I was heartbroken. I was missing you so much I couldn't handle seeing you and pretending everything was fine. I wanted you! That's all I wanted. But the whole stupid scheme was your idea! I was just trying to do what you wanted!"

"I know, I know," Mei said, looking around wildly. Her eyes begged. "I knew I'd messed up, that I was just scared. But I wanted to be generous, and give you time, and not pressure you into commitment. I wanted to know you chose me, that you felt what I did."

It was so strange to know it, now. After everything. To know that Mei regretted it, to know too why she'd started it. The anger and resentment she'd felt, not just from the dreadful lunch with Erin, but from the very start, burst out of her.

"So you just—what? Pressured me into sleeping around? Made me think that if I didn't, I wasn't right for you? Or ready for you?"

It was impossible to imagine how she might be feeling now had she not fallen for Ruth. Had she come to the wedding alone, had she spent the past weeks hoping, longing maybe, to win Mei back. But instead it was so clear that she was done. If there was a decision to make here, she knew without a doubt what her answer was. She didn't want Mei.

"I know. I know, and I'm so sorry. I convinced myself it was the right thing."

Mei hung her head and scrubbed both hands through her hair. It was short, Bette thought, shorter than she had ever seen it. It suited her, looked beautiful with the wide, square neckline of her black dress.

"I don't know what you want me to say. I hope you're very happy with Tamara. She seems great. I hope it was worth it."

"It wasn't," Mei said, grasping Bette's hand. Her touch felt hot on Bette's skin. Electric. But not in the good, sparky, delicious way that tingled through her body. Not the way Mei's touch used to feel. This kind of electricity felt dangerous. This kind could short everything out. This kind could, if she was being dramatic (which she absolutely was), blow everything apart. "It isn't. I—I don't want to be with Tamara. I want—I want this not to have happened. I want to go back to the way things were. I want you."

Bette laughed, hollow and low. She regretted the impulse instantly, but the madness of the moment struck her. A month ago, this was exactly what she would have said she wanted. Exactly the outcome she longed for. And now she couldn't imagine saying yes.

"I don't know that you do, though. What you think you want

is the type of girl you can call to a hospital at midnight. And I get it. I'm that type of girl. But I don't actually think that you want me," she said, squeezing Mei's hand, searching for the right moment to let it go. Mei's eyes were brimming with tears, and Bette felt strangely calm. She needed to say no. Her whole body was saying no. "I miss it. I miss what we had when it was good. But that's—it's not what I want anymore."

Mei shook her head, short static little movements that seemed to be shaking Bette's reply from her mind as she rejected it out of hand.

"I'm sorry," Bette said, and let go of her hand. She looked up, across the moodily lit room, and into the eyes of the only person she wanted to see, who also happened to be the last one she wanted to have witnessed the conversation.

Ruth.

Ruth's jaw tightened, resignation written clearly on her face. This was, Bette realized in a rush, exactly what Ruth had antic-ipated. She'd been preparing herself for this all day. And then across the room she'd seen Mei's hand in Bette's, the two of them deep in conversation, Mei's face apologetic. Ruth was leaving the hall, and Bette had to explain. She ran across the room after her and out through the door to the car park, then regretted their impetuousness instantly. There was a hallway that might be better for this conversation, surely. It was almost November. It was Scotland. It was cold.

"So, yeah. I—I can't do this," Ruth said, turning toward her and looking so apologetic about it that Bette's heart ached. The goose pimples that had erupted over her arms and chest were suddenly the least of her worries. "I just can't. I can't do it again, when you're still hung up on your ex. I promised myself I wouldn't do this again."

"I'm not still hung up on Mei," Bette protested, and Ruth scoffed. It was so important that Ruth understood. Bette was tired of being told how she felt, of being told what she should want. "I promise I'm *not*. I'm angry with her. I'm angry with her for making me feel stupid. I'm angry with her for the stupid plan, and for not listening to what I wanted, and I'm angry with myself for going along with it. But I'm not hung up on her. I'm hung up on you. I've wanted this—wanted you—for months now. Since the start, probably. No, definitely. From the start."

"I—I shouldn't have kissed you back last night. I wanted you too. I want you. But . . ."

"No but!" Bette said, abandoning her desire not to draw an audience in favor of a sincere yell. "No but! I want you, you want me, what else is there?"

"I'm here at this wedding with you because you were so heartbroken over your ex that you couldn't come alone. And now she clearly wants you back. And even if you don't want that to-day, you might tomorrow. I can't risk it again. I can't jump. I can't. It hurts too much."

The worst thing, Bette realized, was that she had already known it. This wasn't news. Ruth had told her, had been so clear about exactly where she was. She had taken things slowly, glacially slowly, with Gabe. That had been her whole thing. He was right for her, and they'd been taking it slow, and now . . . what had she said last night? Not to worry about it? That it wasn't a problem? God. Why hadn't Bette asked a single follow-up question?

Regardless of Gabe, Bette had ignored what Ruth said she wanted, ignored her going slow, and kissed her anyway. Hoping . . . what? That she'd be the exception? Hoping it wouldn't matter? Hoping that Ruth would change her mind? But it felt, last night, like she had. The way Ruth had kissed her back wasn't a performance. She felt it as much as Bette did. And suddenly, Bette was furious. Furious at everyone thinking they were making good, sensible decisions when they were actually just messing everything up.

"This is such bullshit. You can't fall in love when it's convenient to you. Sometimes it just happens! You're just going to walk away from it because you're scared? Because we didn't do this in the way you planned out in your head?"

It was cold and quiet outside the hall, and her words rang out into the darkness. She looked at Ruth, sure this would be the moment she'd see just how ridiculous she was being. Sure that she'd kiss her, and they'd go back inside and dance, and kiss some more, and that things would be exactly as they should be.

But Ruth looked up and broke the long silence between them.

"Yes. I'm really sorry, but yes. That's exactly what I'm going to do."

And Ruth turned her back and did exactly what she'd promised. She walked away.

CHAPTER TWENTY-FIVE

SUNDAY, 30 OCTOBER

...

1 day post-Ruth

In the film version of the wedding saga, Ruth would have run off after their conversation and caught a sad train back to Bristol, leaving Bette to sit alone with her devastation. But it wasn't the film version. Ruth was a PhD student on a budget and Bette had bought non-flexible multi-connection tickets, and the last regular train back south had already departed. And so when Bette made it back to their room, she found Ruth already curled up in bed, facing the window. It was a starkly different scene to the one the night before, and Bette chewed on her lip, holding back tears. She had cried enough already today. There was nothing for it but to get into bed and try to sleep. In the bathroom she brushed her teeth and diligently took off all her makeup, and then pulled back the duvet (how was there a company that sold duvet covers printed with toads?) and pretended to herself that it was possible for her to get any sleep at all.

The twenty minutes between getting out of bed and making it to the train the next morning were some of the worst of Bette's life. The room was too small to avoid each other, but she couldn't think of a single thing to say. She couldn't beg Ruth again. Couldn't ask her to throw caution to the wind, ignore all her instincts and give them a go. There were only so many times you could ask someone to be in love with you before it became mortifying. She'd run out of asks.

The idea of sitting next to one another for the seven-hour journey back south seemed entirely impossible. And so, on their way down the stairs, suitcase slapping against her shins as she maneuvered it awkwardly, Bette proposed the alternative she had thought of when lying awake the night before.

"Look," she said, swallowing again before she continued, trying to force the lump in her throat back down it. "I think we probably both need some time. Alone, I mean. So how about I forward you your ticket, and we just . . ."

She paused, unsure how to say it. It had been so clear in her head.

"Make our own way back?" Ruth finished.

"Yeah."

"I think that would be good for both of us," Ruth said, her voice delicate. Impossibly small. It sounded as though she might burst into tears at any moment. "I should pay you for the . . ."

And Bette couldn't stand it. It's not that the money wouldn't have been useful, not like the ticket had been cheap. She was staring down the barrel of a lean November. But the thought of Ruth paying her out of guilt was too horrible.

"Don't," she interrupted. "That was the deal. You—you came with me, so I didn't have to be alone. I'm really grateful."

Ruth shrugged, misery smearing into calm on her face. They stood in silence, not quite looking at each other.

"Okay," Bette replied. At the bottom of the stairs she handed her room key to Ruth and pulled out her phone. "I'll get on this, and you return those."

She found Ruth's ticket, screenshotted all the bits of it and sent it, then swiped on the litany of messages clogging up her notifications to clear them and pushed the phone back into her pocket. Outside the hotel the air was heavy with November drizzle. Bette could feel her hair frizz almost immediately.

"Well," Ruth said as she stepped out behind her, not quite meeting Bette's eye. "I'll see you back in Bristol, then."

"Yeah. I'll be in touch," Bette said, the words odd and formal and entirely inadequate.

Ruth nodded and turned to leave. Bette watched her turn the corner at the end of the street, willing her to look back, to change her mind. She didn't. Once she disappeared, Bette burst into tears.

BETTE HADN'T BEEN able to think about food in the station and was deeply regretting not having forced herself to pick something up. The smell of the hot sandwiches made her feel queasy and the sight of crisps make her heart ache, and so she was surviving on a diet of tea and Kit Kats, of staring out of the window and feeling sorry for herself.

Finally, an hour or so from Birmingham, she took a deep breath and pulled her phone out of her bag. There was nothing from Ruth, no heartfelt missive trying to find her carriage and take it all back. It was as expected, but it hurt regardless. Thankfully, there was nothing from Mei either. There was a message from her mother, prompting her for details of Christmas plans that Bette hadn't made. And there was, inevitably, a string of messages from Ash that grew increasingly more committed in their use of capital letters. She scrolled back through them, barely taking them in, and then plugged in her headphones and hit the call icon.

"You're not dead then," Ash said, picking up on the second ring. Bette felt a flash of guilt; they always replied to one another. She would have killed Ash if the situation was reversed.

"No. Not dead."

"Well, you'd better be calling to tell me you've been having a frankly disgusting amount of sex. That's the only acceptable reason for ignoring me since yesterday."

"I—" Bette replied, and her vision blurred through her tears. "I—"

"Bette, hey. Hey, what's wrong? Where are you?"

"I'm here," Bette managed, uselessly, and then abandoned her backpack at her seat and stumbled down the aisle, avoiding eye contact with everyone she passed. Once in the vestibule between carriages, she sank down against a wall until her bum hit her heels. She would not sit down on the floor of a Cross-Country train. She would *not*.

"Are you still there?" Ash's voice said in her ear.

"I had sex," she said.

"Okay," Ash replied, leaving space on the line for her to continue.

"Not with Mei."

Ash burst out laughing on the other end of the line, but recovered quickly. "Sure."

"I had sex with Ruth."

"Obviously."

Ash had known, Bette reminded herself. She'd always known.

"I slept with Ruth, and I think I might be in love with her, actually, but Mei wants me back and Ruth saw her holding my hand, and now she doesn't want me."

There was a long pause.

"What?"

"She's somewhere on the train, but I don't know where. We're not traveling back together. But we have to change, like, three more times, so there's a decent chance I'll run into her on the platform. God, we're going through fucking Wales, because they were the only tickets I could afford. We've still got hours to bump into each other. I ruined it all. I never should have kissed her. I—oh god I fucked it up. Ash, I fucked it up so badly . . ."

"Hey," Ash interrupted. "It's okay. It's going to be okay. You're going to be home soon. So soon. We're going to work it out."

"How, Ash? *How* is it going to be okay?"

"Honestly? I have no idea. But you just need to get through the next few hours. And then I'll be there."

The next three hours felt like seventeen. At Birmingham New Street, outside the Pret, Bette glanced to her left and caught a glimpse of the back of Mei's head. She turned away and saw Ruth instead, looking up at the departure board. It felt like an experience she should nod sagely at, as if that's what she should expect after the past forty-eight hours: a heartbreaking not-quite love triangle encounter in a major railway station. It felt like some sort of cosmic bullshit, the universe laughing at her. Except that she didn't believe in that, and actually they were all in the same place and on the same trains because she'd planned all their journeys in the first place.

She made it onto the next train, and then kept her head down and her headphones on, counting down the trains until they hit Bristol. When Bette tapped through the barriers at Temple Meads, Ash was standing there, an insulated cup clutched in front of her.

"I thought you might need a tea," Ash said, taking Bette's case from her and pushing the cup into her hands.

The last fifteen minutes home were, somehow, the worst of all the worst bits. The previous hours paled in comparison with the effort it took to place one foot in front of the other, to keep making her way up the hill. It helped to have Ash beside her, though, even if she hadn't said anything since handing the tea over.

"If it helps, she looked at least as rough as you," Ash said finally, dodging a pedestrian and almost losing the suitcase into traffic.

And it really did. For a moment it helped a lot, made the stupid hope flare in her chest. If Ruth was as devastated as she was, surely it was only a matter of time before she decided Bette was worth the risk. Worth the jump off the cliff. But she extinguished the hope before it could find a toehold. Maybe devastated was simply how you looked, after an incredibly good, impossibly complicated night of fucking at a wedding.

BETTE LIVED SMALL all week. Small and quiet and determined not to lose herself, not to sink into a pool of devastation. It would have been so easy to luxuriate in it, to lean into a heartbroken esthetic again. But she tried hard not to, tried so hard that it felt instead like hibernation, like all her focus and energy went into keeping her vital faculties (showing up at work, eating whatever Ash had cooked, brushing her teeth, sleeping) functioning. She couldn't even watch ice-dancing. Everything in her was frozen. Paused. It was safer than despair.

Eventually, inevitably, it was Sunday again, and a whole week had passed. In a bid to fill her weekend with purpose, with something tangible, Bette decided to visit her nonna. On the familiar train, she watched the countryside slide by. No one needed anything from her, no one started a conversation. She'd searched Spotify and was listening to a playlist called Sad Classical, which ran the full spectrum from moping to devastated. Apart from the regular interruptions by ads for dairy alternatives, it was sort of perfect.

Bette had texted her mother the night before, trying to nudge any Sunday family plans out of her. It was a difficult bit of subterfuge—seeming interested enough in Sunday church and lunch to reassure herself that she wouldn't run into the rest of the family at the care home, but not so interested she ended up with an invitation. She simply did not have the energy to engage with the rest of the family. The possibility of running into them, of being demonstrably miserable, had sat heavily on her. It was one thing to feel like she had to defend her life when she felt blissfully happy. It was another thing altogether when she was heartbroken, when she couldn't talk about why she was sad. When she was alone again, living the sort of life that made it easy for them to pity her. It was precisely what they feared: a lonely, miserable existence. And it wasn't that. But it also wasn't a week when she felt particularly capable of shouting about how great things were.

It was a long, meandering journey to the care home, and it was November. Bette walked with her hood up, the misty rain gradually turning to drops on her skin before trailing down her throat. By the time she arrived, she was damp. The sort of English dampness that wasn't quite enough to count as wet, but was absolutely enough to make taking her coat off a sticky, uncomfortable, horrible sort of job.

There was no one at the desk to witness the coat removal, which was a relief. She'd been waiting only a moment when the matron appeared down the corridor with the same energy as always: as though operating on 1.2x speed, slightly at odds with the world around her.

"Leone, isn't it," she said, the certainty of her tone negating Bette's nodded confirmation. It was her nonna's surname, not hers, but every time she was known and remembered, it squashed down the guilt she felt at not visiting enough. The matron didn't dither, not brusque or cold, just without any interest in extraneous chatting, and Bette was grateful for it; her temperature was recorded, a mask was handed to her, and she was pointed down the hall without any need for small talk.

Her nonna's room was right at the end, close to the large shared space that opened out onto the garden. She made her way past rooms filled with the other residents and their families, trying to resist the temptation to peer into every open door. But her wet footsteps on the squeaky floor attracted attention. Music-loving Mr. Law, who had a record player and a towering stack of jazz and blues by his window, waved as she passed. And then Jean, her nonna's closest friend and a relentless gossip, practically body-blocked her as she walked past her room.

"Little birdy told me you started a care homes project, and we're not on the list."

"Hi Jean," Bette said, and submitted to the hug Jean pushed on her. Bette hadn't been ready for it, hadn't braced herself as she had been doing with Ash all week, and it loosened something within her. She cleared her throat, her voice scratchy and caught after a morning of disuse. "It's regional funding, sorry. We did try! We'll make it a big success and then next year we'll be able to expand it. I'll keep Nonna posted."

"We've got that owl lad, is all I'm saying. Could do with some art. Anyway. I'll leave it with you. I've a face to put on and a date who won't wait."

She bustled back into her room, leaving Bette processing in her wake. She stood for a moment until Marina, her favorite of the care home staff, walked out of Jean's room with a tray beneath her arm.

"Morning, love." Marina was too young to call Bette "love," really, barely in her mid-twenties. But she also wore an engagement ring and the residents adored her and she was so capable and easy-going. Her hair was always twisted up elegantly in a scarf, her winged liner perfectly applied. In almost every respect, Bette felt like a teenager in her presence, someone who barely had her life together.

"Hey Marina." And then, before Jean's words took another loop through her head: "Owl lad?"

"Oh, that's Pascal," Marina replied. "He brings an owl in on Thursdays."

She smiled at Bette as though that explained literally anything.

"Right."

"She had a rough night, love. Your nonna. She was awake a lot, so she's tired. Been up and dressed, but last I checked she was having a little lie-down. Might wake up in a bit though, if you want to sit with her? Sure she'd love to know you're there and chatting to her?"

Bette nodded, aware of the amount of effort it took to smile.

"You can always give us a call and check too, before you come." Marina squeezed her on the shoulder and walked off down the corridor.

She should, of course. Calling made sense. But she also only had weekends, and she was so reliant on the trains, and she wanted to avoid her parents. Really, these Sunday mornings were her only option. And so even when it was a day like this, when it wasn't a good day, when it was a "sitting in Nonna's room and reading in case she woke up for a bit" sort of day, Bette knew she'd happily get on the train anyway.

It was a well-appointed room; enough space for the large bed, a couple of chairs, some small moveable tables and a tall chest of drawers. What made it feel small, as if the walls were forever creeping inwards, was all that was crammed into it; the piles of hand-knitted and hand-sewn blankets and quilts, the well-polished shoes lined up that Nonna rarely put on but liked to see, the crowded collection of framed family photographs that sat on a lace runner. The framed pictures of Jesus and Mary that sat among them, honorary members of the family, their hands hovering over their holy, glowing chests.

In the plastic-framed bed her nonna lay on her side, on top of the sheets, dressed in her regular nylon elasticated-waist trousers and a shapeless lilac jumper. A quilt covered her from her knees to the foot of the bed. Bette wondered if Marina had placed it there, and decided she liked imagining she had. She could picture it precisely: tender, careful Marina shaking out a quilt and tucking it over her nonna's notoriously cold feet.

Her first impulse was to clean, to make sure Nonna's room was the way she liked it, but it was spotless already. Not a frame out of place. There was nothing to do but sit and wait. She slid a chair over to the bed and unpacked the contents of her backpack: a thermos full of coffee (there was a lot that suited Nonna about life in the care home, but the quality of the coffee was an ongoing challenge), along with two slices of cake that Ash had picked up for her at Hart's the day before. She looked down at the box and felt, for the first time all week, truly on the edge of tears. She was so lucky. She didn't deserve Ash.

Bette hadn't felt like reading when she'd left home, but she was regretting not bringing a book with her. Scrolling through Instagram had too much potential to be devastating while she was in this mood. But she needed to do something. Marina had mentioned talking to Nonna; maybe Bette could just . . . talk. It was surely better than dealing with everything swirling around her head. She realized that last time she had seen Nonna she had been heartbroken and hurt over Mei. It felt so long ago, that so much else had happened. But it wasn't, really. And, despite all that had happened in Edinburgh, the pain of that first heart-break still lingered.

It would have been easier, maybe, to be so crushed after Ruth that it pushed everything else from her. But the truth of it was that it was one thing on top of another: the humiliation of everything with Mei, the loneliness, the devastation of starting all over again was all still there, propping up the fresh hurt.

"Ciao, Nonna," Bette said, reaching out to rest a hand on the bed. She cleared her throat again, keeping her voice gentle and low. After the first stroke they'd all talked to her like this. As if she could hear them, as though it might encourage her to come back. "Sorry you had a rough night. Honestly, you're not missing much. Seems like a quiet day here. And it's been a shit week. Sorry. A bad week. Not that I've been keeping up with the news, really, but it all seems pretty doom and gloom. But you probably— you probably know this. And there'll be family news, but you'll have heard it from Mum, and I don't know . . ."

Bette didn't know, was the simple truth of it. Didn't know what she could tell Nonna that she didn't already know. Nothing about the family, that was certain. And it wasn't her family that was occupying Bette's thoughts anyway.

"I lied, Nonna. I told you I'd been all right, last time I came here. I wasn't. I wasn't okay. I was pretty bad at hiding it, so I'm sure it's not much of a surprise. You probably knew. But I was heartbroken. I think I still am, a bit. I had a—thing—with someone, and it ended. And I miss he . . . I miss how easy it was. When it was good. I still don't know how to just—not have it. And be okay with that. Everyone seems to think it's good that it's ended, and I know it's the right thing. It is. But I'm just—I'm really sad about all the things I thought we'd have that we won't now. I'm so sad that it fell apart because we both assumed stuff that wasn't true. I want to stop being sad about it, but it's still there." It was good, she realized. Useful, to say all this without thinking too much about it. To be sad about Mei, whom Ash was definitely sick of hearing about. "I told myself it didn't matter anymore, so I'm sort of angry it does. Because I also—I met someone else. Or, I didn't meet them, but I guess I finally understood how I was feeling about someone. So it all seemed— fast. It felt like I fell for them fast. Even though I didn't. But I messed it up . . ."

She trailed off as her nonna's breathing changed, as the mouth that had dropped open in sleep came back under her control.

"Elisabetta?" she asked, eyes still closed.

"It's me, Nonna. Hi," Bette said, giving her hand a squeeze. "Do you want to get up?"

Her nonna nodded against the pillow, still finding her way back from sleep. Bette moved her chair back to where she'd hauled it over from, looking out of the doors and into the garden. It took a moment to get her nonna settled in her chair, and then Bette sat down in the other.

"You bring—?" Nonna began, trailing off with a satisfied smile when Bette wheeled over the table with the thermos and the cake box. She poured the coffee out into the Willow-pattern cups her nonna liked best, and relayed stories of workshops and work plans. It was easy, for a while, to be distracted. But it felt oddly like a monologue; she'd expected the sort of questions and opinions that her nonna was never short of.

But it was not the conversation her nonna seemed to want to have.

"This person, the one you love? Do they love you?"

Bette's stomach turned over. Of course Nonna had been listening. She'd forgotten, somehow, that they were years on from the stroke now. That she wasn't trying to bring Nonna back into the room. That she was right there, napping. Listening, apparently.

"I don't think so. I mean, they weren't ready for it. They're getting over someone. And I knew that."

"Everyone always getting over someone. People die. People leave. Everyone is sad, but don't just be sad. Might as well love too."

"I'm not sure it's just sadness. More . . . fear. I think maybe if you've been badly hurt, it would be scary to feel like you're falling in love again."

"Who could be afraid to love you?" She reached out and took Bette's hand, her dark eyes sincere. "So easy to love."

There was nothing to say to that, really. Bette shrugged and nodded, like it was true. Like she agreed. Like it truly was that simple.

"What is her name?"

"Ruth," Bette replied, before she could think twice about it. And then she felt, suddenly, as though her face had been ignited from the inside: hot and uncomfortable. Her heart raced, her tongue and teeth felt too big in her mouth. She hadn't—she didn't—how did . . . ?

"A good name," her nonna said, nodding, quiet and considering. "Naomi, Orpah, Ruth."

Old Testament names, Bette realized. She couldn't remember the details of the story. She was too distracted to try.

Her nonna looked entirely unperturbed. Like the information wasn't new. Had it been the gender-non-specific pronouns? Had her mother said something? Had Bette let something slip? She wanted to cry. Wanted to press her nonna for more. But her nonna was sipping her coffee and reaching out for the cake. Maybe drawing attention to it wasn't the right thing. Maybe they could just . . . not. And so Bette pulled out her laptop and put *The Golden Girls* on, and settled back in her chair to laugh along with her nonna as Blanche flirted in dubbed Italian.

After a couple of episodes, her eyes flicked over to the clock hanging above the chest of drawers; she and Ash had an afternoon of house-cleaning ahead of them. There was a train in thirty minutes, and she needed to be on it.

"Your train?" Nonna asked, and brushed off Bette's apologies. "Thank you for coming. For sitting with me. You bring Ash to visit? Next time?"

Bette screwed the top back on the thermos and zipped up her backpack. She pressed her masked mouth to her nonna's cheek and squeezed her hand.

"I promise. Ciao, Nonna."

BY MONDAY MORNING, Bette had made a decision. She couldn't make Ash's life impossible any more. She couldn't be the sort of flatmate who didn't shop and didn't clean and moped around the flat. This wasn't even a breakup, and she was absolutely, definitely not going to mourn it as if it were. And so, when Ash had found her up and dressed in the kitchen before work, Bette had smiled and handed over the coffee she'd made.

"Thanks," Ash said, clearly incredulous. She'd been so careful and kind all week, had sat and talked with Bette after they'd done the cleaning. Later, as she was getting into bed, Bette could see how the rest of the month, the rest of the year, might go. She knew Ash had had the same thought too. She could see the dinners Ash would put in front of her, and the nights on the sofa. Maybe, just maybe, she could skip it. Maybe she could be a better friend and better person than she had been in the past weeks and not make the rest of Ash's November about her too. She could be the kind of flatmate who made coffee instead.

"I was thinking it'd be nice to see Tim this weekend? Feels like it's been ages since I've seen him for more than just a hello or goodbye."

"Okay, stop. What's going on?"

"What do you mean?" Bette asked, keeping her voice perky and bright, fighting the impulse to slip back into the cold allure of hibernation.

"Nothing. Nothing, obviously. This is all entirely normal. We'll just get something in the diary then," Ash said, her voice loaded with sarcasm.

"Great!" Bette replied, confident that leaning into relentless cheer was the only real way to get through this. She was going to fake it until relentless cheer was all she had left.

Ash looked at her, drained the cup and handed it back to Bette. She turned to pull her lunch from the fridge, and then looked back again before leaving the kitchen.

"This was weird," she said, waving her hand as if to encompass all of Bette. "You know that. That was a weird interaction we just had. But I could get used to the morning coffee. If that was a bit you wanted to commit to. Anyway. See you tonight."

It was even easier as the week went on. It felt ridiculous that she'd never really considered it as an option, that she hadn't just embraced this the week before. That instead of feeling absolutely every feeling, instead of collapsing into the sofa in devastation, instead of moping around in bed, instead of shutting everything down and feeling nothing as the only alternative, she could just . . . live.

Despite Ash's clear misgivings about the way she'd proposed it, Bette had messaged Tim midweek and organized a long, wintry pub lunch for Sunday. Being all right again was going to be about filling her time. She needed not to dwell on the thought of Ruth in her bra in bed, her chest flushed, her eyes half closed. Being all right was about making sure she had plans on the weekend and in the evenings, about removing the possibility of wallowing alone. Being busy was the key.

When Ash was at Tim's on Thursday, Bette's first impulse was to order a takeaway: boxes of hummus and stuffed vine leaves and falafel and salads with chopped herbs through them. It would be easy to order something, to collapse into the sofa. But she thought of making the mussels, thought of the satisfaction of lifting the lid off the pan. She thought of being busy and useful, giving her brain something to do. She thought of the train tickets too, of the frugal month she was supposed to be having.

There were books in the kitchen—Ash's, of course—but

she'd find something. The corner shop didn't have everything she needed, but Ash had most of the rest. And the internet was confident that the sauce would work without the marinated artichokes. Bette ate her pasta at their table, music playing from her phone, and then watched *Bake Off* in the bath. When Ash came home the next night, there were leftovers for them in a box in the fridge; they ate them cold, standing up in the kitchen, passing the box and a fork back and forth between them. Ash stuck a Post-it on the recipe in the book, wrote the date and Bette's name, and *v. good (try the artichokes next time)*, and Bette wanted to text Ruth about it. She managed to resist the temptation.

On Sunday there were deeply fine roasted vegetables and surprisingly decent Yorkshire puddings, and genuinely great pints in the pub near Ash's school. It was pretty early in November, but the fairy lights were already up. Signs around the pub promised carol nights and Christmas quizzes and a room for hire at the back for work parties. The floor was wood rather than carpet, Ash's only stipulation. It was busy, every table occupied and a hum of general cheer filling the room. It had been a good plan, a perfect distraction.

It was easy, Bette thought, as she walked across the pub to collect the ancient edition of Scrabble from among the pile on the windowsill, not to be thinking too much about Ruth. Ruth would probably like this sort of thing, but so did lots of people. It wasn't particularly special to have met a woman who seemed like she might enjoy a Sunday roast and a board game. There were loads of them.

It was easy, Bette thought, as she waited at the bar to buy the three of them another round, not to get too hung up on the things she didn't have, on what her life was lacking. It would be nice, of course it would, to be in love with someone who loved her back. That wasn't a unique feeling. It wasn't unusual to want that. It didn't make her special. It hadn't changed anything.

It was easy, Bette thought, as she put *bazaar* over a triple word score and tried not to look too smug about it, to think about the bits of her life that were brilliant and to feel happy to be here in the pub with Tim and Ash on a gray Sunday before Christmas. They'd go home later and Ash would make them watch some twee '50s classic film. She and Tim would roll their eyes and they'd drink tea and it would all be lovely. She didn't need to dwell on a thing that had only existed as a possibility for a couple of hours in her head, one night before a wedding.

And in the meantime she'd won Scrabble, and bowls of pear crumble and custard had arrived. Tim was full of retail capers; his stories always got madder and better the closer they were to Christmas. His knitted jumper looked cozy, and his hair had grown out enough to be pleasantly scruffy. Beside him, Ash had on an oversized cardigan and there was pink blush on her cheeks and she was scraping the last remnants of custard from her bowl. They looked so soft and perfect next to each other that Bette couldn't help smiling stupidly at the pair of them.

"Hey, we were thinking of keeping things small this New Year," Ash said, smiling back, as if she knew exactly what Bette had been thinking. Bette's heart dropped. Most years they had a party of sorts; the size fluctuated, but Ash loved to host and was, incomprehensibly, a fan of New Year's Eve. Bette had grown used to not having to make a plan, knowing the party would happen around her. The thought of having to find something else to do, of leaving them to it, was appalling.

"Maybe dinner just the three of us?" Ash was saying, pulling Bette from her spiral. She felt the relief fill her, warm and soothing, like tea after a long walk.

"That's perfect," she said. "Low-key family dinner is perfect."

Tim smiled at her too, and then all three of them were laughing at each other like idiots. It was cheesy, and lovely, and the best she'd felt in a while.

CHAPTER TWENTY-SIX

THURSDAY, 15 DECEMBER

...

Six weeks later

By December, work was the busiest she'd known it, a whirl-wind of events, projects coming to a close, and the im-minent commencement of their January sessions. For the weeks Erin was on honeymoon Bette had been covering her events too, until she'd returned to the office, face tanned and full of questions about Ruth and Mei that Bette managed to dodge.

Bette arrived at the office early and left late. She cooked for Ash a couple of times, and resisted the temptation to order more takeaway than she could afford. She got into the habit of getting up and making coffee in the mornings before Ash left. Her nail polish was unchipped and she went to bed with her hair mostly dry. She visited her nonna twice more, watched more *Golden Girls*, and took Ash along with her as promised. She thought about getting a subscription to *The New Yorker*, realized it was because Ruth had those well-designed covers framed in her kitchen and decided not to. She did yoga in the leggings that had sat in her drawer all year, rather than in a T-shirt and her pants. She finished three books. She made a plan for Christmas and texted her mother back.

And she booked a ticket to a queer meet-up she found online.

The idea of getting back on an app, of dating someone new, was deeply unappealing. Being on her own for a bit felt like the right thing to do. But she missed the queer presence in her life she'd had since meeting Ruth. She'd come to depend on it. And in the absence of a text suggesting they try being friends again, she needed to meet some new people.

The bar was full when she approached it. It was a Thursday, a week before Christmas, and half the women inside were dressed in novelty jumpers that were Mark Darcy levels of awful. But it was a bar, and it was full of queer women. She hadn't seen that nearly often enough to be put off by the presence of some glitzy pompoms. At the door there was a sticky label to press to her chest, and a cute woman with a pen who blushed and laughed when Bette pointed out that there was a -*te* on the end of her name.

"Name, not verb. Got it. Anyway, this is your drink token," she said, gesturing at the bar behind her. She was in a jumpsuit and trainers and had a warmth and ease about her that suggested she was used to reassuring nervous strangers. "First one's included. A warning: the wine's pretty average. If you like beer, go for that."

"And then I just—I mean—is there like, a format? Or do I just—"

"It's just a meetup tonight. Very low-key," the woman said, smiling reassuringly. It was a nice smile. The woman—Claire, her name tag read—had great lips and a gap between her front teeth she could have passed a pound coin through. "So find a group you fancy joining. Or pick someone who looks nervous. If you're the person looking nervous, one of us will come and find you in a bit."

"I promise I'll talk to someone," Bette said, cringing at her own obvious eagerness to please.

"Okay!" Claire replied, clearly not bothered one way or the other. "See you in a bit then!"

Bette leaned against the bar as the guy behind it filled her glass, and thought that if that was the only conversation she had tonight it had still been worth coming. She'd stepped into a queer space, had put a name tag on her chest that identified her as part of this group. It was a good thing to have done.

"Bette!" she heard from behind her, and she turned to see Heather, in towering heels and black leather trousers, walking toward the bar. Of course Heather was there. Of course she was. "I didn't know you came to these!"

"I don't! I mean, I haven't. But I thought it would be good— good for me."

"Well, there's nothing quite like a fortifying social engage-ment to make you feel good about life."

"Sorry, I didn't mean *good* for me. In a broccoli way. Or any-thing. I meant, like, a good thing to do. That it would be good!"

"I'm teasing you, babe," Heather said, resting a hand on her arm. "Maybe—I don't know—maybe take a breath or some-thing?"

Bette did, and then took another. It helped.

"So, how have you been?" Heather asked. Bette scanned her face, trying to work out how much she knew. But Heather was serene. A swan. If there was any work happening, it was deep below the surface.

"I'm fine," she replied.

Heather nodded, head cocked to the side, and then leaned over the bar and ordered two shots of tequila. She was silent as they were poured out, and then handed one to Bette.

"Oh, I—"

"Look, I'm not going to make you drink something you don't want. That's not cool. Or classy. Very much not my vibe. But maybe you want to?"

She did, sort of. And so she drank it, beer still in her other hand, and winced as it hit her esophagus. She'd always hated tequila. Or she'd always hated the hangover following university nights that ended with tequila. Hated that the last time she had drunk tequila had been with Ruth. Hated that it now reminded her of that night.

"Okay," Heather said, staring intently at her. "How are you? Actually?"

It was a neat trick. Bette's throat still burned and it was too hard to lie.

"Not really that fine," she admitted. Saying it, she wanted it to feel like a weight off her shoulders, to have admitted it here, tonight, in front of Heather. It didn't. It made her feel hollow, and sad, and foolish. "Not really fine at all, to be honest."

"Didn't think so," Heather said, her voice all warmth and empathy. She gestured over Bette's shoulder. "Want to come and join me and the girls?"

Bette's heart raced, certain that if she turned round it would be to come face to face with Ruth. She was aware, all of a sudden, that she wasn't strong enough for that, wasn't ready for it. Would walk out, probably, if Ruth was behind her. She turned.

Ruth wasn't behind her.

Heather gestured toward a group of women Bette didn't recognize. They were dressed as glamorously as Heather, exuding the energy of a girl band who'd wandered into the bar after a gig. As a collective they were intimidating: the only whole group in the room who didn't have at least one member in a Christmas jumper, whose glitzy heels and statement jewelry performed the requisite nod toward the season instead. Bette felt great in the dark jeans and gold top and winged eyeliner she'd put on before leaving the house, but in the midst of this group she was aware of looking more like the journalist on the tour bus, battered notebook in hand.

It was a relief, then, that the group welcomed her in. Heather was clearly greasing the social wheels, and Bette kept glancing around, acknowledging to everyone else in the room that she was aware she didn't belong with the glamorous set. But it was hard to feel that for too long. Impossible, once Zoe had inquired where she'd bought her top, and Ola had asked seven interested follow-up questions about Bette's job, and Molly had grilled her about her at-home, very-much-out-of-a-box dye job.

"Have you all been here before then?" Bette asked. They weren't mingling much, and Bette couldn't quite work out why they'd come if their plan was to stand together in a cluster all evening. Surely there were other bars they could do that in. Fancier bars, nicer bars, with less stark lighting.

The group hushed for a moment, stealing surreptitious glances at Zoe.

"Oh, all right," she said, throwing up her hands, an armful of bangles jangling as she did. "I'm bi. I just came out. Like, a month ago. And so the girls thought we should come and celebrate somewhere. We were looking for a club night or something, but when we Googled things for queer women in Bristol, it was literally just this."

Bette grinned at Zoe, having done precisely the same thing, feeling an odd compulsion to hug her. She wanted to gesture between them and say, *Me too! me too! How could we have missed it?!*

"We've all been friends forever, see?" Heather explained. "Since primary school. And we've been three-quarters queer since, like—"

"Since our second year of university," Molly continued. "Since that drunken party when I kissed Anna and realized I wanted to do it again. But Heather's been gay forever, and Ola's been out since school. And now we've got the whole set!"

"Anyway, it's not a whole big thing," Zoe said, her cheeks flushed. "But I've left my husband at home, and we're having a big queer weekend. This is the first stop. It's probably really rude, to come here and not talk to anyone else. Anyone else apart from you, obviously. But it's nice."

"It is, isn't it?" Bette said. "It's just really nice to stand in a room full of queer women."

"Yeah!" Heather said emphatically. "Gay bars are full of queer guys and straight girls. Which I get! I'm all for a space for queer men to be safe to dance and flirt and fuck. A space where girls can dance without being groped. But there aren't spaces for us, really. We get occasional curated club nights. Not this weekend though, so we thought we'd come here. For Zoe. And then we're going dancing. Because gay bars may not always feel like spaces for queer women, but at least the music is great. We've got an Airbnb for the weekend." She looked at Zoe, the corner of her mouth creeping up. "So ignore her, because it's definitely a whole big thing. BIG! LESBIAN! WEEKEND!"

"Except I'm not a lesbian," Zoe corrected.

"And I'm not either," added Ola.

"Heather's actually the only lesbian," Molly said, shrugging at Bette. "But she did do most of the planning, and this is her city, and we are all technically women who fancy women. So . . ."

"Pfft, semantics." Heather waved her hands lazily in front of her.

They all laughed, and then Ola turned to Bette.

"How do you know Heather, then?" she asked.

She should have anticipated it. Should have planned a non-Ruth-related answer. Of course they were going to ask.

"I met Bette at Jody's birthday over the summer," Heather said, which had the benefit of being true and also leaving out the bit that was making Bette's back sweat.

"Oh cool!" Ola said, and that was that. The conversation moved on. It wasn't all that interesting as an origin story. Not really worthy of note. So it felt ridiculous that Bette could still feel her fingers tingling, feel every breath struggling to work down into her lungs.

"It's such a great house, right?" Zoe said, directing her words toward Bette. "I'm obsessed with their kitchen."

Images crowded in: standing in the kitchen with Heather

and Ruth, the magazine covers framed on the wall, watching Ruth as she turned in the sequined dress, the herbs on the windowsill. Ruth holding her bag of salt and vinegar crisps, Ruth's face as Heather asked her about Charlie, Ruth beneath her in bed.

Ruth.

Ruth.

Ruth.

Bette's heart was pounding in her chest; she could taste it in the back of her throat, iron-rich and heavy. Her face was so hot she felt sure the rest of the group could feel it radiating. She managed to nod at Zoe, trying to turn her mouth up in a smile. It was, based on the faces looking back at her, an unsuccessful attempt.

She needed to get out.

"I—I forgot I have to—I have to go. I hope the weekend is fun. It was really nice to meet you all. Thanks for being so nice," she said, determined to get out before things progressed into a full-blown panic attack. She was due one, probably. Had been saving it up for a moment precisely like this. She pushed past jumpsuit Claire at the door, calling back an apology and then strode off, sucking in lungfuls of air, trying to get a good distance away before she collapsed.

She was halfway along the pier, her coat still clasped in her hand, before Heather caught up with her. There was no preamble, no time for Bette to prepare herself.

"Ruth's not fine either," Heather said, and then ran her hand across her mouth, gripping her jaw as if her teeth ached. "I shouldn't be telling you this. But she's not all right. And if there was a thing you could say to change that, then I think you probably should."

"She made what she wanted pretty clear," Bette said, heart still pounding in her ears. She felt trapped. Stuck. She crossed her arms across her chest. "I don't think there's anything left for us to say."

"The thing you should know about Ruth—I mean, the thing I know about Ruth, the thing that makes me worry, is that she's her own worst enemy. She's so determined not to be hurt again. But not everyone is going to be Martha."

It was the first time Bette had heard her name.

"I put myself out there, Heather, I really did. She's the one who walked away. And I can't *make* her want to be with me."

"No," Heather agreed. "You can't. But also, the wanting isn't the problem. You know that, right?"

Heather reached out and squeezed her arm and then, mercifully, turned and walked back into the bar. There was a tree a few meters away, and Bette stumbled toward it. She rested her forehead against the trunk, the cold air painful in her chest.

She knew it, of course she did. She'd been there the night before the wedding. Ruth wanting her had never been the problem. But Ruth didn't trust Bette, didn't trust herself, didn't want to take the leap. She'd walked away.

SOMEWHERE AFTER THE first perfectly assembled room, Ash slipped a gentle arm through Bette's. Bette knew that the hunt for Tim's Christmas present had been a ruse. The truth was that

Ash was oddly soothed by the winding route of IKEA, by the arrows on the floor pointing the way. She did most of her hardest thinking there. So an out-of-the-blue trip on a Friday evening after work meant a conversation, meant something was on her mind.

Bette reached up and squeezed the hand that was curled around her elbow. "So. Talk now, or over meatballs?"

Ash exhaled and looked up at her. "Meatballs. Is that okay? It's nothing bad. I just want to talk when I can see your face. Once we're properly sitting down."

"Course," Bette replied as they rounded the corner into the sofa section. It was a good hour later when they finally emerged at the checkouts, and then wheeled their purchases up to the restaurant. They had managed to make their way out only slightly weighed down by things they suddenly couldn't live without: a pair of new cushions for the sofa, three house plants for the bathroom shelf, some tumblers that looked fancier than they had a right to, a bag of Daim bars. An enormous stuffed crocodile for Tim ("he reckons he sleeps better when I'm there, so I'm getting him a horrible substitute for Christmas") that poked ominously out of their trolley. They spread out at a big booth table in the restaurant, quiet so close to closing, and Ash queued up for their dinner before wheeling it over.

It was Ash and Tim, Bette was sure of it. Ash had waited as long as she could for Bette to be sorted but now Bette was back at square one and Ash was ready to move in with Tim so they could keep saving for a deposit and move on and Bette was going to have to be thrilled about it which of course she *was* but also she'd been dreading this day for nearly a decade and god she didn't know if she was ready, if she'd ever be ready. And now it was here, and she didn't have a choice.

Ash had been in her seat for less than a minute, had just taken her first bite, when Bette lost the patience she'd been clinging to around the warehouse. "Okay, you have to tell me."

Ash nodded, took a gulp from her plastic cup and set her cutlery down by her plate.

"I was thinking about what you said a little while ago, about Mei being the first person you'd been with where you felt like you could be yourself." Bette felt her eyebrows creep up, felt wrong-footed. It sounded as if this wasn't going to be quite the conversation she had readied herself for. She nodded, running her fries through the gravy, leaning forward so that it didn't drip down the front of her sweater. "And I get it. I remember heart attack, and that faux-feminist swing-dancing Virginia Woolf-obsessed guy, and the one who tried to get you into tennis. You were working so hard to be a perfect girlfriend, to present them with everything they were looking for, everything they might need. I should have noticed at the time, but it's really obvious now that you weren't getting what you needed."

Bette laughed, and Ash rolled her eyes.

"Yeah blah blah blah you're gay. I don't actually mean the sex. I don't think you can put it all down to that." She held up a hand, stopping Bette's rebuttal before it could begin. "I'm not dismissing how important that is. I don't know what it's like to have sex with people I'm not fundamentally attracted to. But there was more to it than that, I think."

She cut a meatball in half and dipped it into the jam, then

speared a few peas onto her fork. Bette waited for her to finish, not wanting her to lose track of the thought. Ash chewed carefully and then set down her cutlery again.

"You're really good, I think, at performing happiness. At convincing yourself—at convincing everyone—that things are exactly as you want them. It's what I was worried about when you were with Mei. You were always in a state before she came round, making the flat perfect or stressing out in the kitchen, and we both know you hate cooking. You shuffled your life around her, making sure you were free when she might want you over. You were always on edge. But as soon as she was there in front of you, you were happy as anything. Everything was perfect. Even if it wasn't." She stared down into her lap, where Bette was sure her hands were probably twisting together, and then looked up and met Bette's eye. "Bette, I wanted to say this, in case you needed to hear it. I love you. Not because you cook dinner for me, or make sure we always have toilet paper, or plan lovely things for us. Or because you're always happy and jolly and up for a laugh. I love you *despite* the fact that you're crap at all of that, and you're often in a really shit mood. You're really crap so much of the time and I truly, absolutely, love you. I mean, I think we'd kill each other if we were dating . . ."

They both laughed, and it eased an ache in Bette's chest that had settled there since Ash had begun talking. She maneuvered some peas onto her fork.

"Anyway. You like to please," Ash said, then stopped abruptly as Bette snorted out a laugh, her mind flashing suddenly to Ruth, to Natalia, to Mei, to Evie, to Netta. And then, painfully, to Ruth again. "Oh come on, that's not what I meant. You're a people pleaser. You have been forever. But I'm kind of worried that you think love is . . ."

"Conditional."

Ash nodded, her face tender. She reached across the table for Bette's hand. "Yeah. And I just want to see you with someone who makes sure you know that theirs isn't."

"It's not Mei's fault." Bette's voice was quieter than she intended, but she wanted to defend Mei, to defend the time she had spent so committedly fighting for her.

"No, of course not. I'm not saying it's all her fault. But it's not yours either. I just want to see you happy. I want you to know that you're worthy of all of it, and not just because you work hard to make sure that the people you date are happy. Not because *you* try to seem happy, even when you're not. But that you're enough. Just you. Even on nights when you've cooked nothing, and you're in a funk, and someone else has to clean the flat."

Bette could tell that Ash was intending for her to laugh. But she couldn't hold it back; tears started running down her cheeks and into her meatballs.

"Bette! No! Come on! I really didn't mean for this to be a crying thing," Ash said, squeezing her hands tightly. "But I promise that there are people who know just how great you are. You deserve to be with someone who loves all the messy bits of you too."

It wasn't hard to work out who Ash was talking about. Bette thought of scrubbing mussels, of watching ice-dancing over and over, of fighting over dinner and making up over dessert, of laughing and kissing and fucking and lying beside Ruth in a panic while she slept.

But she'd played all her cards at the wedding. She'd stood in front of Ruth and said all of it. She'd revealed it all, all the messy shit, and Ruth had walked away.

Knowing she wanted Ruth, that she could make her happy, wasn't enough. It hadn't been enough. How could it possibly be enough?

CHAPTER TWENTY-SEVEN

SUNDAY, 18 DECEMBER

•••

Five months since the break,
ten weeks since the revelation,
fifty days without seeing Ruth,
and seven days to go until Christmas

The Christmas tree in the front room was demonstrably too large for it. Earlier in the month they had looped every decoration they had over the branches, while listening to an album of '90s bands singing Christmas covers, but it had still been startlingly bare. To compensate, Bette had bought six strings of fairy lights; the plug socket they were all patched into hummed vaguely when they were on, as if wanting to show off about the work it was doing.

Bette was arranging place settings and Christmas crackers, rubbing smeary fingerprints from cutlery handles with the hem of her shirt. Ash had planned a Christmas dinner, this final weekend before Bristol lost them all to their respective family homes. School had broken up, Anton and Carmen were coming round, and Bette was in the midst of her bit of the preparation: readying the front room.

The dining table had taken a while to come into their lives, and the front room still wasn't properly big enough for it. They didn't bring it out very often. It mostly sat in a half-folded state, covered in Ash's school planning. Getting the table out was a production, something they'd never do without guests. Today it felt like a real celebration, covered in bits of seasonal tat and glitter and touches of gold. Bette looked around, pleased, and flopped down on the sofa to admire her handiwork.

It was strange to look at the table from this angle, she thought. Oddly removed, like she was waiting for actors to arrive onstage. She was struck with a sense of déjà vu, of having had precisely the same feeling before. And then she saw the table as it had been for the mussels lunch: all of them in their usual chairs, utterly creatures of habit. And Ruth, sitting right there, in the space where a sixth chair might go.

It was no secret that everyone else at the table had wanted to add a sixth chair for ages. It had been good when Mei had filled it; so easy to imagine that that could be it. But Bette thought of the wedding, of Mei standing in front of her, desperate for everything to return to normal. Desperate to win her back.

Thought of knowing, unwaveringly, with pure clarity, that it was Ruth she wanted.

Not because she filled a chair, not because everyone loved her, not because it was easy. Not because she made Bette want to be a better version of herself. But because she made it easy for Bette to be entirely and completely herself.

She wanted Ruth to be able to be herself too. To say what she wanted and to get it. But Bette had kissed her, and slept with her, and then stood in a car park and basically shouted about love at her. It had been the exact opposite of what she needed: the opposite of slow.

And it didn't have to be.

It could all be on Ruth's terms. She could tell Ruth they could take it slow. Let her see that Bette was ready, and that she could trust her. That she wasn't going to fall back into bed with an ex. That it was Ruth she wanted. They could date. Ruth could just . . . come to dinner. Sit at the table. No pressure, no intensity, no U-Hauling, no lesbian urgency. Just two people, taking it slow.

And before Bette could think anymore about the details, could think a plan through, she was walking toward the kitchen.

Usually, when Ash cooked, there was an air of calm that surrounded her. The ease with which she could make things happen, could pull things together, was enviable. But Bette had the sense that she'd perhaps stumbled into a slightly more stressful situation than normal.

"Fuck, fuck, *fuck*," Ash muttered, whisking furiously, her eyes mostly on the open book alongside her. "Fucking thicken my *arse*."

Bette cleared her throat.

"Yes, I know you're there. I can practically feel you vibrating. What's going on? What's happened? Is the table all right?" Ash asked, still whisking furiously at whatever was in the saucepan.

"I think I have to go and talk to Ruth," she said, the words leaving her in a rush. "I mean, I really like her. You know that. And I think I need to tell her. Make it clear we can do it on her terms."

Ash turned off the hob and quietly, calmly put the whisk down on the chopping board. She gripped the counter with both hands, and her head dropped forward. Predictably, the doorbell cut through the silence that had settled, echoing obnoxiously around the hall.

"Bette," Ash began, her voice sharp and dangerous. "Are you

fucking *kidding* me? There have been so many good moments for us to have this conversation. Weeks of good moments. But now there's a whole salmon thing wrapped in sodding pastry in the oven and this sauce will not thicken and guests are at the door. Literally at the door. Right this second." Ash turned, clasping her elbows behind her, as though she couldn't quite trust herself with her own arms. "I want to shake you, you absolute *idiot*."

"I'll get the door," Tim said, seemingly unperturbed by Ash's outburst. Bette hadn't even realized he was there, perched on the windowsill; between Ash's panicked whisking and Bette's big idea, there'd been no emotional space in the kitchen for anyone else. He took a beer from the fridge, levered the top off, kissed Ash on the cheek and stepped quietly out of the kitchen.

"I know this is bad timing to bring it up," Bette said, apologetic. "I didn't mean to. Truly. But I need help."

"Right," Ash said, sounding utterly exhausted.

"If it makes a difference, it was the IKEA trip that kind of started things in my brain. And running into Heather."

"Well—I mean—I'm glad," Ash said, sounding annoyed to be admitting it. "It was meant to help. So what are you going to do then?"

"Oh I have no idea. None at all."

Ash turned toward her, finally. There was sauce splashed on her shirt above the apron, her eyeliner was smudged out toward her temple, and there was something green on her cheek.

"I wanted your advice, actually," Bette admitted, cringing as she said it.

Ash nodded, her eyes closed. "And, again, just to be clear, you picked now, this precise moment, to seek that out."

"No, I'm not an idiot. I would never have chosen right now. There's a salmon thing in the oven and your sauce won't thicken," she parroted, and then regretted it instantly. Ash really wasn't in the mood to be poked and laughed at. "But I was in the front room and had a thought and then . . . I didn't really think. I just came in here."

"Of course you did."

Tim's head appeared round the door. "You're being pretty loud. I filled them in; didn't think you'd mind. Carmen has some thoughts, actually? Ruth-wise? If you'd like?"

"IT'S THE RUN to the airport!" Carmen said as she helped herself to French beans. Her dress was some sort of knitted gold, the fanciest thing at the table, though between the five of them there was a respectable showing of sequins and shimmer and sharp shirts and great lipstick. "That final bit of a romcom!"

"Well, no one's going anywhere," Bette reminded her. "There are no major transport hubs involved. So that's not what's happening here."

"You know what I mean!" Carmen waved her off.

Bette looked at Ash in search of a slightly more grounded reality. It was clear, from the schmalzy look on Ash's face, that she was going to be disappointed.

"Bette, you're going to find her, and tell her, and it's going to be *so* romantic." The cooking was done, and Ash had slipped away to fix her eyeliner just before they'd all sat down. She had changed her top and was cozy and happy and completely clean of sauce. She had also, apparently, changed into a complete sap.

"That's *exactly* it," Carmen said, reaching over for Ash's hand, her eyes practically hearts behind her glasses. It was sickening.

"Guys . . ." Bette started, pushing her salmon around her plate, nerves playing havoc with her stomach.

"It's like the end of *When Harry Met Sally*! You've realized you love her. And now you have to tell her!! You want the rest of your life to start!!" Tim burst out, the third glass of cava apparently fizzing through him and coming out in exclamation points.

Bette dropped her head into her hands. "Again, because you've clearly all forgotten, my pitch to her is 'We can just date for a bit' not 'I want to spend the rest of my life with you.' We're leaving Nora Ephron out of this. Ruth wants to go slow. I don't want to scare her off. Let's dial the intensity down *just* a little."

She was faced with four incredulous expressions.

"Okay, sure," Anton said, his tone long-suffering, as though she were denying him a treat. "I mean, 'We can just date for a bit' is less romantic. But we can work with it."

"Let's work through potential snags. Just so you're ready." Ash said, her tone suddenly practical and businesslike, the exact Ash that Bette needed.

"Well, I've been trying not to think about this but the night we . . . you know," Bette began.

"Fucked," Anton filled in, and Carmen nodded.

"Sure. Anyway, she told me Gabe wasn't a problem, and in hindsight I don't know what that meant. Like, it's not a problem: we're non-exclusive? It's not a problem: we're not seeing each other anymore? It's not a problem: he was tied up in a weird pyramid scheme and has been arrested? It's not a problem: he's come down with scurvy and is being treated in a specialist facility in Switzerland? I have no idea. So I don't know if he's still in the picture."

"I feel like Heather wouldn't have given you a nudge if he was," Ash said with an easy shrug.

It was fair. Practical, rational, obvious. Bette nodded and let out a breath she hadn't been aware of holding.

"You're right."

"So, it's just Gabe you're worried about?" Tim asked as he reached for more sauce. He'd finished his salmon, but spooned sauce onto his plate regardless, then dragged a finger through it. It dripped onto the front of his shirt as he lifted his hand to his mouth.

"I mean, there's a good chance that it's still going to be a no," Bette said, cringing at the vulnerability of it. It was like asking for approval on a selfie; it was clear what her heart longed for everyone to say. She hated to be pitied and cosseted, but this was an ideal moment for some positive reinforcement.

"Well, yeah," Anton said instead. "That makes sense. But you have to try. You just have to show her you really mean it. You need to make a big romantic gesture."

"I mean . . . I *do* really mean it. So I'll just—I don't know, I'll look her in the eyes and just tell her. Right?"

"What, like—at her house?" Carmen said in horror.

Anton cut in before Bette could defend the idea.

"No. No, come on. It has to be bigger than that."

"You could sing something?" Tim suggested, miming on what could only be a ukulele.

"I'm not Zooey Deschanel and it's not 2011. Also, I can't sing."

"You need something she can't say no to," Carmen mused. "A really meaningful gift. Or take her somewhere she'll love for a meal? Tell her over oysters and a cocktail."

Bette couldn't imagine Ruth being swayed by a gift, or by the promise of a fancy night out.

"I think—guys, I think I just need to tell her?" Bette said, aware that there was a real chance this conversation no longer included her.

"You were talking about some cliff thing," Anton said, as though she hadn't spoken. "She wants to jump off a cliff?"

"No, the opposite. She said she couldn't jump off a cliff into a relationship again. That was the whole thing. She needed to take it slow, to know we're on the same page. Honestly, I think the lingering ex in my life is what really freaked her out. So I just need to say, 'Mei isn't a problem, let's take this slow.' But I need to do it now. Before I lose my nerve."

"So, you could take her to a cliff."

There was silence as everyone looked at Anton, trying to gauge how serious he was.

"It's not the cliff we'd need to go to, actually," Bette said, an idea dawning. "I need to show her I can take it slow. Where's our closest beach?"

BETTE WAS BEHIND the wheel of Ash's car, MUNA blasting through the speakers. She was almost at Ruth's, gearing herself up for being her most convincing, charming self. The romantic gesture that had finally received sign-off from the group demanded a specific location. And so the first step was one she had started feeling anxious about: she had to convince Ruth to get in the car with her.

She arrived at the front door fizzing with nerves, her hand visibly shaking as she knocked. It was Heather who opened it, dressed in striped twinset pajamas, holding a mug of tea. Her eyes lit up as she kept Bette standing awkwardly on the top step.

"Jody?" Heather called into the house, her eyes not leaving Bette. Bette heard footsteps inside, too many to just belong to Jody.

"That's not actually what I'm . . ." Bette started.

"Oh, I know," Heather assured her, fully grinning now.

Jody appeared in the hall, an oversized hoodie exposing one shoulder. They were accompanied by someone Bette could only assume was Leon. She remembered him vaguely from the party; he was tall and gangly, with an abundance of hair and a beanie pulled down almost over his eyes.

"No *way*," Jody breathed.

"Yep," Heather confirmed, still watching Bette, as though afraid she might vanish if she looked away.

"It's really nice to see you all," Bette said, digging her nails into the meat of her palm in a bid to get her hand to stop shaking. "I was wondering if . . ."

"She's not here," Jody said, their face painted in delight.

"She's not . . ."

"Not home," Leon confirmed. His voice was softer than she'd imagined. "Hi, by the way. You'll be Bette."

"Yep. And you're Leon? It's really—anyway I came—I'm here

for—" Bette could feel the words sticking together. She took a steadying breath. "Do you know where Ruth is?"

"The ASS Library," Jody said, waggling their eyebrows suggestively.

"Right," Bette said. "So I'll just . . ."

"You could come in?" Heather offered, standing back from the doorway. "You could have a tea and tell us what's got you all worked up. We could text Ruth and get her to come home?"

The idea of having to explain the plan to anyone else, for it to be picked over again before she tried it out on Ruth herself, was appalling. Bette stumbled back, almost tripping down the stairs.

"Or not," Heather said, easily. "Like Jody said, she's working in the ASS Library."

"Should we expect her back tonight?" Jody said. "Only, we've been waiting for her to get back to start *The Muppet Christmas Carol* so . . ."

"She'll be—I mean—I don't know," Bette said. Really, she had no idea how Ruth was going to take any of it. "But I really need to—I'll get her to text you? If I find her?"

"Good luck," Heather called after her, in a way that turned luck into a two-syllable word.

Bette typed the Arts and Social Sciences Library into her maps app and clambered back into the car. There was pressure now, a time limit. She didn't want Ruth to leave the library before she got there, didn't want her to get home to a story about "Bette being weird on the doorstep." She had to find her.

"WHERE ARE WE GOING?"

They had been in the car for close to ten minutes, and barely a word had passed between them. Finding Ruth on the second floor, and her agreeing to the drive, putting piles of paper into her backpack and leaving the table to be pounced on, had been such a relief that Bette had forgotten for a moment that it was only the first step. In Bette's fantasy they would head out of Bristol in companionable silence, along these Clifton streets Bette had once lived on, both excited about all the possibilities to come. She had pictured them with the windows wound down, the air moving over her arm as it rested partway out. Grinning at each other over the console. But, of course, it was December. A week before Christmas. It was freezing; the dump of snow they'd had a week before still lingered in places. The windows were wound up, and they were in the bottleneck that led to the Suspension Bridge. The brake lights of the cars ahead were giving her a headache.

"Bette, where are we going?" Ruth repeated.

She couldn't just ignore her until they got to the beach. There was a chance that Ruth would simply open the car door and walk away if Bette didn't at least try to reassure her.

"You said you love a road trip," Bette said, realizing as she did quite how lame it sounded.

"What?"

"Ages ago!" she said, committing to it. "I was talking about hell coaches and you said you love a road trip."

"I can see your maps app," Ruth said, leaning across in her seat. Bette was tempted to hide her phone in her lap, was attached to the idea of the beach being a surprise. But Ruth couldn't see where they were going, only how long they had left. "And sixteen minutes is not a road trip. It's a commute."

"A road trip is an energy though," Bette argued as they approached the bridge and she tapped her card for the toll. The barrier lifted and they crawled across it. "It's not all about the destination. Look! Look how beautiful Bristol is!"

It was hard to deny, and Ruth watched the city from the bridge, her head turned to look out of the window.

"The bridge is nice, I'll give you that. But driving through Bristol's suburbs on a Sunday evening, feeling like I've been kidnapped, no knowledge of where we're going, is not peak road trip energy." She sounded exhausted, over it already, and Bette wanted to reassure her, ached to keep her onside.

"It'll feel more road-trippy in a bit," Bette hedged. "We're nearly out of suburbia."

It was a hopeful thought. But Bette watched as Ruth's hands anxiously folded over and over in her lap. She was practically vibrating in her seat.

"I think," Ruth said, her voice tight. "I don't—can't we just pull over and talk?"

Shit, shit, shit. No.

"Ruth, it's a red route. I'm not allowed to pull up here. I just—please don't worry. We're going to get there, and you're going to see it, and we can talk. I have—there's stuff I want to say. But I don't want to do this while I'm driving Ash's car. I don't want to do it on the side of the road. I want to be able to focus completely on you."

There was a long silence, and Bette wished that she'd plugged some music in. It would have taken the edge off the tension to have Paul Simon or someone, a good neutral, in the background.

"We're going to the beach," she said, as if that might be enough.

"The beach?" Ruth echoed, and Bette sensed an ellipsis. Of course there were follow-up questions. There were always going to be follow-up questions. "Bette, it's—it's dark. And we're miles from a beach. Are we seriously driving all the way to the beach tonight? Which one are we going to? Which beach is ten minutes away?"

Bette didn't want to tell her yet. The whole point of the thing was that it should be a surprise, should take Ruth's breath away. Should be so romantic and unexpected that Ruth had no choice but to say yes. But she'd already blown it by saying beach, which was the surprise bit, really, and the road wasn't a red route any more. Bette weighed her options. They were approaching the big roundabout, and the signs all made it entirely clear where they were going, which arrow they were following.

"Portishead," Bette said.

"What?"

It was not a curious, happy, interested "what."

"Portishead. We're going to Portishead Beach."

"Why on earth are we going to Portishead Beach?"

"Because we are," Bette replied, stupidly.

"So you've forced me into a car to take me to the worst beach in England. In the dark," Ruth sounded incredulous. "It's not even a real beach, Bette. It's an estuary. You can't swim there. There are boats. And currents. And—and tides. And it's December. So we couldn't even swim anyway, even on a good beach. Which, to be clear, this is not."

Bette passed the sign that welcomed them to Portishead and stopped at a red light. She looked across at Ruth. Anton had been the one to recommend Portishead and suddenly she hated him. Twenty-six minutes had seemed ideal when he'd flashed her his phone. But she really should have looked at some pictures.

"You know a lot about Portishead Beach," Bette said, trying to sound bright and relaxed. "How is—how do you know so much about Portishead Beach?"

"Stop saying Portishead. I can't believe I left a table in the library, an actual *table*, to go to a stupid non-beach with you in the middle of winter."

"Well, only five minutes left now!" Bette said, as though being on the beach Ruth clearly hated might somehow improve things.

There was another roundabout, one that took them away from the town and toward the beach. The car climbed, higher and higher, and then a sharp turn led them down toward a line of empty car parks. It was clear no one else had made a winter-evening plan to be on Portishead Beach. It was hardly surprising: it was all mud and tankers and slushy snow and darkness. It was impossibly bleak.

Bette eased the car into one of the parking spots, halfway down the empty row. She turned off the engine.

"Well, this is pleasant," Ruth said. "Are you going to murder me? Feels like a great spot for it."

"Look, ugh—fuck—I wanted us to take our shoes off!" Bette risked a glance over at Ruth and found her looking back, her eyes wide. "I wanted to stand on a beach and tell you we don't have to jump. That I want to date you, and that we can take it as slow as you like. We were going to walk into the water. The estuary. Whatever. It was going to be really romantic."

She could just make out a bright-yellow sign poking up out of the darkness. It read *DANGER SOFT MUD* in a font designed to be taken seriously. She was going to kill Anton. Kill him dead.

There was an agonizing moment of silence, and Bette refused to give in to the temptation to look to her left again.

"Bette."

Screw the mud. They were doing this.

"So if you'll just come down to . . ."

"Bette."

"I'm sorry. Honestly, I'm really sorry. Sorry for making you leave the library and for not thinking of a plan to make the drive nice, and for suggesting Portishead, which was Anton's suggestion because I wanted a beach that was close, but in hindsight is a really shit place for a romantic gesture. I can see that now, obviously. But if you'll just . . ."

"Bette."

Bette turned to her. Ruth had that look of fond exasperation on her face again, the one from the night they'd watched Tessa and Scott skate. It was unmistakable now, what that expression was. Bette couldn't quite believe she'd missed it at the time. Bette felt her anxious heart melt in her chest, a tub of ice cream on a hot day, sending warmth all the way down into her belly.

"If you're with me," Ruth said, carefully and deliberately, her hands anxiously clasping and unclasping in her lap again, "if you're really with me, and no one else, then we don't have to walk in."

"No?" Bette asked, her brain catching up instantly, her heart full of hope. She reached over and laid a gentle hand over Ruth's.

"No. I was scared. Scared of being hurt again. But maybe I could just try . . . not being scared. Or maybe I can be scared and jump anyway. Off the cliff, I mean. Metaphorically," she added, unnecessarily, though Bette would have jumped off an actual cliff if Ruth had asked. "Probably. I mean, if you like. Honestly, I can't really imagine you being chill enough to take it slow. And I don't just want to casually date you. The thing is, I kind of think we might have jumped already. In Edinburgh. And we're just now—I don't know. Catching up with ourselves. I'm catching up with myself, at least."

"Ruth, I . . ."

"I know," Ruth replied, which wasn't an answer to anything she was going to ask, but also sort of was. And then Ruth leaned over and kissed her. Which was precisely, exquisitely, exactly the answer the Bette had been looking for.

It wasn't anything like she'd imagined, really. They weren't standing, barefoot and freezing and ankle-deep in water, illuminated by the lights of the marina on Portishead Beach, lights that didn't appear to exist. They were in Ash's car, with the little overhead bulb on. The wind was whistling around the car, and her seatbelt buckle was digging into her hip, and the belt itself was still buckled, actually, and hauled her back when she tried to lean closer. But it was also exactly what Bette had imagined. It was Ruth's mouth, hot and wet and clever. Teasing her, and drawing her in. Giving, giving. Giving Bette everything she'd imagined. Giving her the lights and the romance and the thrill of all of it. Bette felt Ruth sigh, the handbrake in the way between them.

"Hold on," Bette said, and kicked open her door, threw off

her seatbelt and ran round to Ruth's side. Ruth was out of the car before she got there, and then was pressed hard against Bette's body, her back against the door to the back seat, her own door still wide open beside them. They kissed again and again and again, Ruth's hands never straying far from Bette's face; from her jaw, from her cheek, from her brow, from her lip, as though she needed to map the details of her. As though she needed to be sure of Bette while her eyes were closed, even as she was pressed tightly against her. Bette released her lips for a moment, biting instead at her fingers, sucking them inside her mouth, running her tongue between them.

"We're not fucking in the car," Ruth muttered, panting against her cheek.

"Agreed. We're grown-ups. Grown-ups don't fuck in cars."

"Grown-ups absolutely fuck in cars," Ruth replied, and Bette felt hot all over. "But we're on the worst beach in the world and this car has a terrible back seat. And even if all of that wasn't true, it's freezing and it's six o'clock and there are probably kids in that skate park. Honestly, I'd much rather get you home and into bed—into one of our beds—than be arrested for public indecency."

"That feels like a good line to have drawn," Bette agreed, shivering in her jumper and tights, now that Ruth had pulled back a little. "No fucking on a terrible beach on a Sunday evening."

"Actually, can we go to yours? If we go to mine then we're going to have to deal with Heather and Jody and a level of excitement that might actually ruin this whole thing."

"We can go to mine. Ash is out. At Tim's. She's not coming home tonight."

"You were that confident?" Ruth smirked.

"No. No, I really wasn't. I was sort of sure you'd say no. But Ash was confident. I thought of the plan over lunch—we thought of the plan over lunch. Oh, I should say—" She was babbling now, could feel her mouth moving too fast, knew the words were stumbling out, tripping over each other, too close together to be smooth. It was hard to care, when Ruth's smile was wide enough to have to leap over. "Tim knows too. And Carmen. And Anton. They all adore you, obviously. They were very keen I didn't fuck this up. Their level of investment here is beyond cringe, honestly. They're obsessed with the idea of you 'joining the gang.' Which is a real thing Carmen said, that I have now repeated to you. Anyway, I took the car and Ash was—she knew. She's known how I felt about you for longer than I have. How I feel about you."

"Oh yeah?" Ruth said, stepping back toward her door, seemingly unwilling to let go of Bette, one hand still grasped round her waist. "And how do you feel about me, then?"

"Shut up," Bette said, flushed pink. "Get in the car. And don't touch me until we get home. Or I may pull over and get us arrested after all."

SATURDAY, 31 DECEMBER

...

13 days with Ruth

The last of their dinner was sitting in the center of the table: a chicken, most of the meat torn from it, a loaf of bread they'd diligently worked their way through, the last few lettuce leaves in a bowl. Their glasses were smudged with buttery fingerprints, and had been topped up with champagne all evening. There was ice cream in the freezer, a cardamom and caramelized milk recipe that Ash had spent all morning on. The candles were low now, throwing shadows around the room.

"Half an hour to go," Ash said, standing up and piling plates haphazardly. "I'll get the paper and pens?"

Each New Year's Eve, just before midnight, Ash corralled everyone in the room to join her in a ritual she'd borrowed from her cousin. One year it had been just her and Bette, so drunk on fizzy wine and Robyn that they could barely pull themselves together to do it. The first year had been at the university, a huge house party, and Bette had looked on in awe as Ash had found kitchen roll and a couple of pens, and had managed to get everyone in the house settled on the floor in the front room. Through the years, whoever they spent the evening with, there were torn scraps of paper, and a collection of wishes and hopes and wants and desires for the coming year, folded away in a little pile. This was their tenth New Year's Eve living together. Bette didn't have to ask what the paper and pens were for.

But there was someone who did need to ask. Someone who would be playing for the first time.

"Paper and pens?" Ruth repeated, looking to Bette with amused eyes. "Are we playing consequences? Have we run out of conversation? Is it time for some doodling?"

"Ash'll explain," Bette said, slinging an arm across the back of Ruth's chair and pressing a kiss to the side of her neck. "It's her favorite thing. She'd happily murder me if I she thought I was taking over."

As promised, Ash returned with a stack of paper in pastel hues pulled from her printer and an old golden syrup tin filled with pens. "I wouldn't kill you," she said thoughtfully, putting everything in the center of the table. "But I'd make next year a nightmare for you. Well, not me personally. But I'd use one of my pieces of paper on it. And the universe would take care of it for me."

"Okay, that's me well and truly lost now," Ruth said, topping up everyone's glasses round the table.

"I hate resolutions," Ash said, as if that explained it.

"Sure," Ruth agreed. "January is a terrible time for resolutions."

"See this is why I'm glad we've got you now," Ash said, clearly pleased, and Bette felt almost incandescently happy. "You're really going to get this."

"Should we have dessert while we're doing it?" Tim suggested.

"Absolutely not. You can't multitask; you need to focus. Dessert after fireworks."

Tim threw up his hands, but there was a smile hidden at the corner of his mouth.

"Okay, so you're going to tear your paper into twelve bits," Ash explained, demonstrating with hers. "And then on each bit you're going to write a thing you hope for, for next year. A good thing, or to let go of a bad thing. Like maybe start tap classes or stop worrying about the stupid Head Teacher on Sundays—"

"Quality, generic, examples there, Ash," Tim said, and Ash put a hand over his mouth and continued.

"Or write a letter to a friend once a month. Something tangible or intangible that you think will make your life better. Or something you want to have done by next Christmas. Anyway, do that first, and then I'll explain the next bit."

Ruth picked a green pen and snorted in laughter.

"Serial killer," she said, under her breath. Bette didn't tell her to swap, didn't warn her that she'd be stuck with something that looked like it had been written in serial-killer green all year. Instead she tucked a hand between Ruth's legs beneath the table, tracing over her thigh. Ruth tensed, trapping the hand, and glared admonishingly at Bette. "Ash said we have to focus. No multitasking."

"That was only for Tim," Bette protested. "I'm perfectly capable of multitasking!"

"Well, I'm not. Keep your hands to yourself. I'm busy."

Ash laughed, heartily and long, and shot Bette a smile so wide and so true and so blissfully pleased that Bette wanted to cry. The champagne had done its thing.

But first.

The first few were easy—yoga, a walking holiday with Ruth

because she'd like it (unfortunately), more books, drive to Wales to swim, visit her nonna every fortnight. The next few were harder to articulate, the sort of wants that scratched at the inside of her skull but which she never properly said aloud. Open an ISA, sure, but also start thinking about the next bit. Talk to Ash about the future. Stop avoiding it, and make a real plan for the next few years. Figure out how to be an aunt. And then there was space for fun ones: let Ruth teach her to bowl, go and watch some drag with Jody, play wing-woman for Heather, go with Ash on one of her weekends back home and eat too much of her mum's biryani. Try more . . . stuff . . . with Ruth. Figure out which of it was her stuff.

It would be a great year, she thought, if she could do everything on her list. A really great year.

"Okay, fold them all up and make sure they're tiny. You shouldn't be able to tell them apart," Ash instructed.

"Do you know that no matter how big the piece of paper, the most times it can be folded is—" Tim began.

"Seven times! Wild, right?" Ruth replied. "Though actually I think there's a girl in America who folded a piece of toilet paper in half twelve times? Kind of blew the whole paper-folding game wide open."

Tim's jaw dropped.

"Oh great," Ash said. "He tells us that at exactly this point, every single year. It's going to become an extended bit now."

But Ruth had already pulled the article up on her phone and was handing it across the table to Tim.

"No way!"

"Right?!" Ruth said.

"Look, I'm honestly thrilled for you both, and you can nerd out

over the physics of paper-folding after midnight, but we only have fifteen minutes."

"Sorry, sorry, sorry," Ruth apologized to Ash. "So now we have twelve hopes? Twelve plans? Twelve tiny bits of paper? What do we do with them?"

"We're going to throw them into a bowl," Ash said, "one by one, until you're left with only one in your hand."

Ruth tossed one in and Bette followed suit. Round and round and round they went, until they were all holding a single squashed scrap of paper.

"We're going to burn those at midnight," Ash explained, gesturing at the paper in the bowl. "Outside on the street. And the universe will take care of them. But that one in your hand, that's yours. You have to be responsible for that."

"Do we . . ." Ruth started, working her paper open. "Do we read it out?"

"Only if you want to," Ash assured her. "I should have said that at the start, so if you don't want to, no pressure."

"I think let's not, this year," Bette said, as she looked at the word "aunt" making itself known through the half-unfolded paper clutched in her hand. She needed to fill Ruth in on her family, probably. With things going as they were between them, it was inevitable. But it wasn't the time. Not tonight. She pushed the paper into her pocket.

Ruth looked over, aware, as if she was entirely attuned to Bette's precise mood, knew that something had shifted. She reached over and took her hand.

"Let's go and burn the universe ones," Ruth said, pushing her own paper into her pocket. "Anyone want a top-up?"

There was a flurry of activity as they made their way outside: glasses were refilled, Ruth pulled Bette in for a quick kiss, Ash found some matches and a saucepan, Tim ran back for a lid. And then they were outside, the streets filled with people finding a perfect vantage point for the fireworks.

"What did your piece of paper last year say?" Ruth asked, slipping her hand into Bette's, twining their cold fingers together.

Bette laughed.

"I can't tell you. You're never going to believe it."

"Ooh, talking about last year's paper?" Ash said, only a step behind.

"Yeah," Ruth said, turning back. "Hold on, do you remember too? You can confirm Bette's story! I'll believe it with corroboration!"

"The corroboration is at home," Bette assured her. "It's pinned above my mirror."

"Well what was it?" Ruth asked. "Come on, did you manage it?"

"I . . . did," Bette said, turning to Ruth, unable to keep the smile from her face.

"Yeah you did!" Ash crowed behind her, and Tim whooped.

"We're going to find a spot," Tim said as he and Ash made their way around them. Ash caught Bette's eye as she passed and the look from earlier was back, the utterly blissed-out, overwhelmed look. Bette returned it.

It had felt too soon, in the past week, to say it aloud. They'd had barely any time together before Bette had traveled down to Devon. By the time she returned on Boxing Day, Ruth was with her parents in London. She knew, of course she did, what Ruth talking about jumping off the cliff meant. They had teased each

other about it. It had been waiting on her tongue for a fortnight.
But Bette didn't want to say it in the flurry of everything being
good, in response to the relief of Ruth agreeing to come back. She
wanted to say it, clear-headed and sincere and so certain that she
could feel it in every part of her.

"Bette . . ." Ruth started, her voice soft, her feet still. "I . . ."

"Last year, my piece of paper said—it said—" Bette interrupted,
desperate to be first. "It said: fall in love, and be beside her at this
party next year."

It so felt good to finally say it: drunk on champagne, at mid-
night, the fireworks over Bristol behind her. And then Ruth said it
back.

ACKNOWLEDGMENTS

This is a debut, but it's also my second novel. I wrote my first paragraph of fiction in October 2016, and spent the next five years carving out snippets of time to work on what ended up being a very sad gay book: set in the past, filled with guilt and yearning, centered around a murder. It's the type of book I love to read, but the brutal truth is that I wasn't particularly good at writing it. My first deeply heartfelt thanks, then, goes to my best girl Ella Risbridger: a dream of an editor; the very first person to reassure me I could write fiction, who laughed at my jokes and was moved by my characters, who read multiple drafts of that first book, who patiently challenged me and problem solved with me, and who also helped me understand that it's not failure to start over. Thanks too to my incomparable agent, Zoe Ross, who read that first book and told me to strip everything back, to work out what sort of book I had been trying to write. It turns out the answer was: the wrong one.

It took another year for me to write the right one. This one.

I'm so lucky to have spent the past eighteen months working on it with a veritable dream team of editors, who understood so clearly the book I had written, who were brimming with enthusiasm from the outset, and who saw the work that still needed to be done: Katie Bowden (and Lola Downes) at 4th Estate, Marie Michels at Pamela Dorman Books, and Bhavna Chauhan at Penguin Random House. There's a word document that exists only on our computers with a comments section covering everything from Caroline Calloway to the best crisps to the reasons Tessa and Scott are magic to the mechanics and choreography of lesbian sex. I am so grateful to have found a team of editors so inspiring, so clever, so funny, and so relentless in ensuring each detail is perfect.

Some more thanks: to Barbara (farewell, great lady Ford, I miss you) and to Rút (my companion, my noble Škoda). The vast majority of this book was planned —and often captured in side-of-the-road voicenotes—while on long drives in you both. Thank you too to MUNA, Kelly Clarkson, The Shirelles, Tegan and Sara, Robyn, Taylor Swift, The Ronettes, HAIM, The Mountain Goats, Lizzo, and (perhaps most of all) Michelle Branch, for providing the soundtrack that's been in my head for two years now.

To Bry and Dan (RomCom Club). I owe you—and the forensic analysis we did of an impossible number of romantic comedies—so much.

I am forever indebted to the friends and loved ones who read very early copies of the book (on phones, on laptops, on printouts done late at night in the office). I'm not naming you all here because I'll worry about leaving one of you off the list, and then simply never sleep again. But know I'm thinking about you, yes YOU, when I say: thank you for giving feedback and advice; for your long voicenotes; for suggesting names when it sounded, early on, as though the characters were all born in 1932; for letting me ask questions about care homes over lunch; for pointing out when I slipped into Australian-ish; for being horrified about brunch dates; for asking tricky questions; for screenshotting your favorite lines; for requesting a redacted sexy-baths-free version; for telling me about the cigarette you smoked after chapter twenty-three; and for talking with me about Bette, Ruth, and Ash as though they're our real-life friends.

I am indebted too to friends and colleagues in publishing and in bookselling, who have been so kind, warm, and excited about the existence of this book, right from the start. It's been a true joy, after years of writing about food, to be able to come to you with a very different kind of story. I am so excited for all the opportunities ahead to work alongside you.

Thank you to my parents (Mum, Dad, Cheryl, Geoff, and Chris) and my siblings (Luce, Anna, and Tom). Thank you for being genuinely extraordinary, for loving and supporting me so well, for wanting to read everything I write (even the apple murder book—thank you, Anna), and also thank you again for skipping chapters eight, fifteen, and twenty-three. Or at least pretending you did.

Finally, thank you to the family I chose, for choosing me: thank you to Ella, Tash, Rich, Andy, Rocket, and Sydney. Thank you for the Janes, for auction graphs and celebratory dumplings and baked potatoes, and for days spent together on various sofas (and on occasional outdoor adventures). Thank you for everything but most of all for the pure *fun*, for filling my life with the sort of love and joy that made it possible for me to write this book. I wouldn't have done this, or been this, without you. Every single day, I can't believe my luck.